A FLORENCE GRAY MYSTERY

GO WITH THE FLO

JUDITH
DECHESERE-BOYLE

For Rick, my best friend

ACKNOWLEDGMENT

It is with the utmost respect that I acknowledge Francisca Melogno, a custodian at the high school where I taught for many years. I appreciate her skill, integrity, kindness, and friendship and thank her being an impetus for this novel.

CHAPTER ONE

FLO

Life is a paradox! How is it that at the exact same second in time one person can be on such a high that she cannot see the ground beneath her and another can feel so low that not a sliver of air could possibly slide between her and rock bottom? How is that?

Flo had harbored this thought from time to time, and recently, given the fact that she was floundering somewhere in the middle, with every good memory locked as tight as tick in the middle of her brain, and with too many bad recollections gone over the proverbial dam and just as well forgotten, she was able to reconsider it. Contemplating life's contradictions, and understanding them, had never been her forte, but recent events had given her a chance to see more clearly. Being on a random plane that for her right now was as smooth as polished glass, allowed her to view life, perhaps for the first time ever, without the usual, annoying filters. God knows she had spent enough time reflecting on her own past and finally had come to the conclusion that it was not her fault. Oh, she had played a part, of course; it was her life. Yet it was behind her and the future existed; she actually had a few plans for that safely deposited, for now, on the back burner. Presently, however, in this particular expanse in time she did not have to dwell for one stinking second on the past or the future. Instead, she had been planted here and now, for some unknown reason, in a position merely to watch events unfold. She need not interfere; she need not judge; she needed only to be still and take it all in. And what was it? Well, in the minds of most people in the community, it was a mess. Yes, a fucking mess, and Flo found herself in a quite unique position to watch it play out like nobody else.

⌘　⌘　⌘

Florence Maxine Gray was old, or so she thought, although she was only forty-five. She felt much older than the calendar years marked and would have had little trouble convincing folks that she was over sixty and nearly ready to retire because experience had hewn and etched deep furrows into her brow and cheeks. Her long, straight hair, as flat as a blade, had turned grey when she was thirty and she never had had the means, or the aspiration for that matter, to do anything about it. Most days she tied it back in a tight ponytail that she then wrapped into a loose bun. Her face was nondescript, the only notable feature being a rather large, black mole that rested at the corner of her left eye like a blob of black tar. It was likely the first thing one noticed about Flo and she was conscious of it, as one is conscious of a gaping wound. It pained her, and although she lied to herself, imagining it as a Marilyn Monroe-like beauty mark, she knew better; so she suffered, and looked sideways at people with sad, brown, emotionless eyes.

She wasn't as spry as she had once been either, the job she held being a constant reminder. Flo was a janitor. The job description labeled her a custodial engineer, but she knew better about this too; she didn't engineer anything. She had been hired by the Center View School District to dust, sweep, vacuum, wipe, empty, and straighten, and to do so without getting in the way of the administrators and teachers who on most occasions did not give her the time of day. She was an expert on cleansers that some distant, district official had purchased by the truckload at a discount rate that mirrored their effectiveness. Some days she would sneak in her own, more potent, cleaning supplies that actually would pull the black graffiti from scratched, plastic desktops or wooden, door jambs and would loosen wads of dried, chewing gum that lined the undersides of desk tops or was smashed into tight tufts of carpeting. Sometimes she felt like a creature on a carousel, continuously repeating her duties over and over to no avail for the graffiti and gum reappeared daily as though she had never been there cleaning in the first place. She certainly felt no sense of accomplishment and was rewarded only with demands from school officials to do a better job, and to do it quickly. To that end, she was frustrated and a bit sad; yet she completed her tasks with bored efficiency that kept her out of the line of fire most days and in the most unique setting to be a watcher, and watch she did.

Why only last night, at the exact moment she was schlepping a heavy vacuum from a science lab into an empty hallway, she heard voices.

"I can drive you home," a man's voice said.

"No, I'll walk."

"But it's dark out, and cold."

"I like to walk."

Flo seized up abruptly in the doorway, afraid to move forward, afraid to retreat. She listened though, and recognized the voice. It was Jack Mitchell, science teacher, administrative designee, divorced, and impulsive . . . and the girl? She was a petite blond. Cheerleader. Overachiever. Flo had noticed her before but didn't know her name, not until Jack unwittingly revealed it to her.

"Angie, I can't have you going home alone at this hour. The town's not safe. You ought to be smart enough to know that! There's not a female in town that should be out alone in this town after dark, not with what's happened around here," Jack admonished, his eyes narrowing knowingly.

Flo bit her bottom lip as she watched Jack Mitchell seize the girl's arm and pull her to him. She sucked in her breath, holding as still as a sentry though her gut churned. Jack's behavior toward the girl stirred an unwelcome memory or two.

"Besides, I have something I want to give you." His voice took on a lusty tenor and Flo shivered inside her dingy cardigan.

"Mr. Mitchell, I . . ."

The girl could not finish. Jack Mitchell pulled her quickly into his classroom, the only sound being a distinct and jarring click as the door sealed. The two were in the room for only moments, however, before the door flew open again and Angie tore from the darkness, and ran down the hallway, slipping at the end of it on freshly waxed linoleum. She fell heavily onto her back, her head snapping sharply on the floor. Surely she was dazed, for she lay still for moments, giving Jack time to reach her there and gather her into his arms as though she were a lifeless puppet. He pushed her hair from her face and grinned down at her roguishly.

"I'll give you a ride," he told her firmly, ignoring the probability that she was injured. Lifting her to her feet, he hefted her backpack to one shoulder and with the other arm, pulled her up. Flo could see the muscles in his back and arms bulge with his effort as Angie swayed uneasily in his grasp for a moment. When she could steady herself, he drew her to him and kissed her forehead as though she were an obedient child, and perhaps she was, for the two of them left the building, his arm clutching her shoulder protectively as they stepped into the swirling fog that danced around ethereally in the evening cool.

Flo hovered silently in the hallway listening to her heartbeat reverberating in her ears. She had avoided detection. Fortunately Jack had been so immersed in his own doings that he had not seen her. Generally speaking he never gave her a second glance anyway, not these days, and for that she was grateful, to say the least, for she had insight into Jack Mitchell that few people could possibly know and that burdened her hatefully. Thinking about him now made her stomach churn.

⌘   ⌘   ⌘

Hollow Vista High School may have seemed an average, even quite ordinary place where students, teachers, and parents went about fulfilling their assignments, duties, and obligations, but Flo knew that simmering beneath this seemingly mundane place was a cesspool created by more than one misguided soul. As she had witnessed the night before, Jack Mitchell was one of them.

She had chosen not to mention the interaction between Jack and Angie to anyone, and although guilt for not doing so tormented her conscience ever so slightly, she told herself she was right to remain silent. She convinced herself, that her own bias about the man surely had stirred her imaginings; yet she shuddered involuntarily as she recalled the teenager who had been led away in his grasp.

⌘　⌘　⌘

Interestingly Flo had known Jack Mitchell for more than thirty years and when she thought about him, even now, her stomach tightened. She never had known him well, but years before, they had been classmates at the very same high school where he currently taught science or, on occasion, assumed administrative duties, and where she vacuumed his classroom and emptied his trashcans every day; but she remembered. It did not take much for her mind to pull out that record and put her right back in time.

"Ho-Ho-Ho. Here comes Flo. Ready to blow . . . me," he had chortled more than a few times when she had slid past him and his pack of friends who lined the entrance to the main hallway of the humanities wing of the building that was closest to the street. It was the corridor where students, too many to count, entered and were intimidated mercilessly by Jack and his buddies. His slurs had been lined with innuendo and had made Flo blush crimson.

Even now, she flushed with the memory.

His harassment had not stopped there either. Later in English class, where he had sat behind her, he had jammed his desk into the back of hers and had slurred, "When are you going to let go, Flo? What do you have to show, Flo?"

And when his hand had inched forward to grab a strand of her hair, she had twisted around angrily, annoyed by his startling touch. Why was he constantly toying with her, with her name, inanely attempting to find a rhyme for it, for no rhyme or reason other than simply to be cruel? She had known he had no real interest in her. Why would he? He and his friends were jocks, with all the popular girls and dimple-faced cheerleaders clamoring for their attention. So why had he chosen to torment her, a nonentity sporting a black blob on her face? She keenly had come to understand, in no time at all, that she was only target practice.

"Oh, no, Flo. Got to go," he had laughed, grabbing his crotch, leaning back forcefully in his desk, and staring at her coldly.

He had been a stupid boy and, in Flo's opinion, had grown into an equally foolish, insensitive adult. As though the passage of time had afforded him not one degree of wisdom, he was at this very moment, smack-dab in the middle of the current affair that had turned the town of Hollow Vista upside down. And even now, as though he was completely oblivious to his predicament and the accusations that were being launched his way, he was carrying on as he likely always had, drawn into a behavior that he clearly could not stop. Had she not witnessed it the night before?

CHAPTER TWO

MIDGE

"The guy's going to go around ruining lives everywhere he goes," Midge said, looking intently at the vulnerable, young woman in front of her. It had been early January.

"It's as though he has his head in the clouds, high above everyone else and he is unable to see through them to the real world below. And it wouldn't matter anyway. Not for him. He has one intention, and that's to satisfy his own ego-centric, selfish desires. He doesn't feel it a need to consider anyone else; probably couldn't if he tried. It's not in him." Midge McGrath was talking about Jack Mitchell. In her own deep-seated, calculating manner, she maligned him.

Midge had been teaching for over twenty years and the time devoted to the profession had earned her a reputation: hard, unyielding, and self-righteous. She was. She had her opinions and was quick to size up both her colleagues and students, using them or abusing them as she saw fit, keeping the ones she detested in their places and allowing a few to enter her inner circle. She did have one nagging trait, however, that irritated her like a boil; she had a soft spot for people in pain. She had been hurt herself growing up and could read volumes in the sad eyes of more than a few colleagues around her. She felt somewhat smug harboring this secret proclivity, but in actuality would have loved to be done with it; like a bee drawn to honey, however, she could not help herself. Honing in on some poor soul enhanced her sense of superiority and sharpened her skills in digging for dirt as it were. Knowledge was power to Midge; it didn't matter if what she learned came from her studies or from the revelations of the sufferer at hand. She ambitiously acquired all the information she could and stored it safely. She remembered. Oh, how well she remembered.

And so it was, that she had pulled Melody Miller aside and offered her counsel at the beginning of the new semester. After all, the girl had made a spectacle of herself by openly moping, and even breaking down in tears in front of a group of students who simply had asked her what was wrong. More importantly, though, was the bruised eye socket, still bearing a tinge of purple and yellow that she had tried to disguise when she returned to school the first Monday after the holiday vacation. She had smeared her cheek, forehead, and eye socket with thick make-up that drew more attention than the bruise itself would have. And she bore an abraded forearm like a badge, not having sense enough even to cover it with a long-sleeved blouse or sweater.

Does the girl not have the sense to come in out of the rain? Midge had been appalled when she saw Melody, a first-year, temporary teacher, sniffling at the door of her classroom while curious students filed past her on the new year's first day of classes. In Midge's opinion Melody's behavior had sealed her fate. Clearly she would not be offered an invitation to return the following year. Gossip had been circulating at warp speed around the faculty lounge and next to the teachers' mailboxes throughout the fall semester and the rumors continued still. Everyone knew Melody had been smitten with Jack Mitchell who clearly had been manipulating the young woman as though she were a chunk of clay from the very first moment he had lain eyes on her at the year's first, faculty retreat way back in August.

Melody's battered face and arms, at the hands of Jack Mitchell, were the result of a misunderstanding of sorts that had occurred on New Year's Eve. Melody had confided her secret to Midge whose interest in the poor girl was tinged with her own desire to bottle up such disclosures for safekeeping. The revelation had, at the time, made Midge wonder about her seedy, and, in her mind, clearly reprehensible colleague as never before.

Seated in the corner of the empty classroom, Melody looked at Midge with sad, brown, doe eyes. Melody was a plain, young woman, whose round eyes, round face, and out-of-date, poufy, pageboy haircut reminded Midge of a female version of the Pillsbury doughboy. The only defining features in her unremarkable face were deep dimples that were fixed in her pale cheeks as though they had been punched in place there. Midge was torn between wanting to hug her or slug her in the belly. And who had named her Melody? The name simply didn't fit; she was a tense and melancholy figure most days, rolling her head to the side and gazing glumly into the space before her as though searching for answers to questions she quite likely never could have articulated. One could have assumed that a person called Melody might have grown into such a pretty name and worn it like a song, but instead, she was the antithesis of it: moody, sullen, and sad.

Midge looked at Melody and tried once more.

"It's not your fault, Melody. You wouldn't have been able to stop him from doing what he did. Nobody could. It's as if he can't control his impulses. He's addicted, you know, to the intrigue of it all. He likes the rush! And when the newness wears off, he's done. Ready to move on. It's what he can get away with that makes all the difference."

"I thought we had something," Melody said forlornly, unable to unwrap herself from the tangle of self-loathing that had consumed her.

"I'm sorry to say it, but you did have something, but it was a one-way street." Midge addressed the girl bluntly, harboring a growing distaste for her. "You had something he wanted. He was too selfish, always has been, to see beyond his own self image and now you're hurting. I'm sorry, Melody, but you need to get your head on straight. Stop thinking about that asshole and start taking care of yourself. Nobody's going to do it for you."

The words slid over Melody like scalding water and she visibly flinched. Midge made her rage inside, but she didn't know where her anger should be directed: at Midge, at herself, or at Jack.

⌘ ⌘ ⌘

Now it was May. Nearly a full school year was complete, and it was ending on a remarkable note, the likes of which even Midge McGrath could not have foreseen.

Midge's annoying, contrived concern for Melody had disappeared completely after only one or two sessions with the girl. Instead, as was the entire community, she was caught up in all the hoopla involved in an investigation. Numerous people, including, quite notably, Jack Mitchell, had been questioned. She mused over Jack's arrogant, but simplistic claim that he had been at home alone, sick with the flu on the day all hell broke loose in Hollow Vista, for she wanted to believe more than anything that it was he, Jack, who had something, if not everything, to do with the crisis, indeed the tragedy, that had the small town of Hollow Vista blistering with outrage, accusations, and absolute, unbridled fear. She detested Jack that much. *He's a bastard, but he's weak, all bravado and no follow through.*

She had noted that Jack appeared rather unaffected by the goings-on that had everyone, from the mayor and the police chief, from students to adults, abuzz with assertions and gossip, none of which clearly, to this point, had been sorted through or analyzed with any degree of thoroughness. The state of affairs was all too new. Jack's demeanor, however, had Midge quite nonplussed.

His alibi to the authorities surely appeared weak and questionable. *Sick with the flu.* Midge found him annoying. She had known the man for years and was aware of his ability to squirm his way in and out of sticky situations like a serpent. Was he perhaps, for once, telling the truth? The notion knotted her stomach.

CHAPTER THREE

MELODY

Melody Miller grew up to be a teacher. Her father, the well-known Harold Miller, had been a principal for over thirty years at the esteemed Black Basin Boys' Prep Academy in the central valley; her mother was a kindergarten teacher . . . still, and, as if osmosis were working at its very best, Melody had absorbed the profession despite having had secret dreams of dancing under bright lights on a stage somewhere spectacular. Fourteen years of tap and ballet had planted that seed, but she hadn't grown tall enough, couldn't master pointe, and lost her edge when her breasts grew too big and her face retained the round cheeks of a cherub. So, at the age of seventeen, when she graduated from high school, she tossed her ballet shoes into a waste-basket outside the dance school's back door, smashed her tights and a tutu or two into a Goodwill bag, and set her sights on college.

She had had no idea what she wanted to study. She abhorred math, was bored with history, and was too confused herself to think of mastering sociology, psychology, or doing social work, so she settled for what she knew better than anything else: English. Reading was not something she loved doing; it made her sleepy, but her parents had read to her from infancy, and she had tolerated and half-heartedly read a number of the classics required in high school, so to that end, she considered herself somewhat prepared to venture into the study of her own language and eventually, she assumed, to find some place to teach it, if anyone would have her.

Unaware of her daughter's clawing doubts, Melody's mother was delighted. "Oh, darling," her mother had said, "I believe this is an excellent choice."

Her father had guffawed deeply and added, "Well, of course it is, Loretta. It's in her blood. Why, she has to keep the family tradition. We're educators, and fine ones at that. What would the neighbors think if she had chosen to pursue any other career?"

Harold Miller had never been able to get over himself and had run his home the way he ran his school, flaunting his knowledge, and posturing himself arrogantly in order to maintain power and control. Under his tutelage Melody had floundered as a young girl, seized with over-sensitivity and burdened with self-doubt. Though her mother tried to encourage her, her efforts were tepid at best for she was struggling herself to maintain a sense of autonomy. It was not surprising to anyone who knew the couple well, why when Harold Miller retired, Loretta continued working. She had just inched into her seventies.

With her father's approval, Melody entered a state university not far from home, but distant enough to put space between herself and her parents. She savored the freedom but struggled to keep her focus. College was hard, not like her high school had been, and she was distracted by the social scene that offered way too much stimulation. As a result, she missed a few classes, drank too many beers, smoked pot, and slept with three different men from her dormitory the first month she was there.

Yet, the fact that she could not let her parents down pressed on her conscience. She was an English major; she would become a teacher. She would make them proud. When her first college essay was returned to her, awash in red ink and baring a broad, heavy D in the upper margin, however, she was stunned. Beneath the grade was a scrawled message, "Certainly you can do better than this, Ms. Miller!"

She was shocked at the cruel assertion, but moreover crushed and ashamed, spending days afterwards wallowing in self-pity. *I am so stupid.* The words spiraled inward and stuck there, festering.

⌘ ⌘ ⌘

I'm so stupid. The phrase surfaced once again as she slipped out of Midge's classroom into the dusk when Midge had ended their conversation with a stiff squeeze to Melody's shoulder. She had been telling herself the same thing, reciting those exact, self-critical words continuously for years and had come to believe them. Certainly, her sudden dismissal by Jack Mitchell had been enough to solidify her own pronouncements about herself. It was bad enough that since the end of the holiday break Jack had offered not even a modicum of attention to her. The fact of the matter was that he coldheartedly had ceased acknowledging her existence entirely, ignoring her as if she were invisible, and the obvious rebuff had done in poor Melody like a sad song, the refrain endlessly playing in her mind. As a result she was exhausted and so anxious that she wished for nothing more than to crawl out of her body altogether and hide from the world.

Wish to hell I hadn't let Midge in on all that has happened. Stupid. Midge doesn't care about anything or anyone but herself. Melody's was a sudden, typical admonishment, yet it held an intuitive truth. To that end, then, it suggested perhaps that she wasn't so stupid after all.

CHAPTER FOUR

FLO

Flo finished her late evening chores at midnight, checking the alarm and locking the science wing's outer door carefully. She wandered through the dim campus toward the parking lot where her dented, burgundy Honda was parked right in the middle of the lot. She was fortunate to have moved into Rob Green's parking space in the faculty lot that day, as she had become accustomed. Not everyone was so lucky for generally the spaces were filled from 7:30 a.m. every morning until well after five o'clock when most bedraggled teachers headed home. While she didn't take stock in the attitudes of a good number of teachers who barely acknowledged her presence, she had noted over the years that most worked hard, much harder than the public was apt to give them credit. Oh, a few were not worth a pinch of salt, she knew for sure. Why old Mr. Green had probably never corrected a paper in his life. Flo knew this to be a fact. She had hefted trashcans filled with unmarked essays and ungraded tests into the outside dumpster more times than she could count. And, Mrs. Cummins couldn't make it through the afternoon without a nip or two of the vodka she deftly concealed in an ancient perfume bottle and stashed in the bottom drawer of her desk. Mr. Lindsey slept during his prep and lunch periods, snoring soundly and drooling thick swaths of saliva onto the desktop when he wasn't issuing silent farts into the air around him. He blamed the stench of his classroom on the chemicals lodged there, but Flo knew better. She hated cleaning Mr. Lindsey's classroom each evening more than any other.

She both admired and feared teachers with reputations such as Midge McGrath's. It was widely known that Ms. McGrath was as tough as nails and didn't let a thing slide past her eagle eyes or eager ears. Flo never had met the woman, but had caught wind of her reputation. Midge listened to those around her, gathering more gossip about the goings-on at the school than anyone, and she bore her predilection for amassing rumors, true or otherwise, like a medal of distinction. It gave her power. Midge obviously basked in her knowledge, whether it was verifiable or otherwise, and her ability to use it in any way she thought fit, clearly must have armed her with unquestionable clout. Others were aware too, Flo had observed, and others were afraid. How a person such as Midge could manage to manipulate situations by what she knew fascinated Flo, who, despite herself, in a much simpler and unsophisticated manner, was learning the ropes.

New teachers were always interesting to observe as well. They generally were cautious and alert, their eyes darting to make sure the coast was clear, having little sense as to what the tide might bring in each day. They simply knew they had to be ready. The one exception, Flo had noted, was a young, rather bland, round-faced woman who couldn't seem to focus on anything. And who could blame her? Everyone knew she had had a bout in the fall and winter with Jack Mitchell, and what a round it must have been, for the girl bore the scars, both physical and emotional, for weeks. Flo had never spoken to the teacher but she had seen her with Jack earlier in the year. Their relationship had caused Flo to ponder, and she wondered still, for she had not seen them together all spring and clearly Jack's interests were elsewhere. Hadn't Flo taken in that tidbit earlier in the evening?

As she reached for the door of her ancient Honda, Flo recognized her exhaustion, a tiredness that was exacerbated by the gnawing image of Jack Mitchell and the girl named Angie who had disappeared into the night air in front of her as if they had never existed at all. Given what she had heard through the grapevine recently, combined with memories of her past encounters with Jack, should have been reason enough for Flo to react or to act, but she had not. Instead, at the end of this work night, she simply slipped her aching body into the front seat, turned the key, and as the engine sputtered into action, closed her eyes. It was only for a moment, but was enough. She would go home to a bite to eat, a glass of cheap, red wine, and sleep. Tomorrow she would repeat the routine with likely only a minor adjustment or two.

⌘　⌘　⌘

When Flo reached the door of her tiny, stucco house that was situated next to a mature and aged, grape vineyard in a small, silent lot at the edge of town she was annoyingly awake. The short ride home in the cold Honda had stripped her of her fatigue, at least momentarily. Heavy fog obscured the moon and stars and when she turned off the headlights of her car all was pitch black. She stepped out into a cool night so dark she could hardly make out her front door. The trek from the car to the porch was so familiar, however, that in only moments her key was twisting in the lock of the door and it fell open revealing two, small, yellow globes shining in the shadows. Freddy, her ancient, tabby cat meowed loudly just as Flo flicked on the light. Home. It was her special place, shared now with only her cat after the horrid death of her husband of twenty years just before his fiftieth birthday last January.

Randall Gray had been a painter, and a good one. Though he never had had the ambition or wherewithal to start his own business, several, different, painting companies had provided steady employment for him over the years. Painting was his life, he often said, and at the close of a day, if he had the inclination to talk, he might even explain.

"It's the motion of painting that pulls on me," he had confided at first, only to his wife. With the passage of time, however, he divulged his reasoning to anyone who would listen. "I love hearing the swish of the brush or being perfectly precise so I can cut a color right into a tight spot. The physical labor doesn't matter to me. It's what I see that counts. On a big project watching one color overtake another simply at my command is almost a violation of sorts. It arrests me and holds me in awe. It's the same with my artwork. It's magical to me how a canvas is transformed with only a quick flick of a brush and with the slice of an X-acto knife I can chip a color away in a flash. Why, even altering a tint can cast me into a bad mood, or a good one. It's real simple Flo, and you know it. When I paint, I'm happy as a pig in shit."

Most folks who listened to Randall Gray's ranting thought he might be just a bit off kilter, and perhaps they were correct. God only knows he had inhaled enough paint fumes to fill a hot-air balloon. His warped reasoning enabled him to lose himself in his sketches and drawings when a day of work was done, however. For hours on end he created lavish, oil paintings and pastel watercolors, completing them painstakingly and stacking them against the wall of his living room or in the shed out back, until there were hundreds of them. He never sold a single one, though, although Flo had encouraged him to try.

"Don't need to sell them, Flo," he told her time and again. "Just have to paint them. I can't help myself. I'm drawn to that canvas like I'm drawn to you." He would grin at his absurd assertion and then slap his wife happily and inappropriately on the ass.

"Randall Gray. Don't know what to do with you and don't know what I'd do without you," Flo retorted.

It was the truth. He had been Flo's only lover, her best friend, and her worst nightmare. They had loved and hated each other with equal intensity, each morning waking up with affection to push them into the day, and each night sinking into sinister sadness induced by too many worries, not enough money, and too much alcohol. Randall didn't care what he drank. Whatever was available was just fine with him, but he did love Scotch whiskey, and he loved it straight. He didn't even bother pouring it into a glass. A swig or two of the stuff directly from the bottle was sufficient to lower his stress, his sense, his sensitivity, and his tolerance. Flo took the brunt of his abuse, with Freddy, the cat, having an innate instinct to sneak under the table or behind the couch for safety. Flo, on the other hand, endured years of Randall's belligerent behavior, detesting, tolerating, and loving him, until one day he fell head-long, right behind her back, onto the kitchen floor and could not get up.

The result was not a pretty picture.

"You have bladder cancer," an elderly doctor told him at a sprawling, community hospital in Stockton after a battery of tests had been completed. "It's in the prostate too, and I'm afraid it has metastasized to your liver. You should have come in months ago, Randall, for a check up. In cases like this, procrastination is a patient's worst enemy. For ignoring your symptoms you're paying the heftiest price possible."

The old doctor shook his head slowly from side to side and stared at the couple in front of him with sad, blue eyes. His mouth fell slack and his hands worked each other. *I'm getting too old for this kind of work.* The silent musing, pushed aside, gave way to spoken words that he knew would create the kind of pain he was certain he had no power to heal.

"I'm afraid there's nothing we can do for you. Your occupation and your lifestyle, without a doubt, have contributed to your illness. I'm sorry, Randall, but I have to be frank with you, and you, too Florence. Your husband doesn't have long, a few months. Time to get things in order, my man."

It was a blunt and brutal revelation that left Randall quivering on the exam table and caused Flo to dissolve into tears, one of the few times that had occurred in her lifetime. Just when the two had perfected their dance of life, however perverted and destructive it had been, they faced its end. The one, flimsy consolation was that they would be together to see it through. The fact of the matter was, that with dysfunction at its core, Randall and Flo's marriage had slipped into a comfort zone that neither could have explained. The news from the doctor shocked them beyond belief, but facing the destruction of their rhythm together caused the most pain. Their tango had taken a twist and turn down a road they never could have imagined and they were catapulted into new territory that offered them no route around what was inevitable. Despite tepid attempts to alleviate the pain associated with Randall's disease, it was hopeless and he withered into a skinny frame over which taut, yellow skin clung like tough leather. Flo sat beside his bedside day after day until the onset of the proverbial death rattle, that gurgling sound in the throat, that launched her into hysterics. She flew from the room to the back yard, vomiting and dry heaving into the yard until she was awash in perspiration and smothering on snot and tears. When finally she made it back into the house that day, to the bedside of her lover and tormenter, he was dead.

She had his body cremated and secretly scattered his ashes in the vineyard next to the house. It was important for Flo to have the only man she had ever loved nearby.

CHAPTER FIVE

JACK

Jack Mitchell was up at dawn as was his usual habit, ready to begin his day. The silence of the morning seemed to wash him clean and he sorted out his demons by jabbing a heavy, punching bag that hung from a thick chain in the corner of his garage and by doing one hundred push ups, twenty or more performed one handed. He groaned and perspired with the effort, but when he was done he launched into a fast walk for forty-five minutes on his treadmill. He would shower next in water that was so hot it scalded his back and chest, and he would lather his testicles with soap, caressing his penis and scrotum with pleasure, closing his eyes and concentrating on the gentle power of his touch. When the morning ritual was complete he could face another day and the job he had grown simply to tolerate, for the excitement and passion he once had possessed for teaching had waned in recent years. He was forty-five now and his age in numbers was a reminder that he was no longer young. Watching some of his male students saunter into class, all arms, legs, and muscular maleness irritated him. They reminded him of what he had been, of what, despite his efforts to maintain, he was losing. It grated on him.

Jack had been a jock himself at the very high school where he had taught physical science and biology for twenty years. He had played football at Hollow Vista High School, quarterbacking the team to the state finals; he had played shortstop on the baseball team as well, his agility and quickness often putting him in the spotlight. He was not quite tall enough, not quite stocky enough, and not quite muscular enough, however, to be considered seriously by colleges to compete there, and certainly not by a professional team of any kind. He was resigned then to participate in intercollegiate sports that did little for him other than keep him in shape and in the eye of a few, young women on campus.

And speaking of young women, he was finding it harder and harder to quash his fantasies about some of the young girls he had as students. Certainly the girls with whom he attended high school years before did not look like these girls with their long, thin legs, firm arms, large breasts, silky hair, and perfect, blemish-free faces. No, he had gone to school with the likes of Florence Gray, old Flo, who for some reason was still in his world dragging a vacuum around his classroom and dumping his garbage at night. What a despicable character she was! While he in no way remembered tormenting the poor woman when she was a teenager, he had not been able to forget her, for she was there, day after day, a woman who had grown old before her time and who was an annoying reminder that the passage of the years was inescapable for him as well. The fleeting thought of the woman, even now, irritated him, but he conveniently shoved her hideous face from his imaginings and replaced it with that of Angie Murphy whom Jack had discovered just the night before, to his demented dismay, was smarter than he had expected.

⌘ ⌘ ⌘

Jack arrived on campus before seven, slipping into the principal's office where Cora Davies, the school's head secretary offered him a cup of hot, black coffee and a wary stare. Cora had been at the helm of the school, more or less, for eons. In Jack's mind she was ancient, nearly sixty-five. She had begun her stint at the school when Jack himself had been a freshman there. Probably five or six principals and even a greater number of assistant principals had come and gone under her watch. She knew none would stay for long because school board members and administrators at the district level stymied their power and bolstered their longing to move into higher, more prestigious positions themselves. It was as predictable as clockwork.

The current principal, Roger Cunningham, was an insipid, uninspired man who certainly, not by choice, was caught up in a crisis he now was attempting to understand. Jack Mitchell, his golfing buddy and friend, among several others at the high school, he knew, was being scrutinized, as never before and in all honesty, Roger was not quite sure how to handle the matter. It was not within his power to subdue the turmoil that in recent days had locked his staff in suspense; nor could he eliminate the gossip and innuendo that was running rampant among them. He was left simply to watch and wait, hoping desperately that no one he knew, particularly his friend, Jack, had been involved.

Roger had latched onto Jack the first month he had been hired in a friendship that to onlookers was quite out of the ordinary. Roger was very tall, nearly six feet, four inches, and as thin as a rod. His hair was conspicuously absent, his balding pate shining like a polished apple. He shaved away what little hair sprouted around his neck and ears, but sported a thin mustache and goatee that fortunately gave his face some color, for he was pale, his skin maintaining the same pallor in summer as winter. His sallowness strangely mirrored his demeanor: quiet, cool, and generally calm, although in recent days his gut had begun to churn in the face of matters he could not comprehend or control. Roger was a family man too. His wife, Regina, was a teacher as well, a short, plump woman who loved nothing better than coddling her first graders and taking care of the couple's own trio of children at home.

So it was odd that Roger and Jack, who still carried himself like the athlete he once was, had established such a bond. Jack had no family to speak of, having divorced his wife of seven years some twelve months before when he accused her of having an affair right under his nose with the family's gardener. Whether his allegations were true or not did not matter at the time, although in recent days, knowledge of his claims would have gained more than a modicum of attention. He never could have admitted the truth though. The fact was that being stuck with a demanding and assertive wife who made him feel inadequate and insecure had caused a silent rage to ignite inside him. As a real estate broker in town, she made much more money than Jack ever would. She was often away, on the road with a colleague or client, and Jack's hidden self-doubts about his own competence got the best of him and filled him with anxiety. He didn't like the feeling. His contrived accusations, however, only exacerbated a secreted fear and pain that had rested within him for years.

The angst that plagued him took him back to his childhood, to a mother whose job was tending the bar at Joe's Place out on Highway 65, and to the men, one after the other, she brought home to their single-wide trailer for one night stands. He recalled the sounds of their sexual play, the snide glances directed his way, and one incidence in particular that he had shoved into the deep recesses of his mind, but which surfaced relentlessly from time to time, nonetheless.

Jack was eight years old when his mother, Marion Mitchell, came home one evening, earlier than usual, with a bear of a man, smelling of whiskey and sweat right behind her.

"This is Burt," she had told her son. "He's going to be resting here for a bit while I go back to Joe's to close things up."

Burt had said nothing, looking at Jack as though he were a speck, and had collapsed on the small, tattered settee just inside the flimsy, trailer door. Instantly he had fallen asleep, one hairy arm thrust over his head and the other hand landing on the bulge in his trousers. Jack retreated to his tiny room, stripped to his underwear, and crawled into bed covering his head with a pillow. He knew it would not be long before his mother returned and the moans and groans to which he had become accustomed would fill the night air.

Sleep had evaded him for some time, but eventually it settled in, heavy and deep. Jack had dreamed that night of transforming into an eagle, soaring the sky in search of prey when the unspeakable happened. The thin, wool blanket that had covered him was yanked away and he felt the pressure of one, great hand on his back, pressing him unmercifully into the mattress, and the other tugging at his underwear until it wound around one, bare ankle.

It was then that Burt, panting and dripping perspiration, shoved his penis, thick and erect, between Jack's legs, finding its place deep in Jack's anus. Though Jack attempted to escape, screaming in pain and fear, he was held fast, his head pushed into the mattress that became the receptacle for his tears. The pillow over his head stifled his cries until the assault was over.

He oddly still could remember the sensation of the release of pressure when Burt's hand left his back, for it had given him freedom to move ever so slightly and vomit into the wrinkled sheets. He had heard Burt exit the trailer moments later, slamming the door with staggering might, his heavy footsteps crunching the gravel outside until he was gone for good.

Alone, Jack had managed to turn over on his back where he lay in the shadows for long minutes, breathing shallowly and holding his nose from a stench he never could have been able to decipher, for the alien smell of vomit, semen, fecal matter, and blood all mingling together putridly, had enveloped the air.

When Marion Mitchell had returned that night, she was so intoxicated she fell directly onto the dirty settee on which Burt had slept just hours before and did not awake until noon the following day. By that time Jack had managed to stand and find his way to the shower where he cleaned his aching bottom, assessed the damage as only an eight-year-old could, and determined finally that he would not die.

"You must have a flu bug," Marion had said when she noticed the vomit covered sheets later in the day and followed the terse remark with, "Guess Burt didn't want to hang out here. Came back to the bar last night for a few beers."

Jack had not replied to his mother's clueless comment that day but simply had looked at her despondently. Sadness was the only emotion he knew to feel for he loved her and hated her equally and to that end, Jack purposely did not reveal to her the rape he had endured at the hands of one of her lovers. That little boy made a few decisions then, however. He would build up his strength, carry wariness as a weapon, and make sure he always had the upper hand. Not one person would take advantage of him ever again. And as for women, his mother became his model. He would tolerate them, but they were toys to be used and abused as he saw fit.

⌘ ⌘ ⌘

Since being done with Sherry Mitchell, Jack had attempted to play the field, but the crop of available women was small in the valley town so he was left to his fantasies and to a few weekends away in San Francisco when he had the extra cash to hire an escort service to satisfy his sexual desires.

When he had sighted the fledgling teacher, Melody Miller, at the faculty retreat at the beginning of the school year he thought perhaps his luck had changed. She was not his ideal, but she was female and available. It hadn't taken much energy on his part to have the young woman acquiesce to his overtures. He had intercourse with her within days of their introduction.

"Oh, Jack, it's too soon," she had protested halfheartedly when his flirtatious advances had morphed into more. On a slow walk around the retreat grounds at dusk the second night there, Jack had invited Melody to his private room in a rustic cabin at the edge of an area dense with thick Manzanita, Yerba Santa, buck brush, and poison oak. "No, baby, it's never too soon," he had responded. "Besides, if you don't make love to me now, you'll regret delaying the inevitable."

"How do you know it's inevitable?" she had asked coyly.

"I just know. You'll be miserable wondering what you're missing and then asking yourself why we waited. We can't have that, can we?" Jack had questioned her with a twisted grin lingering on his lips. He breathed heavily into her neck as he pulled her to him briefly and a bit too roughly stroked her back and bottom before pushing her firmly onto his bed.

That wasn't half bad. Jack had chuckled to himself when he was done with her for the night. He did make sure she reached the retreat complex proper before leaving her alone to find the way to her own cabin in the dark, but beyond that, any real concern for the woman slipped from his mind like melting ice. He'd play this one later, picking up where he left off when the need arose.

For Jack now, that initial liaison was only a dim recollection. The retreat had been set in the tranquil foothills of the Sierra, miles away from the valley. The principal, Roger Cunningham, hired ten years prior, had arranged the event in hopes of creating trust and collegiality among his staff. In the ten years he had been at the helm of Hollow Vista High School, Roger was acutely aware that few teachers had forged compatible, working relationships, and, in fact, they often were openly at odds with one another simply to promote an agenda or two. As with his former high school, a major metropolitan campus where he had been an overworked, assistant principal, the staff was equally as disparate and divided. He naïvely had hoped that at a smaller school such antagonism would be lessened if not absent altogether. He was so wrong. The retreat at the end of August had been Roger's somewhat desperate attempt to engender some productive change in his staff's professional and personal rapport. Jack was afraid, however, that his poor friend was living life wearing blinders. Not one teacher at Hollow Vista High was about to give an inch, save Melody Miller, perhaps.

⌘ ⌘ ⌘

"You have to be straight with me, Jack," Roger said, the dull lining of his words betraying the anxiety he felt inside. "How much do you know about this mess?"

"Roger, I've told you. I've told the cops. I've told practically anybody who'll listen. I don't know shit! I haven't talked to Sherry for months, not since we separated for good. The only time I've seen her is on that preposterous billboard with her picture right smack dab in the middle of it. You know the one, out by the Interstate. Ridiculous if you ask me. Never could get enough attention. Always wanted to be in the limelight, Sherry did. Well, she sure has the attention now."

Jack's eyes had not settled on Roger or on anything else in the room during his tirade. Instead he searched the corners of the tiny office for answers that did not come easily, not for him anyway, for the fact of the matter was, and God forbid that anyone might find out, but he was afraid. A madman had been out there. Anyone could be next. He had to be careful. Everyone did. Isn't that the reason he had wanted to take Angie Murphy home just last night, to protect her? "God knows who might be lurking around outside," he had told her and then pushed her, a bit too forcefully, into the front seat of his black, pickup truck for the ride home.

"I didn't have jack shit to do with what happened," Jack added once the random thoughts that were swirling in his mind settled for a moment. "Don't have a clue who would have the wherewithal to do such a thing. I suspect it might be that handyman Sherry hired a while back or the son-of-a-bitch's son, maybe."

"How would you know she hired a handyman if you haven't seen her for months, or that he had a kid to boot?" Roger asked, wondering intuitively if perhaps he had caused Jack to stumble.

"She hired him before the divorce. We weren't living together then and I never met the dude, but knew she hired someone to do maintenance on her house and a few other properties. Found out more shit from his kid," Jack was quick to continue, hoping that his uncharacteristic blathering would distract from an issue of prickly heat that had crawled to his neck.

"Guy's son, little ass wipe, goes to school here; kid's got problems. Probably because of the way he showed up here – hair matted down, scowl on his face, overalls. He's always complaining about being picked on by somebody. Probably makes shit up. Just wanting attention. Name's Willard Dunn. His old man moved the whole brood – wife, five or six kids, and a dog or two out West from down South somewhere. Kid's damn near illiterate. Suspect the old man is too."

"You found this out from the boy? How'd that happen?" Roger questioned.

"Yeah, I did. I have the kid in biology this year, but last spring when you attended that administrative conference down in San Diego I was filling in as an admin, doing some discipline action. Kid was sent down from Carol Cummins' class. God that woman couldn't keep her class under control if her life depended on it," he digressed.

"You're losing me, Jack," Roger stated.

"The kid came in practically crying. For God's sake, I hate seeing a boy, especially one in high school, blubbering away. Guess Brad Browning and some of his buddies got in Willard's face for something. You know how some of those jocks like to throw their weight against the little guys. They were just playing around and the kid couldn't take it. When he finally settled down, the first thing he blurted out to me was, 'Mr. Mitchell? Ya' know a lady named Sherry Mitchell?'"

"He pretty much spit out the name like it was a piece of dung. I told him I knew of her. Didn't say more, but I watched the kid squirm. 'My dad works for her. Seein' how ya'll have the same last name, thought ya'll might be kin,' he said. The kid was scowling like crazy. That's when I figured I was right. Sherry was screwing the guy. I could read the anger in the kid's eyes – little daggers out of the blue. He probably knew his old man was off fucking Sherry, swimming in that fancy pool, taking liberties, while his poor mother was stuck home with a slew of other brats. Kid probably can't read a third grade level book, but he isn't stupid. I'm pretty damned sure I'm not far off the mark. Don't know what Sherry could possibly see in a fucking handyman, horny bitch!"

"I think you'd better keep that opinion to yourself, Jack," Roger warned sharply. "And you sure as hell better not go off half cocked and implicate some kid from our school. Implying that one of our students had something to do with this crime is absurd. What you're spouting here is just pure conjecture, and coming from an ex-husband it doesn't look good. For Christ's sake, Jack, what are you thinking? Investigation's just beginning. The police are looking in your direction too, you know."

"You know damn well I was home sick as a dog for two days when all this shit came down," Jack sputtered, squaring his shoulders and sucking in his bottom lip for a moment. "The only thing I saw that day was the goddamn toilet. Heaved my guts out for two days straight."

"I'm just saying, Jack. Sounds like you already have a wild hair up you butt. Don't go saying too much. Keep a lid on it. As your friend, I'm telling you." Roger took a swig of creamy coffee from the mug on his desk. Finally it had cooled a bit, but was warm enough still that he could feel the liquid coat his tongue before sliding slowly down to his stomach.

Roger looked at Jack Mitchell across the desk and sighed. Why he had been drawn to the man, he did not know. They were opposites. Jack was crass, crude, and always on the fringe of controversy. He carried his attitude in his swagger, in his steel blue eyes, and in the ominous twist of his mouth when he was honing in on something he wanted, whether it was the perfect drive on the golf course, the authoritative control of his classroom, or, he could imagine, the masterful command of a woman.

Roger, on the other hand, always had played it safe, never wanting to ruffle feathers. He had had only two women in his life, his childhood friend's adolescent sister, and his wife of twenty-five years. The primary rushes in his life occurred the moment his golf club impacted the ball before a line drive or early, Sunday morning sex with his wife. Beyond that, he was a stolid, quiet man who was committed to his family, his profession, and the truth. It was the latter, at this point in his life, he longed for most. For the question of the moment for everyone in the normally quiet, valley community was, as of yet, unanswered. Who was the person, Roger wanted to know, who had fired a bullet right through the forehead of Jack's former wife, Sherry Mitchell?

CHAPTER SIX

MELODY

At six o'clock when the alarm spewed startlingly loud, rock music into Melody's bedroom, she nearly jumped out of her skin. She had been awake, but unsuspecting of the time. Sleep eluded her night after night, and as a result she was constantly exhausted, emotional, and irrational. Ever since the New Year's Eve confrontation with Jack Mitchell, Melody's mind had been unable to clear itself of the events of the evening and the awful words Jack had shouted at her.

It had started so innocently.

"Why, aren't you a pretty picture?" he told her when she opened the door of her apartment to face him.

"Hardly," she mumbled, flinging off his compliment as if it were a speck of dirt.

"Why do you say that?" he confronted.

"Well, it's true, isn't it?" she whined.

"You know, Melody, the more you say it, the truer it is!"

Jack dropped the subject, but the fact was that Melody's continuous, self-deprecating comments were beginning to exasperate him. She was the antithesis of his former wife, Sherry. Sherry was diligent, self-assured to the point of arrogance actually, and beautiful. He would never forget the first moment he had seen her maneuvering a grocery cart down an aisle at the brand new, organic market in town. Oblivious to anyone around her, she had been piling produce into her cart, smelling the cantaloupes, searching for the perfect batch of asparagus stalks, and plopping fat, Fuji apples into a paper bag. Her face was tanned, her lashes ebony and thick, and her hair the color of dark chocolate. He had not been able to see her eyes, but imagined them blue, deep pools that would draw him to her. He had watched her that morning for a full minute before she responded to his stare. He remembered. She actually had smiled.

Jack had not apologized for gawking at her so unabashedly, but instead had said, as only he could, "You're a vision, there, Miss. Couldn't help but notice."

She had shaken her head at him as if he were a bad boy, scooted past him, and said nothing, but her eyes, that were indeed a deep, azure blue, had danced with his words. Jack had noticed.

He had made sure he was behind her at the checkout stand that day where again, he smiled, this time offering not a word. *She'll have to make the next move, and she will.* To that end, Jack's arrogance rivaled Sherry's, and outside of the store, it had happened. She spoke to him.

"Okay. My name's Sherry," she had said, tossing her hair with her hand and squaring off against Jack as if it were a contest. "I sell houses, and I'm a broker."

"Jack. Jack Mitchell. Teacher," he had admitted. He instantly was not sure what he was up against with this woman who oozed confidence. He always had been equally as self-assured though, so to that end, there was no competition. That, for Jack was fortunate because before either of them knew what had happened, they were in bed, he fucking her and she reciprocating more wildly than either had experienced in their lives. It had seemed the perfect beginning, and with the summer before him, Jack made sure, between hours spent on the golf course, to squander time, precious time, with Sherry. The days had inched by with afternoons spent making love or lounging by the pool at Sherry's house. In August she invited Jack to move in with her, and on the first day of December they were married by a Justice of the Peace at the county courthouse. The ceremony was over in a flash and the two settled into a routine that was both comfortable and concerning, as misgivings and suspicious began slowly to taint their world.

⌘ ⌘ ⌘

Melody's dinner on New Year's Eve had been a disaster. *I should have known the night would end like it did. I can't cook worth shit. I even told him. It's Jack's fault. He insisted we stay home.* It was the morning after. *And now, with what he said and did, it will never be the same. It's probably over.* Melody began bargaining. *Will he take me back, especially if I say I'm sorry?*

She was still in bed on New Year's Day at noon, nursing a bruised cheek and eye socket and abraded arm. Her physical pain paled in comparison, however, to the emotional stress, a tangle of anger, fear, shame, and sadness that knotted inside her.

"Better to stay in," he had told her the week before. "Biggest storm of the year's predicted for New Year's Eve.

We can do dinner at your place and then move on to better things," he had added lustily, although, if the truth were known, he was tiring a bit of sex with Melody. She was inhibited in her sex play and self-conscious about her body. He had heard her whine more than once, "My hips are too big. My breasts are too small. I'm not pretty enough for you."

Her anxious, self-deprecatory remarks had found a home in his head. They irritated him. After a dynamo like Sherry, Melody's insecurity was wearing him down.

Though Melody would have preferred a night out, or a party invitation, neither had surfaced, so she had acquiesced to Jack's demand. She prepared what she hoped would be a gourmet treat, but the baked potatoes were overcooked and mushy, the artichokes undercooked and hard, and the New York steaks, fresh from the butcher at Safeway, so tough that eating them took effort even Jack Mitchell could not muster. He definitely was a "meat and potatoes" man, but this meal was enough to make him consider veganism.

He chewed on a piece of steak that grew bigger in his mouth as he attempted to eat it. Eventually, not so discretely, he spat the wad of the masticated meat into a napkin. *She'll have to do better than this.*

"It's awful, isn't it?" Melody sighed. "I'm not much of a cook."

"Maybe it's just the cut," Jack said attempting to placate Melody's obvious embarrassment, but added, "but it is like trying to eat shoe leather." He chuckled then at his own trite remark and scooted away from the table.

"Think I'll stick to the wine I brought," he said smugly.

His comment was enough to push Melody into one of her sullen snits and she glared at Jack, her brown eyes betraying her anger. *Asshole.*

She said instead, "I'm so sorry, Jack. I've never liked to cook, and my mother never taught me much." As was her nature, Melody placed blame.

It was another trait that irritated Jack. Nothing was ever Melody's fault. She simply did not take responsibility for anything. Botched lesson plans were the result of professors who did not prepare her; unruly students were the fault of poor parenting; a poor performance review was because the administrator didn't like her; an irate parent thought her child could do no wrong, and a dirty classroom was the result of shoddy work by inefficient, lazy custodians. The excuses seemed never-ending.

By nine o'clock in the evening the first bottle of wine had been consumed and a second well on its way. The champagne was still chilling, three bottles lying in the refrigerator like ice-cold torpedoes ready to explode.

Though he had planned to have Melody in bed the first moment after midnight, Jack did not wait. Rather, he led her to the couch, poured yet another glass of wine for each of them, and threw his arm around her shoulder. In only moments his hands began to roam her body, his touch harsh and anxious. His unusually forceful advances initially startled Melody, but after minutes she softened to his touch. He made his move then, pulling down her jeans, pushing up her sweater and, like a teenager, soon was humping her on the floral couch. Though his knees were sliding uncomfortably into the space between the cushions, he could not wait. He was consumed with desire. A sudden, unexpected vision of his former wife, Sherry, flashed into his mind, just as he jabbed his penis roughly into Melody's vagina.

"Ow, Jack. You're hurting me," she squealed.

"It's good. It's good," he said, ignoring her cry, and driving into her violently until he was done.

He lay on her for moments still panting in the aftermath of his effort. Tiny beads of perspiration had formed on his forehead and when he reached to wipe his brow, his body shifted, shoving Melody awkwardly to the floor.

"Jack! Shit!" she cried.

"Come on, silly. Get up," he directed abrasively, pulling her into a sitting position beside him. Clearly he was oblivious to her discomfort or embarrassment.

"Silly?" she replied, glomming onto the negative.

"Yeah. You're being silly. Grow up, Melody," he snapped.

With this bout of sex behind him, and he did expect another round much later that night, Jack quickly grew impatient.

"But you hurt me. You pushed me onto the floor," Melody complained. She was not letting up on him. "At least you could apologize."

"Goddamn it, Melody. You fell half a foot."

"It still hurt," she said, biting her lip and willing a few tears to form, "and besides, I'm cold."

"Well, get us a fucking blanket then," Jack barked as he careened carelessly from the couch. His foot brusquely raked Melody's body, and he stomped to the bathroom, slamming the door hard.

Jack's impulsive behavior pitched Melody into an emotional frenzy and when he reentered the living room, he found her sobbing uncontrollably. She had cocooned herself in a soft, purple blanket, filled another glass of wine, and sat blubbering into a pillow. Jack looked at her and seethed. *What a fucking, spoiled, little bitch.* He sat down next to her not uttering a word.

Eventually the crying stopped and Melody silently stared at the television that was broadcasting the escapades of New Year's Eve revelers in New York City. Her sullen, forlorn face was the antithesis of those of the partiers on the screen. Jack wanted to slap her.

Instead, he said, "I'm going to be heading out, Melody."

"Why?" she asked with a look of inane surprise.

"Because this is not my idea of a great New Year's Eve."

"Mine either," she pouted. "I count too."

"You count for one thing," he blurted, "to be a fucking pain in the ass!"

Melody's face flushed a deep red.

"Why are you being so mean to me? I just made love to you and now you're treating me like I'm nothing to you."

"You call that making love?" Jack started. "That was not making love. That was plain, old fucking, simple as that. I made love to my wife, not you."

Melody blubbered a response, "Jack . . . I."

"You repulse me," he continued. All of his pent up frustration and irritation with the girl finally had erupted and his ruthless arrogance bore down on her like an awl. "You're right, Melody. Your ass is fat. You don't have good tits, and you smell. For God sakes, why don't you clean yourself up?"

Melody stood then and her blanket fell away revealing her pale, nakedness. "Jack, I love you. You have to know that. Why are you treating me like this?"

She moved closer.

"Don't be stupid. You don't love me and I sure as hell don't love you. Right now, I don't give a shit about you."

"Jack. But I thought we had something. We've been making love for months now."

"Fucking. We've been fucking," he told her. "I made love to my wife," he said again, "to my beautiful Sherry."

In reality, sex with his wife was a distant memory, but it had been torrid, frequent, and good. And for Jack, now, it was sufficient ammunition with which to attack the woman who stood naked before him like an imbecile.

Melody reached for him then, but he grabbed her arms so that she could not touch him. He held her there and she grew rigid in his grasp.

"Jack," she yelled. "You're hurting me. Let go."

"I'll be happy to let go, you stupid bitch."

His dropped his hand from one of her arms and twisted the other firmly behind her back. Why he did it, even Jack never could have explained, but at that moment he felt as though he had been sprung from a trap. He was filled with such hatred for Melody, for her round, dimpled face and dull, brown eyes that he struck, his fist bashing into her cheek and eye socket.

Melody reeled backwards, falling into the arm of the couch and then twisting onto the floor. Blood oozed from her nose and she lay sprawled there, knocked almost unconscious until she heard the front door open. Jack was leaving her.

She raised her head slightly to see Jack's return. He looked down at her, his mouth twisted into a snarl and his eyes alit with anger and fear. "Don't say a fucking thing to anybody," he said. "I'll deny anything you say."

"I wasn't even here," he continued, conjuring a lie as he turned. "I was with my beautiful wife, Sherry."

CHAPTER SEVEN

MIDGE

Midge had never been fond of Sherry Mitchell, likely because her aggressive demeanor and uncompromising business transactions were like a slap in the face to Midge. Midge had learned the hard way.

In actuality, the two could have been clones in regard to their outlooks on life, as they both equally were driven for reasons neither was likely to be able to explain. Sherry was a wake-up call of sorts to Midge, a reminder of her own predilection for wanting control. Unfortunately, power for Midge was illusive to a great extent for much of her world was restrained or dominated by others: administrators, school board members, parents, and unruly students. As a result Midge was frustrated and a bit angry. Unlike Sherry, who found countless outlets for her assertiveness, Midge was bound up, unleashed fury silently churning painfully within her.

When Midge's husband of twenty years had left her ten years prior for no particular reason at all, Midge had been forced to sell her lovely, country home and move into a small cottage nearer town. She had been completely confounded by her husband's flight, and truly was unable to understand why she had been abandoned so abruptly. It wasn't as though another woman was waiting for Fred McGrath. He was, after all, in Midge's mind, a hapless, uninteresting man with little education and with few skills, save for understanding the flora and fauna of the foothills and Sierra that lured him to them more often than not.

Need to be away, now, he had scrawled on a note left on the kitchen table those many years ago. *No need for hard feelings. It's not you.*

Yet Midge knew that was a lie. She knew Fred resented her education, her drive, and the respect she had earned not only as an outstanding, high school teacher, but as an activist in the community where she found time to organize book fairs for the public library and to campaign for local politicians who caught her fantasy. In contrast, Fred had been a floater in life, unable, and more likely unwilling, to settle. Any concern for a secure job simply eluded him. He had worked for a time as a warehouseman at the cannery on the edge of town, had stocked shelves at the bustling, new Safeway store, and before his departure had even secured a position at Midge's high school as a custodian alongside Frank Sutter, a dull shell of a man who wandered the school in the late afternoons and evenings completing his janitorial duties.

"That Frank's a mystery to me," Fred had said once of the man. "He must have been brought in with the foundation. Don't have a clue what he's thinking."

"And why on God's Earth would it matter, Fred? He's a custodian!" Midge had retorted insensitively, wondering momentarily why the man cared for one second about old Frank Sutter, and furthermore, oblivious to the look of disbelief that slipped across Fred's face like a shadow. With dull anger and incredulousness, he absorbed his wife's flagrant distain for both Frank Sutter and his occupation, a job that incidentally he currently shared.

"It doesn't matter," he had answered, his eyes losing contact with Midge's face. "Just wondered about him. Always works with his head down, his eyes half open. I imagine he's seen a lot more than he ever bargained for when he came to Hollow Vista as a janitor though. Probably true for any of them that work in the district. Jesus Christ, they work like dogs and get abused like them too. Most folks look at janitors like they're a piece of shit. Can't tell me they don't have their eyes open, claws retracted, ready to snap some day."

Though perhaps an overstatement, Fred comments were perceptive. He understood a bit, having attempted to master the mundane tasks, that to him were tedious, uninteresting, and, in actuality, quite disgusting. Simply being employed in that position had made him feel more inadequate than at any time in his life, but the job itself was not the cause. Rather in all probability his sense of ineptitude could be attributed to Midge who clearly found his presence at her school, working in what she clearly deemed an inferior capacity, an affront to her sense of importance. To that end, she avoided Fred at all costs, slipping into the restroom if she saw him sweeping a hallway near her classroom, or quickly turning and hustling away in the opposite direction if she saw him out and about on campus.

It had been shortly after he left his custodial job, offering no notice at all to the administration that he disappeared from Midge as well. He quite likely was done with it all, for in the ten years he had been gone, not one person in the community, Midge included, had heard from him.

With no husband, no extra income, however sporadic it had been, and an unquestionable but secret fear of being alone in the sprawling, country, ranch house, Midge had moved, hiring Sherry Mitchell to sell her home. Not only was Sherry's expertise as a realtor and broker well established, contracting with her had been Midge's ploy of sorts to find out more about Jack Mitchell, the then young, science teacher who was married to Sherry at the time.

It didn't take much time at all for Midge to determine that their marriage was, without a doubt, broken already. Sherry dominated, wheeling her credentials, her influence, and her money as though they were the very breath of her life. Jack, it seemed to Midge was only along for the ride. Clearly Jack adored his lovely wife but his attachment to the woman appeared unhealthy. Sherry was overbearing, Jack overly accommodating, and while she was quick to judge, he was more interested in avoiding confrontation. He acquiesced to her wishes unabashedly and watching that interaction time and again grated on Midge like fingernails down an ancient chalkboard. And even though Jack was as arrogant and handsome as Sherry was assured and beautiful, she had the man licking from the palm of her hand.

"Jack, do go grab some dinner for us, won't you? You're off work so early, and well, clearly I'm still at it," she smiled condescendingly.

"I just walked in, babe," he said, gently closing the office door behind him. "Thought we could spend a few minutes alone."

Although Midge was in the room, seated directly across from Sherry, her back was to Jack and she did not see him lick his lips distastefully at his wife.

"Really, Jack. I have a client," Sherry huffed, sighing audibly, and eyeing him dismissively.

"Go buy yourself, us, some dinner. I'll be home later. Midge and I have a bit more to discuss." Sherry's eyes bore into Jack. "And you've interrupted us."

Though Midge had not turned to look at Jack's face, she could imagine the anger lodged there, for she heard him suck in his breath and click an unclear, mumbled retort between clinched teeth.

"Later," he managed, the word *bitch* accompanying him out the door.

Midge had observed more than a few such interactions during the course of her business dealing with Sherry. Her realtor's arrogance made her seethe, but Jack's reactions to his wife made her stomach churn. The couple's blatantly hostile behavior towards one another irritated Midge although she couldn't put her finger on why. She pondered, for longer than she should have, how two, such individuals ever could have married, much less even been attracted to each other. Yet the irony that lay within such judgment was astounding, really, because Midge did not possess the wherewithal to see that their relationship mirrored that of Fred and hers exactly. And where had that taken them?

When the haggling over a sales price was over, Midge stood by and watched silently as many more folks than she could have imagined entered her home, a place that had been her private domain with Fred for years. They trampled dirt on clean carpets, ran hands over her Formica, kitchen countertops, and eyed her belongings and décor with obvious dislike, palpable aversion, or indifference.

Weeks, months passed by before an offer was made. It was way below the asking price.

"You've priced too high, Midge," Sherry told her. "I believe I warned you about that."

"But this is a beautiful home," Midge argued. "I've lived here for twenty years."

"Therein lies the problem," Sherry said bluntly. "This was likely a nice house years ago, but it's dated. It needs work, upgrades. It shows wear and tear. You need to lower your expectations."

Midge bristled with Sherry's words. *How dare she say such things.*

"I think it's priced right . . . " Midge began, but was instantly interrupted.

"Look, Midge. I can't work with you if you can't be reasonable about this. I am the expert here."

Midge stared at Sherry unable to absorb her words quickly enough for a retort.

"So if you'd like to find another agent, do so. You decide." Sherry ended her comments there and walked out the front door to her Mercedes. Within seconds she had backed down the driveway and was gone.

It took four weeks for Midge to give in. The price was lowered to what Midge considered rock bottom and sold to a middle-aged couple with five children ranging in age from two to fifteen.

God only knows what they'll do to the place. Midge mourned her loss as she signed the closing documents. *Oh well, it's done. The bitch had me hogtied. Time to get over it.*

Midge did move into her new cottage, but she did not get over what she saw as a bungled, real estate transaction that had stripped her of valuable equity by selling the house to the couple for thousands of dollars less that Midge felt it should have been. Sherry was to blame. Midge was not about to forget.

CHAPTER EIGHT

ANGIE

Angie awoke feeling dirty. She wasn't of course, but she felt it, inside and out. Violation was not new to her. She had experienced it before with Jerry Gerard when she was only ten, and then over and over, really with Brad Browning, her current boyfriend who didn't seem to understand the word *no*. Last night had been different though and the newness of the blatant abuse lodged in her gut like hot lead.

Practice with the other cheerleaders had run late more because of constant bickering among the girls than for any other reason. Angie was weary of it. The routine was as synchronized as it would ever be, but Suzie, the captain of the squad, kept pushing. "This isn't good. We can do better," she badgered over and over until the others simply balked at her nagging.

"I'm out of here," Angie finally told the group. "Need to get to the science wing before it's locked. My backpack is in the lab."

"Need a ride home?" her friend Cynthia asked.

"No I'll walk. It's not that far."

"You sure you want to do that, walk alone, after what happened last week to Ms. Mitchell?"

The reminder of Sherry Mitchell panicked Angie for a moment. Chills crawled onto her arms and neck.

"It's okay. I'll walk," Angie said again, this time a terse assertiveness in her voice.

She turned quickly away from Cynthia and rushed, not looking back, toward the building. She could feel her throat tighten and her eyes burned with unwanted tears. Sherry Mitchell, a now very dead Sherry Mitchell, had hired Angie three years prior to answer the telephone, file, and do other mundane tasks around her thriving, real estate office. Angie worked weekends during the school year and more often in the summer when the demands of multiple, honors classes and extracurricular commitments diminished. Sherry was a demanding boss though who had high expectations, was often verbally abrasive, and actually quite hateful, finding fault at every corner. Angie knew she was an easy mark for the abuse, being young and a bit anxious, but she endured the woman's ill treatment and was, on the outside, courteous and accommodating. Inside, however, Angie seethed, bubbling with resentment that often churned a maelstrom of self-deprecating disgust for putting up with the woman's mistreatment. Yet she did, out of principle. She was not about to let Sherry Mitchell know how badly her words and actions hurt.

"Nitpicking bitch!" Angie had muttered under her breath more times than she could count. *No wonder Mr. Mitchell dumped her ass.*

As months moved into years Angie continued working at the busy, real estate office, tolerating the job that provided a little extra spending money and gave her some sense of importance and autonomy, however ridiculous that notion was. For Angie was hardly independent. Her father, a detective for the small police department in town, made sure she was either at school, cheer practice, at Sherry Mitchell's office, with close friends, or home. George Murphy loved his daughter with every ounce of his being, but he was a cop at heart, always surveying the environment around him, often tense, and constantly controlling. He considered it his duty to observe closely, for he had become the sole provider for Angie when her mother, Linda, died only an hour after Angie's birth from extensive hemorrhaging that could not be controlled either by the paramedics who delivered her to the hospital, the young doctor on call, or by a bevy of nurses on hand to assist at the time.

"I'm sorry," the doctor had told him dolefully. "The complications, combined with the normal stress of childbirth caused . . . "

George stopped listening. He refused to hear, for his world instantaneously dissolved in pieces at his feet. Despair was not a word he could possibly have understood until that very moment. He suddenly was awash in perspiration and yet he was cold. His hands found each other and curled inward in his lap. Nauseous and dizzy, he lowered his head and breathed, taking in air so rapidly that he was sure he would heave his heart out in pieces. He sat alone for minutes, his thoughts a tangle of memories: her long, auburn hair, her smell, the smile that never ceased to make his heart flutter, and her brown eyes glistening with joy when she had told him, "I'm pregnant, George. We're having a baby. I'm so happy."

For seven and a half months they had waited and planned. Rotund and radiant, she had blossomed with the pregnancy until that unforgettable day. One misstep was all it took. She had tripped on the tail of her nightgown at the top of the stairway and had tumbled down a flight of stairs where she had lain for moments stunned. She had been alone. Cautiously, after many minutes, she had managed to scoot to the phone and dial emergency. Paramedics had arrived in minutes, but by then she was faint and weak. Blood had begun to seep down her legs and when lifted gently onto a gurney, a greater gush had intensified the crisis. The birth had been rapid and intense, the baby whooshing into the hands of the doctor only minutes after Linda had been wheeled into the delivery room. The infant, who had not uttered a sound yet, had been whisked away to an incubator in intensive care and George had been shoved forcefully from the delivery room away from the frantic, medical staff now concentrating on Linda. Their efforts had been to no avail, however, and she had been pronounced dead by the young doctor whose face, stricken and pale, had informed George that the bleeding could not be stopped. George would never be able to erase that absolute nanosecond of time from his memory for the rest of his life.

In the aftermath, he had sat alone, demanding his privacy until a nurse had tugged on his shirtsleeve, had touched his hand gently, and had led him into the nursery. She had helped him into a gauzy, green gown and had ordered him to sit. George had been unable to do anything but obey, for he was numb from the inside out.

"You have a baby girl," the nurse had told him, placing the newborn tenderly in his arms.

In his muscular grasp, she had felt like a feather: light, fragile, and delicate. And she was his: his child, his responsibility, and his incredible new love. George had looked at the tiny face, the eyes tightly closed, the lips pursing, the cheeks flushed pink, and had been overcome with an emotion he never could have articulated. He had felt a sensation of floating, buoyed by hope and love for this tiny infant that his lovely Linda had given him. So contorted had been his feelings then, of love and loss, that he could hardly breathe, but he had, in and out, as great tears of joy and sadness had slid down his cheeks onto the soft, pink blanket.

⌘　⌘　⌘

"Get in," he told her.

Jack Mitchell had a firm grasp on Angie's arm when he unlocked the door of his pickup truck and pushed her firmly into the front seat. In seconds he slammed the door shut, rounded the back of his vehicle, and climbed in.

"There," he said. "Got you where I want you."

"You don't have me anywhere, Mr. Mitchell," Angie began, her heart pounding more with anger than fear. She was conscious of a dull pain in her neck, a result, surely, of her backwards spill on the slick, hallway linoleum just minutes before. Gingerly she touched the back of her head that had taken the brunt of the fall. It was tender and she winced with the touch.

Jack's voice softened. "I'm just worried about you, Angie. Now look at you. You're hurt and I need to get you home safe." His right hand moved from the steering wheel, reached her face, and grasped a thick strand of her hair. "You really have turned into a beautiful, young woman," he told her, his eyes falling to gaze at her breasts as his mouth twisting tastelessly.

For a moment she felt trapped and then she knew exactly what to do. Her chin tilted upward and her eyes fired daggers. "What do you want?" she asked, those simple words taking her back in time.

Angie had been cornered once before in her life, seven years before when she was only ten. She had been alone, sitting in a rounded, wicker chair on the front porch and was engrossed in reading Wilson Rawls' *Where the Red Fern Grows* when Jerry Gerard, a notably, wayward, neighbor boy sauntered up the steps. She had been startled.

"What do you want?" she had asked him hatefully.

Angie had been aware of Jerry's reputation. His propensity for troublemaking and complete disregard for anything intellectual had made him a dubious star at Hollow Vista High School.

"I hate that school. Those fucking teachers don't teach me shit," he had said more than once to anyone who would listen.

His innate belligerence clearly had clouded his ability to understand that his instructors did not, in fact, hold all the keys to learning. Nonetheless, miraculously he had graduated the year before likely as a result of a well-thought out, but tacit decision by the administration. If he were passed on, he would be gone. His counselor had confirmed as much in a private conference with the principal. "It's a no-brainer," the man had muttered, washing his hands of the kid.

Months later, with no job and college out of the question, Jerry had not yet committed to his future.

"Just seeing what's up, Angie," he had said, leering at her through heavy-lidded eyes.

"Go on away, Jerry," she had told him. "I'm busy."

"Don't look busy to me."

He had leaned against the railing that surrounded the porch and had ogled her for a full minute, rubbing his chest before his hand slipped lower to his groin.

Angie had stared at him and her heart had begun to race uncomfortably. A mass of unkempt, yellow hair had fallen over Jerry's forehead shadowing his face that was sallow and pocked from adolescent acne. He was skinny as a rail and thin faced with a hawkish nose. He was an ugly, young man.

"Your dad home?" he had asked suddenly rubbing the bulge in his jeans more vigorously.

"Not yet," she had replied and then tensed. She should have lied, should have told Jerry her dad was asleep or showering. Anything. It was too late though.

"Well, that's a good thing," he had snickered, his amber eyes narrowing to sinister slits.

"Why's that?" she had questioned. "He'll be home any minute."

"Yeah, right. Don't lie, you little bitch. Don't you ever lie to me," Jerry had snarled, his angry words wrapped up like coiled snakes.

"What's your problem, Jerry?" Angie had asked, her voice feigning composure. She had been anything but calm by then though, for adrenaline had its grip on her. Jerry had not been behaving normally. He had looked evil and mean and she had begun to quiver.

"Why are you shaking, Angie? What are you afraid of? There's nothing to be afraid of. I want to show you what's up," Jerry had sneered.

In that instant he had grabbed her skinny arm, spinning her upward from the chair, and then had pushed open the oak, front door, dragging her behind him. He had powered into her then, pushing her to the floor, pulling down her shorts and panties, digging between her legs with dirty fingers, and then jabbing her there with something hard. It had hurt and she had squirmed beneath his grasp, crying in pain and fear. Jerry's hand had muffled the noise until his assault was over and then Angie had let loose with screams that continued unabated until her father stood over her twenty minutes later. He had arrived home on time, but he had been too late, for his innocent child, bloody and bruised, had been raped and traumatized by God only knew.

It had not taken long for George Murphy to find out the truth, but between the instant he had found his daughter and that moment of unequivocal veracity, lay an uneasy, expanse of time during which George had berated himself for being a horrible father, for not observing well enough, for not taking better care, for not preventing a heinous crime on his daughter, and for being unable to protect her innocence. He had been unable to save his wife years before, and now this. He had been ambushed by feelings of failure and though he had wanted to lash out in rage, he had known he could not. Not then.

An ambulance had reached the scene within minutes, Angie had been eased onto a gurney and with one hand in her dad's and the other in the hand of a female paramedic, she had ridden silently to the hospital for treatment. When hours later she had found her voice, she told her father what had occurred. DNA evidence, in time, corroborated her story.

Jerry Gerard had been arrested that very evening, an eighteen-year-old molester who had found his future.

Though years had passed, neither Angie, nor her father would forget. Their love and trust was forged even stronger after that day, but George's protective instincts took precedent over all else. He would never let any man hurt his daughter again. Angie understood that as well as she could recite her name. And so it was, that Angie Murphy knew exactly what to do when Jack Mitchell advanced on her.

"I'm getting out of this car," Angie told her teacher "You won't stop me and you will never touch me again."

"Now, listen," Jack smirked, his putrid breath fouling the tiny space between them. "I'm just going to drive you home."

"No. You are not. I am leaving this truck now. You will not follow. You will not." She said the words her father had taught her.

Angie opened the door then and quickly stepped out holding her backpack between her body and Jack as though it were a weapon. She backed slowly away from the truck and then she ran. She sprinted five blocks in the dark night and swirling fog to her home, arriving just in time to meet her dad, her friend, and her confidant. She did not tell him about Jack Mitchell, however. She would protect him from that. It would have shattered him had he found out once more that he hadn't been watching closely enough.

CHAPTER NINE

FLO

Flo's car circled the faculty parking lot ten minutes be-fore she was due to sign in for duty at Cora Davies' desk that sat smack in the middle of the front office of Hollow Vista High School. Every weekday afternoon she was there seconds before 3:00 p. m. when the final bell rang. As was usual, Flo gripped the steering wheel and looked for Rob Green's tall, skinny figure that almost without fail was in the lot minutes before students were let go for the day. She would watch for his fedora hat, fixed on his head like a lofty helmet; it was his trademark. When he came into view, Flo would drive to within a car length of his parking space and wait. He'd back out; she'd pull in. No glances and certainly no words ever were exchanged, but their trading of plac-es was like the changing of the guard: quick, abrupt, and staid. Flo was unsure, of course; it was none of her business, but Rob Green's rapid and timely exodus every day led her to believe that he had not set foot in a faculty meeting or study session after school for years. As with the reams of Mr. Green's ungraded assignments that she had tossed into the dumpster year after year, his ability to avoid duties other teachers would not possibly attempt gave Flo reason to believe he had the goods on somebody. She would never have given voice to her thoughts, but she wondered nonetheless.

Once inside the aging office, Flo stepped up to Cora Davies. Old Cora was the cornerstone of the school in Flo's mind. She'd been there forever, even when Flo, herself, had been a student at Hollow Vista over thirty years before. Though Cora's face was etched with wrinkles now, and though the skin on her neck fell in floppy folds, her hazel eyes were warm and her greeting always positive, at least to the students and support staff, and always to Flo.

Flo could remember still Cora's greeting the first time she had set foot on the intimidating, high school campus when she had been only fourteen. Flo, unaccompanied by parents, unlike so many other students who had been flanked by one or two, had looked frightened and forlorn. Racked with shyness, she had been dressed inappropriately in wrinkled, corduroy pants and her father's faded t-shirt. Her attire, combined with hair that had been tied back in an unkempt knot on the back of her head, had been the clear antithesis of the other girls who had worn pleated skirts, soft blouses or sweaters, and had their hair coiffed to perfection. Within the confines of the office a small throng of girls had smiled, chatted, and giggled, clutching and picking at each other like frantic monkeys. It had not taken long until they not so discretely had ditched their parents turning their backs and rolling their eyes in disgust at actually having been caught there with them. Each girl's reaction was so similar to the next, it had been almost laughable to Cora Davies, but she had grown use to the dance played out every year by a new set of freshmen girls who wanted so badly to be grown up; yet, although their lashes were heavy with mascara and the office laden with wafts of their perfumes, they were merely children who could not see beyond the moment. They had snickered and leaned into each other that day, eying a pack of upper-class males strutting outside among the mass of students like princes. Flo had watched but did not move, standing still just inside the office door, not knowing whether to move forward or step back.

"Hi there, honey. Can I help you?" Cora had asked that distant day so long ago.

"I . . . I . . . I'm here to register for high school," Flo had told her, her hand subconsciously reaching for her cheek to touch the big, black mole that was stuck there.

"I can help you. Your mom or dad couldn't come with you?" Cora had asked.

"No. My parents both work days down at the cannery, so I came alone."

Flo had felt momentarily defensive, believing that the woman may have thought she was neglected or unloved; despite the fact that she had been on her own that day, however, she never felt alone. Her parents doted on her when they could, but having little themselves in the way of money and precious time, they could only do so much. Flo accepted their affection in small doses, returning their love unconditionally.

"If they could have been here they would have," Flo had mumbled quietly in deference to her parents.

"I'm sure they would have," Cora had smiled, intuitively interpreting the girl's discomfort. "Well, let's get started, then," she had added, gathering a stack of papers from the counter. "What's your name, honey?"

"Flo. Florence. Florence Gray. Maxine Gray," she had mumbled.

Cora had looked up that day, a quizzical gaze glazing over her face. "Florence or Maxine?" she had asked.

"Both," Flo had replied. "Florence Maxine Gray. Everyone calls me Flo."

"Well, Florence, Flo, let me help you," Cora had said, her sweet smile providing the young girl a momentary modicum of relief. Flo never had forgotten Cora's goodness. She had patted Flo's hand and had led her away to a table where the two had filled out sheet after sheet of redundant information required by the school. They had attempted to concentrate, but had been distracted more than once by a parade of boisterous students who clutched completed paperwork and passed by, ogling the woman and girl. Flo had made it a point to try to avoid direct eye contact with the other students who brushed by, but, nonetheless, painfully had observed each stare, each smirk, and each unspoken judgment. Flo's sensibility had been tortured that day and as a result she had grown small.

"Look, Janice. Look what the cat dragged in," she had heard a shrill voice whisper much too loudly.

"Next homecoming queen?" another had chimed in, looking directly and unabashedly at Flo.

"Lots of fashion sense, that one has," voice one had added, amid giggles and guffaws.

"Move on, girls," Cora Davies had spat. "Take your conversation out of the office."

Cora's eyes had squinted disgust as the girls retreated. "Sometimes I . . . " she had started, and then stopped, turning her attention again to Flo whose face had blushed pink, and whose eyes had become glassy with tears. Her hand had moved again to the black blob on her cheek. "Don't pay any attention to silly girls," Cora had stated firmly that afternoon. "You hear me? Ignore them."

Cora had known then that Flo would become a target, if not for any other reason than for malicious practice. The little girl beside her was naïve, and shy. Cora could only hope she would survive the slurs that surely would continue. All some heartless girls needed was a direction in which to aim their taunts and insults; it had been clear to Cora that they had found one before the school year had even begun. It had made her heart sink.

⌘   ⌘   ⌘

"Hey there, Ms. Davies," Flo said, pulling a clipboard from the wall next to Cora's desk.

"Hi Flo. How are you today?"

"I'm doing fine. And you?"

"Myself? I'm good. As for everything else around here, I'm not so sure. I'm sure you know what I mean."

"Got an idea," Flo said with a half smirk. "Not much to do but stand back and watch."

"I believe you're right about that, Flo. I feel like I'm right at the hub of a big, old carousel just watching a bunch of animals going around in circles with their emotions so up and down they don't know what to do." Cora's analogy was perfect in her mind, for it seemed to her, that since Sherry Mitchell had been found dead just days before, every person at the school had taken on the bearing of a carousel creature: tight-lipped, glassy-eyed, uncommunicative, not glancing aside, simply moving through the day, any would-be errant feelings tightly bound inside.

"Well, have a good evening, Flo."

"Thanks," Flo replied simply, clutching her lunch box close to her chest to avoid colliding with a teacher who had stomped by aiming for the principal's office. The woman's cheeks were red and puffed out, a load of words and rumors she was likely to be harboring, stuffed there.

"Midge, you need to wait," Cora cautioned. "Detective's in there."

The woman stopped immediately and glared at Cora as if she were the devil himself. "Well, you let me know when Cunningham's free," she spat. "And it better be soon."

Cora remained silent. *I'd like to give that Midge McGrath a piece of my mind. What a witch she's become over the years. Ever since old Fred left her high and dry, she's been angry at the world. Takes it out on anyone who gets in her way.*

Flo watched Cora's cheeks blaze red. *Got an idea what's going on in Cora's mind right now.* Flo backed through the swinging door onto the campus. Through the scratched, glass window she could see the ruddy-cheeked teacher circling, a coil of contention ready to snap.

I wonder what's gotten her underwear in a bundle. Doesn't really matter, but she looks like she's about ready to burst. Poor Mr. Cunningham's likely to get an earful.

Flo continued staring into the office as she stepped backwards directly into the path of Jack Mitchell, the top of her head whacking into his chin. "What the hell, Flo. Watch where you're going, you klutz."

Flo's body tensed immediately. She was mute.

"Well, the least you could say is sorry, you idiot," Jack continued. "God, some things never change."

He pushed past Flo then, shoved open the office doors and was sucked immediately into the tornado that was Midge McGrath.

CHAPTER TEN

MIDGE

Twenty minutes elapsed before Midge was able to see Roger Cunningham. By that time she was seething and her heart raced. She watched Detective George Murphy exit the principal's office, his eyes perusing the area from the front door, past the teachers' mailboxes, to a back door that led onto the campus. He was not smiling and his dark eyes flashed in recognition as they scanned past Midge standing, frumpy and clearly edgy inside the door. He noticed her arms first, crossed and locked tightly across her ample bosom; he saw her thin face, a deep red, with eyes that were dark, narrow slits. Her lips were tightly pursed. God only knew if she released her hold what might leach out. Lastly he noticed her feet; one wide, leather loafer was tapping the floor with dull thumps. It didn't take a mastermind to see that she was angry. George imagined he knew exactly why, and at this moment had no intention of saying a word. He had dealt with the woman just the evening before, learning very quickly that she was a badger, ready to eviscerate anyone who did not meet with her standards or who simply might not understand the power she ostensibly wielded. Though he had held his own with the woman and would never have let on that her behavior had scathed him, if only slightly, he had gained a new respect, however negative, of her. And so it was that he chose to depart from the high school office that afternoon, not saying a word. Midge McGrath was not, however, removed from George's ever expanding awareness of just who, indeed, inhabited his town. He kept every word and every nuance of Midge's demeanor categorized and filed in his mind, just as he had the others, later to be typed with care into reams of notes that he hoped in time would allow him to sort out details in order to solve the murder that had racked the town and made him more than a bit uneasy about the vulnerability of many folks in town, his daughter, Angie, among them. Midge was not the only individual he had questioned, but she had been the last.

⌘ ⌘ ⌘

Roger Cunningham sighed heavily, taking only a moment to relax after the departure of Detective Murphy before he drew up again, a tense coil of battered nerves that had nowhere to spring. Midge McGrath swooped into his office with her hollow cheeks blazoned ruby and her lips pressed tightly together in a hideous frown.

Roger would never have uttered the words aloud, but his thoughts were very real. *God, she's an ugly sight.*

"Three things, Roger! Three things!" she started, bearing down on the desk top with a clenched fist.

Roger sat back in his leather chair bracing for the on-slaught. Midge's approach to speaking with him never altered much and though she offended him to the core, he deferred to her ranting and simply listened. She was perhaps the most intense person he had ever met.

"What's the problem?" he asked, his insipid words a cover to the emotions that churned inside.

"First, are you aware, Roger, that that nasty Detective Murphy came to my house last night? Are you aware of that?" Midge had not sat down but instead was leaning over Roger's desk, leering at him.

"Sit down, Midge," Roger demanded weakly.

"I'll sit down when I'm ready," she replied and then did so, complying subconsciously. Her fist remained on the edge of the desk.

"Well, answer me, Roger. Were you aware that that detective detained me at my very own home last night?"

"Detained? No . . . " Roger was not allowed to continue.

"Well," she began again. "He was there, right about dinnertime, pounding on my front door, and demanding to have a word with me. I'm not a criminal, Roger. Why in God's Earth was he hounding me last night? Me? I'll tell you I won't put up with that kind of treatment." She spoke about the detective as if he were a delinquent student. "Did you put him up to this?"

Midge stared directly at Roger with such animosity that he shivered, belying what in his wildest imagination he inanely desired; a right hook into the woman's ruddy cheek would have set him in a better frame of mind.

"He's doing his job, Midge."

"Doing his job? Going around insinuating absurdities, conjuring nonsense about innocent people? Making judgments he has no right making?"

"Was he insinuating something?" Roger asked, prying.

"He certainly was! I believe he might have been trying to connect me with Sherry Mitchell's murder. Where were you the night of . . . whatever? How well did you know Sherry Mitchell? In what capacity did you know her? And aren't you a colleague of her ex-husband? How well do you know him? On and on he went, Roger, until he had me quite discombobulated if you can believe that! I will not put up with such disrespect. Did you put him up to this, Roger?"

"I'm not a detective, Midge, far from it. I will comply with requests from the police, though, and to that end I gave Detective Murphy a list of our faculty. What he does with it is his affair, not mine." Roger was as forceful as he had ever been.

"Well, you need to know I am deeply offended," Midge sat back then and stared, her lips still drawn, her eyes darting from one corner of the room to the other.

"I'm sorry you were uncomfortable," Roger offered. "Was there something else?"

"Oh, yes, yes indeed there is. You have a new teacher on your staff, Roger, who has been behaving in quite a disconcerting manner. Ms. Miller. Melody Miller. You know the girl I mean . . . the new English teacher. I'm not sure she even knows what she's teaching, but beyond that, her wretched behavior here at school is atrocious, an embarrassment both to her and to the rest of the faculty. Why, even the students are talking about her. Up and down. Up and down. Her mood swings and her emotional outbursts have to be stopped. Are you aware of her at all, Roger?" Midge spat.

"I am aware that we have an English teacher named Melody Miller. Yes," Roger replied. He was not about to offer more to Midge McGrath. Roger had been informed

with more detail than he wished he had been of the goings on between the young teacher and his friend, Jack
Mitchell. A round of golf and a few beers had Jack expos-
ing and elucidating events between the two in vivid images.
Roger knew theirs had been a brief, torrid relationship that
had ended sourly, but he had only Jack's version of the story. Beyond that, he knew little about the girl other than that
her parents were educators and that her evaluations had
been satisfactory.

"Well, Roger. That girl does not hold the standards
necessary to be a part of this faculty! Why, from what I've
observed, she's rather peculiar to say the least, not to mention she's unprofessional. I simply must put in my two cents
about her. You're not going to retain her to teach again
next year are you?"

The question bordered on a threat.

"The administrative and district staff will decide that,"
Roger stated dully although at the same time he bristled a
bit with Midge's bullying approach.

"Well, Roger, as head of the English Department, I
would hope I'd have a say," Midge continued, pushing.

"When the time comes, and that's not now, we'll talk,"
he said. He was quite done with the angry, callous woman
in front of him.

"You said you had three things you wanted to discuss,"
he added, hoping to divert this conversation into a new
direction.

Midge sat for a moment, brooding before blurting, "Yes.
One more thing."

Roger simply looked at her.

"Carlos. That custodian. Can't understand a thing he
says, his accent is so thick, and he's doing an awful job
cleaning up. Doesn't even vacuum under my desk. I want

you to reassign him. Give me someone new. That tiny, little limp rag of a woman, anyone will do. Just not him."

For the second time during his interchange with Midge, Roger wanted to do harm to her but he stifled the alien, emotional, and distressing response and thought instead of the custodian Midge had lambasted. Carlos Ortiz was the kindest, gentlest man in the world and in Roger's view worked harder than any custodian he had ever seen. Beyond that, his wide smile and deep chuckle carried through the hallways announcing the man's presence long before he arrived himself.

"I'm not sure, Midge," Roger said. "The custodians here all have their own niches. They do a good job."

"Well, that Carlos doesn't." Midge snapped again, "Look into it, would you Roger?"

Roger Cunningham leaned back in his chair and actually closed his eyes against the woman for a few seconds.

"Is that all?" he said finally.

"Yes, it is," she replied smugly

"You know, Roger, you're not above replacement either," she spat into the space in front of her as she stood. "And I have no intention of going away anywhere, as you well know."

CHAPTER ELEVEN

MELODY

Melody could not pull herself from bed. "I just want sleep," she mumbled to no one. Myriad, invasive musings prevented her wish, however. Thoughts tumbled, barreling down on one another, an avalanche with no sign of stopping: school; friends or the lack thereof; foes, Jack Mitchell seemingly the most recent; her parents whose ongoing pressure and demands haunted her. "Why don't they leave me alone? I'm an adult now," she murmured. "They don't trust me though, even now. I'm so stupid. They know."

Audible self-talk was common in Melody's world. It often filled the silence around her. This day was no different and the words threatened to settle spitefully yet again. They gave way instead, however, to additional, arbitrary, and invasive thoughts: tasks, so overwhelming she could not conceive how to begin; inconsistencies, most recently in the form of Midge McGrath who it seemed had lost interest in her, just when Melody had divulged too much;

loss, conjuring Jack Mitchell's visage again; and self-image with merciless judgments of her own creation. On and on random reflections rolled through. She could not stop the onslaught and was annoyed.

"I just want sleep," she grumbled again, squeezing her lids tightly and focusing on amoeboid shapes and flairs of mute colors dancing in the space captured there. She became aware of the tenseness of her body, her hands fisted, teeth clinched, and her knees drawn up toward her chest. She had rolled to her side into a fetal position that mirrored her absolute sense of helplessness to thwart her current, bewildering, yet not, uncommon state.

Melody had been prone to such malaise often beginning when she was only fifteen and continuing to the present. No one had known, not for years.

"She's a typical teen," her father, Harold had proclaimed years earlier when her mother had broached the issue of their daughter's mercurial temperament. "My Lord, Loretta. I'm an educator, an administrator. Do you think I haven't seen worse? Why, I've been working with teenagers for years. Know them all too well. Kids get moody. Up, down, all around!" he had chuckled. "Give it time. She'll grow out of it."

The fact was, though, that nobody – not her parents, her teachers, even her friends – could possibly have understood the demons that plagued Melody. No one knew, not until the moment Loretta Miller had pounded on Melody's locked, bedroom door a week after Melody's seventeenth birthday. Inside the room Melody had slumped on the bed, semi-conscious, having ingested pill after pill after pill, all ransacked from her father's medicine cabinet just hours before. From the place where she had lain, still and unmoving, as if anchored there, the sound of the knocking had roused her only to the point of hearing. The noise then had grown distant and faint. She had felt as though she was sinking into quicksand and quite willingly had given in to her wish that it soon would be over.

Melody had awakened in the hospital, oxygen flowing freely into her lungs, her head now dizzy, and her mind confused. One wrist had been tied firmly to the railing of a gurney, and the needle of a port had been jammed into her vein, carrying glucose and other nutrients into her body that shuddered erratically. She was alive. *Shit!*

Rounds of counseling sessions, cries from her mother, harrumphs from her father, and even a visit from the family's priest were useless. Melody's mood swings dominated her days and threatened her nights. Either she could not sleep at all, staring wide-eyed into the darkness, or she would aimlessly tiptoe barefoot up and down the hallways of her parents' once elegant, now aging, Victorian home, a mansion that had seen better days. And so it was with Melody. What had happened to that carefree childhood when she had hiked the foothills with her father, had baked chocolate brownies and fat, apple pies with her mother, or had painted watercolors at an easel placed perfectly at the corner of the front porch? From her perch behind her paintings, she had looked endlessly, and appreciatively, taking in the colors of the California landscape: the tinder dry hillsides awash in golden hues and sparking beneath the hot, summer sun and patches of pale, green grasses interspersed with weeds and low, fruitless brambles displayed in myriad shades of browns or bleached and parched to an off-color white. She had loved every facet, every nuance of the scene before her all of her life until one day quite inexplicably she did not.

Perhaps it had been then that Melody's mind initially had cuckolded her, for almost instantly the land she had so loved once lost its appeal. She could almost remember the exact day in late August. From behind her easel, on a stiflingly hot afternoon, everything changed. Her watercolor, half-completed, was a dull wash of russet, beige, and grey. *Ugly. Of course it's ugly.* She perused her work and the yard beyond her. *Just look out there. Ugly. It's ugly there, and ugly here, just like me, inside and out.*

She had ripped the entire pallet of paper from the easel, had thrown it on the cracking slats of the porch, and never had retrieved it. By November, the pad had pulverized into a sodden mound, having been drenched by early, winter rains. The easel had stayed put as well, disintegrating into a heap after a year or two.

And so it was with Melody. She felt as though she was rotting from the inside out. She simply could not tolerate the person she had become. Every attempt to move normally into a day was thwarted by her mind and the pain that resided there. It would not go away. No amount of reasoning, no amount of analysis could change the emotional abyss into which she fell time and time again. It is not to say she did not have happy moments. Her seventeenth birthday had been happy. Four, loud, chatty girlfriends had taken her to a movie and they had stuffed their mouths with chocolate cake and ice cream later at Melody's house. Her parents had stood by smiling. When the friends had departed, however, and when her parents had settled into their soft recliners for a glass of port and the evening news, Melody had said goodnight.

She had fallen instantly to sleep, satiated by too much sugar, and her head swirling with adolescent gossip. In an hour, however, she had aroused not because she wanted to be awake, but because the unrelenting anguish she felt inside was too intense to set her free. So, she had sat for hours, propped up by pillows, her knees drawn up to her chest, crying, sobbing really, until the first morning light. Though she had attended school that day, she had not made it through second period algebra.

"I'm nauseous," she had lied to the teacher, fleeing from the classroom and into the hallway where she had stood against the wall, sweating and shivering at the same time.

Avoiding detection by the campus supervisors and circumventing the main office to check out officially, she had wandered home in a daze. She remembered. The early morning mist had given way to warmth by the time she reached the house, even though the sun shined dully, an opaque, amorphous sphere in the autumn haze. Rummaging under a frayed mat at the end of the porch, she had found the door key, had entered the house, and had stumbled up the stairs to her room, the sanctuary that would save her, at least for a time. She had cried herself to sleep that day, sleeping for hours until her mother had arrived to find her in a disheveled heap on the bed. When she had seen her mother's face, Melody had been filled with two emotions: anger and sadness and she wasn't even sure why. Her attempted suicide had followed two days later.

⌘ ⌘ ⌘

Now, years later, the disturbing thoughts of distant days combined with current, nagging pressure had anchored Melody between the sheets for much longer than they should have. She heard the squeal of her alarm clock once more. It was seven o'clock. School began just shy of eight. She would be late.

"Shit," she sputtered aloud. "I'm never going to make it on time. Stupid. Why do I do this to myself? I'm a teacher now. Need to be smarter."

Melody slid from bed, stood slowly, and sighed, the sound she issued a blend of melancholy and anxiety that froze her once again. *I just want to sleep.* She actually closed her eyes momentarily in the still of her bedroom.

"I can't though. If I hope for one second to have a job next year, I at least have to show up for this one." That perhaps was the single, rational statement she could manage.

She skipped a shower, teased her hair into its customary pouf, and dabbed on mascara, blush, and lipstick before attempting to select an outfit to wear. She settled on black slacks, a white blouse, and grey sweater. *Perfect. No one will notice me, not that they do anyway.*

She thought then about Jack Mitchell wondering wistfully what he had ever seen in her in the first place. She lit then on the simple truth. Sex. *I'm so dumb.*

When she arrived at her classroom doorway it was five minutes before the final bell. Students already were outside the door leaning against the wall or squatting, their butts pressed to the wall. Few were smiling, save for Angie Murphy who was leaning into the broad chest of Brad Browning, whose claim to fame was his prowess on the football field in the fall and winter and whacking at a baseball in the spring and summer. In between those activities, however, it was clear to see he had enough to keep him occupied. Brad towered over Angie and clutched her close, looking into her face approvingly, all the while allowing his hand to slide to her bottom where he unabashedly kneaded her there through skin-tight jeans. With Melody's arrival Brad looked away from Angie. He watched Melody's eyes glance the couple's way and he winked seductively at the young teacher before she turned abruptly, fumbling with her keys before unlocking the classroom door.

God, these kids! Think they can get away with anything.

With the classroom now available, the students filed in, brushing by their teacher as if she didn't exist. After the first twelve or so had herded through, Melody looked from the doorway into the hall, perusing it for stragglers, Brad and Angie among them. Her attention was drawn, however, to the figure standing just outside the adjacent classroom. Midge McGrath stood staring at Melody, her lips contorted in disgust, her eyes livid, and her face red. She made no attempt to hide her distain for her young colleague's tardiness and, what she quite certainly must have deemed, a lack of professionalism. Though the girl had confided in her candidly just a few months before, and she had listened, Midge was not impressed. Furthermore, and more importantly, she was very aware that the brief interaction with the silly, young teacher had ignited her own, long-standing tendency for caring unduly for the odd underdog. She aimed to quash that annoying bent immediately at all costs for she had paid an enormous price for such a predilection when she had married poor Fred who, although certainly not worthy of her time or faint affection, had humiliated her by disappearing to God only knew where. As a result she had existed alone, crammed full of bridled rage, for too many years,

Unwilling to cease glaring at Melody, Midge heightened her abuse. She shook her head from side to side in blatant revulsion, a clear message to the girl that she was faltering in more ways than one.

Melody could not bring herself to respond in any way to Midge McGrath or look further for slacking students. Instead she turned quickly into the classroom and shut the door. At her desk she emptied her briefcase, began shuffling through papers, and mumbled, "Okay, it's time. What in the hell are we supposed to do today?"

CHAPTER TWELVE

JACK

Jack had been loitering around the teachers' mailboxes for twenty minutes waiting for Midge McGrath to finish her business with Roger Cunningham. He suspected Roger was knee deep in gossip, innuendo, and demands from the woman whom Jack had held in contempt for years. The very fact that Midge had pried into his private affairs when he had been married to his wife, Sherry, made his blood boil even now.

He recalled initially meeting Midge the year he began his teaching career at Hollow Vista. Having already established her position, she quite simply was a younger version of the meddling, arrogant woman she was today, and then as now, he wondered how on God's Earth such a creature had been created. She was plain to the point of being homely and as abrasive as a grindstone. He and the other staff members had learned to expect her fierce, in-your-face manner though, and for the most part, tolerated it.

It was not until much later when Sherry had been commissioned as Midge's realtor that Midge truly had set Jack off. Again, it was the abrasive attitude: demanding results, insisting on having her way, assuming she knew more than his wife, Sherry in regard to real estate issues, and inquiring into personal matters that clearly were not her business. Jack had been in love with Sherry at the time, or at least he believed himself to have been, and had become defensive when Sherry complained about Midge's requests and ultimatums regarding the sale of her country property after her old man, Fred McGrath, had disappeared into nowhere. If she had been angry before his flight, his absence only exacerbated her negative bearing that was now a trademark.

"That woman's going to drive me crazy," Sherry had complained, filling a hefty glass of merlot and collapsing onto the couch. "You know me, Jack, I don't easily acquiesce to anybody, but I'm about ready to throw in the towel after dealing with that bitch!"

"Do," Jack had replied tersely, yielding to Sherry's rant.

"Ah, the sale of her house is one thing, but that's not the half of it. She's a nosey, old snit! She's asked more than once about how we met, how you are around the house, if you really like teaching, if we plan on having a family. Shit, she has no business knowing our personal affairs. She even asked how I felt about being the major bread winner."

Sherry had continued.

"Midge actually said to me, 'I do know what a teacher's salary is, you know. I'm sure you make much more than that!' She had the nerve to insinuate that I looked down on you because I make much more money."

"Then she said, 'Well, education's important too. At least Jack's a college graduate. Are you?' Ah, just thinking about that witch pisses me off!"

Midge knew how to strike a nerve and had done just that when she snidely alluded to Sherry's education, or lack thereof. The fact of the matter was, that Midge could not have had a clue as to the degree of schooling Sherry had had, but that made no matter. Her innuendo was poised perfectly for a reaction, and when Midge saw Sherry's neck and cheeks tinge red, she knew she had hit a home run.

Why that particular conversation, spoken so many years ago, popped into Jack's mind at this moment was an unanswerable question. It had though, and with it, the realization that Midge had tapped into a truth. The fact that Sherry made much more money than Jack, as well as the fact that she was an autonomous and aggressive woman in her own right, had become paramount in the demise of the marriage. When it ended, Sherry had stated coldly, "You never did quite make it, did you, Jack? I can't keep picking you up financially or otherwise. You're just not good enough for me, Jack. I need more."

He had not forgotten her words. Moreover, the deprecation of his worth melded into hatred and festered inside so intensely that it engulfed not only Sherry, but Midge McGrath as well. In Jack's mind, Midge had been an instigator, and to that end, the root cause of his divorce. Though even Jack had questioned his sincere capacity for experiencing true love, he did know, without a doubt, that he had never adored any woman as much as he had his stunning Sherry. In truth, he secretly had wondered from the beginning if it would last, but the dissolution of their marriage was a profound disappointment that burrowed its way to his heart and lodged there.

⌘　⌘　⌘

Jack took one look at Midge as she left Roger's office and knew she had done damage. Her entire body communicated it: arms tense and crossed across her chest, lips drawn tightly, eyes narrow slits, and her cheeks crimson. Looking at no one, she stomped past Cora Davies without so much as a glance and pushed her way out of the heavy, office door toward the humanities wing. Whatever had transpired in the principal's office had not been completely left there. Midge carried her hostility like badge of distinction.

"Better go on in there, Jack," Cora said bluntly. "You might need to pick up the pieces."

Initially Jack looked at Cora blankly, but quickly offered her a drawn smile. *The old gal knows more than she lets on.*

Jack entered the office, closing the door behind him. He watched Roger look around the room as if searching for specters, and then sigh heavily.

"Jesus Christ, Jack. That woman is a jack hammer!" Roger blurted. "Sorry, Jack, poor analogy, I guess. Didn't mean to use your name in vain."

Roger's comment made Jack grin, if only for a moment. "What'd the bitch want anyway?" he asked.

"Oh, different day, same old stuff. She's irate because Detective Murphy questioned her last night. 'I'm not a criminal,' she said. 'I won't stand for that disrespect,' on and on. Then she was maligning your favorite, English teacher, Melody Miller, but we don't need to go into that. Then to top it all off, she had the gall to ask me to remove Carlos Ortiz from his custodial position in her wing. Said she couldn't understand him. 'Can't understand a word the man says!' Guess that makes him worthless? Jesus Christ, he's the best custodian we have!"

"Oh, by all means, switch him with old Flo. She gives me a pain in the ass just looking at her," Jack replied snidely.

He was careful to avoid commenting on Melody Miller or Detective Murphy though. He wanted to avoid each of them with equal intensity.

Roger could do nothing but shake his head at the teacher in front of him. Jack was a piece of work himself, but for some odd reason, Roger liked his friend. Roger reached into the deep recess of his bottom drawer then and pulled out a bottle of Jack Daniels whiskey. "Don't do this very often, but, Jesus Christ, Jack, I need a snort!"

"Don't mind if I do," Jack replied, accepting the silent offering with a wide grin.

⌘ ⌘ ⌘

At home later that evening, Jack's mind betrayed him. For reasons he could not have articulated, memories stirred a hornet's nest there. Sherry's face, in every image imaginable, appeared relentlessly to torment him. Though he and Sherry had been apart for over a year, he was convinced he would never find another woman who could replace her. Jack had so idolized his wife that any substitute virtually was impossible; as a result, more than a few females he even remotely considered, paid the price of his loss. Melody Miller was the last in a sporadic batch of women he had charmed and then taken to bed multiple times until he tired of them. Not once did he feel remorse for his rakish, callous behavior that left more than a few of his victims injured mentally if not physically as well.

The local news was garbled noise in the background and Jack was reading in his leather recliner, sipping a cold Budweiser, when the unexpected happened. His throat tightened, his fingers twisted, and he began to sob. Not even when he and Sherry had said their final good-bye, did Jack cry. Now, however, his shoulders shook with intensity as the grief he had never expunged took precedence and he was caught in its snare. Jack's tears flowed untethered down his cheeks and onto his shirt, his nose filled with mucus that drained into his throat, and he began to cough violently. In anger at his inability to control his emotion, he grasped the beer can so tightly that it crumpled beneath his force, and the foaming liquid spurted upward, showering him.

"You fucker!" he shouted into the room as he hurled the half-empty can across the room. It landed askew at the base of a bookcase where the remaining contents soaked into the carpet there.

For agonizing minutes more, Jack cried. When he thought he had gained control, another remote image of Sherry would filter though his mind bringing on another onslaught of tears. He was undone. Eventually, he was able to compose himself for a moment, but just as quickly his sadness was replaced with anger, anger at the man he knew he had become. His heart pounded and be began to sweat. Never in his life, save for the moments after his mother's abhorrent acquaintance had abused him so many years before, had he been filled with such sensations. The horrific attack on him as a child had been buried deep, and now, perhaps for the first time, in the midst of this emotional breakdown, he admitted it was an integral part of his angst. Grief for a tainted childhood had lain fallow for much too long. And on this night that realization, compounded with the still-raw death of Sherry, caused Jack to ponder whether life need go on at all.

CHAPTER THIRTEEN

ANGIE

Angie Murphy and Brad Browning entered Melody Miller's classroom just as the final bell blared. Angie found her seat quietly. Brad, on the other hand, kicked his desk noisily, and bellowed obnoxiously, "Good morning, Ms. Miller!" He then winked at his teacher once more and flopped into the desk next to his girlfriend. He scooted it closer to her, draped his arm around the back of Angie's desk protectively, and perused the classroom to make sure he had gained the attention he so adored. Not yet finished with his antics, however, he inappropriately gestured to one of his football buddies, flipping his middle finger so all could see, before slouching into his seat. He dropped his free hand then and began caressing his crotch.

"God, Brad!" Angie hissed, "Get a grip!"

"Just what I'm doing, baby," he replied, licking his lips provocatively.

"What are you looking at, jackass?" Brad muttered hatefully to Willard Dunn who had been staring with wide-eyed discomfort at Brad's behavior. Willard reacted immediately, his shoulders inching upward and his head jerking forward toward the front of the room. "You look like a goddamn turtle," Brad continued. "Eyes to the front, turtle boy," he hissed to Willard who was seated to Brad's right, much too close for Willard's comfort.

If Ms. Miller had heard Brad's denigrating attack on Willard, she ignored it, but Angie did not.

She squirmed in her desk, "Cut it out, Brad. Willard hasn't done anything to you."

"Oh taking up for old country boy, are you? Got a thing for old Willard, old Willie, old turtle boy?" Brad asked, bullying her.

"Brad," she whispered, "just stop."

Angie turned her head away from him then and pretended to listen to Ms. Miller's assignment. She could tell already what was coming. Ms. Miller planned to have them writing again, an in-class essay on the novel they all supposedly had completed. *Didn't get her lesson plans done again. When all else fails, think up something really fast. Make us write all period long.*

"You should have finished reading *Lord of the Flies*," Melody began, "William Golding's work is a classic. It truly delves into the intricacies of human nature. How civil are we anyway? Do all people have a dark or savage side? It's something to consider. Just look at what's happened here in town recently. There's been a murder and someone's guilty. I think it's safe to say we're all a little on edge. Of course what's happened here is a different story, but it makes a person think. Do we really know the people around us?"

"Sounds a little paranoid," Angie whispered to Brad.

"Yeah," Brad answered, his voice low and husky. "She's scared – a little too close for comfort maybe. Heard she was messing around with Mr. Mitchell a while back."

"Yeah. Well, he's a creep," Angie stated tersely before continuing. "Wonder if Ms. Miller knows Sherry Mitchell was his wife?" Angie murmured behind her hand, pondering for the first time why her boss had kept using Jack Mitchell's last name as her own after the divorce was final. *Odd.*

"Brad, Angie. Enough of the conversation," Melody uncharacteristically asserted. "Anyway," she said, directing her words to the entire class, "what I want you to do is to write about what you believe is the theme of *Lord of the Flies.* Explain why. Back up your thoughts with examples of events you recall from the text. You have the entire period to write. Get busy."

Several groans and sighs were audible around the room including one loud moan from Brad. He hadn't done the reading, Angie was sure. Angie had though. Grades were important to her and she wanted that A.

"Can we use the book?" Brad asked, this time with a polite plea.

"I suppose, if you must," Melody replied. *Brad needs all the help he can get and little Miss Cheerleader won't be able to write this essay for him.*

Melody Miller was not fond of Angie who was what Melody had never been: cheerful, bright, outgoing, and popular. Just looking at the girl, made Melody despondent. And although Angie would never have let on, the feeling was mutual. Ms. Miller was the antithesis of Angie herself, always upset or depressed, and clearly unsure of herself. Angie grew tense just being around the woman.

⌘ ⌘ ⌘

With English class over, Angie and Brad parted ways, he to gym class and she to math analysis. She made it through the day, not pestered by Brad whose classes took him in a different direction. Her last class of the day was biology. She loved science, but detested the teacher. For the first time since Mr. Mitchell had physically forced her into his truck a few days prior, she would have to face the man again. A bubble of anxiety toyed with her. *I'll just ignore him. I'll look around him, not at him. I'll talk to Suzie, or there's always Willard.*

Willard Dunn, the unfortunate student who had been the brunt of Brad's barbs during English class that morning, had been matched up with Angie as her lab partner. It was an uncomfortable pairing for both of them at first, but Angie adjusted quickly to the young man's southern twang and insecurities. Willard had arrived at Hollow Vista High School just days after the start of the year, from Alabama. The poor guy was ridiculed from the moment he arrived for more reasons than Angie could count. First, his appearance made him stand out. He came to school the first day wearing faded, blue overalls and a plaid shirt buttoned neatly to the top. His dusty, blond hair lay in wide, flat chunks as if a comb had never touched it, but otherwise he appeared clean, save for his large hands that were rough and calloused with age-old dirt hiding in the crevices. His eyes were an icy blue color, a shade that either repulsed people or drew them to him and his smile, crooked and timid, revealed a chipped front tooth in need of dental care.

On his first day in the biology class Mr. Mitchell had squared Willard up in front of the other students and humiliated him with his introduction.

"This here's Willard Dunn," Jack Mitchell said in an affected Southern drawl that he wisely and quickly dropped. "He's moved out West from the deep South with his family. Get to know him. You might learn something about another part of the country. That is, if you can understand him!" Jack had chuckled at his inane joke while Willard had blushed red, fumbled with the leg of his overalls, and scanned the room as though wishing for a magical exit to appear.

Angie cringed. *Mr. Mitchell is such a jackass.*

"Willard, you're going to have a lab partner, and to start, that'll be Angie Murphy," Jack Mitchell stated with a smirk. He knew correctly that the new student would be tongue-tied alongside the pretty, popular cheerleader. The thought of the kid's discomfort gave him a perverted sense of pleasure. Jack did not know his student, Angie, very well however.

Jack Mitchell's demeaning insults toward Willard lodged in Angie's mind. She was determined. In no way would she be a part of her teacher's inappropriate and insensitive play. Angie remembered that day very well. When Mr. Mitchell had finished his remarks, a few chuckles could be heard from students in the room and Suzie had skewed up her face in disgust. Angie could read her friends' thoughts: *Good God, poor Angie. She's like the most popular person on campus and she's stuck with this nerd every day in biology. She's going to hate it.*

Angie did not hate it. She took the assignment in stride gesturing for Willard to join her at the shiny, black lab table in the back of the room.

"Hey, Willard. I'm Angie Murphy. So where is it you're from? How long have you been here? Do you have brothers and sisters?"

Angie peppered Willard with questions, before he gave up. He smiled.

She learned that he was from Alabama. His family had moved to California for a new start. His dad was a handyman who helped with small house repairs and was a whiz at landscaping. Willard's mom stayed home taking care of a two-year-old, baby boy, and a four-year-old girl. "Charlie and Massie," Willard told her. "I have two other sisters in grade school. They're eight an' eleven, named April an' Cindy. They're pretty much a mess."

"So you're the oldest of five kids?" Angie could not imagine being part of such a family.

"Yeah. All spread out from two t' seventeen. What about your family?"

"It's just me. No siblings," Angie replied. "Just me and my dad."

"No mama?" Willard asked as if he had been struck.

"She died just after I was born," Angie said stolidly, her smile disappearing for the first time. "I don't talk about her. Don't remember a thing. My dad tells me stuff, but we don't talk about the past too much."

"I'm real sorry ya' lost your mama," Willard said quietly, fidgeting with the new biology book he had been given.

Angie grinned again. "It's okay, Willard. Like I said, I don't remember. Thanks though."

"Guess we're the two O's," she added somewhat childishly. "The oldest and the only."

That was the beginning and for Angie and Willard first impressions were important although at that time they never could have told each other so.

Willard seems like a nice guy. He's easy enough to talk to anyway. He's really shy though. Guess he could use some help to come out of his shell. Hope he doesn't get picked on too much. He could be a target.

Willard had mused about their meeting as well. *Nice girl an' real pretty. It's real nice of her t' talk t' me. Maybe we can be friends.*

CHAPTER FOURTEEN

FLO

Flo stood silently at the door of the custodial closet in the science wing and watched the students exit. The initial rush caused her to hold her breath, for as was usual, the students, some gabbing or shouting, others silent as the dead, pushed and shoved each other through open classroom doors and down the hallway, like lemmings to an open tundra beyond. Such moving masses of high school humanity had intrigued Flo for years and, if triggered to do so, she could remember still being an integral part of the lot over twenty years before. Even then, certain behaviors mirrored those of the students that at this moment were alone in their togetherness, each one pressing forward with a mute and individual intention to be somewhere, to meet someone, or simply to escape the confines of school. Flo had been one in the latter group, simply wanting out of the place that continuously reminded her of her imperfections. High school for Flo had been synonymous with pain.

From the first day of classes students had gawked at her, snickered behind her back, and been outwardly cruel, as Jack Mitchell had been. She had not forgotten and likely had not forgiven, although as a widowed, forty-five year old woman simply trying to get by, she did not dwell.

With the first, explosive exodus over, the remainder of the students left their classrooms and wandered alone or with a friend to the double doors that led onto the campus. Among those strolling along were Angie Murphy and her boyfriend, Brad something. Flo didn't know his last name and wouldn't have given the boy a second look save for the fact that he was an annoying reminder of Jack Mitchell, cocky and arrogant. Almost every day Brad slipped into the hallway of the science wing, having escaped his class early to gather his prized possession, Angie. On this day he stood next to her biology lab class door for many minutes before she slipped out, thankfully with her backpack in tow. He enveloped her with his huge arm and pulled her to him assertively. As they walked away his hand slid to her butt and rested there until they were gone. Looking on from the doorway of the science lab was the lone figure of Willard Dunn, although Flo did not know the boy's name, not yet anyway. He stared at the couple in front of him, a look of mild displeasure clouding his features. Flo noticed.

Willard sauntered slowly toward the heavy, exit doors, and surprisingly slammed them open with such an angry force that Flo was startled. He then launched into a sprint. When the doors had suctioned shut behind him, Flo turned immediately to her duties, but strangely could not forget the image of the young man in flight.

⌘ ⌘ ⌘

After only an hour, Flo's nightly ritual of emptying trash-cans, scrubbing graffiti, and vacuuming was interrupted. She heard footsteps pounding down the polished linoleum and turned to see the faces of the head custodian, Carlos Ortiz and the principal, Roger Cunningham. The two were a study in opposites. Roger, at well over six feet in height, towered over Carlos who likely was only five and a half feet tall on tiptoes. While Mr. Cunningham, as thin as a rake, strutted into the room, Carlos waddled alongside him, his belly distended, and his cheeks shiny and rotund. The principal, who always appeared pale and solemn, looked even more so next to Carlos whose skin was a dark bronze and whose smile was wide. Their entrance together startled Flo. *Am I in trouble?*

"Good evening, Flo," Roger began.

Flo stared at the two men, not knowing whether to look up into the eyes of the principal, or lower down to the face of Carlos. "Good evening," she said.

"Flo, we were wondering, well, Carlos and I were discussing, well, I've been considering the possibility of reassigning you to the humanities wing for a month or two, maybe longer," Roger stammered, his voice a dull monotone.

"Has there been a complaint?" Flo asked, color rising onto her cheeks. Her thoughts went instantly to Jack Mitchell. *He's probably the one.*

"Oh, no," Roger told her. "Nothing like that. Everyone knows you do a fine job."

"Then why?" she asked.

Roger was not about to admit to either Flo or Carlos the reason for his decision to switch his custodians to different areas. He would never embarrass Carlos by revealing the content of Midge McGrath's rant about the man, but more importantly he could not admit that the woman had coerced him into making the change. Just that morning, a letter had been shoved at him. Midge would be taking her complaint, in the form of a grievance to the union if Carlos Ortiz was not removed from her area of the high school. She had offered a litany of reasons why, all of which had been fabricated of course, but her threat was real. Roger certainly did not need more problems with which to contend, so he acquiesced to her intimidation although it made him sick to his stomach to have to do so.

"I attended a conference recently," he lied, "about managing high school logistics, maintenance being one component. The suggestion was to rotate custodians on a regular basis, so as to acquaint them with the entire staff, to help them understand the school as a whole, and to avoid complacency, not that I think any of my custodians are doing a poor job."

Flo looked at Roger Cunningham as though he were invisible. She could see right through him. His feeble reasoning was clearly concocted, but she was not about to complain. She knew her place, at the bottom of the pecking order. She would tell the truth, however.

"I'd rather stay put," she said. "I have a pretty good system in place for handling all the messes that occur in the science wing, but I'm willing to go wherever I'm needed. When will this change occur?"

"Monday, after the weekend," Roger said docilely, the sound of his voice deceiving his authority.

Flo continued staring at him as though he was an unwelcome menace. He understood. He had given Midge McGrath an identical glare after having read her letter earlier that day. Had he been a stronger man, perhaps he would have contested her demands, but his hands were tied. And so were Flo's. She had no choice but to follow directions.

After the men left her, Flo walked slowly into Jack Mitchell's classroom for the last time. At least she would be out of his line of fire for a while. Monday would bring her new assignment into better focus. She simply would have to wait and see.

⌘ ⌘ ⌘

Flo had never been one to meddle, but on this night, she did. She wandered to the front of the classroom where Jack's desk was angled into the corner. From the chair behind it she could tell that Jack comfortably could peruse and monitor the lab, his miniature dynasty with all its subjects, as he saw fit. Flo imagined his sense of power. She looked at a pile of ungraded notebooks on one corner of the desk and a neatly arranged collection of science books lodged between wooden bookends on another. Slowly she circled to the back and sat gingerly in Jack's chair. She stared out at the empty lab, wondering, when Jack was present, what he observed. *On whom did his eyes fall most often? The likes of the pretty, little Angie most certainly had gained his attention, but how well did he see the others?* Every year students shuffled through. Face after face passed by until the memory of them must have become a blur. Flo could only assume that was the case for Jack, because it certainly was so for her. Oh, a few students were memorable, even for Flo, but for the most part, faces and personalities were forgotten the moment the bell rang for the last time each year.

Uncharacteristically for Flo, minutes ticked past and she did not move. Finally she did, but not to resume her duties. She slid open the top drawer of Jack's desk. It was cluttered with pens, pencils, post-it notes, paper clips, and motes of dust and dirt. The other drawers were equally untidy with papers shoved into manila folders or folded into rectangles and shoved into deep recesses that likely had not been cleaned for years. Flo pawed through the mess. The papers there revealed phone numbers without names to accompany them; notes that must have been snagged from the hands of bored students; short, self-directed memos to Jack himself to remember this, that, or the other; and various photographs of students, usually senior portraits of smiling faces on the front, and lines of endearments to the teacher on the back. Flo continued her shuffling, her fingers finally alighting on a smudged photograph of Jack with a dark haired woman whose eyes were startlingly blue. Her face bore a broad smile, as did Jack's and in their hands they held crystal, champagne flutes. *Was this Jack's wife? Was this Sherry Mitchell?* Flo stared at the picture for a long time before she turned it over. Bold letters scrawled there revealed the answer to what Flo had wondered: *Wedding Day – Sherry and Jack.* A swath of red ink had crossed out Sherry's name and beneath it the word *bitch* had been penned in bold, black, perfectly printed letters. Flo subconsciously ran her fingers over the ink for a moment and then turned the photograph over again, mesmerized by Sherry's eyes. She shivered slightly as she stared, for she was taken aback suddenly by the knowledge that the advent of fate's fury, unbeknownst to the smiling faces in the picture, had been at work, poised to change everything. Simply the consideration of such a notion made Flo feel small. Suddenly, without deliberating, for a reason she never could have articulated, she slipped the photograph into her pocket, closed the drawer, and scuttled back into the hallway.

CHAPTER FIFTEEN

ANGIE

Angie wandered into the cold, quiet kitchen having dropped her backpack and jacket at the bottom of the stairway where they would stay put until later when she made her way upstairs to her room. For now, all she could think about was food.

I don't know what's gotten into me, lately. I'm always hungry for some reason. What sounds good?

Angie plucked a tangerine from a bowl on the table. "I love these things," she said aloud. She ate one, and then a second. She savored them, licking at the sweet juice that lingered on her lips, all the while staring out of the kitchen window at the expansive back yard. The grass had not needed mowing all winter, but sprouts of green abounded now. Soon her father would be outside cutting and edging the lawn and trimming the bushes to perfection. In the spring and heart of summer, George Murphy spent hours caring for his little corner of paradise. It gave him comfort. His wife, Linda, had loved being outside too, and had spent hours planting flowers, pulling weeds, and on unbearably hot days, sitting in a lawn chair in the shade of a sprawling oak tree, a tumbler of lemonade in hand. After her death, George frequently found himself drawn outside. It was almost as though Linda's spirit was still there and when grief overwhelmed him as it often still did, he found peace minding the half-acre of land she had adored. Angie had followed in his footsteps. From the time she was a toddler she was her father's shadow and had grown to love the land with the same intensity.

At the far end of the lawn was the garden that Angie and her father tended together throughout each summer. For the entire winter it had been unattended, a mass of drooping, nearly lifeless plants that in late fall had stopped producing plump, red tomatoes, green and jalapeño peppers, and more crookneck and zucchini squash than they could have consumed in a full year. Angie knew that she and her dad soon would be working again, side-by-side, planting seeds and bedding plants for another round.

She noticed two pumpkins that never had been harvested lying like huge orange spheres in a tangle of brown, shriveled vines and leaves. Seeing them there conjured a memory. In the fall, she and her dad had picked several other pumpkins, lugged them into the house, and pulled the seeds from the guts of the squash. Once cleaned and salted, they had baked the seeds on cookie sheets. She could almost smell the rich aroma now. Munching the freshly roasted seeds had been an annual treat since she was a little girl. Then the two had carved the pumpkins into jack-o-lanterns to set on the front porch for Halloween. It was a tradition they still maintained although Angie was much too old for trick-or-treating. Still, she dressed up sometimes, usually as a welcoming witch, and doled out candy to the children in the neighborhood as her father stood by solicitously. Though she was warmed by the memory, she suddenly shivered.

The recent murder of Sherry Mitchell was a reality that pushed its way into her mind much too often. Ridding herself of thoughts about the successful and vivacious woman who had been her boss had become impossible and this tormenting shift had thrown Angie off balance. And if her life had been altered, certainly others in the community suffered as well. *Would folks lock their doors and keep the children close or would people stifle their apprehensions and carry on as always?* The thoughts were unsettling. Angie was consumed without warning with a wave of emotion that brought tears to her eyes and she sank, sobbing suddenly, to the linoleum floor of the kitchen. She was crying so hard that she did not hear the front door open; nor did she see the anguished look on her father's face when George Murphy slipped into the room and found her there, slumped on the floor in the dim and dusky light.

⌘　⌘　⌘

Angie had walked home alone that day after leaving Brad at the door of the gym. He had football practice, and for that she was thankful. She liked Brad, maybe even had loved him once, but his constant presence, either in a class they shared, or waiting for her at the door of one they didn't was becoming an irritation. Such behavior on his part was new and annoying, for Angie had many friends, male and female, and she always had enjoyed her autonomy. She gained energy from interacting with other people whether it was the squad of cheerleaders who chattered and bickered at practice, her girlfriends who gathered in the bathroom to primp and share gossip, or her classmates, many of whom sought Angie's friendship in an effort to gain popularity themselves. She even enjoyed talking to her lab partner, Willard Dunn, who in the recent months seemed to have adapted to life in the central valley town and who talked to her openly at the corner lab table they shared each day during biology class. He still was the brunt of snide remarks from the likes of Brad and his buddies, but he was stronger than his attackers may have thought. Initially Angie had seen Willard's face scrunch distressfully and his eyes shine with tears, as he reacted to his tormentors. He at first had pulled his shoulders upward and scurried away to put distance between himself and the taunts that followed him. More recently, however, he had mustered the wherewithal to simply ignore the remarks that still routinely were aimed at him.

"Turtle man! Never have seen a turtle move so fast!"

"Look at him go."

"Where are your overalls, Willard?"

"Did your mommy buy you some new clothes at the thrift store?"

"Guess you got nothing to say. Doesn't matter. Can't understand a word that comes out of your mouth anyway."

"Where are you going, turtle man?"

"Go on. Move a little faster!"

The jeers were sport for insensitive boys who should have known better and they were bait for the girls who looked on, laughing in agreement in order to gain their own approval. The verbal attacks had diminished in recent months, but still occurred from time to time like a bad habit. The slurs had done their damage, Angie was sure. She had watched in disapproval, but had said nothing and for that she was a bit angry with herself. Willard, she had come to know, was a very nice person. She liked him, and was more than certain that the feeling was mutual. So her stomach knotted when Willard became a target for the likes of Brad and his buddies. It was a sensation that had surprised her.

⌘ ⌘ ⌘

George Murphy's throat had tightened at the sight of his daughter sobbing almost uncontrollably in the kitchen that evening, but he managed to find words that he hoped would console her.

"Angie, honey? What's wrong?"

"Oh, Dad." Her words were so soft George almost could not hear, but when she gazed up at him, he knew she would confess.

"I'm just feeling a little miserable right now. I don't know why, really. I came home and was staring out at the yard, thinking about our gardens, about picking our vegetables all summer long, and carving pumpkins in the fall. I was thinking about all the normal things we've done every summer and fall, and then I realized nothing is normal any more. Are people going to take their children out on Halloween next October? Do you think they'll be afraid to? Are we going to make jack-o-lanterns for them, or is our tradition going to end because of the . . . what happened to Sherry? I guess I sound like a baby, but I love that time of year and I don't want to give up our traditions. Are we going to have to? What's going to happen, Dad?"

George kneeled on the floor beside Angie and patted her knee. His forehead was lined with worry and his eyelids were half closed, a clear sign of the exhaustion and frustration that he felt.

"I don't know what's going to happen, Angie. I'm doing everything in my power to find some answers, but it's difficult. Hard to know when folks are telling the truth or just blowing hot air. And I'm learning that teachers are an interesting and evasive lot; at least the ones at your high school are."

Angie realized her dad had tunnel vision. Summer gardens and Halloween, all the traditions they had shared, were far from his mind. He was looking for only one thing, the truth, the answer, and the name of the person who had killed her boss in what appeared to be cold-blooded murder. Her stomach tightened as she looked at George's weary face. He was getting nowhere fast in his investigation. She was sure of it.

She allowed her dad to pull her from the floor and he patted her cheek. "Want to order a pizza?" he asked. "Doesn't look as though either one of us is in the mood to cook tonight."

"Sounds good," she answered dully. "You want to order, or should I?"

"I will."

He looked into Angie's face, so pretty now, a little girl who had grown up much too quickly. He brushed her hair from her face. "Are you going to be okay?"

"I think so. Think I'll go upstairs and take a shower," she managed. "I just feel so tired, and so sad."

George did not reply. He could not find the words, but he hugged Angie to him, patting her back lovingly as he did.

She did not resist.

⌘ ⌘ ⌘

In the warm shower, Angie's tears finally subsided but her forlorn and confused emotions persisted. She felt lost and empty. As she wrapped herself in a large, soft towel, she examined her face, a somewhat blurry reflection in the mirror. It was a pleasant enough face, she thought, but her eyes, ever-changing from green to hazel, had lost their sparkle in recent weeks. *I look sad.*

She dressed in her favorite, comfortable sweats and slippers, and sat on the edge of her bed. Her hands lay limp in her lap for a moment and then she held them up and inspected them as if for the first time. Small with thin fingers, her hands were completely the opposite of her father's that were large, short-fingered, and thick. *I must be more like my mother. Wish I had known her.*

The fact was, however, that she had not known her mother, ever, and to that end perhaps she subconsciously had carried the burden of loss for a lifetime. Angie knew her mother, Linda, had died from extensive blood loss less than an hour after her birth. She had been told that much. Aside from old photographs of her, though, Angie had nothing: no memories, no feelings, really, and no significant woman in her life, save perhaps Sherry Mitchell, the arrogant boss she had both revered and detested. Certainly Sherry in no way had imparted a single modicum of nurturing warmth to her, but she had been a successful, feminine role model.

Angie relied then on her father, whom she loved deeply, for virtually everything. Her dad never had remarried after the death of his wife, but instead had concentrated solely on his daughter. It was a conscious decision on his part, and in that respect, perhaps, without fully understanding himself, compensated for unrealistic guilt and unparalleled grief he had never been willing to relinquish. He was painfully aware that he had not been able to protect the woman he had adored with every ounce of his being, so he focused on their child, doing double duty by playing the role of two parents the best he could.

Angie thought about her father, George Murphy, so courageous, determined, and dependable, and so perfect in his profession as a police officer and detective. Unfortunately his need for control and a sense of protectiveness played out at home as well. Angie had learned to live with that, although in her younger, teenage years she had, at times, been resentful. She admired her father's tenacity though, and she understood his resolve after the horrific attack on her as a child. This was yet, she realized as if for the first time, another traumatic loss: her purity, her virginity, essentially her childhood, had been snatched from her when she was only ten. In a very real and agonizing manner she had lost her innocence at the hands of Jerry Gerard, a wayward teen with no conscience.

Angie shivered, remembering.

CHAPTER SIXTEEN

JACK

Jack did not move from his recliner after his emotional breakdown. He couldn't. It was as if he were glued to the chair, so he gave in to the sensation that immobilized him, closed his eyes, and eventually fell asleep, though fitfully. He dreamed of Sherry.

They were together, at a carnival somewhere, sharing an enormous swirl of pink, cotton candy. The sticky sugar melted on their tongues and stuck to their lips and when they kissed he wanted to believe they would never be able to draw apart. Their gummy fingers found each other too, and they held on, not wanting to let go but did when they were attracted to a rickety, wooden, roller coaster. The rough ride forced them together and jarred them apart as momentum carried them up, down, and around in wild circles until they were dizzy. Stumbling off the ride, Sherry listed sideways, grabbing Jack's hand instinctively for balance. His arm encircled her and she looked up at him as she had on the day they had married, her eyes sparkling, and her smile wide. Jack felt as if he were falling forward and melting right into her.

Sherry motioned toward a bright, yellow, painted bench. "Let's sit," she said.

"Your teeth are pink," Jack laughed.

"Yours too," she retorted. "We need something to drink."

"Don't you just love cotton candy?" he chuckled, heading for a concession stand for water.

"Imagine the damage to our teeth, not to mention our insides," she giggled as he moved away.

For long moments the two sipped bottled water and watched as a parade of people passed by. Parents of every size and shape ambled along the pathway carrying or tugging their little ones while older children pranced and ran around them in circles. It was a cacophony of joy. Jack was captivated, and then he heard his name.

"Jack! Come on! There's a Ferris wheel!"

Sherry was skipping toward the ride like a little girl. They stood in line for only a short time before a gruff-voiced worker ordered them into a two-person swinging chair that rocked to and fro forcefully as their weight settled.

"Get on in there, folks. Can't keep the wheel waiting!"

The old codger locked a steel bar across the two of them and then pushed them forward. "Off you go," he laughed.

The Ferris wheel carried Jack and Sherry up, up, and farther up until they could see beyond the carnival entrance to the Sierra foothills that lay beyond. At least ten rotations had been completed when it happened. Sherry was hurled from her seat and into the air, alone. She floundered for a moment, glanced back at Jack quickly, and then, as if escorted by angels, floated away into the heavens.

Jack was trapped at the top of the wheel, his seat, unbalanced and rocking uncontrollably. He watched until Sherry was a speck in the sky before he felt downward movement again. By the time he

*reached the platform to escape the ride, his heart was racing and he
dripped in perspiration.*

*"Sherry!" he called. "Sherry!" Over and over he shouted her
name and he ran, pushing into families, shoving children, and
crying hysterically.*

"Hey, watch it, buddy!"

"What in the hell are you doing, man?"

"Have you lost your marbles, dude?"

*To get away from the jeers, and moreover from what he could
not possibly understand, Jack searched for a place to hide – a bush,
a trailer, a building, anything. He ran headlong through a narrow
doorway that almost magically appeared before him. It led to a hallway, and then another, and still another. Every corridor was lined
with mirrors. At every corner he ran into himself. He could not get
away. The more he ran, the more he panicked until finally he spied
a slice of daylight. He stumbled forward with weak legs and at
last located a sheath of curtains that surely had to be an exit. He
shoved the drapes aside and fell to his knees horrified. Surrounding
him were clowns, hundreds of them, sneering, laughing, gawking,
and screeching. Although caked in makeup and fanciful paints,
some faces were familiar. Beneath the disguises were people he knew:
Roger Cunningham, Midge McGrath, Cora Davies, old Flo Gray,
Melody, Angie, and his dead mother. Their faces were contorted,
their mouths grimacing, and their voices cackling and hooting,
louder and louder as if to outdo each other. Above them all, bigger
than life, was a drunken Burt whose hideous, drooling mouth was
chortling the hardest.*

And Jack remembered.

He awoke bathed in liquid, for in his frightful sleep he
had sweated profusely, urinated on himself, and to his horror his bowels had released as well.

⌘ ⌘ ⌘

Jack scooted from his recliner to the bathroom, carrying the stench of his accident with him. He turned on the shower, waited for warm water, and then stepped in fully clothed. When he had stripped naked, he allowed the water, hot now, to pepper him clean. He stayed there for nearly half an hour, rubbing a bar of soap over his body time and again, trying desperately to find satisfaction. When he was ready, he turned off the water, scrubbed himself with a stiff towel, and then wrapped a thick robe around his bare body. He looked at his clothes, a sodden heap on the shower floor and began to cry once more. *What has happened to me? I don't have anyone. Sherry is dead. My mother's gone. Both gone. Bitches!*

Anger set in. As if on cue, he straightened his body, ceased crying, and walked back to the recliner. With a damp cloth he vigorously wiped the soiled chair clean, and then sat in it once again hoping for rest, yet fearing sleep. The nightmare had rattled him to the point he was numb. Quite undone, his thoughts went to his mother, the woman who had given birth to him, had provided him a place to live, however wretched the single-wide trailer had been, and had allowed him free reign to make his own way. She had cared as much as she could, he supposed, because her interests had lain elsewhere: to the job she clung to desperately, to men she courted recklessly, and to the alcohol that became her true love.

Marion Mitchell had been a pretty woman with green eyes and long, curly red hair she wore clipped on the sides with barrettes, the mop of curls cascading down her back to her waist; or she would gather it into a fat ponytail and tie it with colorful scarves. She had been tall, thin, well proportioned, and loud, often inappropriately so. She had adored the attention her off-color jokes and outbursts of profanity afforded her.

"You cocksucker, Bill (or Joe or Tom)! Get your filthy, fucking hands off me!" she'd say in mock dismay.

"Can't help myself, Marion, baby," was a typical response.

"Been thinking about putting my hands on you all day," was another.

"You're a looker," Jack had heard men say.

"Easy on the eyes, and well, just easy," others chuckled behind her back.

So the parade of men had become a mainstay in Jack and Marion's life and as the years passed, Jack had grown aloof and angry while Marion had maintained she was doing all she could, given the fact that Jack's father, whoever he was, didn't know Jack was alive.

The two had lived in mutual tolerance of each other until Jack completed high school at seventeen. Though Jack had been an athlete and something of a star in high school, Marion never actively had supported his endeavors.

"Can't be at your games," she had told him over and over. "Somebody has to work and put food on the table around here."

Jack had known then, as he knew now, that her assertion was a half-truth. In reality, he had been quite clear for many years that his mother's lovers had taken precedent over him and to that end he had released his resentment by punishing others on the football field or by hitting a baseball with such intensity he was the coach's dream.

Although Jack's athletic aptitude had made him more than a bit cocky and arrogant at school, at home he had felt defeated. He was caught in an awful snare and understood that he had to be his own advocate. If his prowess in sports had taught him nothing more, it had taught him tenacity, and with dogged resolve, he set his sights on college.

"I hope you know I won't be able to help you," his mother had told him.

"Don't need your help," Jack had replied defiantly. "I'll get by. I can work."

Driven by anger and motivated by a desire to put distance between himself and his mother, Jack had moved to San Francisco where he found work at a gas station, lodging in a small room atop a garage, and single-mindedly had completed class after class. He even had played a bit of intercollegiate football, scrimmaging with acquaintances that were never allowed too close, and partying with girl after girl whenever he could. In that respect, he was not much different than his mother.

Marion died only four months after Jack had left. She had finished her shift at the bar late, having partied with several fellows that night, and stumbled to her old pickup in a daze. She was tired, drunk, and dejected because when it came right down to it, her offer of sexual favors that night had been rejected. The man of interest had been too inebriated to stand up and she had been undeniably let down. Though she had driven home from the bar thousands of nights in varying degrees of intoxication and knew the road well, this night she had faltered. Driving much too fast through fog that swirled eerily across the road, she had swerved into the path of an oncoming big rig and had been killed instantly. Jack had not been allowed to identify his mother's remains because her truck had been so mangled that authorities, of necessity, had extricated her body from it in pieces.

A somber, police officer had given Jack the news of Marion's accidental death. Jack had driven home from San

Francisco because he had been directed to do so. He had been the only surviving relative and with that, he had inherited the old mobile home and three hundred dollars in cash. There had been nothing more. One final walk through his old home had been enough. He had grabbed a few books, one photograph of Marion, and had slammed the rickety door behind him. It was over.

CHAPTER SEVENTEEN

MIDGE

Midge had ended this trying and wearing week of school with a victory. With cat-like stealth and ingenuity she had shoved Roger Cunningham into a corner where he had squirmed under her power until he gave in to her demand to oust Carlos Ortiz from her wing of the building. She didn't have the absolute proof yet, but she knew her threat to involve the union in supporting her, had been genius itself. In all honesty it was quite likely that she might never have followed through with her intimidating demand, but Roger Cunningham didn't know that. So she gloated and waited. She would get her way. She was certain of it.

That morning Midge had arrived on campus early . . . early and prepared. She had stayed up late brainstorming, conjuring false complaints and accusations against Carlos Ortiz, and finally processing her letter and printing it out on school stationary. The letterhead was emblazoned with Hollow Vista High School in bold, red and gold print, and was followed below with the words: "Providing Quality Education". *What crap that is. Certainly quality occurs in my classroom, but several teachers I know should have been dismissed long ago and a few never hired in the first place.* She thought of Melody Miller immediately and mentally put her name on an intangible agenda as her next devious undertaking.

The front office of the school had not yet filled with the teachers who loved to mill around the mailboxes gossiping and complaining before they moved on to their classrooms. In fact, only Cora Davies had been there, sitting in the middle of the office as she had for years, like a black widow spider sending her authoritative spinnerets off in every which direction with absolute precision and control. Though in Midge's mind, Cora was only a classified employee, a secretary, for God's sake, she was well aware that the woman dutifully and efficiently had managed the goings-on in the front office, if not beyond, forever. Midge fortunately had not needed to ask permission from Cora to enter Roger's inner office when she had pushed open the heavy, swinging door at seven o'clock, for he had been standing right by Cora's desk deep in conversation. He had looked up as Midge walked in and had blanched noticeably causing Midge's heart to flutter with satisfaction.

"Here Roger," she had stated emphatically and without hesitation. "I believe you will want to take a look at this letter before you start your day."

Roger had glared at Midge as she shoved an envelope at him. He had dropped it immediately as if were hot, but quickly had retrieved it, retreating into his office without saying a word. He had been inside only long enough to read the letter that she had filled with her brilliant and fabricated claims against Carlos Ortiz.

"Midge," Roger had begun when he walked out to face her.

"I'm quite serious about this, Roger," she had interrupted. "You don't have to think twice about me following through with a formal grievance with the union."

"You know this is wrong," he had replied, thinking of his devoted custodian who had been at Midge's beck and call for several years.

"I think I have every right. Every right. I will not be kowtowed into accepting substandard services any more. Do you hear me, Roger?" she had bullied.

Midge didn't have a leg to stand on and she knew it. She could easily have been accused of intolerance and racism, but Roger Cunningham was not man enough to stand up to her threats. *What a mouse.*

She had stared at the man. *No matter. I'll get my way.* Her eyes had dropped to observe his hands, trembling now, with what she had surmised could have been one of two emotions: anger or fear.

"I'm truly saddened by this, Midge," Roger finally had managed. "I'll see what I can do."

That had ended it. She had strutted silently past Cora Davies who clearly had heard the entire interchange. Cora couldn't possibly have known then what the problem was, but Midge astutely assumed that in no time at all, she would, and would weigh in with her opinion, as was the norm. No matter. She was simply a secretary, nothing more.

⌘   ⌘   ⌘

Midge sat now in an absolutely quiet, empty classroom at her desk basking in the memory of the morning interaction with her principal.

"What a mouse," she repeated, this time aloud.

She walked to a window of her classroom that was located on the second floor of the building. It was a corner room with windows on two walls, a luxury that let in intense sunlight on remarkably striking, spring days, such as this one had been. A cool morning had given way to an unseasonably hot afternoon. She placed her hand on the windowpane, feeling lingering warmth there and watched the sway of tree branches that recently had transformed from spindly, bare boughs into radiant, chartreuse and celadon wonders. The view from her window always had allowed Midge to monitor the seasons that melded one into the next ever so quickly with the passing of each school year. Well over twenty-five years had elapsed since she had begun teaching at Hollow Vista High School and she did not see an end in sight. She needed the income and would have found herself empty of purpose if she were unable to teach, indeed educate, her students year after year after year. And speaking of students, quite a crop of misfits had filtered through recently.

Kids are behaving worse and worse. And they dress as if they've crawled out of a gutter, some of them. Don't know what's going to become of this generation. Midge often mused hatefully about her students, wondering about their private lives, their families, and their homes. She knew many had a rough go of it. This was a poor, farming community where generally both parents worked and too many teenagers were left on their own, doing God only knew what! A collective lack of ambition among many students burdened Midge at times, but she could do nothing with young people who had no understanding of the value of education. She had washed her hands of them years ago. Instead, she concentrated on those who had potential and at least an nth degree of drive and desire to make something of themselves.

Earlier, moments after the final bell, she had stood exactly where she was stationed now and had stared through filmy glass as hordes of students had rushed through the campus to escape the confines of school. After the initial rush, small groups or couples had meandered down the concrete sidewalks to their destinations. A group of cheerleaders had commandeered a somewhat private patio adjacent to the science wing where they jumped, strutted, and flailed their arms into the air in front of tall windows that reflected their movements.

What an egocentric assembly that is. Can't get enough of themselves. 'Mirror, mirror, on the wall, who's the fairest of them all?' Words from the childhood fairytale spun in her head, tormenting her for a moment until she spied the swagger of Jack Mitchell approaching the girls. He walked up to them, said something that made them twitter and giggle, and then he made his way inside the building.

Jack Mitchell. What a creature, he is. He'll be inside staring down on them until they're done for the day, I imagine. And in this case, though she was only projecting her negative view of the man, Midge had struck on a truth.

She also recalled seeing Brad Browning, the muscular athlete and his diminutive girl friend, Angie Murphy, clutching and pawing at each other in front of the cheerleaders who regarded them indifferently.

"Those two!" Midge huffed audibly in disapproval. *That Brad. His hands are all over her and she lets it happen. Neither one of them seem to care if they have an audience or not. That little slut is going to be in trouble if she doesn't watch out. It's another example of poor parenting if you ask me.*

"Angie Murphy. Murphy. Murphy," Midge mulled, while speaking the name out loud. *Ah, Detective Murphy. Her father, I bet . . . that arrogant, pushy son of a bitch.*

She suddenly seethed as she recalled the detective bombarding her with question after question as to her knowledge of Sherry Mitchell: "Where were you on April 13th, the day the body of Sherry Mitchell was discovered? How well did you know her? In what capacity did you know her? Oh, so she was your real estate agent. Was she congenial, easy-going? Did you find her supportive and accommodating in your dealings? When did you last see her or converse with her?"

And he had continued, prying, meddling, and firing question after question that she had considered intimate and intruding, about her life, her routines, her friends and colleagues, her husband: "So, you are estranged from your husband? When did you last speak with him? Do you know his current whereabouts?"

The detective had had a limitless number of annoying questions and insinuating inquiries that to Midge had seemed absolutely irrelevant to solving such a case and pushed her to the point of panic. She had found herself muttering inane, half answers until she was quite tongue-tied. She always had prided herself on her aptitude for flawless articulation, but Detective Murphy had rendered her helpless to do anything but stammer. As her frustration had intensified, her face had grown red and sweaty, her lips had pursed into a tight pucker, and she had leered at the man acerbically.

Clearly the detective had been cognizant of her discomfort, but he smugly had feigned a disregard to her demeanor, focusing instead on a small pad where he had jotted what she assumed, he had determined was relevant information. Midge had been able to do nothing but watch, fuming.

Murphy. She began muttering aloud. "I need to find out for sure if Detective Murphy is Angie's father. That little Murphy girl worked in Sherry's office. I remember seeing her there quite often, shuffling papers, delivering us coffee, answering the phones, and smiling that smile that surely was her orthodontist's dream of perfection. I wonder what she knows about the investigation into Sherry Mitchell's murder?" *Hum.*

⌘ ⌘ ⌘

Midge had watched that afternoon as Brad had kissed Angie hungrily, his hands grabbing at her thighs and butt, before she pulled away. Angie actually had placed her hand on Brad's chest and backed away.

Well, enough is enough, even for Angie.

Midge had snickered but in that moment her attention had been diverted. From the direction of the science wing, she had spied Willard Dunn, that somewhat timid student who had been harassed unmercifully by Brad and a few others, charging toward the doors of the humanities wing. Midge knew of the bullying only because she had heard a few comments from a distance. She had not interfered though. He was not actually her student and certainly not her responsibility. Willard had been running in the direction of Brad and Angie, but when he saw them, he had stopped short as if he had collided with a wall. He had stood perfectly still until the two had walked away, side by side, toward the gym where, of course, Brad would work out with the other athletes until it grew dark.

⌘　⌘　⌘

It was dusk now. As was her habit, Midge stayed in her classroom late each afternoon, correcting essays, preparing lessons, ruminating on the day's events, and from time to time, positioning herself at her window to observe the goings on about the campus. In Midge's mind, she simply was being prudent. Astute observation gave way to knowledge, understanding, and, more importantly, power. In the past, as with her husband, Fred, she had erred by not watching closely enough. It had been a hard lesson learned.

Below in the darkening campus, Midge suddenly saw what she had been anticipating. Roger Cunningham, who towered over short, pudgy Carlos Ortiz, was headed with the custodian to the doors of the science wing.

He's going to break the news to that female janitor. She smirked, knowingly. *I'd bet a million dollars that little speck of a woman will learn about her transfer in just a few minutes. Whether she likes it or not she'll be cleaning my section of the building come Monday. Ha! And old Jack Mitchell will be dealing with Carlos Ortiz.*

Midge moved quickly away from the window so as not to be seen by the two men, gathered her briefcase, and strode to the door. She snapped the light switch with triumphant force, stepped into the dimly lit hallway, and sighed.

And another one bites the dust!

CHAPTER EIGHTEEN

MELODY

Melody darted from her room into the hallway only fifteen minutes after the bell had rung. She had stuffed her briefcase with ungraded essays as the students hurried out, clearly as eager to start the weekend as she was.

"Friday. Thank you, God," she murmured to Cheryl and Michelle, the last two girls to leave.

They both glanced back at her and grinned. "Have a good weekend, Ms. Miller," they said in unison.

"I will," she answered. "You too."

The idea of a good weekend had become alien to Melody in the months after New Year's Eve, after Jack. During the winter she had met a few men at Two Timers, a respectable bar, despite its dubious name, downtown. Those encounters had resulted in nothing more than one-night stands, however, that left her feeling used and exacerbated her depression.

Though she was shy, self-conscious, and reticent about entering any bar alone, Two Timers was a decent establishment and she had been subconsciously drawn there for potential thrills that eluded her elsewhere. A few beers lowered her anxiety and she found herself smiling and flirting unabashedly until she was escorted out on the arm of a man she did not know. Spying two, male staff members, Rob Green and Chuck Lindsey, at the bar in late March had put a sudden stop to Melody's risky, amorous adventures though. She could not afford gossip. Whether the teachers had seen her or not, she was not sure, for she had backed out of the door as quickly as she had entered. She had made a rapid about face toward the parking lot, run to her car, and sat inside, breathing heavily. *Shit. I'm so stupid.*

⌘ ⌘ ⌘

When she stepped outside of the humanities wing, the warm, afternoon air caressed Melody's skin like velvet, lifting her spirits if only slightly. She knew her contract called for her to remain at school for at least a half hour after the final bell, but this day had been hell for Melody. Waking up late was the first problem, being unprepared to teach her classes a second one, and realizing that her students could see right through her and her impromptu assignment was a third. She had heard the groans when they had been told they had to write an essay, but she simply couldn't tolerate embarking on a discussion of *Lord of the Flies* when she knew half the students had not done the reading. She wasn't prepared herself to fill in the blanks. She had heard twittering comments between Jennifer and Kerrie, two students who

Melody was sure, thought they were smarter than God and had shown their animosity toward Melody more than once.

"She's a dumb shit," Melody heard Jennifer say during the first week of school.

"Got her credentials from Incompetence U," Kerrie had replied haughtily.

The two had continued their insults all year, issuing them quietly, hands covering their mouths, but loud enough for Melody to hear. Their words were hurtful though Melody did not allow them the pleasure of knowing. Somehow she managed that feat, but she was bitter nonetheless, harboring intense dislike for the girls that spilled out in acid comments scrawled at the bottom of their essays: *You need to read more closely." "Your argument is illogical." "Flesh out your ideas before considering them complete." "Really?" "Proofread!" "Your words, or someone else's?" "Back up your assertions with specifics from the text." "You're dead wrong here!"* It really was the only recourse Melody could contrive to get back at the conceited girls whose barbs bore in and festered.

As Melody walked toward the front office she hoped she would not run into the principal who though polite, intimidated her. He seemed a brooding man whose very nature depressed her. Besides, she knew he was a stickler for following the rules. He would not be impressed to see her leaving school so early.

To her dismay, not only did she encounter Roger Cunningham immediately upon entering the office, but Jack Mitchell as well. The two had their heads together, staring at a document in Roger's hand.

"What a witch," she heard Jack say.

"My hands are tied, Jack," Roger replied glumly, looking up at Melody and then gazing at the large, round clock that dominated the wall above Cora Davies' desk. It was ten minutes after three.

Melody cringed.

"I have to leave early, Mr. Cunningham," she lied. "I have a three thirty appointment. Only time I could get."

Melody's cheeks flushed pink. She was a horrible liar. Jack could vouch for that. Her lies had dominated their brief relationship.

She never would be able to forget. After coyly resisting Jack for a week or so, she had given in to his advances. On the night they had had sex for the first time, he had pulled a condom from his jacket pocket, toying awkwardly with the packaging. She had watched him anxiously for a moment before blurting, "No need for that, Jack. I'm on the pill."

He had looked at her dubiously. "Just want to stay on the safe side," he had replied.

"Really, Jack," she had said again. "It's okay. Do you think I want to get pregnant? I've been using contraceptives for years. Heavy periods. The pill helps."

For over six weeks they had unprotected intercourse and with each time, Melody had closed her eyes tightly, hoping, even praying to become pregnant. Jack had stolen her heart immediately. He was handsome, masculine, athletic, and eager. Never in her life had she had such a man show interest in her. She would do anything she could to snare him.

Melody was quite sure her prayers had been answered when only two months after she and Jack had been dating she had missed her period and had awakened headachy and nauseous. A quick pregnancy test at the local clinic had affirmed her suspicions.

"Jack, I'm pregnant," she had told him demurely after arriving without warning to his classroom after school.

He could not possibly have known that she had squealed to herself, bubbling with joy just minutes before she saw him. She had run toward him that afternoon, ridiculously expecting a welcoming embrace. Instead he had stood unmoving, his arms crossing his chest in definite defense. His face instantly had grown slack, his eyes had glared at her hatefully, and he had pushed her away from him as though she were dirty.

"You lied. You said you were on the pill," he had snapped.

"I am," she had fibbed again. "I must have missed taking a pill for a couple of days when we went to the coast last month. That must be what happened. I didn't mean to."

"Well, deal with it," Jack had barked.

Melody had looked at him with utter shock. "Deal with it?" she had replied, feeling a flutter in her heart. Immediately her mind had become a tangle of disappointment and dismay.

"Get rid of it."

"But, Jack. I can't do that."

"Yes, you can. I'll tell you this. I'm not marrying you just because you're a stupid bitch. God, Melody. I don't want a fucking kid."

It had been the first of December, only a month before Jack's attack on her, but it was the beginning of the demise of their relationship. Melody was sure of it even though she was not ready to admit it. Instead she did exactly what Jack told her to do.

I'm so stupid. The refrain played yet again. She had not spoken another word but had turned her back on Jack, leaving him red-faced and livid in his science lab.

Unaccompanied, she had driven to San Francisco, located an agency that would abort the baby, and had spent three days in a shabby motel alone crying and verbally abusing herself for her stupidity. She had never mentioned the abortion to a soul, nor had Jack spoken to her about the incident again.

Now, in front of Roger Cunningham, with Jack at his side, Melody squirmed.

"I'm sorry. I should have told you, uh, asked you earlier," she mumbled.

"That would have been appropriate," Roger stated bluntly. "Go on. Do what you have to do."

"Thank you," Melody said, glancing at Jack who smirked at her knowingly.

When she reached her car, Melody tossed her briefcase into the trunk, slid into the front seat, and immediately started the engine. She leaned her head against the closed window for some moments before mumbling to no one, "I have to get the hell out of here."

When she drove away that day, despondent and ashamed, she had no idea that another's eyes were watching.

CHAPTER NINETEEN

FLO

Flo stood just outside the janitor's equipment room having gathered the supplies she needed for her evening duties. She felt uncharacteristically uneasy but she couldn't put her finger on just why. Perhaps it was the fact that on Monday she would be assigned to a new area of the building. Change had never been comfortable for her, so for many years she had wrapped herself in routines that she hoped would eliminate surprises that in the past had thrown her for a loop.

Even as a child she had felt a need for order. She never had had much in the way of toys or books, but what she did have was arranged neatly on a small cabinet in the corner of a tiny area that had been curtained off, making a small bedroom for her, adjacent to the kitchen. She had two dolls, Rosy and Dolly that were bookends to the ten books she prized. Rosy and Dolly stared out at her with unmoving, glass eyes, becoming something of a conscience for Flo as she performed tasks at home while her working parents were gone for long hours. She was a good girl and an obedient child, but the solitary hours alone exacerbated her natural bent to be introverted, inhibited, and shy. Aside from the time she spent at school, she stayed home. She learned not to ask for frivolous items that she knew her parents could not afford. As a result her wardrobe was scant, changing from year to year only to accommodate growth spurts, and remained the same once she turned fourteen and did not grow another inch. She was five feet, one inch tall and wispy thin, but she was strong.

As she grew older she made lists to organize her life, cleaned the house, and prepared dinners for her parents who dragged home, tired and aching, from the local cannery where her mother worked on the assembly line and her father stacked cans into boxes before loading them onto trucks that would transport the goods throughout the country. At home, Flo planted a small garden in a plot behind the house, harvesting the plants and saving the seeds for the following year. The vegetables she grew supplanted the items her parents never could have afforded to buy. In the evenings, Flo and her folks sat at the kitchen table together, exchanging stories about events of the day until it was time for sleep, although at times, Flo's father hefted an old guitar, his only luxury, to his knee and eked out a tune or two, singing in a sweet baritone, and joyously filling the house with sound. Flo cherished those moments and still could conjure them in her mind although with the passing of the years some had faded into a vague and distant blur. She actually wondered at times how much of it really had happened.

One event however, a hideous memory for her even now, had created the first, nearly unbearable change in

Flo's life. On June first, a week after she had turned eighteen, and two days after her graduation from high school, Flo's father, Charlie Carter, had been involved in a horrible accident. Flo had been at home when it occurred, but she felt almost as if she had witnessed the tragedy first hand, for the plant manager had delivered the news to her in vivid detail.

From the safety of the cab of his semi truck, an unseemly driver, bent on heading back out on the road in a hurry, had begun shouting curses at what he clearly deemed as slow and careless cannery workers.

"Get out of the way, you goddamn sons of bitches! Get your lazy, fat asses out of the way of my truck! Now, you bastards!"

Without looking back, the man had spat a wad of chewed tobacco out of the window before shoving his enormous vehicle into reverse. He had revved the engine until it screeched, had planted his foot on the gas pedal, and had sped backward with no warning, slamming into Charlie and two co-workers, crushing them against the concrete dock. The men did not know what hit them, their bodies so pulverized they were unrecognizable. The families had been given no choice but to bury the three men together in a communal grave.

The death of Charlie Carter had killed his wife as well, not physically initially, but mentally. Ruthann Carter was never the same after the day her husband died, and if the truth were known, Flo was not either. Ruthann, almost instantly, had transformed into a ghost, silent, staring into the air in front of her blindly, and wringing her fingers together until they were raw.

Flo had tried her best.

"Mama, you have to talk to me," she had begged. "Mama can you say just one word?"

Ruthann had said nothing. She had refused to feed herself as well, forcing Flo to pry open her lips and shove spoons full of applesauce or oatmeal into her mouth. She had forced water by the spoonful down her mother's throat simply to keep her alive.

"Mama, you have to eat. Please Mama."

In a month's time, Flo had given up. She had had no choice but to place her mother in a charitable, nursing facility where she had lingered for two more months until she died.

While her mother had grown weaker, Flo paradoxically grew strong. It was as though the loss of her parents had freed her from an untenable lifestyle of her own creation. She no longer was restricted to her parents' home, cleaning and cooking dutifully. Instead, with her parents gone, she took long walks, read her books, and grieved silently. She also continued making lists: the emotions she felt, the foods she would eat, activities she wanted to pursue, and places she wanted to go. Her lists guided her in ways she herself did not understand but they moved her forward. Perhaps simply processing what she was thinking, writing it down, and making it somewhat tangible made all the difference.

⌘ ⌘ ⌘

In late summer Flo fortuitously was hired by the Center View School District as a custodian at the high school where she had just graduated. She moved from the old house to a small duplex in town taking with her, her dolls, Rosy and

Dolly; her books; the only clothes she owned; a few pots, pans, utensils and linens; and her father's beloved guitar. She no sooner had settled in to her first real job and her own home, than a brand new, life-changing episode blindsided her. She fell in love.

Flo met Randall Gray during the summer a year after her parents had died. He was a painter, hired along with a few others, to paint the outside of the sprawling, high school. He walked directly up to her the moment he saw her.

"Hello," he said, glancing at the cart of cleansers, rags, brushes, and brooms that Flo, only moments before, had pushed through the door into the science wing. "Looks like you have your work cut out for you."

He smiled a slightly crooked grin but looked away from her for a second when her mouth fell open, just a tad, and she stared at him without saying a word.

"Randall. Name's Randall Gray." Tall, slender, and clad in paint-splattered overalls, he tucked in his chin to look down at her. A shock of dark hair fell over his forehead when he did.

"Flo," she answered, looking up into Randall's sleepy, hazel eyes. "Florence Carter." Flo's hand went immediately to her face to touch the mole lodged high on her cheek. Her eyes darted, looking to see if she and Randall had been observed, and her heart raced. She was very aware of the alien sensation, so very new and unexpected. No man had ever paid her the least amount of attention unless, of course, it was to make a snide or off-color remark. She had practiced dodging interactions with men to save herself. She had wounds enough for a lifetime.

So why is this man talking to me? She began fussing with and needlessly rearranging the cleansers on her cart.

"Do you work here? Are you a custodian? A janitor?" he asked, bobbing nervously first on one foot and then on the other. "Never have seen a woman janitor before."

"Yeah. Got hired a while back."

"Pretty hard work, isn't it?"

"It's not bad," she said. "I like it. Keeps me busy. I like the solitude, the quiet."

He continued gazing at her as if she were an enigmatic presence.

"And you're a painter, I see," Flo managed. "Big job, painting this huge building."

"It's okay. I like the routine," he told her. "And like yours, it's a job that keeps me busy. I can think. Don't like being bothered by needless chatter."

That was the beginning. Randall Gray had taken a chance. He had known only one girl before in his life and she had been spirited away by a former acquaintance before Randall knew what had happened. It had been a disappointment that had crushed what little confidence he had possessed, so he had avoided women for several years, finding solace in his acrylics and watercolors that swallowed up huge chunks of time and became a substitute for other pleasures.

Why this girl, this young woman named Flo, had appealed to Randall Gray, he was not sure. She was not beautiful but she possessed a simple cuteness that had made him curious. And her eyes - big, brown, and sorrowful - had captured him. He had no choice; nor did she. The attraction was a mystery and it was something of a miracle for them as well. What inexplicable workings, in a universe neither of them understood, had brought them together? It was a question both debated mutely, separately, and alone.

In two months they had married and embarked on a childless, but loving and chaotic journey that tore into their spirits, but that undeniably bonded them for twenty-five years and beyond. Even after Randall's untimely death just over a year before, Flo was bound to her husband. She was certain no man would enter her life again, and with that, she was satisfied.

⌘　⌘　⌘

"Flo? You okay?"

Carlos Ortiz tapped Flo's shoulder. "You look like you're in a trance or something."

Flo's mind had been awash in memories; yet, paradoxically, at the same time, she was very present. For several moments she had been observing a fledgling, female teacher, who, she believed, had been Jack Mitchell's former squeeze, hurriedly walk from the main office to her car in the lot. Flo had watched as the young woman forcefully threw her briefcase into the trunk as though ditching it there was of acute urgency. She then had opened the car door, had slid inside the front seat, started the engine, and sat for a few moments unmoving. If she had been in a hurry, she must have forgotten her intent, for she had leaned her head against the window as if it were her only support. Moments later she had driven away.

"Sorry, Carlos," Flo answered, jumping slightly with his touch.

"I was just watching the parking lot, watching teachers leave, and I was thinking about the change next week. Hope it will work out for us. I've never been one much for changes, especially sudden ones. I still am not quite sure why it had to be done."

"I'm not sure either, Flo, but we'll adjust," Carlos smiled. "The principal seems to have his mind set."

"He does that. Guess we'll make do," Flo agreed, tentatively. "We always do. No other choice really."

CHAPTER TWENTY

ANGIE

Angie sat perfectly still staring at her reflection. Her face was pale, her usual bronze skin having lightened throughout the winter months. Without make-up she was plain, but not in an unattractive way; in fact, she was actually quite lovely. Her almost white-blond hair, straight as a blade, fell below her shoulders to the middle of her back. Her hazel eyes were almost green this night, a color that matched the light, olive shade of her sweater.

"I have no brows," she mouthed to her image. "No eyelashes either." While that certainly was an exaggeration, it was true that both were very, very light, only a shade darker than her hair, a strand of which she twisted tightly around one finger until it hurt.

A string around a finger . . . I can never forget. Suddenly a ghostly likeness of Sherry Mitchell materialized ethereally before her, and for the second time in a week, she began to sob.

⌘ ⌘ ⌘

Earlier in the evening, Angie had been with Brad. They had attended an impromptu party at Jimmy Nelson's house. Jimmy's parents had left for the weekend, as they often spontaneously chose to do, to their mountain house near Kings Canyon. They had a habit of leaving Jimmy on his own, trusting him to take care of their faux-rustic, chic estate outside of town. Jimmy's folks had more money than anyone Angie knew and flaunted it with expensive cars and a stable of racehorses managed by their handpicked trainer. When his parents were absent, parties at Jimmy's place were common especially among the popular crowd from high school: the football players, the cheerleaders, and a few girls who made the grade because of their good looks or sexual favors.

Jimmy was Brad's best friend, but would have dropped Brad cold if he could have had his way. The fact was that Jimmy secretly had lusted after Brad's girl, Angie since all three of them were freshmen. While Angie instinctively understood, Brad seemed oblivious. Fortunately for her boyfriend, Angie wanted nothing to do with Jimmy Nelson whose prowess among the girls at school matched the intensity with which he played his other favorite game: football. Simply being in the same room with Jimmy made Angie uncomfortable, for he looked at her as though she were naked, his steel, blue eyes staring shamefully at her breasts, her waist, and below.

"Don't really like Jimmy much," she had whispered to Brad after they had entered the house where already an untapped beer keg sat square in the middle of the expansive kitchen. A large bowl of marijuana had been placed on the counter alongside an assortment of opened bags of chips and pretzels.

"Dig in," Jimmy chuckled. One of his thick hands wrapped around a mug of beer and the other was kneading Angie's friend Suzie's backside.

"Don't like Jimmy? What's wrong with you, Angie? He's the best dude I know, my best friend. Besides he's fucking rich! Why wouldn't anyone want to hang out here in this place?" Brad answered a bit too loudly, looking around the room as if he were in Disneyland.

"There's more to life than money," Angie replied, thinking immediately and somewhat unexpectedly of Sherry Mitchell.

Why now? Why had Sherry's face come to her at that very moment all of a sudden? Was it because of the decadence surrounding her here? Was it because of Jimmy's cocky attitude? Or was it something else? Angie could not place reason; yet the woman's image stubbornly lingered in her mind for several moments. Sherry Mitchell, like the Nelsons, had acquired more money than she seemed to know what to do with, but it clearly had not brought her happiness. Angie always had considered her boss to be arrogant, aggressive, and angry especially after her divorce from Jack. Any joy in life seemed to have eluded her. Money certainly had not provided her with the perfect existence. Perhaps that was it. No matter. None of that was important now, for Sherry was dead – stone, cold dead – and here, now, for Angie, the empty power of wealth was stifling.

"I don't know," Brad answered. "I think money is basic to life. Least it seems to be everyone's goal to make as much cash as they can."

"Well, it's not mine," Angie snapped, somewhat appalled by Brad's callous viewpoint.

"Oh, Angie, don't go turning into a bitch tonight," he replied and pulled her close. She cringed under his touch, a reaction that actually surprised her. This place, this house, in this boy's arms is not where she wanted to be, but she acquiesced to Brad's touch and moved with him up the stairway where bedrooms had been made available for the taking.

"First come, first serve," Jimmy laughed tensely as he watched the couple mount the stairs.

Brad and Angie found their way to Jimmy's parents' bedroom, the focal point of which was a king sized bed piled high with pillows of multiple shapes and sizes. The walls of the bedroom, lined with heavy, oak chests and bookcases, had been painted burgundy, a color that would have made the room appear cave-like had it not been for an expanse of windows that opened onto an upstairs deck. Even at night, diffused illumination from the moon, combined with lights blazing from the heart of town only two miles away, cast the room in pale, golden hues.

Angie pushed open a door to the balcony and stood, quietly staring at a corral not far from the house itself and at the dark pastures beyond. A light was on in the barn in the distance. Clearly a trainer or handyman was tending the horses there. Angie was envious.

"Come on, Ang," Brad said, pulling at her arm. "We don't have all night. Need a little penal stimulation, baby."

"God, Brad!" Angie bit back. "You are fucking gross sometimes."

"Just love you, baby," Brad slurred. He already had consumed the equivalent of a six-pack. He wouldn't be long for this night.

Angie slid her jeans to the floor, flattened herself in the middle of the bed, and closed her eyes. Brad groped her awkwardly, pressing on her breasts and kneading her thighs as he kissed her greedily, forcing his tongue deep into her mouth. Angie felt smothered and twisted away from him, burying her lips into a scratchy pillow.

"All right, then," Brad smirked, a bit taken aback by her abrupt movement. "On to the main course."

When he was finished, he lay atop her breathing heavily into her ear. She felt trapped, and indeed, she was, in a relationship that increasingly made her uneasy. Brad was not the boy she had been attracted to years before. The funny, engaging, adorable kid had changed, in time, into a cocky, sharp-tongued jerk. *It's plain and simple. It's not that I don't like him. It's worse. I detest him.*

Nor did Angie like herself. She felt used, abused, and sad. *Well, Angie, what did you expect? You put yourself here.* The words lay still in her mind, too heavily immersed in truth to vanish. They tormented her.

Wedged beneath Brad's shoulder, Angie could hardly move. She stared at the cedar ceiling of the room and held her breath. All was quiet now, aside from a remote and pulsating rhythm of music in her ears, and the distant din of youthful conversation below.

"Brad," she whispered. "Move, would you?"

Brad said not a word, but complied, rolling onto his back and tugging at the bedspread to cover himself. His eyes were open for only a moment before they rolled back a bit and closed. He threw one hand over his forehead and with the other clutched the folds of material that lay near his crotch. When Angie was certain he was asleep, she eased her body from the bed, slid into her jeans, donned her sweater, and wandered again to the balcony. The cold, night air refreshed her, yet she shivered. Something was amiss. She heard voices and snickering. What was happening out there in the dark?

Below, at the far end of the immaculate lawn, near a low-lying hedge that separated the main house from the swimming pool, she saw movement, and then more. Someone was throwing items into the pool. She watched as towels, clothing, or fabric of some kind sailed over the hedge, actually fluttering in the light breeze and then landing and floating on the water before they sank. She heard splashes too. Shoes. Someone's shoes had been tossed into the drink as well. What was happening? Her heart pounded.

"What the hell?" she muttered, focusing further on the melee occurring on the lawn below.

She clearly could hear Jimmy laughing as he booted at something on the ground. What was it? His chortles grew louder as he kicked at what Angie could see now was a nearly naked person scooting along on his knees in the semi-dark yard. Several people stood in the shadowy periphery, not involved directly in the abuse, but observing it. She heard giggles, and gasps, but no one moved forward to assist whoever it was. Light, cast from the kitchen, helped Angie's eyes adjust to the darkness.

"You're a dumb shit, turtle butt," she hear Jimmy holler. "Get on out of here as fast as you can."

Angie gasped, "Willard!"

Within moments, she had run down the stairs, passed through the kitchen, and was out the door.

"What the fuck are you doing, Jimmy?" she yelled, rushing to Willard's defense.

"Just having a little fun with old turtle man," Jimmy slurred. "Stay on your knees, turtle boy. Don't you be trying to stand up."

Angie was horrified.

"You are such a jackass, Jimmy," she shrieked, pushing him, an athlete who outweighed her twice over, with all her strength. Jimmy was so intoxicated he staggered backwards with the firm force of her touch but steadied himself quickly.

"Get the fuck out of my way, Angie," he yelled.

"I'm not getting out of anyone's way," Angie replied angrily, clearly driven by the adrenaline that rushed through her.

She pushed her way between Willard and Jimmy, but was shoved roughly aside. She found herself reeling sideways for a moment, but Jimmy grabbed her before she fell.

"Sure love your spunk, baby," Jimmy said, holding her firmly against him. His breath was warm, and he stank of sour beer and rank perspiration.

"Let me go, Jimmy!" She had attempted to shout but her voice failed her, the words issuing outward in a guttural growl.

"Got you and turtle boy here just where I want you," Jimmy sneered, staring with insensitive cruelty at the girl he clutched. "Where's your big, old boyfriend anyway?"

Angie's glanced quickly at the balcony. "He's right up there. He'll be down in a second," she lied. She knew Brad was sound asleep by now, satiated by a six-pack worth of brews and a quick screw.

"Let me go, Jimmy," she demanded again at the exact moment another hand grabbed her shoulder. Willard. He was on his feet, wearing nothing but his briefs, and tugging Angie backward toward him. If he were embarrassed, he had stifled the emotion, intent instead on pulling Angie away from Jimmy's grasp. The fact that he managed just that was something of a miracle, but in only seconds Angie was stumbling backwards into Willard's arms. Both fell to the ground, hard. It was then that laughter engulfed the scene. Not one partygoer held back.

"Are ya' okay, Angie?" Willard's voice was low and husky. As though he were in a bubble of his own, he seemed to be oblivious to the taunts and guffaws that filled the air.

"I'm okay," she said without looking at him.

Her face flamed red with anger and humiliation. From the spot where she had landed on the ground, she looked up at Jimmy who was grinning callously at both Willard and her.

"Get your dumb asses off my property," Jimmy snarled.

"Where are Willard's clothes?"

"Oh, shucks, now, I do believe they took a swim. Probably at the bottom of the pool by now."

"Get him a towel then, or a robe," Angie demanded.

"Turtles can go without," Jimmy answered hatefully.

Angie was incensed by this time, not just at the party's host, but at everyone there – her friends, her classmates, the people who adored her.

"Suzie?" she suddenly questioned. "Are you out there?"

Suzie stepped forward, her eyes meeting Angie's for only a second, before she cast them downward shamefully afraid to hold contact.

"Get a beach towel, will you, please, Suzie? A towel. A robe. A coat. Something," Angie pleaded.

Suzie turned then, raced into the house and was back in moments with a long, trench coat she had pulled from the front, hall closet.

"Here," she offered, her mouth drawn into a serious line.

Angie said nothing, but turned to Willard, helped him with the coat, and immediately turned back toward the crowd of students that had grown strangely silent. The horrid spectacle was over.

"And now, we'll need a ride home," she stated coldly.

She stared once more at the horde of faces hidden in the shadows. She and Willard waited an awkward, half minute before hearing a voice.

"I'll drive you home."

It was Cynthia, from Angie's cheer squad.

"Come on," she muttered. "Let's get the hell out of here."

To avoid the bright lights of the kitchen, Willard and Angie shuffled instead around the side of the house behind Cynthia. Angie found Willard's hand. It was freezing cold but she did not let go.

"God," Cynthia managed. "What a fucking mess."

⌘ ⌘ ⌘

Once inside Cynthia's tiny Toyota, the trio breathed more easily.

"What the hell happened, Cynthia? How did this happen? How could anyone have let this happen? And how did you get here, Willard? Who brought you?" Angie assailed her friends with questions.

Willard spoke first. "Suzie passed me a note t'day at school. Told me I was invited t' a party here. Said Jimmy, Brad, all of ya'll wanted me t' come. I believed it. Guess that was real stupid."

"Suzie? Suzie did that? God, Cynthia, what was she thinking? Bet Brad and Jimmy put her up to it. Jimmy was all over her tonight too. What the hell's wrong with her? She could have refused. She knows what jerks Brad and Jimmy can be, especially to Willard." Angie began shivering again. "How'd you get here?" she added quickly.

"Walked – two an' a half miles in the dark. I reckon I'm a dumb shit."

"You're not dumb, Willard. It's just that some people are jackasses. Real honest to goodness dicks." It was Cynthia's chance to chime into the conversation. "And aren't you pissed, Willard?"

"Yeah, of course I'm mad, real mad. The worse thing now is that I have t' get int' my house somehow without my fam'ly seein' me an' makin' a big fuss. My dad keeps real calm, but my mama will throw a hissy fit. Don't like t' see her get her dander up. It's not pretty. Gosh darn it, I'm not sure how I'm goin' t' tell my mama I lost my shoes." By this time, Willard clearly was speaking out loud what he was thinking. His family was poor. In his mind, he had let them down.

"We'll make sure you get shoes tomorrow," Angie told him.

"Why?" he asked. "Why would ya' do that, Angie?"

"Because I like you, Willard. I feel horrible about what happened tonight. I'm disgusted with my friends, some of them, not you, Cynthia, but Suzie, and Jimmy, not that he was my friend, and Brad, all of them. What the hell went wrong tonight, Cynthia? How could decent people become such shits? Doesn't anyone have feelings any more?" Angie's ramblings took on a suppliant tone. Any semblance of understanding had evaded her.

"I don't know, Angie," Cynthia began. "People got drunk and stoned. It was Jimmy's show. He planned the whole thing, I guess. He has more money than he knows what to do with, and he's a jock, a stud, can get anything he wants. He wanted to be the big man."

"What happened anyway, Willard?" Angie asked.

"Jimmy saw me walkin' int' the back yard. Strutted right up t' me callin' me names, ya' know, *'turtle boy'* an' shit like that. I told him t' stop, but he didn't. Then out of nowhere, he slugged me, once in the stomach an' then in the head. Knocked me out, I guess, because when I came to I was down t' my underwear, naked. 'If you don't want more,' he said, 'get on your knees.' I did. I didn't want t' be hit again, but when I was on my knees, he pushed me down flat an' started kickin', over an' over. I couldn't breathe. I could hear him laughin'. An' then, thank goodness, I saw ya' comin' toward me, Angie. God knows what would have happened next if ya' hadn't shown up."

"Well . . ." Angie could not respond.

"What happened with Brad?" Cynthia asked suddenly. "Where was he?"

"Upstairs," Angie replied, "Drunk. Asleep. Sleeping it off."

"Probably good he was," Cynthia said. "He would have been knee deep in the whole fiasco."

She turned at the next corner and stopped in front of a small, wooden, frame house. "Here you go, Willard. You're home," she added.

"Thanks, Cynthia, for the ride," he said. "Thank ya' both."

He then touched Angie's cheek softly. "Bye," he whispered before stepping silently out of the car and fortunately walking to the door of a dark and quiet house.

"Hope he makes it in without another scene tonight," Cynthia muttered.

"Me too. Thanks, Cynthia. Thanks for all of this. You're a good friend."

"I got caught up in all this too, Angie," she admitted. "I didn't act quickly enough. I'm ashamed. I didn't do what you did. You did what was right."

"Willard's a nice guy. He didn't deserve this. Nobody would."

"I know. I know that for sure. And for some reason, I feel I've had the shit kicked out of me too, just like Willard. You know?"

"I do," Angie replied. "I know exactly."

Silence consumed the girls until Cynthia pulled her Toyota to the curb in front of Angie's house. The front porch light flickered slightly, but inside the hallway was bright. George Murphy had made sure.

"I'm breaking up with Brad," Angie blurted.

Cynthia actually gasped. "Why? You two have been together forever."

"I'm just sick of him, of his arrogance, his attitude. I feel like I'm always the one giving, and I'm tired of being used. He's not the same guy he was, Cynthia. I don't know. I just feel smothered by him. Need some freedom."

"Does he know?"

"No. Not yet, but he will, soon enough."

"He's going to be pissed," Cynthia warned.

"He'll get over it," Angie replied. "It would have happened sooner or later anyway. We're going to graduate, go in different directions. I'm definitely going to college and he, well, he didn't get a football scholarship. God only knows what he'll end up doing. He hates school."

Cynthia snickered. "I do know that! He's been copying my history notes for ions."

"I know he's never read a book from cover to cover," Angie said. "He lives for Spark Notes! I guess I shouldn't run him down. It's just that I'm tired of everything, the sex, the way he paws me in front of people, the way he treats some of my friends."

"Would that be Willard?" Cynthia smiled.

"Well, yes, it would. I like Willard, Cynthia. He's a nice guy, and I don't like the way Brad treats him."

"Well, be careful, Ang. If Brad thinks you have a thing for Willard, the shit really will hit the fan."

"I don't have a *thing* for Willard. I just think he's nice. Don't you?"

"I really have no idea, Angie. He seems cool enough, once he got use to how life is around here, once he got rid of the overalls." Cynthia laughed again. "Look, he was nice tonight, and pretty brave too for dealing with Jimmy's abuse. Hope this doesn't spill over into school next week. You know everyone will be gossiping."

"It won't be a big deal at school. Jimmy will make sure of it. The last thing he wants is trouble, and if anyone says a word, Jimmy will take care of business. Every kid at school knows what he'll do if one word is mentioned about what he did to Willard. He has that much power. You know it. I know it." Angie sighed. "Look, I know for myself, I'm keeping what happened on the down-low. I don't want to have to deal with Jimmy, and Willard doesn't need any more humiliation. Poor guy."

"You're right about that!" Cynthia agreed.

"Thanks again, Cynthia, for stepping up for Willard and me tonight, and for the ride home. I hope I can sleep tonight. I feel really empty inside, like all my emotions have drained out and there's nothing left to feel."

"Yeah, I'm right there with you. Take care, Ang," Cynthia said as Angie stepped out of the car. "See you Monday."

Angie walked quickly to the door, slipped her key in the lock, opened the door, and turned to see the red taillights of Cynthia's car disappear as it rounded the corner.

Once inside, she climbed the stairs to her room, stopping by her father's open, bedroom door on the way to her own.

"Hi, Dad."

"Hey. You're home early."

"Yeah. It was a dumb party. What are you doing?" she asked.

"Just going over notes. Still working on the investigation," he said. "Did Brad drive you home?"

"No. Cynthia did. Brad stayed at Jimmy's for the night. Drank too much. Couldn't have driven if he tried."

"Well, I'm glad you were smart," he said.

"I don't know how smart I am, but I am glad to be home. Good night, Dad. See you in the morning."

"Sleep well."

Angie did not. Brad, Jimmy, Willard, her classmates, Sherry Mitchell, all, set up camp in her mind, and like the party she had abandoned earlier, created chaos there. The only release she could find, for the duration of the night, was in her tears.

CHAPTER TWENTY-ONE

JACK

A new day did not bring relief to Jack Mitchell. He awoke cold, sore, and achy in a grey room diffused in dawning light. He twisted from the chair where he had spent a fitful night and stood shaking a bit from both the chill and the horrific memory of the unmitigated mess he had created only hours before. He sniffed the air, a putrid smell permeating his senses. It was all around him, in his nose and his mouth, on his tongue. Shit! The whole room was infused with the stink. Yet he was clean, wasn't he? He had showered the night before and had scrubbed himself, the floor, the leather lounger, everything in sight before he had sunk, dismayed and distraught into the chair that mercifully cocooned his quivering body. He had dragged two, heavy, woolen throws with him, curling like an infant into a fetal ball, his head lying on the thick arm of the chair, legs drawn up tight, and bare toes bandaged into the folds of the fabric. Sleep had come quickly, but was brief and then intermittent at best as he had tossed and turned the whole nightlong.

As was his routine, he moved slowly to the garage where he stared for a full minute at the huge, hard, punching bag that hung motionless before him like a mammoth phallus. "Don't mock me!" he stammered inanely at the thing as though it were an animate object. And then he was upon it, his ungloved, unwrapped fists flailing at the leather surface with unbridled force. He pounded and pounded until the ragged seams abraded his knuckles and blood oozed through his fingers and dripped on the concrete floor. The sight of the crimson drops ceased him abruptly. His unrestrained fury had dazed him, and he was angry, incensed by his stupidity. How would he explain the mangled hands to Roger, to his students, to that jackass of a detective who couldn't seem to get enough of his excuses, his alibis? He caught his breath then, gasping in deep, heavy gulps, as perspiration slid from his face and neck to mingle with the blood on the ground. He stared until the moisture was a blur, until an intense feeling of despondency enveloped him causing him to shiver in relentless quivers despite the radiant heat that emanated from his body.

How in God's Earth did I get to this place? He staggered back into the house. *And what the hell am I suppose to do with this day?*

⌘ ⌘ ⌘

Jack did not have to do a thing with the day. The day did it to him. It was Sunday, a time that generally had him lounging around his house from the moment he awoke. Mornings were spent sleeping late and afternoons were filled with football games blaring the excited voices of announcers who appeared awestruck by tackles, scores, and infractions made by one team or another. The wide screen television bolted to the living room wall was actually quite often Jack's focus. Earlier in the year, Melody Miller might have joined him for a few beers and a bout of sex on the floor, but those days were long gone. While he still could have used her body, he had no use for her otherwise, so was satisfied when she finally had disappeared as a central figure in his life.

On this particular Sunday, however, Jack left his house before noon. He had no plans, but found himself, almost without thought, driving into the parking lot of Hollow Vista High School for no specific reason. He exited his pickup truck and wandered the campus toward the science wing. Once there, he unlocked the door, scurried to the panel that housed the security system, and switched off the alarm. The place was as quiet as a grave, save for a sharp echo that emanated from the click of his heels as he ambled down the polished, hallway floor to his science lab. *Old Flo has the place all spiffed up. Guess she's good for something.*

He entered his classroom, stood momentarily at the door, and stared at the empty desks. Tomorrow at this time they would be filled with students – bored, impatient, uninterested students. He was getting tired of the little shits and their arrogant attitudes that indicated to him that they had better things to do than to waste time listening to his lectures. At his desk, that was positioned at an angle in the front corner of the room Jack sat. Before him, in a haphazard stack, were student notebooks, all baring an originality that could have identified a kid almost without looking at the name that was scrawled or neatly pinned on the front cover. Jack generally leafed through the notebooks two or three times a semester, putting a check in red ink here or there to suggest that he had been there, that he had looked. Seldom did he actually read the lines that were a regurgitation of the notes he wrote on the white board or definitions of scientific terms he assumed most of his students would not remember at the close of the school year. Occasionally he spotted a superfluous comment that had absolutely nothing to do with science and he would pounce then, circling the statement with his heavy hand and scrawling a sarcastic comment there. *"Science, really?"* *"What does love have to do with it?"* *"Football folly."* *"Did you think I would not read?"* *"Fools' names, like fools' faces . . ."*

Jack had never graded a paper on the weekend in his life, but began leafing through the books one by one until the afternoon was spent. By the time he was finished, the sun was low in the sky and he stood staring out of the west window, feeling oddly satisfied. As he had skimmed the notebooks, he had pictured each student: Suzie – her voluptuous breasts and pouty mouth too often provoking an uncomfortable arousal; Brad – the athlete, dumb as a donkey, his brain in his pants; Cynthia – too sweet for her own good and likely to pay dearly for it; Jimmy Nelson – a spoiled brat, smart, conniving, and so full of himself he stank; poor Willard Dunn – the new kid who certainly was not as ignorant as he had first appeared and who likely would one day lash out at the likes of Brad and Jimmy who harassed him unmercifully; Angie – stunning Angie. Oh, what he would like to do with her. And there were others, faces that in a few months would be gone and forgotten save for a few who would reside in rusty recollections, their vague visages washing into his mind and then receding like tepid and sleepy waves on a distant shore. In time they too most certainly would slip away forever, just like the others, into the depths of a dark and murky memory.

When he had gazed for long enough at the empty campus that was as familiar to him as his own body, he turned back to the desk. He sat down again, opened the top drawer and began shuffling through the clutter there: notes, hall passes, paper clips, pens, staples, post-it notes, a broken pencil, crumpled memos, and photos, lots and lots of photographs of students who had come and gone. He picked up one and then another until he had a stack of nearly thirty pictures in his hand. Some were faded, some glossy, and all bearing an endearment of sorts on the back: *To the best teacher ever. Thanks for the laughs. Thanks for passing me. You rock, Mr. Mitchell! You made biology fun! I'll never forget you or this class!* Jack read every single message, put the stack on his desk, and fumbled more through the drawer. As he rummaged through what was left, he was weakened with sudden, unexpected alarm. For a moment he struggled with the sensation, but was sucked further in when he realized that something was wrong. His face suddenly flushed, his neck grew itchy, and his hands tingled. Something was missing. It was gone. Sherry. Sherry's photo, the one he gazed at day after day after day, sometimes with anger, often with remorse, and most recently with sadness had disappeared.

"What the fuck?" he said out loud. "It was here on Friday."

Jack sat very still. Then in a mild panic, he began to dig again through the rubble, finally becoming so agitated that he yanked the entire drawer from the desk and dumped it onto the floor. On his hands and knees he searched longer, realizing at last that Sherry, in every sense of the word, was gone. She was dead, her photograph, taken with him, had vanished, and he had no idea where. He began to shake. *Someone's been . . . who the fuck has been here?*

He glared into the room as though the culprit might be hiding there, but his classroom was empty. He was met with nothing but an acute silence that agitated him further. *Some little shit has been in my desk. Who? Was it that jackass, Brad? Jimmy?*

A simple, misplaced photograph had wrenched Jack into a confused state of anxiety. He felt strangely violated and afraid, fearful that someone now knew that in a moment of anger and regret, a year before, he had defiled his beautiful wife, Sherry, in the only way he knew how. She had rebuked him, embarrassed him, sent him packing, and like a child, he had thrown a tantrum. He remembered precisely the moment he had cried, looking at the photograph of the two of them smiling on their wedding day. Her eyes, as blue as a summer sky, captured forever in the bliss of their beginning, were frozen in time there. When it was the end, those ice blue eyes had stared at him mockingly. He could recall the exact moment when he had slammed the photograph face down and read the words – *Wedding day – Sherry and Jack*. He had drawn a thick line across her name and, like a bad, little boy replaced it with the word *bitch*, and though it had been over a year since their divorce, he had looked longingly at the image of Sherry's face daily since the moment he had degraded her name. *God, what a stupid ass I was . . . am. Should have thrown it away a year ago. Something like this probably would be just the ticket to provoke Detective Murphy into pressing charges.*

He wondered more. Had his friend, Roger, been going through his desk? Had he let that awful cop into his classroom? Certainly Roger would not allow that. It was an invasion of privacy. But who had taken it? A creeping obsessive need to know grabbed hold.

"I'm going to find out who did this one way or the other," Jack mumbled out loud. *Until I have that picture back in my possession it's potential trouble. God knows what some people might make of this, especially now, though I don't think that jackass detective has a clue who popped Sherry. For God's sake he's been talking to everyone and their brother for days. I'll sit back. Watch. Listen. Stay quiet. But, sooner or later, I'll find out who's been into my shit.*

It was all Jack Mitchell could do, but the rumbling in his stomach assured him it would not be as easy as he might think.

CHAPTER TWENTY-TWO

MIDGE

Midge McGrath routinely spent Sunday afternoons cooking. Why? She had no idea save for the fact that it helped pass the lonely afternoons and gave her ready-made entrees for the week ahead.

From the time she was a small child she had hated Sundays. In the mornings her parents had forced her to accompany them to the small, community church in town. It was a non-denominational affair that catered to poor, lost folks who in winter enjoyed the warmth offered by the huge, wood-burning stove that had been stoked by the minister himself, and in the summer shaded them from the searing sun. Midge doubted, even at a young age, that the parishioners gave a rat's ass about religion. More important was what occurred after the minister had said his last *Amen.* Pot luck dinners served by the ladies of the church after each service filled the bellies of more than a few, transient, cannery and field workers and proffered plenty of introductions that led them to a more permanent status in town. Farm girls in the county were a dime a dozen and most had no clue what their futures held until a sly glance, a touch on the elbow, and a hasty invitation to a movie in town by one of the young men who wandered through gave them some semblance of hope. In that regard, the young men and girls were as similar as two peas in a pod. The couplings became routine, with some moving on to San Francisco or beyond, and some staying put, laying down roots, and procreating like rabbits.

Midge had had no interest whatsoever in following suit. Instead, she had her sights set on college, thinking to herself there was no way in hell she'd spend the rest of her life in the crummy town where she had lived since birth. Furthermore, she smugly and silently concealed her intention for more – to use her education and her intellect to become a power broker over those she assessed as inferior, hateful morons. The very thought had warmed her.

"I'm going to be a teacher if it's the last thing I do," she had told her mother.

To that end, at least her mother had been supportive, urging her in her studies, and scrimping and saving every nickel so that education became a reality. While the other girls had ogled the workers at the afternoon, church socials, Midge had scooted away as quickly as she could to her home and to her books. In her youth, Sunday afternoons had been spent reading and reading more. She had never been lonely then, not as she was these days, because novels that took her places she never could have imagined, satiated her. Books had been a salvation then, an escape from the others who thought her more than a little bit odd. *I'll show them. I'm smarter, better. I don't care what they say behind my back.*

While that bold, self-assured assertion had been fabricated, she had wanted with every ounce of her being to believe it to be true. Unfortunately, the fact was that she had cried herself to sleep too many nights to count and had created imaginary images of revenge on her classmates that she never could have revealed to a soul. With the auspicious passing of time, though, she finally ventured away to attend college in San Francisco where she completed a four-year program in three years simply because she was that driven. Ideally she would have stayed in the city, but jobs eluded her and when her money had been depleted she went home to live with her aging parents in the very house where she had been raised.

Midge had no sooner settled in, than she met Fred, who was the epitome of what she had hoped to avoid in a mate and who was, in essence, a carbon copy of the workers she had shunned as a young girl. To further the irony of their pairing, their first, chance encounter, had occurred at the same, community church she had attended with her parents as an adolescent. It had been Easter and the place was packed with women and children dressed in frills, ruffles, and wrist-length, white gloves. The men sported wrinkled, seldom worn, summer suits, many wearing white shirts with collars that exposed dirty, yellow, perspiration stains that never had been scrubbed away.

Fred had been late that day, and as Midge learned in the years to come, that frequently was the case. Punctuality was not his strong suit. In fact, in time, she determined it was a hallmark of his personality and an anchor that weighed him down to such a degree that he had never been able to secure a job for any length of time.

On this Sunday, harried and sweating profusely, he had moved into the pew beside her in a space at the end of the row too small to prevent their arms from touching, and though she had slipped a quick look from the corner of her eye to see, indeed, who the intruder was, he had done quite the opposite. He had turned almost sideways and had gaped at her as if she were the only woman in the room.

"Hello," he had said too loudly, just as the pianist began pounding the keyboard with a slightly out-of-tune rendition of *How Great Thou Art.*

"Shhh!" she had responded.

"Shhh!" she had reiterated.

The two had sat, side-by-side for an entire hour while the minister gave a short sermon, read a Bible passage or two, and led the congregation in song. At the moment the service was over, when Midge had turned to move into the aisle, Fred had stood his ground.

"Hello," he said for the second time.

He had nice eyes. That was the problem. Midge impetuously had fallen, at that very second, in love with a man whose name she did not yet know.

⌘　⌘　⌘

Though she had berated herself for her silliness later that day, the damage had been done.

"Hello," she had answered softly, looking from side to side to ascertain whether anyone was observing their encounter. Fortunately no one had appeared to notice the two for the throng of worshipers was fleeing the stuffy church as quickly as they could in search for fresh air.

"My name's Fred. Fred McGrath," he had told her.

"Midge," she had said, not offering her birth name.

"Are you a Margaret?" he had asked.

"Yes."

"Ah! Pretty name. My mother was named Margaret, but folks called her Maggie. Midge is nice though."

The eyes, those soft, brown eyes lined with long, straight, ebony eyelashes had rendered Midge still and speechless.

"Cat got your tongue?" he had grinned.

It had been unbearable. Midge, never in her life, had felt as she did at that moment, completely confused both by his overture and the sensation that made her knees weak and her heart pound. *For Christ's sake, Midge, get ahold of yourself.*

"I . . ." she had started. Words abandoned her though and instead of completing a sentence, she had lunged slightly toward him, dizzy.

He had grabbed her shoulders firmly to stop her momentum forward, but did not let go when she was motionless once more.

"I'm sorry," he had offered, gazing down on her with a look of love and lust, "but I won't ever let you go."

It was a lie, of course, but neither he nor she knew that then.

Fred and Midge had left the church that day both a bit taken aback by what both of them considered later as pre-ordained. Fred had known they would marry immediately. It had taken Midge more time although she could not deny that she was not the same young woman she had been when she had walked into the church that day as she was when she had departed on the arm of Fred McGrath.

⌘ ⌘ ⌘

The memory of her first encounter with Fred was a common recollection that often cast Midge into melancholy. That had not always been the case, but since the day he wandered out of her life ten years earlier as abruptly as he had drifted in, she could not shake the emotion. So, she cooked on Sunday afternoons to keep her mind occupied and she remembered, stewing over the fact that he was gone, she had no clue where, and she refused to speculate why.

"We were happy enough," she said aloud. "Weren't we?"

That was true for several years. Midge secured a teaching position at Hollow Vista High School in a tiny town farther East at the valley's edge, just before the earth edged up into the Sierra foothills. Fred amazingly found an abundance of work, none of it lasting for long. He was a truck driver who delivered potable water all over the county first, before finding work in a cannery, a shoe store, a Safeway market, a Texaco service station, at Two Timers Bar, and at quite a few other random businesses before finally landing a janitorial position for a short time at the very high school where Midge taught. What an embarrassment that had been! In between jobs, Fred floundered, and Midge seethed. She began to grow weary of his lack of ambition, a one hundred and eighty degree departure from hers. Though they had been in love and happy enough for a time, Fred's ambivalence for years, countered by Midge's condescending need to control, began to destroy the very union both had thought an act of fate. The excitement and newness of nearly nightly sex for the first two years waned in time, and like the fragile love that had brought them together, grew unimportant.

While Midge taught English during the day and corrected papers or continued her studies well into the evenings, Fred found delight in wandering the Sierra foothills, following the footprints of myriad animals and photographing or sketching from memory those he found. In no time he had albums of drawings and photographs of the critters: coyotes, deer, squirrels, foxes, rabbits, lizards, and snakes. Fred wasn't particularly fond of snakes, but had run into a few rattlers, coiled in high grass and ready to spring or stretched out across a path warming in the sun. He had learned to watch his step. He gathered leaves for another collection and plucked seedlings from the ground to take home. Before too many years had passed, the perimeter of the back yard was filled with buckeye trees, Ponderosa pines, western redbud, yarrow, lupine, mule's ears, and Manzanita, all of which delighted Fred when they flourished. He brought home wilted bouquets of wildflowers he thought a perfect demonstration of his affection. Midge thought otherwise and fumed at the assortment of flora that began to clutter the back porch or was piled and left on the kitchen table.

"Enough, Fred!" she lambasted. "What am I supposed to do with a bunch of dead weeds?"

"Look, honey. Look here. This is a golden violet. Here's a shooting star, a rose clover, a columbine, and a four spot. And you know California poppies when you see them. This is miner's lettuce, and this here's a pretty face, just like yours."

This here was all Midge heard.

"Fred!"

Poor Fred was unable to stop himself. He was drawn to the hills and all that he treasured there in the same way Midge was lured to her books and her library fund drives. He made a half-hearted attempt to work but after twenty years of suffering job loss after job loss he gave up. Midge had looked at him with disdain for years and he understood.

He sadly but truly did. He humiliated her, and though his love for her remained intact, on the day after their twentieth anniversary he walked away leaving a pile of freshly plucked wildflowers and a note printed in an effeminate scrawl: *Need to be away now. No need for hard feelings. It isn't you.*

Midge never got over his disappearance and this early spring Sunday, despite her attempt to avert the inevitable, her mind again had been bombarded by hateful memories. Melancholy overwhelmed her. She bitterly was aware of what was behind her, but what lay ahead? God only knew. For the first time in her life, Midge understood that she never really had controlled a thing, and with that realization she panicked. Hot tears burned her eyes and she muttered aloud in an empty room, "What in the hell will become of me?"

She was terrified.

CHAPTER TWENTY-THREE

ANGIE

Brad was on Angie's doorstep at noon on Sunday.

"Where'd the hell you go last night, Ang? Heard you left with Cynthia and that creep, Willard? Why the fuck did you do that?"

"You were drunk, Brad. Passed out. Besides, I'm sure you've heard all about what happened last night," Angie said, biting her lip. The burgeoning and burning disgust she harbored for her boyfriend had her fuming inside, but if he were in any way aware, he ignored it.

Instead he laughed. "Sorry as hell I missed it! Heard it was a great show!"

"It was sickening," she said. "Jimmy's a jerk. I told you how I felt."

Brad chuckled more. "Jimmy was just having fun with old turtle boy. Willard's a stupid jackass."

"No. You're the jackass, Brad. You and your misguided friends make me sick. I'm over it. I'm over you. This is it. We're done."

There. She had said it. A brief look of shock passed over Brad's face and his eyes widened. Then, as if overcome by some alien presence, his features grew dark. He smiled a twisted, ugly smirk and grabbed her arm.

"Don't go fucking with me, Angie."

"Let go, Brad."

He squeezed harder.

"I said, 'Let go, Brad.'"

"What are you doing, Ang? You can't break up with me," he threatened.

"I can and I am. I'm done, Brad."

"But you love me. I know you do." The grip on her arm loosened slightly but he did not let go.

"No, I don't love you. I haven't for a long time. I've wanted to tell you . . . "

Brad's very countenance, his stance, his attitude intensified before her. Was it disbelief? Perhaps at first it was, but it took only seconds for him to puff up with anger so intense that he pushed her backwards into the house and then stepped forward. His fists became clinched weapons and his body began to quiver as if he might not be able to stop himself.

"Brad!" Angie managed, as she took another step backwards, panicked. She had been here before. Suddenly the faces of Jerry Gerard and Brad Browning melded into one terrifying visage and she braced herself for an onslaught of abuse. *Oh, God. My dad . . . where is he?*

George Murphy was nowhere near his home at that moment. He was away, consumed by a murder investigation, and obsessed with finding a killer. He had left at daybreak.

"Brad," she said again. "You need to leave."

And in the back of her mind she heard her father's advice: *If you're ever in a situation where you feel threatened, be assertive and say what you mean. Stand your ground, but be smart.*

Brad pushed her roughly into the wall and held her there, seething. His big hands pressed her shoulders firmly and his mouth found hers. It was not a kiss, but a forced and brutal osculation that mashed her lips against her teeth; it hurt. He let her go then, so suddenly she could hardly stand.

"You're a bitch, Angie. How dare you to try to make a fool out of me. Don't forget, you little cunt, that I know who you are. I know more about you than your old man, your friends, God. You fuck with me, Angie, and you will pay."

Never in her life had Angie seen Brad in such a state. It was as if she was seeing him for the first time ever and he was frightening. His words, though lacking of substance, stung, of course, but his bearing was much more alarming and held her rapt. She could not move.

A full, tense minute passed before he spoke. "Now, you fucking twat, tell me again that you're done. Go ahead. Tell me."

Brad towered over Angie, his words as looming as his body.

"I'm . . . I'm not."

"Not what, you bitch! Not telling me or not breaking up."

Angie was not stupid; nor was she crazy. She clearly was in a predicament she had not imagined occurring. Cynthia had been right and she remembered her friend's words: *"Brad's going to be pissed . . . be careful."*

Backtrack. Backtrack. Tell him what he wants to hear. You can break up later. Calm the jerk down. She looked up at him, willingly softening her voice, so that he could barely hear. "I guess not."

"Guess not, what? Say it!"

Brad was not going to stop his intimidation, not now, not ever. It was a very real, and very arresting realization for Angie, so she did what she had to do.

"I'm not going to break up," she told him. "I was just mad at you."

"Now that's better," he said, grabbing her upper arm again forcefully. "Don't let this shit happen again, Angie."

Angie did not reply.

"Now get upstairs," he told her. "Give me some stuff."

"No, Brad. I have homework."

"Don't fucking tell me *no* again," he hissed.

"My dad will be home soon," she lied.

"Your old man won't be back until dinner. He's out finding killers," Brad smirked. "Now get upstairs."

Angie was trapped. *One more time . . . one more time and I can get him out of here. One more time and then we're done.*

She trudged slowly up the staircase to her bedroom, feeling Brad's hands possessively gripping her waist. Once inside, she stripped naked, lay on her bed, and closed her eyes until it was over.

⌘ ⌘ ⌘

When Brad finally left for home an hour later, Angie took a shower. Water, soap, and shampoo were not enough. She scrubbed her legs, her under arms, her breasts, and between her legs over and over. She felt filthy and ashamed.

Moreover she was angry with herself for not standing up to the boyfriend she detested. Why had she given in to him? Why had she let him intimidate her? She knew. She knew. She was scared. Ever since the assault years ago by Jerry Gerard, she had been afraid, actually quite terrified, not openly, but deep inside. And no one knew. She had even managed to lie to herself. She was lucky, wasn't she? The façade she presented had always worked well for her. She had a nice home with an adoring, protective father, was a popular, successful student, and had plans for her future.

She stared at herself again in the mirror. Why was she constantly drawn there? It was as though her image pulled her in, for a peek deep inside herself, but all she could see was that she needed help, and despite the devotion of her father, she felt lost. She gazed for minutes, but this time did not cry. Rather, she felt numb and resolute. *I don't want to exist like this any more. It's not that I want to die. I want to live, but I want to live unafraid. I just don't know how to do that, not any more, not with what's happened around here. And now there's more. There's Brad. How am I ever going to get away from him?*

⌘　⌘　⌘

The memory of Brad's heinous behavior, not to mention her pathetic, gutless acquiescence to his sexual demands, tormented Angie the rest of the afternoon. She attempted to study, but her natural aptitude for focus and concentration abandoned her. Instead her thoughts drifted to Willard Dunn. Where was he this Sunday afternoon, and how was he feeling after his humiliating experience at the hands of Jimmy Nelson? God only knew how the kids who had been covert participants (to some degree as guilty as

Jimmy by not taking action when the disgusting scene was completely out of hand) were tending to their own consciences this day. Or perhaps they weren't. Last night the whole, drunken group of them had appeared to be devoid of any principles whatsoever. Angie thought immediately of Suzie. How was she coping this day after having observed, first-hand, the violence her would-be boyfriend, Jimmy, was capable of delivering to an innocent victim? *She's not the least bit concerned. Suzie's fine. She didn't give a shit then; she doesn't now. She only wants to be the light in some wealthy, popular jackass's eye.*

As the handsome, cruel face of Jimmy Nelson worked its way into her mind, Angie sadly envisioned her friend, Suzie, as well. Only now, it was in a new light. Her two classmates suddenly were uninvited evils, dominating her thoughts and making her heartsick. It was so very clear that the very notion of Suzie and her having a viable friendship again was gone forever. It had slipped away into the shadows of Saturday night's fiasco. *Maybe it wasn't a friendship after all.*

And Cynthia? Cynthia had done what was right. She had. Yet Angie wondered if their relationship would be altered too. Did Cynthia regret what she had done? Popularity was paramount to Cynthia; Angie knew that for a fact. Would her joining with Angie in coming to the rescue of a battered acquaintance, tarnish her reputation? Surely Cynthia would take a heap of criticism for asserting herself, even though tardily, to help a student named Willard Dunn, a kid not one other person, save Angie herself, had given a chance.

Angie's musings were interrupted by a noise – a shuffle on the front porch. The doorbell rang. She trotted down the stairs, praying it was not Brad again. From inside, she peered out the window, and there he was. Willard. A strand of blond hair had fallen onto his forehead and he gazed from side to side, uncertain. Angie quickly opened the door to face him.

"I see you found some shoes," she said, grinning.

⌘ ⌘ ⌘

Willard felt nervous standing at the front door of Angie Murphy's house for the first time ever; however, he returned her grin with his familiar, crooked smile and responded immediately to her comment. "Yeah, bought some this morning," he said, referring to his new, tennis shoes, replacements for his old ones that on Saturday night had settled to the bottom of Jimmy Nelson's swimming pool. In all likelihood they still were there.

Willard glanced down at his feet when he spoke, but quickly looked back up at Angie. His blue eyes seemed almost translucent in the late afternoon sunlight and she was a bit entranced by them. She tilted her head and stared fleetingly at him before blurting, "Come in. What are you doing here?"

"Well . . ." he started.

Maybe I shouldn't have come over. Willard's face grew serious, reflecting his doubts. *Was this a mistake?*

"Would have called ya' first but didn't know the number," he offered.

"It's fine, Willard. I'm glad you're here. Just surprised."

"Well," he began again. "I came here t' thank ya', in person, alone, for standin' up for me last night. It was real nice of ya'."

Willard's southern vernacular was pleasant and soothing. For the first time all day Angie felt a welcome calm.

"Oh, Willard," she began, "I don't even know what to say. I did what I had to do, what a whole bunch of other people should have done. God, Willard, the whole thing makes me sick just thinking about it!"

"Try bein' in my shoes!"

He chuckled for a moment at his own unintentional reference before he spoke the truth. "God Angie, I feel like a jackass, an' I'm humiliated. Feelin' stupid. Sure not lookin' forward t' school tomorrow, facin' all those kids, Jimmy."

"I can imagine," Angie sympathized. "Look, Willard, fortunately the whole school wasn't at the party."

"Seemed like it," Willard murmured.

"I know, but they weren't. And take it from me the ones who were will keep the gossip on the down low, at least at school. Jimmy will make sure of it. He could be in a shitload of trouble for what he did and he knows it. Fact is he probably wants the whole thing forgotten as much as you do, as ironic as that sounds."

"Oh, Jimmy's not about t' forget, Angie. I'm just another notch in his belt."

"You mean he's proud of it?"

"Hell, yeah, he is! I'm sure I'm not the first person he's assaulted like that. Won't be the last either." Willard's eyes grew glassy and sad. He knew he was speaking with absolute certainty.

"I never have liked Jimmy very much!" Angie admitted. "Probably shouldn't go on about it, but he's so spoiled and arrogant. Thinks he's God's gift."

"He's a jerk, plain an' simple!"

"After what he did to you, after Saturday night, that's an understatement," she added shaking her head in disgust, and then she fell silent.

Angie and Willard stood facing each other at the bottom of the staircase. Each was looking at the other openly for the first time ever. A full minute elapsed before she spoke again.

"Willard?"

She reached for his arm and felt it tense slightly with her touch. He was taller than she had realized, but on tiptoes she could reach her mark. She leaned into him and kissed him lightly on the neck. He smelled of soap.

He looked directly down at her taking in every detail of her face. "You're real beautiful," he said in a whisper before pulling her gently to him and kissing her with such tenderness she was not certain she would breathe again.

⌘   ⌘   ⌘

Angie stood at the front door and watched Willard amble down the front sidewalk to the street an hour later. Before leaving he had gathered her hands in his, holding them as though they were porcelain, and then he had kissed her once more, this time sweetly and softly on the forehead. And then he was gone. At the edge of the road he turned, waved, and smiled. She watched him walk for a short distance before he broke into a slow run. It was growing darker now and he had a mile to go.

"I'll call," he had told her, "when I'm home."

"Please," she had replied assured that he would. Her phone number had been tucked safely into his wallet.

Angie sat on the stairs once the door was closed. "Willard," she uttered aloud.

One word. Saying it made her feel as she never had felt before in her life, empty and full at the same time.

⌘ ⌘ ⌘

The phone call Angie had been anticipating came three hours later. In between that time, Brad called twice, once to tell her he needed her biology notes and the second time to moan about his geometry class. It was as far as he had made it in the math department and it wasn't looking good.

"That fucking Mrs. Cummins! She can't explain shit. Called my house today. Told my mom I was failing. Said I had to show up at her class tomorrow morning, first thing. Bitch! My mom's all flipped out. Thinks I won't graduate and with family coming from out of town for graduation, she's going crazy. 'Brad, this, Brad, that!' She's been yelling at me since I got home. Anyway, Ang, bring those notes. Meet me before English. Wait for me out in the hall. Don't forget."

Angie began to reply, but Brad cut her short. "Gotta go," he blurted and the phone went dead. That was it.

"Brad, you're such a jerk. It's all about you, isn't it?" she mouthed at the cell phone adding, "Jackass," for emphasis.

When her cell rang again, she cringed. *Oh, please, not Brad, again.* It was Cynthia.

"Hey, Cynthia here," her friend began. "Hey, just wondering. Did you talk to Brad?"

"Yeah. Didn't get far," Angie admitted.

"Told you. Brad's not going to let you out of his sight. Was he pissed?"

"Yeah."

"I knew it. Knew he would be. What are you going to do?"

"I'm breaking up. Tomorrow. For sure," Angie said though her words felt hollow.

"You don't sound too certain." Cynthia began prying, "Hey, by the way, did you hear from old Willard?"

"Old Willard? What do you mean by that?" Angie was instantly irritated by Cynthia's use of the adjective.

Cynthia unmistakably sensed her friend's annoyance. "Oh, I didn't really mean anything. You know. You know how it is. I'm just used to Willard being called, old turtle man, old, old whatever!"

Angie sucked in her breath. She did not reply.

"Angie? What the hell? You saw him didn't you?" Cynthia gushed as if she'd won a prize.

"Yeah, I did. He stopped by."

"Your house?"

"Yes. My house. He stopped by to thank me, us," Angie embellished, "for standing up for him."

"Is that all? Does Brad know?"

"That's all." Angie was not about to tell her friend about the kiss. "And no, Brad doesn't know. No one does."

"Thank God for that," Cynthia continued, "Guess old Willard, uh, Willard is braver than I thought. Hope he got some shoes."

"He has new shoes," Angie told her. "Look, I have to go, Cynthia. Need to do some reading for English. See you tomorrow."

"Okay, Angie. You can fill me in then. Can't wait for the details! Bye!" Cynthia was giggling as the conversation was ended.

Angie sat for a moment incensed. *How is it that a person can be so helpful and sincere one moment and revert right back like the others the next day? God, I am so sick of high school. Can't wait to get the hell out!*

When her cell phone rang for the last time that evening, it was Willard.

"Hi," he said. "It's me."

They talked easily then until it was late. Angie heard a female voice in the background holler, "Willard, ya' need t' be off that phone! The babies need quiet."

"My mama," he said.

"It's okay," Angie replied. "It's late. I'll see you tomorrow, Willard."

"Yeah," he answered. "Bye."

Angie brushed her teeth, set her alarm, and climbed into bed. She held Albert Camus's *The Stranger*, the next novel on Ms. Miller's reading list. She wanted a head start and hoped reading would settle her mind and put her to sleep. It did not. Instead, just before midnight she wandered to her father's bedroom. He was awake, as usual, pouring over his notes, processing information into his computer, stopping only to catch a bit of news on his television or to sip one of two beers he allowed himself at night.

"Dad?"

"What, Angie? You're still awake? What's up?"

"Can I talk to you about something?"

"Sure, honey. Anything. Are you okay?" George Murphy dropped what he was doing immediately and directed his attention to his daughter. He realized how fortunate he was that she had not walled herself away from him as so many adolescents did with their parents. Instead, she communicated with him on a daily basis, at times about issues for which he felt completely unprepared. He was a man, after all, but he always had done his best as a single parent to fill the role left vacant when Linda had died giving birth to their daughter. His commitment had remained unwavering from that moment until now.

"What's up?" he asked again.

"Dad, how did you know you were in love with my mom?" Angie never had asked such a question of her father. It had not seemed necessary. Having always lived only with her dad and not ever knowing her mother, Angie had not dwelled on the fact that her parents, indeed, had begun a relationship at some point, and a loving one . . . not until today . . . and why today? Angie was not sure, but the question had bubbled to the surface as unexpectedly as Willard's appearance at her door. She needed an answer in the worst way.

George smiled and his features softened.

He's still in love with her.

"We met, of all places, at the station. She had come in to apply for a job in personnel; I was a young officer. She was the prettiest girl I'd ever seen."

Angie grinned.

"What happened?" she asked, moving closer to her father.

"Well, she got the job, and I got the girl," George chuckled. He tipped his head slightly and gazed blankly into the space before him. Angie watched, sure that her father's thoughts had transported him back in time. "Asked her out for coffee. That was all it took, for both of us. I felt so lucky, and was so happy until . . . she was the love of my life, Angie."

George didn't say more. They both knew the ending of the story and neither wanted to go there.

"Why are you asking about this all of a sudden?"

"Oh, I don't know really. Something happened," she admitted.

"What? What happened? Is it Brad?" George questioned, thinking of the cocky athlete who had been Angie's boyfriend for longer than he had wanted or approved.

"Did Brad do something?"

George realized that his conversations these days consisted completely of questions . . . questions followed by evasive answers or vague explanations, dubious alibis or blank stares.

Angie gave him none of those though. Instead she told him the truth.

"I tried to break up with Brad today. I've wanted to for awhile now, but he won't let me."

"Won't let you? What do you mean, 'won't let you'?" George asked, both annoyed and bolstered by the news. "He doesn't own you."

"No, he doesn't, but he thinks he does. He's been getting more possessive, pushy. I feel smothered," she said. "And he's a jerk!"

George did not reply. He was listening. Angie knew it.

"And there's this guy, from school, new this year, from Alabama, nice, my biology lab partner, kind of shy, gets picked on, Dad. He doesn't deserve it. And, Brad . . . Brad's one of the worst offenders."

"Anyway," she continued. "Willard . . ."

"Willard?"

"Yeah. His name is Willard. Kind of an odd name for a kid my age, I know. Maybe it's big in Alabama," she smirked. "But, anyway, Willard stopped by today."

"Here?" George questioned.

"Yeah. Brad came by early, being his typical, demanding self. What a jerk! When he left, I felt, well, angry, frustrated. He told me there was no way he would let me break up with him. He was mean, Dad."

"He didn't hurt you, did he?" George was suspicious.

"No," Angie inserted the lie. Her dad would come unhinged if he thought for one second that Brad had harmed her, although Angie knew, deep inside that he had, in more ways than one. The culpability lay with both of them however; the veracity of that fact stung.

"He finally left, thank goodness, and a while later Willard knocked on the door. I was so surprised. 'Cause he's shy, you know, not like Brad. Willard's the total opposite."

"What happened?"

"Well, I invited him in, and we talked, just about school, and stuff."

"What stuff?"

"Oh, just about how he feels about school, about the other kids, about being bullied." She stopped for a moment. "I like him, Dad."

"How well do you know this guy? And how much do you like him?"

"I don't know. I'm confused. He kissed me, Dad." Angie sighed. "It was special."

"Special?"

"It was sweet and tender . . . kind of special." She paused again. "I can't believe I'm telling you all this, but I can't get it out of my mind. I've never felt like this before. He called me tonight. Brad did too, twice. Brad was all demanding and angry, but Willard was . . . well just Willard."

George had no idea how to respond to his daughter. She had grown up so quickly, a young woman now, with adult feelings, and maybe even in love. His heart ached for her. He understood completely both the delicious emotion and the potential danger that lay in feeling so deeply for another human being. He had experienced both during his life with Linda. The love had given him strength and the loss had rendered him powerless, his emotions raw at each end. It had been Angie, a tiny infant, who had rescued him. He could recall the moment he held her, feather light, for the first time. An amazing nurse whose name and face he could not remember had insisted. "You have a baby girl," she had said. "Hold her." He had, and he would until it was time to let her go.

"Dad?"

"Ah, Angie, I wish I had all the right answers. I do know this though. Don't stay with someone you do not love, someone who is, in your own words, a *jerk*. You deserve better. Cut him loose."

"It's not easy with someone like Brad."

"Angie, in my line of work, I've seen grown women stuck, unable to free themselves of bad situations. And I've seen a few men in the same state of affairs. Some think they can change the other person. I've heard it more than once. Women often say, 'Things will be better if and when . . .' If and when never seem to happen though. So my advice is to be strong. Know who you are, and don't settle for less than you deserve."

George leaned forward in his chair, hands clasped, eyes intent. "Don't mean to lecture, honey. I just love you. Don't want you hurt . . . by either of these guys. Better to be safe than sorry, as ridiculously trite as that saying is."

"Is that why you didn't marry again?" Angie asked, truly considering the question for the first time ever.

"Maybe," George admitted. "Guess I didn't think I'd ever love another woman the way I loved Linda. Guess I didn't think it was possible. And, of course, I had you, a beautiful little baby to love, and a responsibility that I was not about to take lightly." George's eyes softened.

"Thanks, Dad," Angie said, standing to hug him. "You're the best."

"And you are, too," he answered. "But you need to get some sleep. It's late."

"Yeah, I'm going." At the door she turned. "You look tired," she told him.

"That, I am. I'll be turning in soon too. Tomorrow will be another busy day."

CHAPTER TWENTY-FOUR

MELODY

"Jeez Louise," Melody exclaimed audibly. "What a way to spend a Sunday afternoon!"

From the living room window of her apartment she watched the tall, wide-shouldered detective march down the sidewalk that ran the length of her apartment complex to his car. Anxiety had been her companion for a lifetime, but at this moment she felt smothered by it. The man's line of questioning had intensified her stress as the afternoon waned. With his leaving, her wildly beating heart finally settled a bit. Her breathing, on the other hand, was suddenly labored and difficult. She panicked. Something awful was not allowing her a normal intake of air. She was suffocating. She began to pace. *Breathe. Slow down and breathe.*

She could not slow down, however. She needed to keep moving, walking, even if in circles, taking in air, staying alive. She dared not stop; she dared not close her eyes. If that were to happen the dreadful interview she had endured over the course of several hours that afternoon might simply cease to exist for her and she could not let that happen. She had the ability to erase it, to bury it. She knew she could, as she had with other ordeals in the past. She had learned and practiced not remembering. *Forget if need be. It's a choice, really.*

And so it was. In forgetting, Melody was an expert. Some experiences, she had discovered, could be pushed away permanently into a dark corner of her mind. She was sure of it, wasn't she? A niggling doubt pestered her though. Was this power she maintained, this ability to discount what she wanted, another one of her lies? Was this the biggest lie of all? Perhaps it was, but who was she hurting?

The absence of truth isn't always a lie, is it? Melody toyed with the premise she wanted so badly to be the truth, again this day, as she dwelled on the long, tedious inquiry that was finally over.

⌘　⌘　⌘

Detective George Murphy had appeared at her door at nearly one o'clock. It wasn't a surprise. He had phoned first, warning her that he would be stopping by.

"To get a little information," he had said. "As you may know, I'm in the process of speaking with all of the staff of Hollow Vista High among, of course many other individuals."

That comment, *to get a little information,* was an understatement, for although Detective Murphy was polite, the visit had been far from pleasant for Melody. The detective, quite deliberately, she was certain, had failed to alert her to the fact that he planned to grill her with question after question in regard to her knowledge of Sherry Mitchell.

"I don't, didn't, know her," she told Murphy definitively although he noticed a slight quiver in her voice as she spoke.

"But you know of her."

"Yes."

"And what do you know about Ms. Mitchell?" George Murphy asked. The man's eyes did not leave Melody's face. Instead they bore in on her, searching for any movement, any alteration in her speech pattern, any flushing of her skin, anything that might give him a clue as to the validity and reliability of her answers.

Paradoxically, while she gave him what he wanted in terms of her absolutely manic manner, he came away with nothing that could possibly implicate her in the crime, save perhaps that she was jealous. Hers was a baffling performance of sorts that left him absolutely empty-handed as to whom this young woman was and what she might possibly have had to do, if anything, with Sherry Mitchell's murder.

Yet, the woman, a girl really, not much older than his Angie, captured his interest immediately. It was her absolute unease that did it. Melody had shifted in her chair, squirming with every question, her eyes darting to the ceiling and then to the floor. The idea that the poor, young woman could possibly have made eye contact for even a fraction of a second was not in the realm of possibility, he concluded rapidly.

"While I'm not interested in your personal romance," Murphy stated, "I have gained a bit of information regarding a relationship you had with Sherry Mitchell's husband, Jack Mitchell."

"Well, it wasn't an affair," she barked. "He was divorced."

Melody's face flamed crimson at this point. Whether she was angry or embarrassed, the detective could not determine. He did take careful note of it, however. In addition, Melody's body language was cause for attention. Once seated, she had pulled her knees up to her chest and wrapped her arms around her body protectively, and while she replied to his inquiries, her soft voice and stammering diction had him leaning forward to better understand. For a high school English teacher, her ability to articulate even one rational, well-thought-out statement was alarmingly absent. *How in the hell does she get along in a classroom? I'll ask Angie. I think she has Ms. Miller for English this year.* He made another notation.

Whether Detective Murphy simply exhausted his list of questions or grew tired of trying to pry information from her, Melody was unsure, but the man finally stood abruptly, stuffed his papers into a thin, leather briefcase, and departed from her apartment without so much as a handshake. He had been there for nearly three hours, never moving from his place at the end of the sofa, the same couch where she and Jack Mitchell had made love or had sex, whatever it had been, over and over. In fact, Melody covertly had envisioned her sexual escapades with Jack while Detective Murphy had been there. How ironic to recognize that the rhythm of their mutual, carnal movements oddly mimicked his to some degree. The notion had fascinated her. Time and again, Murphy had reclined back somewhat awkwardly and then leaned quickly forward, back and forth, to and fro, in keeping with his investigation: question, answer, backward, forward, question, answer, back and forth until it was over.

⌘ ⌘ ⌘

Though she should have been exhausted, the moment Detective Murphy was out of her sight, Melody was alert and fidgety. His questions, her answers were all a fuzzy haze that she wanted to forget. He had asked what? She had answered how? It was all a blur. She had felt assaulted and defensive, but it was done. Or was it? The afternoon had dredged up memories most of which she wanted to forget and she was quite good at that. Some things she could bury forever but others, such as her memory of sex with Jack Mitchell was alive and well. Of course, the detective knew about that. He had to. She and Jack had had what Murphy called *a relationship.* That meant sex, plain and simple. Perhaps the detective assumed there was more substance to their affair, but in all honesty Melody couldn't remember if he even had alluded to that. It didn't matter, really, for Melody knew the truth. From early on, she sadly realized that Jack had wanted her for nothing more than his own selfish need for physical release. He could not possibly have committed to more for it was clear that Jack never had felt remotely near the depth of passion for Melody that he had for Sherry. He had said as much, and Melody remembered. It had made her sick to her stomach to hear him blather on and on about his beautiful Sherry, but he had. He had.

"And he made my heart ache," she said aloud in the empty room. "It ached with real pain. Ah shit, it's cliché as hell to say, but it's true. It fucking hurt."

All she had to do was to think about Jack and she was back, steeped in sadness. *Let it go.* She wanted so badly to do so, but she could not help thinking again about the detective's barrage of questions. *God I hope I didn't make any mistakes today. Did I say too much?*

She began to pace faster. She clinched her teeth and then stopped still staring for a full minute at nothing until her eyes burned and stomach pitched. "I'm going to be sick," she grumbled out loud.

Melody spun around, confused, as if she had no clue where she was.

Finally her eyes focused. There. The bathroom was to her right. She reeled sideways through the doorway and fell onto her knees in front of the toilet where she wretched and wretched until her throat was raw and her stomach was sore.

She crawled on her hands and knees, sweating and dizzy back to the couch where she lay until the nausea faded and she could breathe more easily.

"Fucking-A," she whispered. "I have to get the hell out of here."

⌘ ⌘ ⌘

Melody cleaned herself, brushed her teeth and hair, and slid on a short, black leather skirt that caressed her thighs. Black tights and high heels made her legs look longer than they actually were and a deep purple, cashmere sweater added just the color she needed. A little lipstick, mascara, and blush and she was set to go. She truly had no choice in the matter. It was preordained. As if possessed by an unspeakable, untenable force, she moved forward. The inevitable was about to happen and she silently and submissively accepted it.

Though she had warned herself not to go there again, not alone, this Sunday evening she could not help herself. In half an hour she stepped through the front door of

Two-Timers Bar. The place was nearly empty. *Shit. This may not be so easy.*

She was wrong.

From the corner of the bar, she saw movement, and watched as almost in slow motion, a tall, well-built man made his way toward her. In only seconds he was beside her and, as if he could smell her need, he touched her arm ever so lightly.

"I'm Tom," he told her.

"Melody."

"What do you do, Melody?"

"I teach."

He grinned down at her. "I bet I know what you teach, too."

She blushed. The innuendo floated like a feather between them.

"And you? What do you do?" she asked, pretending to disregard his remark.

"I'm an attorney," he lied. "Just passing through on my way to San Francisco."

"And you practice there?"

"Yes, but I can practice here too," he smiled.

Tom was a handsome man. Perfect, in fact, with ebony hair, blue eyes, and the wide shoulders of a football player. He rubbed the side of his jeans boyishly, feigning a shy streak.

"Oh, God," Melody gushed. "Maybe you can help me."

"I would so like that," he replied.

Melody was caught in an all-too familiar snare that had pulled her to this place many times before. From the time she was an adolescent she had sought relief in the arms of a boy, or of a man, any man. It didn't matter who he was as long as he could take her away from the reality of her life, if only for an hour or so. Already on this Sunday, Melody had found herself at the mercy of another man, the investigator, who had clawed at her unrelentingly trying to discover a truth, and in so doing had dredged up the past, putting her back in the clutches of an illusory Jack Mitchell, the man who had confirmed to her for months that she was worthless. And now, she would prove him right.

"Where can we go?" she asked sweetly, fleetingly meeting Tom's eyes with her own.

"I have a place, a room," he said, placing his arm around her and touching the small of her back. "Let's go there."

"Okay. Let's," she sighed.

⌘ ⌘ ⌘

Melody woke up before dawn in an empty, dirty, motel room that smelled of vomit and feces. She was naked, her clothes in a heap on the floor. An empty quart of vodka lay on its side at the edge of the bed. She could vaguely remember drinking some from a paper cup Tom had found in the bathroom.

The sex had been fast, hard, and bordering on brutality, and when it was over, Melody had cried, before passing out cold. She could remember the tears. Rolling slowly onto her stomach, she lay still for a moment, assessing her condition. Besides a throbbing headache, she seemed to be all right, although her upper arm bore a faint bruise. When she stood, she swayed slightly, before reaching for her clothes. Dressing quickly, she surveyed the room for any other belongings, and spied her bag, the contents dumped on the top of a chest of drawers. Nothing was missing except her money – five, crisp twenty dollar bills she had obtained at the bank kiosk before heading to Two-Timers.

"Jackass," she said of Tom, all the while knowing full well that she was the one responsible for it all. Her current predicament was the result of a self-fulfilling mission she had created all on her own. She had been here so many times before it was ridiculous, ridiculous and sad. She would move on though. She always did, a façade of innocence disguising the depth of her pain.

She peeked outside at the parking lot that was lined with dented cars and pick-up trucks. It was a trashy place and on this early Monday morning she fit right in. Her mantra, unspoken this time, unsurprisingly resonated in her ears. *I'm so stupid* it said with unconditional veracity.

Melody didn't have to say a thing.

CHAPTER TWENTY-FIVE

FLO

It was Monday morning and everything was in flux. Along with her new assignment in the humanities wing, Flo had been given new hours. Rather than beginning her workday at three o'clock when the students were dismissed, she was told to arrive at noon. That would present a parking problem if nothing else. Old Rob Green would no longer be surrendering his space to Flo each day. She'd make out, though, somehow. She always did. This Monday meant new surroundings, different classrooms, bathrooms, and hallways, unfamiliar faculty member to assess in terms of their demands on her, and students, more than she was used to, complicating her work area simply with their presence. Though Flo was an adult who had been around adolescents for a lifetime, she always had sought to keep her distance. She knew how they could be.

This particular Monday also brought torrential rains to the valley. Such precipitation was unusual this late in the year; usually spring rains were light and sporadic not gulley washers as the weather anchor had warned on television the night before.

"With the ground already saturated from months of rain, we could see some mudslides, rockslides, and downed trees. It will be raining heavily all night but the brunt of the storm will hit the area early to mid morning. Expect high winds, blowing rain, perhaps some hail, and very slick roads. Be careful out there, folks."

"Just when school starts," Flo had replied a bit caustically to the screen. "Great! Oh well, we'll manage."

With years of experience behind her, Flo knew what to expect. Mud would be everywhere and Flo understood for a fact that the hoards of kids from the valley ranches would be tracking the thick muck with them into school. It wouldn't bother them one bit.

"What's a janitor for, anyway," she could imagine some kid saying.

⌘　⌘　⌘

"It's really strange to see you here so early," Cora Davies said, greeting Flo with a smile when she walked into the front office to sign in for her shift at noon. "Wild weather out there," she added when a gust of wind and blowing rain blasted through the door of the office behind Flo.

"Sure is," Flo replied looking quickly and somewhat nervously behind her as if she were being shadowed by an unknown, hidden danger. "It's already flooding down by Manzanita Creek. Kids who live down South of it are going to have a tough time getting home. Thank goodness most of them drive 4x4 trucks. At least I found a parking space. One of the teachers must have left early. Got the spot."

"That would be Ms. Miller's spot," Cora whispered, her eyes scanning the room for would-be listeners. "Believe she must have had quite a weekend by the looks of her this morning."

"I wasn't sure who it was. I thought it was that new teacher's car, but she wasn't driving. It was an old fellow who drove off in it," Flo answered insipidly in an attempt to evade Cora's insinuation as to Ms. Miller's character. The fact was though that Flo knew exactly whose parking space she had taken. It definitely had been the bright lime green Volkswagen that belonged to the young, English teacher. She had observed the obviously flustered and emotional Ms. Miller departing school early on Friday; the girl had seemed angry and upset. Flo recalled watching, strangely attracted by the woman's frantic behavior. Today, according to Cora, Ms. Miller had not been able to make it even to the beginning period her first morning back after the weekend. *I wonder what her problem is.*

"That girl has issues," Cora mouthed.

Flo shrugged. Cora was apt to be correct in her judgment, but Flo didn't know Ms. Miller at all. She had observed the young teacher but planned to keep any speculations to herself. Fortunately Flo knew her strengths. She could be as restrained and silent as a monk.

"By the way, Flo," Cora began again in a hushed voice, "the teachers in the humanities wing are quite the group. Lots of sparring going on for position and I dare say, power. Not bad people, just agenda biased, if you know what I mean. Be careful not to step on toes."

"Thanks for the heads-up, Cora."

Flo truly was grateful for Cora Davies. She had been Flo's advocate, her protector, and her advisor since she was fourteen years old. She had never let Flo down and Flo was confident that Cora's advice was sage indeed.

"Have a good afternoon," Cora said, eyeing the black sky and the deluge of rain that followed a clap of thunder.

"I hope to," Flo replied, pushing her way outside.

⌘ ⌘ ⌘

Hope. As she sprinted to the custodian's supply station in the downpour, Flo wondered about her use of the word. Hope had never been an outlook that held much substance or strength in Flo's mind. To her it seemed an overused term that lacked force or validity. Hope was a toss-up of sorts. It was like throwing one's intentions into the wind with no idea in which direction it would go. Hope was not dependable. That was a certainty. Hope clearly did not always result in happiness or joy. How many times had it ended with despair, with disappointment, or with regret? Flo considered hope to be useless. It was essentially empty.

Hope can go fuck itself. Flo sniggered to herself. She seldom, if ever felt the need for profanity, so simply to use a little, to tease her mind on this day that had Flo just a little unsettled, made her feel good.

⌘ ⌘ ⌘

Flo entered the custodial station in a rush. She wasn't late, but she wanted to be prepared, primed for anything, before she started her new position. It had taken the entire weekend for her to accept the change mentally, but she was ready, and actually nervously excited. Who knew? Working in the humanities wing might open up a whole new world to her. As she piled her cart with a variety of cleansers, soaps, sponges, and brushes, she recalled Cora's warning: "Be careful not to step on toes."

She imagined replying, "Don't worry, Cora I plan to keep my nose to the grindstone."

"Hey, Flo!"

She was startled by the voice of Carlos Ortiz behind her.

"Scared me half to death, Carlos!" She punched her friend playfully on the shoulder, noticing as she did, a man standing quietly behind him.

"Flo, this is Kirby. Kirby Dunn."

"Nice to meet you, Kirby."

"Yes, Mam. Same," Kirby stammered, his head cocked to one side.

Flo stared at the man. He was tall, surely over six feet, and lanky as a monkey. Although he was slightly balding at the temples, his hair, otherwise, was thick and brown with flecks of gold here and there, and his eyes were lazy, with lids half closed. His shy, tight-lipped grin was genuine though. She noticed his hands too. They were large and rough, with big knuckles and a few nicks, long embedded with dirt. His were worker's hands. Flo took it all in, in seconds.

"Finally found a replacement for old Frank, let him rest in peace. Kirby here is from Alabama. Had a job with that Sherry Mitchell woman, handling all the repairs on her rental properties, but, well, you know. Due to what happened to her, well, due to circumstances, he lost his job a couple of weeks or so ago. He's got kids, a family to feed. Saw our ad and came here looking. No other applicant has been worth a damn, so no need for an interview panel.

Principal wanted to hire Kirby on the spot. Got Human Resources downtown to cooperate for once. Put a rush on the fingerprints and as of this morning we're good to go. Should work out for us. Lots of experience." Carlos ran his thoughts together into one, long-winded explanation as to why Kirby Dunn was standing behind him . . . as if, in Flo's mind, it really was any of her business.

Flo did notice, for some reason, one interesting aspect of Carlos's convoluted introduction of Kirby Dunn though: his inability to articulate unequivocally the obvious fact that Sherry Mitchell had been shot dead. That simple detail struck her as odd although she realized that voicing the words tended to make the tragedy all the more real. Carlos had a wife, children; they had been frightened like a whole host of other folks in town whose initial shock and terror had found consolation in rabid gossip and animated conversation; the emotions had transformed since then into quiet whispers or absolute silence regarding the matter. Perhaps the fact that Carlos did not fill in the blank was absolutely apropos.

"It'll be nice to have you around," Flo said politely. "And Carlos and I sure can use the help."

That was an absolute truth. Carlos and Flo had worked with the help of a few, inept, substitute custodians for a few months after aging Frank Sutter passed on from old age. The old fellow had been a janitor when Flo was in school and he was ancient then so it was not a surprise to anyone that his time had come. For the first day in years he didn't show up for work in mid October. His wife, as old as the hills herself, had found him that morning in bed . . . cold, blue, and dead.

"It's a blessing," she told everyone. "I loved him more than life, but he was a mean bastard from the beginning.

Guess in time, the meanness finally got plum worn out of him and he couldn't go on without it, God rest his nasty soul."

"Now that's a proud and practical woman, if you ask me," Flo had told Carlos when she heard Frank's wife's words. "She's loved, accepted, tolerated, and probably despised her old man, and now that she's lived to tell the tale, she can say it straight. Takes guts."

Guts didn't amount for much though.

A small group of friends, including Flo, Carlos, and the principal, Roger Cunningham, had watched Frank's casket lowered into a dank grave in the county cemetery outside of town. Two days later Frank's wife followed him as she always had. Their daughter spotted the deceased form of her mother slumped forward on the porch swing Frank had anchored to the ceiling sixty years before. To folks who had known the couple well, her demise was no surprise at all.

Frank's good wife's sudden passing had dredged up, for Flo, the memory of her own folks' deaths years before. Though it had been longer than two days, Ruthann Carter had died of a broken heart, Flo supposed, only three months after her husband, Charlie, had been killed, crushed against the cannery loading dock in an accident so abrupt and bizarre that people still talked about it.

The similarity in the timing of the events threw Flo into a frenzy of thought that lasted for a long while. Such love and attachment was an enigma to her. How was it that any woman could give herself permission to renounce her existence, to abdicate life completely after the death of a mate? Flo's husband, Randall, had passed on too, horribly, consumed by cancer, and though their marriage had been a dance of love and loathing, affection had dominated. And Flo had grieved. She had. At times she still did. Giving up on life, though, had not been an option. Flo had known that from the beginning, at the exact moment when Randall's lifeless body had been carted off to the mortuary. Any notion that she was ready to give up on living had been out of the question, and it still was. She wanted to go on, listening, watching, and waiting to see what would happen next. And so she did. Flo had existed on an even keel for years, simply taking life, with all its contradictions, as it came, day after day. Was anything wrong with that?

⌘ ⌘ ⌘

"Flo. You're doing it again."

"What am I doing, Carlos?"

"Staring into space, like you did on Friday. You okay?" Carlos asked.

"I'm fine. Good. When you mentioned Frank, I couldn't help thinking about him, his wife, you know," she revealed.

"Was odd, wasn't it?" Carlos said and then looked at Kirby Dunn to explain. "Frank and his wife died two days apart, almost like they planned it."

"Well, we'd better get moving," Flo managed, wanting to quash the memories and end the conversation.

"One thing," Carlos began again.

Flo gazed at him wondering what was next.

"Kirby here has asked that we not use his last name in front of the students and teachers."

"Why's that?" she asked.

"There's a reason," Kirby said timidly. "Look, if ya' could just not use my last name, Dunn, it would be better. Call me Mr. Kirby, or just Kirby if ya' will. See, my kid goes here.

Name's Willard, Willard Dunn, an' well, he's had a rough time with some of the kids here."

Flo listened. She had been there herself.

"I don't want t' make a big deal," Kirby continued, "I haven't even said a word about the harassment t' Mr. Cunningham, but I think if whoever is tormentin' my boy finds out I'm his dad, it could be worse. Ya' know, some kids might have a heyday with it. I reckon some kids think bein' a janitor is a stupid, petty job for knuckleheads. No offense t' ya', Flo, or t' Carlos either. I know better."

"None taken," Flo answered. "I know how hard we work. The students and half the teachers don't have a clue."

"You're right about that," Carlos added, puffing out his chest with pride.

"What's been going on, if I might ask?" Flo was interested on a deeper level than she would ever divulge.

"Seems a few of the football players, some of the popular kids, have been pickin' on Willard, callin' him names. Came home Saturday night pretty messed up. I didn't know 'til Sunday mornin', but some character gave him a real bad time. Took his clothes, shoes, beat him up pretty bad."

Flo's stomach lurched and her throat tightened. It felt as though her heart wanted to make a home there.

"Finally I pried part of the story out of him Sunday mornin'. He wouldn't name names though. Only one. A girl named Angie. Said she was the only one t' help him. Called her an angel. Reckon he might have a little crush. This Angie, an' some other gal, drove my boy home. When he woke up in the mornin', he was wrapped in some stranger's trench coat without a stinkin' stitch on otherwise, except for his underwear. Made me sick."

An avalanche of words had been dislodged. Kirby continued. "Do ya' know what it's like t' see a seventeen year old boy, a smart boy, a good kid, cry like Willard did Sunday mornin'? He tried not t'. 'Don't tell Mama,' he begged. An' then he sobbed. He was embarrassed an' ashamed. All I could do was hug him as tight as he'd let me, pat him on the back, tell him it would pass. I'm not sure it will, an' I'm not here t' spy; I just don't want t' add t' his troubles."

"Got it, Kirby," Flo said simply before adding, "There won't be a peep from me, but I have to tell you, I'll be watching. Can't help it. Been there myself." Her hand subconsciously rose to her cheek to touch the big, black mole that lodged beneath her eye. The motion was as deliberate and expected as taking a breath.

CHAPTER TWENTY-SIX

JACK

Jack awoke strangely refreshed on Monday morning. He finally had slept. No nightmares. No accidents. No shitting and pissing. Just sleep. He was ready to go, with a silent mission giving him a sense of direction for the first time since Sherry's murder. It wasn't much, but it was something.

I'm going to find out who stole that fucking photo or else. His was a ridiculous quest. He knew it, but it was something. It quieted his mind and quashed the memories.

His workout that morning was easier than it had been in recent weeks. Perhaps it was the sleep. Perhaps it was the passage of time. Perhaps he was over the hump of despair, seemingly having hit rock bottom two days prior.

"God, what a mess," he said out loud, embarrassed by the thought that he had been unable to control even his most basic urges. *I couldn't help it. I was asleep. I was sick. I couldn't help myself. It was an accident, pure and simple.* He was bargaining. *But I don't understand. Why? Why did it happen? Thank God no one knows.*

Jack's interior monologue did not stop. *Sherry would have laughed. She would have made a mockery of me. Bitch!* His thoughts twisted, toying with him. *No. Not Sherry. She would have felt sorry for me, wouldn't she? 'Are you ill, honey?' she would have said. She would have understood. Once she would have. Once. Once. Once she would have.*

Grief overwhelmed Jack at that moment, threatening to destroy his rare, acceptable mood. He stood still, his breath slowing, a vision of Sherry materializing before him as if she were actually there. Her face was radiant, her long, dark hair cascading over her bare breasts, her aqua eyes filled with love, with affection for him. A golden glow silhouetted her body and he reached for her. *Sherry?* His fingers tensed, grasping nothing in the empty space. She was gone. *Oh, Sherry. Why did you go away? Why did you let it happen?*

Jack's moan was audible and so plaintive that it jarred him from his reverie.

Jesus Christ, Jack. Get your shit together. You have those brats at school lined up like soldiers; they'll do whatever you tell them. Then, you get home and fall apart. Well, it's not going to happen again. Not again. I'm a new man, now. The past is done.

⌘ ⌘ ⌘

"Jesus, Jack, rough weekend?" Roger Cunningham asked when Jack made his usual stop in Roger's office later that morning. "Here, have some coffee."

The remark surprised Jack because for the first time in weeks he felt relatively energetic. Clearly any vigor Jack had felt that day eluded Roger though. He responded verbally to exactly what he saw. A quick note of Jack's drawn face and tired, spiritless eyes told him something was very wrong . . . still.

Initially the raw news of Sherry's sudden death had slammed Jack into a near state of shock, and not unexpectedly so. After all, she had been his wife for seven years. Her murder had alarmed everyone, the entire community, in fact. It was unheard of for crimes of any significance, especially one as horrific as a killing, to occur in the quiet, valley community. Roger knew not one person, acquaintances of Sherry's or strangers, who had not reeled in horror at the revelation that the woman's body had been found lying in a sea of blood in her office. It had been on a Saturday morning just three weeks prior.

Jack had wept openly when Roger cautiously apprised him of Sherry's death. Although a police officer had been by his side, Roger, as Jack's boss, had been given the dubious task of breaking the news to him. Jack's emotional reaction actually had been a surprise for Roger who believed the romance between Jack and Sherry had been dead for several years before they actually called it quits. Sherry certainly had made it clear she was finished, long before the divorce papers were filed. Toward the end, it had not been uncommon to hear her both privately and publicly, make rude or snide remarks about her husband. Jack absorbed the abuse long enough to become embittered, but did not strike back. Instead, he grew silent and brooding. Roger recalled wondering if Jack ever would release his real feelings. It seemed not. Rather he stayed quiet and appeared to move on. Very quickly Jack shifted his attention to other women, many of them. His was a blatant display of poor judgment, in Roger's view, but he assumed it was an outlet for Jack's pain. Though Jack rarely mentioned in great detail anything about the women he was courting, Roger was certain not one of had enlivened Jack as Sherry had, and to that end, Jack's loss never could be relieved.

Roger looked at his friend, now, waiting for a response to his remark.

"It wasn't bad. Not a bad weekend at all." Jack hedged. He wasn't about to tell the truth. Not one person, not even Roger, could know.

"Actually spent a little time in my classroom yesterday," Jack blurted.

"In your classroom? Are you going nuts?" Roger chuckled.

Though his words were innocent enough, they burned into Jack like a scalding awl. Jack squirmed inside himself. Was he going crazy? The events of the past weekend had him wondering.

"Ah, football's over. Felt caged up at home for some reason. Went out with no destination in mind and ended up here," he said. "Got some notebooks graded."

"Well, I'll be damned!" Roger chortled again. The mere thought that Jack Mitchell might spend a perfectly good Sunday afternoon in his science lab was almost laughable.

"How about you? What did you do this weekend?" Jack asked, seeking to change the subject.

"Not much. Kids had some games on Saturday. Regina said she needed a drive up farther into the foothills on Sunday. Wanted to get out of town. Think all this uncertainty about Sherry's . . . well the speculation, is getting to her. She knows I'm stressed, worried about what happened. Poor Detective Murphy is all over the place, asking questions. Think he was going to talk to Melody on Sunday."

"Melody? Miller? Really? Why her?" Jack didn't like hearing that the detective, or any officer for that matter, might be speaking with Melody Miller. She was a loose cannon and was apt to say anything. Sometimes Jack wished he'd never laid eyes on Melody. She was bad news.

"Don't know. Think he's checking in with the whole staff," Roger continued. "For Christ's sake, he's glommed on to you more than once, hasn't he? I mean, I hate to say it, Jack, but you have to believe the guy's interest in what you were doing when Sherry was killed has not let up one bit."

"I've told the jackass time and again where I was – puking my guts out at home."

"I know. I know," Roger replied. His response was a glum reminder, however, that, in fact, he knew nothing for certain about Jack's unusual, two-day absence during the exact period of time when his former wife, Sherry, likely had been shot. A niggling fear began to grow inside Roger, for he realized, at that moment, that in the ten years he had known Jack, not one other sick day, aside from the two just over three weeks ago, had ever gone into the books.

⌘ ⌘ ⌘

Jack stayed in his classroom all day. Torrents of rain held him captive there. No matter. The conversation with Roger had zapped the spunk he had enjoyed early in the morning, and as a result he lethargically endured his classes all day. By the time sixth period rolled around though, he was antsy, just like the students. The entire lot of them behaved like restless, caged animals, ready to strike.

The final bell rang at 3:00.

"Stay seated!" Jack shouted loudly. He stood, feet planted, arms crossed in front of the exit door.

The students had sprung to their feet ready for freedom, but halted immediately, thirty bodies bobbing in place like marionettes held by invisible strings.

"What the hell?" Jack heard a voice whisper.

The faces of startled, incensed students stared at him. A few sat down, many moved toward the door, and one, Jimmy Nelson, had his say.

"That was the bell. You can't keep us here. We've got shit to do."

"Watch the language, Jimmy."

"What'd I say?" Jimmy had not a clue.

"I'm expecting better behavior tomorrow," Jack began.

The class had been a chattering, gossipy mass that day. Something had them as astir as a swarm of buzzing bees. Jack had been unable to curtail their incessant whispering for a second. He actually had initiated a conversation, up close and personal, with a few students in an attempt to ascertain the reason for everyone's manic behavior that afternoon.

"What's going on with you guys today?" he had inquired. "Something's got the whole group of you going."

He had been met with a blank stare from Jimmy; Cynthia had not even looked at him and Suzie had simply smirked, rolling her eyes to the ceiling. Not one word.

"Well whatever it is that's caused this uproar better be set aside by tomorrow," he had snapped.

As the end of the period neared, Jack was at his wit's end. He had intended to chastise them more, but thought better of it. Instead, he punished the class with an assignment made up on the spot. "Pick up your notebooks on the way out. I expect a reaction report, five hundred to a thousand words on Chapter twenty-five no later than Wednesday. Put some effort into it."

Groans could be heard throughout the room, but the students dutifully, if not disdainfully, shuffled to the front of the room where the notebooks lay in three haphazard stacks. Jack moved to his desk to avoid the fray of figures charging the front table and watched with aberrant satisfaction as the students pushed and shoved each other.

"Hey!"

"Stop pushing!"

"Get out of my way, bitch!"

"Give me that, you dick. It's mine!"

"Jackass!"

The flurry of comments filled the air for several minutes until at last the final two girls, Cynthia and Suzie, pushed their way out of the door into the hallway.

Nice ass. Jack looked squarely at Suzie's butt as she exited. Suzie cast a brief glance over her shoulder just in time to see Jack's garish expression.

"Pervert," she said under her breath.

Jack sat at his desk for a few moments, his palms flat, his head tilted downward, and his eyes closed. He was exhausted; the energy he had enjoyed early in the day had drained from him and he was empty, empty of feeling, of thought, of emotion.

"Guess I'll head home," he murmured. "Last place I want to be."

It was true. Home had become a prison for Jack. He was pent up there, strangled by uncertainties and very clear he had no means to get away from what mystified him the most: himself.

CHAPTER TWENTY-SEVEN

MIDGE

Monday. It was uncanny, but virtually every Monday of her teaching life, Midge found herself reciting the words of author Ken Kesey's infamous character Nurse Ratched of *One Flew Over The Cuckoo's Nest* fame. In her biting manner, the nurse's comment, " . . . *mean, old, Monday morning, you know, boys . . .* " spun into Midge's mind on cue and lay riveted there until the day was well under way. Why the line lodged there Midge McGrath had no idea. Quite likely, she unwittingly identified, or perhaps more certainly admired the nurse's proclivity and, indeed, gift for controlling her domain. Such an aptitude was appealing; feasibly and more importantly, for Midge, it was worthy of emulation. Of course, Midge did not oversee patients in a mental facility but on some level she sometimes felt that way. *God forbid if any student, or parent for that matter, could read my thoughts . . . especially today.*

The weekend flurry of memories, both sweet and devastating, had unarmed Midge to the point she was not sure she would be able to look a single soul in the eye and that would be a disaster in itself. Boring in and bearing down on her victims had been Midge's forte for years. As a young teacher she had practiced on students, but as the years progressed, Midge's expertise at disarming and alarming youngsters, as well as adults, had filled her to the brim with self-satiating power. To that end, she always had been quite puffed up with herself. This day, however, a silent, confounding, and inexplicable shift in confidence had Midge questioning her own ability to manage even herself. Her students were another issue.

"Damn you, Fred," she said under her breath as she stepped out of her car in the school parking lot. Swirling rain pelted the umbrella she hoisted above her head. "You're the cause of it all. Damn you! If it hadn't been for your sorry ass, I sure as hell wouldn't be standing here, in front of a crummy, valley, high school, of all places, stuck, with no where to go. Damn you!"

As was her nature, Midge always placed blame on someone else for the slighted infraction. Today was no different. In her current state of consternation, however, she was so intent on vilifying the husband who had abandoned her that she did not even notice the onlookers. Several parents, standing only thirty feet away under a covered walkway out of the downpour, had been watching with interest and slight amusement as the old teacher clearly was giving some imaginary being an unmitigated piece of her mind.

⌘ ⌘ ⌘

At her desk later, Midge sat silently, savoring the quiet, half hour before the classroom would begin swarming with students. She had skirted the principal's office, slipped by Cora Davies' desk, and gathered her mail without speaking to anyone that morning. The emotional weekend had denuded her of the clout she generally harbored, leaving her exhausted and edgy. She simply didn't feel she had energy enough to face any adult. Certainly the power she had wielded over Roger Cunningham the week prior had dissipated; it was gone as if it never had existed. The last thing she wanted this day was to face the man, even though she reminded herself of her success in unrelentingly manipulating him. She finally was rid of Carlos Ortiz, the janitor she had labeled as a do-nothing. In her heart she knew she had been unfair, but that didn't matter now. She had gotten her way. In the heat of her attack on the man, Midge had been acutely aware that her purpose in pursuing his ousting from the humanities section of the building had nothing whatsoever to do with the quality of his work. No. She simply needed to exercise her ability to dominate and defame. She didn't for one second consider hers an evil bent, but a necessary one that kept her senses sharp and her defenses keen. She loved honing her skills. And Melody Miller would be next. An image of the young, English teacher flashed into Midge's mind, at the exact moment Melody fleetingly peered through her open, classroom door before scooting on down the hall.

"What the hell?" It took effort for Midge to silence her voice. *Melody has shown up to teach wearing that?*

Midge jumped from her seat and scuttled straight to the door where she glanced out to see if, indeed, she was seeing properly. "Oh, dear," she mumbled.

Melody was wiggling into her room wearing a skimpy, very tight, leather shirt and a very wet, deep, purple sweater that clung to her body like a glove. Her hair, knotted in back with a bright, red, soggy scrunchy, looked otherwise completely unattended.

She's a sight! Midge did not hold back. She was upon the girl within seconds. Pushing Melody into the classroom, Midge reached for the doorknob and pulled the door shut as sharply as she could. The heavy, hydraulic hinge offered a strong, inanimate resistance that seemed to mock her effort.

"Come on! Close!" she hissed.

When the door sealed shut, Midge locked it from the inside and turned on Melody Miller like a wildcat. "Ms. Miller, for heaven's sake, what are you thinking? You look like a hooker right off the street in that get-up!"

Midge stepped closer. "And you smell! You reek of semen and sweat and booze. And look at you. Huge bruise right there!" She pointed to Melody's temple. "Oh, and my God, your neck . . . purple . . . here, here. Disgusting. Did you spend last night in a brothel? How dare you show up at a comprehensive high school looking like a whore!"

Melody dropped on her knees to the floor in front of her mentor; her legs splayed outward and her hands lay limp in her lap, the palms facing upward as if in supplication. Midge was stunned when Melody raised her head to look at her. Her sad, round, doe eyes were glazed, red from crying, and ringed with dark, black mascara that had been smudged all the way to her cheeks.

"You look like a blasted raccoon! Where have you been, Melody? What have you been doing, and for Christ's sake, why in the hell did you show up to teach looking like this?"

Midge was incensed both at the girl and herself for actually having listened once and offering advice.

"Here, get up, get up." Midge continued to berate Melody who had not uttered one word. "Sit in this desk and don't move. I'm calling the office."

In no time, Midge had contacted Cora Davies, apprised her of the situation, and instructed her to have Roger Cunningham accompany Ms. Miller's class to the library. "Tell him she's sick, throwing up, something, but then, Cora, you need to come over to humanities, second floor," she demanded. "I have a class to teach and someone needs to be with this girl until she can be escorted, the hell, out of here. Bring a coat and something to clean the girl's face. I only hope the students don't find out about this. They'd make this fiasco the highlight of the year."

Fortunately Midge's final words softened her orders somewhat. Cora was at the door in minutes. The look of shock on Cora's face warmed Midge's heart. *That little twerp, Melody, will be out of here soon, really soon. Cora will make sure of it, if Roger won't.*

Midge, perhaps, should not have been so sure.

CHAPTER TWENTY-EIGHT

MELODY

Cora Davies slipped into Melody Miller's classroom like a thief. Only then did the blustering, red-faced Midge McGrath exit, slamming the classroom door behind her without uttering a sound. Cora and Melody were alone. Melody gazed inanely at the school secretary, a woman who seldom had offered her a word, and suddenly slipped from the desk to her knees on the floor as if pushed there by an invisible apparition. Cora bent down immediately beside her. She smelled of stale coffee and her breath prickled Melody's cheek offensively. Cora grabbed Melody's arm then, her long fingernails boring through the purple sweater into her arm.

"Ouch," Melody whined.

"Look, girl," Cora whispered through clinched teeth. Her voice was like cracked ice. "Keep your mouth shut and your head down. Don't move one inch. You hear?"

Melody stared at the woman's wild eyes and complied not because she wanted to obey, but because she had no choice. Her head had started to spin and a taste of bile rose in her throat. She leaned forward and stared numbly at the linoleum tile until the flecks of brown and charcoal imbedded there became a swirl of muddy color. Her stomach lurched and she began dry heaving with only strings of slick saliva slipping from her lips to the floor. By the time she was through, she was on her hands and knees, vomiting in earnest, too dizzy to move at all. She flinched when she felt Cora's touch again. Although the woman tapped her quite softly this time, it was enough to cause Melody to tumble sideways on her side. She immediately drew her knees up to her chest and fell unconscious. Her short skirt had crawled to her waist revealing bikini panties pasted beneath torn nylons. Her face had blanched white and her hair, matted and dirty, settled into the puddle of her own spittle and vomit. Lying there, she looked like a corpse.

"Jesus Christ," Cora sputtered at the girl. "What a stupid little twit."

Cora covered Melody's body with a stained overcoat she had snatched from the lost and found before leaving the front office. She then phoned for help. It was fortuitous actually that Melody had passed out. Her unconsciousness could be attributed to any number of contrived ailments that would counter the fact that the girl was hung over and stank of perspiration and alcohol. Her lurid condition, with a bit of prudence from Cora, easily could be concealed from nosy students and gossiping parents. The contrary could be disastrous and certainly the high school did not need any additional scrutiny. Cora knew that much.

She voiced her thoughts to no one though. *Yep, surely it will be much better to have her carried out of the building by medical personnel than to risk anyone, particularly a student, getting too close. What a ridiculous thing for her to do.*

It took fifteen minutes for paramedics to arrive and assess the situation. During that time, Melody did not move an inch. Nor did she flinch when two men hefted her onto a gurney. She was covered, trench coat and all, with a blanket and then a silver tarpaulin, strapped in place, and wheeled away.

"Good heavens. Could things get any more bizarre around here?" Cora asked Roger Cunningham when she returned to her post. Not wanting the eager ears of anyone to hear, she apprised her boss of her findings behind the closed door of his office only minutes after the ambulance drove slowly out of the school parking lot in the pouring rain.

⌘ ⌘ ⌘

Melody was taken to a holding bay in a small, local clinic not too far from the high school. The nearest, all-inclusive hospitals were miles away, in Stockton to the North and Fresno to the South. It had taken only minutes for the paramedics to determine that critical care was unnecessary. They bypassed the urgent care area and slid Melody off the gurney onto a narrow bed in a quiet space adjacent to the bustling, emergency room.

"The female in question simply needs to sleep it off," one told an aging physician who had followed closely behind them.

"Must have had quite a night," the other added, smirking at the doctor.

"I'll examine her. Thanks, fellas," the doctor said, looking at a chart of paperwork that had been handed to him. *From the high school . . . a teacher? Hum. Young. Looks young enough to be a student, and she was at school in this condition? Holy cow!*

⌘ ⌘ ⌘

Melody awoke alone, still nauseous, her head pounding. One arm had been secured to the metal railing of the bed, and strips of translucent tape held a needle in place in the vein of her arm. Through blurry eyes, she could see the IV line that connected a flaccid bag, nearly empty of its contents, to a cannula, also fixed in place.

She opened her eyes more widely.

"Hey!" she yelled. She was panicked. She attempted to assess her condition, but could not. Where was she? Her heart was racing and she could hear the throb of her pulse reverberating in her ears.

"Hey!" she yelled again.

A tall, slender male nurse poked his head into the room.

"Settle down," he ordered. "Why are you yelling?"

"Where am I? What am I doing here?" Melody struggled to sit up but she was too groggy. Her head fell heavily back onto the pillow with a thud, pinning her there. She attempted to move her arm, but it was held fast.

"You were brought in this morning," the nurse said, "from the high school where you teach, where apparently you teach."

"What time is it?" Melody mumbled.

"It's two o'clock. Early afternoon."

"Why am I here?" she asked again.

"You evidently fell unconscious in your classroom. We've had you on intravenous therapy for dehydration. Do you remember what happened?"

"What happened when?"

"At school. Before you got to school."

"Oh . . ." she said aloud and then mumbled, "I'm in deep shit."

"Excuse me?" the nurse questioned.

"Yeah, I think I remember," she admitted. "And I said, 'I'm in deep shit.'"

⌘ ⌘ ⌘

Melody did not return to school for four more days. The principal, Roger Cunningham, had gone to the clinic out of curiosity as much as courtesy, to check on her. She had refused to see him, however.

"No way. Not like this," she had informed a nurse on duty. "Tell him to go away."

Without protest, the nurse delivered Melody's message.

"I wouldn't expect your Ms. Miller back at school for a few days," the woman informed Roger. "Just so you know." As required by law, she offered no specific explanation and Roger, being astute enough to understand, simply nodded, turned, and walked out into the squalling rainstorm without saying a word.

Going to have to handle this. He was resolute. *Watching me deal with this Melody Miller situation will make that witch, Midge McGrath, as happy as a clam in high water. How is it that a person like Midge obtains what she wants sooner or later?*

⌘ ⌘ ⌘

With no other choice, Melody phoned her mother, Loretta, who picked her up at the clinic and drove her to her apartment late in the evening. Apprising her mother of what she had done, combined with needing to plea for her help, had pained Melody tremendously. She was quite aware of how her folks were likely to respond to her latest folly. First she would see her mother's drawn face, pursed lips, and sad eyes.

"Oh, Melody, dear," Loretta would coo. "What on Earth have you done to yourself? And aren't you concerned, at least a bit, about your reputation? And ours?"

Her father, on the other hand, would bluster his disapproval. "You're never going to amount to anything, Melody Clarisse Miller. I don't know what you're thinking sometimes. It's a miracle you've actually been able to maintain a position at that high school in town. And now look at this foolishness. You'd better be careful, young lady. You're becoming an embarrassment!" She braced herself for the condemnation she was certain was coming. She had fallen victim to the likes of this current, imagined diatribe many times before.

While Melody was correct about her mother's reaction, she had misjudged her father. Though he had rescued Melody's car from the school parking lot and met the two at Melody's apartment, he said not a word. He was so incensed by Melody's most current escapade that he could not even look in her direction. Instead, he set off down the street, his shoulders hunched and his trench coat flapping in the wind. He reminded Melody of a lost dog.

"I'd better get to your father," Loretta Miller told her daughter. "Get on into your apartment now. We'll talk about this later."

Melody said nothing but shook her head in a motion of acquiescence. She had not heard the end of this and she knew it. *I'm so stupid.* Although numb with disgust for the behavior that had brought her to this moment, she was, at the same time, stimulated by her actions that had more than a few people pulled into the drama of her life.

Once inside her apartment, Melody stood staring inanely at the couch where Detective Murphy had settled in to question her for the bulk of the previous Sunday afternoon. Recalling his tall, hulking body, glaring, green eyes, and huge hands, furiously filling in the pages of his notebook, frightened her still. She trembled involuntarily as a mirage of the man's unsmiling face fantastically loomed like a phantom in front of her.

"Go away!" she shouted at the vision. "Why did you do this?"

She wanted so badly to fault him for what she had done, but reluctantly recognized he had been only the catalyst that had caused her to turn, almost without thought, and certainly without control, into the brazen creature who had wanted nothing more than a night of sex with any man, anywhere.

"Oh, God," she whispered, defeated.

Melody was powerless against what had become a curse, a pattern of baffling behavior over which she had no conscious restraint when the switch was flipped. Indiscriminate, self-defacing liaisons with strange men and boys had occurred so often since she was sixteen she had stopped counting.

Only for a short time had she not fallen victim to her torment, and that was when she had been seeing Jack Mitchell. She thought of him now with sadness and loathing, the two emotions intertwined with a perverse affection that had never fully dissipated. And why? Why did he still have a hold? His physical and verbal cruelty had stung her deeply and she had sworn revenge.

"You'll be sorry, some day, you bastard," she had cursed. "You may just pay in the worst way."

She had cried then, mumbling Jack's name in anguished dreams, hating and loving what she would never have again. And, this night she cried again. Her pain, her confusion, her embarrassment, her self-abhorrence, and her irrational passion for Jack Mitchell were too much to bear.

CHAPTER TWENTY-NINE

FLO

Flo's first task when she arrived to her new work site in the humanities area of the building was to mop to the side of the hallway great swaths of mud that had been trampled in there by the students, teachers, and a few, unexpected visitors, paramedics, Flo learned, who had been called in to fetch the unconscious form of one of the teachers. Cora Davies had provided Flo with a few details about what had occurred but overall Flo ascertained very little information and had not wanted to learn more. She was told only that to avoid detection, a young, English teacher, named Melody Miller, had been whisked away when students were in class. Beyond that, Flo was in the dark and that suited her fine. She had an innate and honest aversion to gossip, although in her position at the high school she had been privy to more than her fair share. The hallways and faculty rooms often were a cesspool of chatter and hearsay, the conversations and whispers spilling over into speculation and conjecture, real or otherwise, about one poor soul or another. The worst offenders were the ones who laughed the loudest or spoke without letting another person edge in a word; they held their hands over their mouths, gushed insinuations with satisfaction, and ogled their victims without shame. Perhaps in the grand scheme of life, it didn't matter. Flo had learned early on that more than a few human beings, young and old, loved filling the air with sound, their own voices resonating much more joyfully to them than a melodic refrain or the harmonies of nature. Flo was quite sure of it. Individuals such as those clearly had concluded over time that if an embellished tidbit or an exaggerated anecdote made for a good story, it was worth the chance of annihilating anyone who got it their way. For some, it was a game, played with humor; for some it was a test of skill; for some it appeared the essence of their existence. It was the latter group that frightened Flo the most. She had forced herself to keep a distance.

⌘ ⌘ ⌘

Flo entered Melody Miller's classroom a short time later, sliding immediately on a ribbon of sticky saliva and bile just inside the door. She caught herself before falling, fortunately, but slammed her hip into the side of a student desk.

"Ouch!" she squealed, grimacing with the impact. "Better get this cleaned up before someone has a law suit."

She donned gloves to avoid any possible contamination from the bodily fluid, sprayed the affected area with disinfectant, and scrubbed. A vile odor wafted to her nose. *Whew, it's so potent after all these hours. God only knows what the girl ingested.*

When she was finished, she perused the room. Unlike the rows of chairs lined in neat order next to countertops that were anchored to the floor in the science department, here the desks were arranged in five, wavy queues, the last ones in each row slammed against the wall under the window. At the front was the teacher's desk, Ms. Miller's of course. A row of textbooks and dictionaries were stacked neatly in the front, but otherwise the desk was bare except for a floppy, brown, stuffed monkey, its head leaning to one side. The animal's eyes were wide, fixed black circles and the mouth bore a broad, toothy grin. Taped to the skinny chest was a sign that read: *Take me to your bathroom.*

Real sanitary. She left her judgment at that though. She had seen worse bathroom passes than this silly monkey.

Aside from the putrid-smelling puke that had been wiped from the floor, the room was clean, so Flo closed and locked the door. Once in the hallway, she stopped immediately. Staring at her from the next classroom was a grey-haired woman who Flo was quite sure was Midge McGrath, the aging, English teacher who was both revered and feared and who had taught at Hollow Vista High School for many years. Flo's prior sightings of the teacher had been from a distance, however. She was uncertain.

The woman may have been fifty and could have been sixty-five. Her face was quite gaunt and her neck long, but the rest of her body did not follow suit. Instead, the woman's shoulders were rounded and her breasts sagged heavily to a high waist. They rested on a thin, red belt that was cinched there. Her hips were wide, but she was not fat. Her legs bowed so conspicuously, however, that her ankles were turned awkwardly outward. The woman's feet were stuffed into sensible, black, flat-heeled shoes like the one's Flo's mother had worn on the assembly line years before. That tiny connection made an unexpected, cruel cut.

"You must be my new custodian," the woman said.

"Yes, I have been transferred to this wing of the building," Flo replied, taking note of the teacher's possessive use of the pronoun.

"Well, come along on into my classroom," she demanded. "I want to show you how I want things done."

"My name is Midge McGrath, by the way, although you may know that already. You'll want to keep me happy."

Flo followed the woman dutifully although Midge's arrogance and attitude of superiority were like salt in a wound. It burned a bit but wasn't surprising; Flo had experienced such an approach many times before. She knew, with little effort, she could work around it.

Midge guided Flo around the classroom pointing and gesturing here and there. "I want the trash cans emptied daily and lined with clean, plastic bags. Otherwise, they become filthy and smell. I detest foul odors in my room. Check the desks each day for graffiti. You won't find much because my students know better than to soil my desks, but it's been known to happen. Generally it has occurred when a substitute teacher is present. Most of those people have no clue how to control a class of high school students, even excellent classes like mine. Now, I want my desks to be placed in straight rows, six across and six back. They must not touch the wall. That results in scratched paint and is unsightly. I do not want my white board touched. My assignments are posted there. And the windows . . . clean them, will you? That awful Ortiz fellow never touched them. They can be a sight when the weather is inclement. What else? Oh yes, I expect my room to be vacuumed spotlessly every day. I do not want to see litter anywhere when I arrive in the morning. And, do not touch my desk . . . outside or inside. That area is exclusively mine."

Flo had been listening politely, but the mention of Midge's desk as her private domain, caused Flo's attention to falter. For a moment her mind took her back to the science wing and to the clutter she had discovered in Jack Mitchell's top drawer. Flo's hand slipped subconsciously into the deep pocket of her frock. The photo of Jack and Sherry Mitchell that she had pilfered on Friday was still there and as her fingers slid over it, she felt a touch of abashed shame. *Oh well, what's done, is done.* She suppressed the annoying recollection.

"And what am I supposed to call you?" Midge asked suddenly, interrupting Flo's thoughts.

"Flo. My name is Florence Gray," Flo said, "but I go by Flo."

"All right, Ms. Gray," Midge replied. "I believe we will manage to get along. Anything is an improvement over what help I had before."

"You may go now." Midge then said dismissively. "I don't want you cleaning when I'm working in my room. It's a distraction. You'll have to work around my schedule. I'm usually gone by five o'clock."

Flo found no words, which was of no consequence anyway for Midge clearly had moved on to other matters. She had turned her back immediately and had hastened to her desk where she began rummaging through a stack of hand-written essays. She was quite finished with her new custodian, at least for the moment.

⌘　⌘　⌘

Flo spent the rest of her first day in the humanities wing of the building wandering the halls between classes, meeting several teachers, most of whom were more gracious and friendly than Midge McGrath had been; some, however, were evasive to the point of being rude, not even looking up when Flo entered their classrooms. At least they weren't demanding. The humanities wing, she discovered housed the English classes, social studies classes, and the art department. English and social studies classrooms would be relatively easy to maintain, but art?

Flo peered into the last of three art rooms that had been deemed as studios by signs above the door. All, Flo noted, were in similar states of disorder. *This will be a challenge.*

The rooms were large, sprawling affairs packed from corner to corner with so many art supplies, equipment, and other paraphernalia that Flo had difficulty deciding where to look first. Four rows of stationary counters with high stools were in front and several round, wooden tables encircled by chairs were placed in the back. All of the furniture had been badly scratched; most had scribbles and initials, quite likely long ago carved there, the wide grooves filled with black dirt and ink. Several easels, all splattered with multi-colored drops of paint, were lined next to dirty windows, translucent to the point that very little, natural illumination brightened them. *Now, isn't that odd? Seems a little daylight would be nice in here, but what do I know? I'm a custodian. Not an artist.*

She found herself turning in circles though, awestruck by the chaos around her. *How do kids manage to get anything done here?*

In this setting, her innate inclination for wanting to keep things orderly, clean, and neat, was creating a modicum of unexpected anxiety. She turned once more. Against the inside walls were long counters that were overflowing with newsprint, newspapers, construction paper, and tissue paper. Pens, brushes, scissors, and pencils stuffed into plastic tubs lined the wall. A paper cutter had been placed smack in the center of the untidiness. Not one space of countertop was uncovered. The walls were a haphazard array of student artwork, some of which Flo found rather intriguing. Other pieces sadly looked as though a kindergarten child had been at work.

"See anything you like?"

Flo jumped visibly when she heard a male voice behind her.

"Oh my goodness! Scared me half to death," she managed, her hand sliding up to the mole on her face.

The man was grinning at her. He was tall, slender, and wore his hair in a ponytail held at the back of his neck with a rubber band. He had a sparse beard and moustache that gave him a slightly unkempt look, but at the same time his appearance was appealing. His eyes looked tired and glassy, but that did not distract from his overall good looks. Flo estimated that he was quite young, in his mid-thirties perhaps, and yes, handsome.

"Well, I kind of like this one," she said, pointing to a pen and ink drawing of a vineyard, the gnarly plants in ordered rows with a squat line of trailing, rose bushes inked into the foreground. It was a symmetrical drawing, the vanishing point evident even to Flo. It reminded her of a piece her husband, Randall, would have created.

"Yeah, new kid did that. Willard Dunn. Kid's got talent."

Kirby's kid.

"Are you the new custodian? Heard we were getting a new person."

"Yes. I'm Flo. Florence Gray. Folks call me Flo." She wondered about the teacher's comment. What discussions had circled the English, social studies, and art departments with Carlos's departure and her arrival? Changes certainly made people uneasy, it seemed.

"Well, Flo, welcome to the chaos," the man chuckled. "My name's Michael Campo. Been teaching art here for ten years. Seems like more sometimes!"

"Nice to meet you," Flo replied.

"I'm not sure where to start here," she added, rubbing her hands as if anticipating how she would ever sort out the clutter.

"Don't worry too much about the art rooms," Michael advised her. "You'll just need to vacuum and empty the trash. These rooms are always in a state of disarray. Just the way it is. Creativity somehow finds its way out of the confusion around here."

"I understand that one," she blurted. "My husband was a painter . . . and an artist."

"Was?"

"He passed on a few years back," Flo stated, a sudden tremor of emotion rising in her chest. It was unlike her to reveal so much to a stranger, but Michael Campo seemed an easy and relaxed conversationalist who allowed her to feel comfortable. This encounter was one hundred and eighty degrees from the one she had had earlier with Midge McGrath.

"Oh, so sorry," Michael muttered. His face had grown serious.

"Oh, it's okay. It's been some years now," she said, attempting to ease the man's clear discomfort. "He painted everything from houses to watercolors – was a painter by profession and an artist by choice. Passionate about it, he was."

"Must have been an interesting man," Michael said almost apologetically before changing the awkward subject. "Speaking of interesting, have you talked to Detective Murphy yet – the guy investigating the murder?"

"Not yet," Flo admitted. "Heard he's making the rounds, though. Talking to everyone on the staff."

"Well, I just got back from spending a hour with the guy. Intense fellow. Sure wants to get to the bottom of this. Can't blame him. Pretty serious stuff for a community like this. Wonder who did it?"

"I wouldn't have a clue," Flo admitted, "but I'm sure we'll find out eventually."

Without thought, her hand again slipped deep into the pocket that held the photograph of Jack and Sherry Mitchell. She could not help but silently speculate still what had possessed her to take it in the first place.

"Can't imagine who'd do such a thing," she said emphatically.

"Me either," Michael agreed, shaking his head from side to side.

"Well, I'd better get on with it. Trashcans won't empty themselves," she said. "I'll see you again, I'm sure."

"That's a fact. Feel as though I live here sometimes," Michael laughed. "The job's not exactly what I thought I'd signed up for, but, what the hell, I like the kids."

Flo answered him with a closed-mouthed smile.

CHAPTER THIRTY

JACK

Once his students were gone that Monday, Jack sat in his lab brooding as he watched heavy rain pelt the windows. He had been stuck in the classroom all day due to the unrelenting storm with more than a few bratty students talking shit, yelling obscenities, milling around the hallway, and flipping parts of their lunches against the walls just for fun. He would have liked nothing more than to drop kick a few of the worst offenders right down the highway. It was nearly four o'clock; staying there so late was unusual for him. Generally he would step across the hall just after the bell rang and have a word with Chuck Lindsey, the only other biology teacher at Hollow Vista before heading home. The two had a guarded friendship of sorts based in their appreciation for the sciences and their need to work together collegially in planning curriculum, but an undercurrent of animosity burned below their complicated rapport as well. Jack was certain that Chuck thought he was the superior teacher, above Jack as well as every other teacher in the science department.

"I don't simply teach and oversee a lab," Chuck often said. "I educate my students. They leave here after my tutelage clear on the fundamentals of life science. They will carry that knowledge with them for a lifetime. I make sure of it."

You're full of shit. Jack had wanted to reply in those exact words countless times, and perhaps, in some ways, he wasn't far off the mark. Chuck's classroom smelled of chemicals and lethal, silent farts, the latter of which, Jack was certain were issued from Chuck himself. The students eventually adapted to the odors that crept around the room like death itself, but not everyone was so adept at adjusting. Jack could remember old Flo Gray remarking a time or two.

"Hate cleaning Mr. Lindsey's lab. Smells like the devil," she had complained.

The old broad's gone now. Out of here. He thought of Flo with mixed emotion. *Seems as though she's been my shadow or a pain in my ass for years now, but she did manage to do a decent job cleaning the place. I wonder who'll replace her.*

In moments he had the answer.

"Mr. Mitchell?" Carlos Ortiz was at his doorway with another man who towered over him. Of course anyone would tower over Carlos.

What a fucking, little shrimp. "What's up, Carlos?" Jack asked aloud.

"Wanted to introduce you to Kirby our new custodian. He'll be working in the science section of the building along with me for a few weeks, just until he gets the hang of how we work around here."

"Finally got a replacement for Frank Sutter?" Jack asked the question before adding, "Should make the work load better for you and old Flo."

"Yeah, it'll be nice to have more help. Took some time though. Can't believe how many losers out there think all a custodian does is push a broom. Couldn't find anyone worth a damn until Kirby showed up in response to our newspaper ad two weeks ago. Handyman experience, too," Carlos said.

"Handyman, huh?" Jack liked that news. "Got some cabinet doors that need adjusting. Damn kids slam the hell out of them or kick them shut and they get all out of whack. They're the one's at the back of the lab. Maybe you can check them out. It'll be obvious."

"Sure. I'd be happy t' do that," Kirby nodded.

"Well, guess I'll head out. This fucking rain hasn't let up all day. See you around Carlos, Kirby," Jack said, throwing on a raincoat and leaving otherwise empty handed. It was a rare day that Jack took schoolwork home. It simply wasn't his style.

He hustled to the main office just as a clap of thunder rumbled ominously overhead. It was followed by a loud crack and a streak of bright lightning.

Ooh! Close! He was not fond of thunder and had been skittish of lightning since he was a boy. Once through the office door, he stopped still, his coat dripping on the tile floor.

"Jack Mitchell, you're soaked!" Cora Davies hollered, her eyes flashing disapproval at the puddle forming at his feet.

"You think maybe? Storm hasn't let up all day. I couldn't even leave the science wing. All I had to eat was a crappy, fried egg and mustard sandwich I slapped together this morning," he answered.

"Wondered why we hadn't seen hide nor hair of you," Roger Cunningham said, stepping out of his office. "Come on in for a second. Want to talk to you."

Cora passed a cup of coffee for Jack through the door a short time later. "Heading home now, Mr. Cunningham," she said. "See you tomorrow."

"Okay. See you then. Drive safe. Hope Tuesday brings a little less excitement around here."

"God forbid, yes," she answered. "Don't like being taken out of my element."

⌘ ⌘ ⌘

It took little time for Roger to apprise Jack of the commotion his former girlfriend, Melody Miller, had created that morning before school had actually started. He had his reasons for cluing in his friend. Though Jack had broken things off with Melody several months before, he had known her intimately. Perhaps he would be able to shed light on what possibly could have precipitated such behavior on the young woman's part. It appeared so incongruous. She came from a good family; her parents were well-respected educators. Surely she knew better. Melody Miller always had been polite and reserved in Roger's presence. *She must have a dark side. Jack has eluded to it, not that I totally trust his version of what happened between them. Jack's been known to embellish a bit, if not lie completely.*

Jack's perspective on Melody Miller's temperament would be helpful though, and conceivably would counter, at least to some degree, the viewpoints of Midge McGrath and Cora Davies who mutually asserted that the daffy, young woman was a definite menace to Hollow Vista High School's reputation. Roger was unable to pinpoint definitively why he even wanted information that might refute the women's interpretations of Melody's character. Though he was reluctant to acknowledge the fact, perhaps it was simply a ploy to neutralize a predicament that had blindsided him and had sent the parties involved reeling. He always had been one to placate others, smooth out the rough edges, and sweep unwanted predicaments under the proverbial carpet. Clearly this was one of those times. If word got out to the general public about what had occurred, a few heads would roll. He didn't want his to be one of them. He had to be careful.

Roger had been given every, grim detail of the morning incident, from the tight, purple sweater and scant, leather skirt hiked to Melody's waist, to the torn nylons, and bikini panties. The women expressed utter revulsion when recounting the dreadful smell of booze that seeped from Melody's pores and the vomit matted in strings of saliva that she spewed on the floor of her very own classroom.

"The little tramp could hardly stand," Midge had reported. "That teacher, if I dare grace her with that title, is clearly a liability."

Midge had not let up. "My heavens, Roger, you simply must do something about her. I've warned you once. You know quite well that ignoring such egregious behavior could cost your position here." Midge's threat had not gone unheeded, although Roger had answered her in his typical insipid manner.

"The matter will be handled, Midge. We can't get ahead of ourselves; could be extenuating circumstances. We don't know all the details yet," he had told her.

"I know the details," Midge had huffed indignantly. "It did not take a genius this morning to see that that woman is a drunken slut."

"Watch yourself, Midge," Roger had replied.

Cora had been less aggressive, but made her point nonetheless.

"The girl tumbled completely out of the desk, retching on her knees until she fell over unconscious," Cora had told Roger. "It was absolutely disgusting. And what was she thinking, actually arriving here to teach in that condition?"

Roger was quite exasperated by the two women. Though he appreciated their timely assistance and input, he had questions. Why, he wondered, had neither of them uttered not one caring or concerned word for Melody? Rather than pausing for a moment to consider that an explicable reason for the young woman's conduct could possibly have existed, they immediately had condemned her without question and appeared driven instead to annihilate her. Why was that? Both Midge and Cora had borne down on Roger describing the chaotic scene and narrating each, juicy element of the near disaster that had been averted in the high school he administrated because of their quick action. The women were so puffed up with self-righteousness that Roger was quite sure each of them would have agreed to a holy anointment of some kind if that had been possible. Certainly, he would assume, they both expected that a confidential, personal award or other accolade from him would be in the offing. Midge McGrath, in particular, would not let up until she was acknowledged properly, and in this case, Roger had concluded, Midge would settle for nothing less than the ousting of the girl.

⌘ ⌘ ⌘

Without saying a word, Jack absorbed Roger's vivid rendition of his former sexual partner, Melody's latest escapade. Though her apparent intoxication and appearance at school, dressed in inappropriate attire, had been shocking to Roger, Jack found it absolutely amusing if not a bit stimulating. His groin stirred as he listened to the story. Roger's description was picture-perfect and though Jack couldn't hide his smile, his lust, even for a woman he had convinced himself was repugnant, was secure.

"I hate to say it, Roger, but it's pretty fucking hilarious," he snickered.

"Jack!" Roger stared at Jack incredulously. "This could have turned into a huge fiasco . . . still could if anyone finds out about it."

"Who's going to find out? Medics won't say anything. Docs can't. Cora won't. Surely Melody wouldn't. Can't put any bets on Midge McGrath to keep her big trap shut forever, but for now she'll stay silent . . . just like a snake. Just give her what she wants and stay out of her way." Jack paused. "By the way, Roger, don't get too comfortable riding in old Midge's back pocket."

The inference to the principal's current acquiescence to Midge brought a slight blush to Roger's cheeks. He didn't like Jack's smug attitude. He glared.

"Look, Roger," Jack added. "I've known Midge forever . . . for . . . ever! She's a bitch, plain and simple. Never has been the same since her old man walked out on her years ago. She's a viper. She'll strike when she can and you, as well as a bunch of other people, are well aware of the venom she can spew."

"Never heard you so eloquent," Roger said sarcastically.

"Look, Roger, didn't mean to piss you off. Just wanting to keep things in perspective," Jack offered earnestly. He really did like his boss, and he didn't want hard feelings, especially now.

Roger dropped his shoulders, leaned back in his leather chair and sighed loudly. He was calming for the moment although he was not sure he could take the pressure of too many more extraneous issues impacting his school. He had enough on his plate: teacher evaluations, district office pressures, budgets, facility upkeep, union demands, badgering parents, and a diverse student body that always kept him on edge. Roger watched the kids roam his school with a combination of feelings: awe, appreciation, admiration, aggravation, distaste, and fear. No one had warned him that a career in education would be such a mixed bag.

"I'm wearing out, Jack," Roger confided honestly. "School's one thing, but with Sherry's unsolved murder still a focus, and now this Melody Miller situation . . . well, I'll tell you one thing. I'll be glad when this year's graduation is over and done. I'm ready for some down time."

Jack winced visibly when Roger mentioned Sherry's murder, but Roger clearly was being so introspective, he didn't seem to notice.

"Look, Jack, is there anything you can tell me about Melody that might explain her behavior?"

"Sorry, I can't help you much. She's young. Maybe she was just out having fun, got carried away, and used poor judgment," Jack reasoned.

"You know her better than that," Roger said. "I was hoping you could tell me about her character. She's always been respectful to me but I'm not sure I can renew her contract given what she's done. I want to be fair though. If there is anything you know that will help me understand . . ."

"She's a decent person, though I'd say she has self-esteem issues. She's moody, high strung, and, well, was too temperamental for me. Had to cut her loose. Don't need that shit." Jack said, adding, "She fucks like a rabbit though."

"Great, Jack. That last remark's going to help me a lot!"

"You never know!"

"Jesus, Jack!"

CHAPTER THIRTY-ONE

MIDGE

Midge was satisfied, at least for the moment. She was actually more than satisfied; she was pleased. Midge hadn't needed to do a thing to end Melody Miller's teaching career, at least as far as her position at Hollow Vista High School was concerned. And if word got out about the morning's near-disaster, which it just might, Melody would be hard put to find a teaching position anywhere. *It's hard to believe really. All I had to do was sit back and wait. The stupid girl has done it to herself. What a ridiculous individual.*

Midge could not help but gloat. *It's been a good day. That little slut will be out of my sight forever at the end of the year. I knew I was correct about her from the beginning. And, of course, I know quite a few spicy details about her life that I can use if need be. I certainly have a trump card. The girl dumped a substantial load of baggage out right in front of me . . . and I don't forget. Yes, everything is working out just as it should.*

Midge's thoughts shifted. *No doubt about it. It's been a fortuitous day. Not only did Ms. Miller seal her own fate, but I also have a new custodian who appears to be perfect, a meek little mouse. Ms. Gray. What an appropriate name.* Midge had seen Flo skittering around the hallway that afternoon, dodging into one doorway and then the next, her eyes shifting, and her head turning left and right as if she were afraid she'd be caught.

"Timid? Skittish? Insecure? No matter," Midge said aloud. *She can possess all those traits. It won't change a thing. She'll be catering to my every need and demand in no time. Think I've sized up little Ms. Gray precisely right. Doubt if she has the gumption to get out of her own way.*

Whether either of Midge's assertions was true was questionable, of course. A debate however would have required another individual to buy into an argument and Midge wouldn't have wasted her time. She was right. She was certain of it. That was all that mattered.

CHAPTER THIRTY-TWO

ANGIE

Angie arrived at the door of Ms. Miller's English class on
Monday to find it locked and the room dark inside. It was
not unusual for Ms. Miller to meet the students at her classroom door just as the bell rang, but this morning she was no
where to be seen and a substitute teacher had not arrived
either. Angie herself would have liked to be anywhere but
at school today. She sadly knew gossip among the students
would be rampant and she was not prepared to listen. *Poor
Willard. This won't be an easy day.*

A number of other students milled about the hallway,
in pairs or trios, deep in conversations, many complaining
about the unrelenting rain that had left them drenched,
and of course, some rehashing, in hushed whispers, the goings-on that had occurred at Jimmy Nelson's raucous party.

Angie stood alone. She was saving her voice for the inevitable discussion she intended to have with Brad Browning
later that day. Moreover, she simply was not in a mood to

talk to anyone. She still was harboring resentment and bewilderment at the conduct many of her classmates had exhibited on Saturday night. Jimmy Nelson's bullying was one thing; the lack of concern and respect for another human being who was enduring a cruel attack was another. She was sick over it.

Angie leaned against the wall and closed her eyes, dropping her heavy backpack to the floor as she did so. She was tired, having stayed up late talking with her father. The memory of their conversation warmed her. She was so lucky to have him and loved him deeply but she worried about him too. He was tired. She knew. He had become obsessed with solving the Sherry Mitchell murder case, with no firm leads as of yet.

"Feel like I'm fishing in a cesspool," he had told her days before. "Whatever comes up is sure to stink. That's for sure."

Angie was pulled from her reverie by a rather unfamiliar, male voice. "Good morning, students." It was Roger Cunningham, the principal. The hallway quieted immediately, although several students ignored the man and chattered on inconsiderately.

"Ms. Miller fell ill suddenly this morning and will be out for a day or two," he said. "A substitute teacher has been called, but won't be here until second period, so those of you in Ms. Miller's first period English class will be enjoying the library this morning."

Twitters of relief and groans of mild annoyance melded together filling the hallway with noise again; the difference in the students' reactions clearly was predicated upon who had done the homework.

"Thank God, Ms. Miller. What a perfect day to be sick. This works out great for me. Now I have time to get some reading done for my stupid, government class. This past weekend kicked my ass," Suzie blathered thoughtlessly, giggling and turning as she did to see who was listening.

Angie glared at her. Their friendship, however shallow and superficial it had been anyway, was over for good. *What a bitch. Does she think anyone's going to admire her for being a slacker? And yeah, I bet the weekend did kick your ass, Suzie.*

Angie felt smug for a moment. *Shit, Angie. You're just as bad.* She thought of Brad. *What a jackass. He hasn't shown up yet. Bet Ms. Cummins is giving him fits for slacking off in her geometry class. Would love to see it.* The idea of Brad kowtowing to anyone, especially a female teacher, provided Angie with instant, spiteful pleasure.

Better be careful. It was a silent warning. *Brad probably will retaliate any way he can the minute he's out of there. God help the person who gets in his way. She thought of Willard then. I wonder where he is. He's usually here by now.*

With her mind awhirl, Angie followed the principal and the other students to the library that fortunately was situated adjacent to the humanities wing. A covered walkway connected them. At least the rain, that had been relentless since the middle of the night, would not soak them once again.

Once inside, Angie sat at a large, round table with two other students. Luckily the library was quiet. Even Suzie had stopped talking and actually was reading. Looking at her now, Angie was filled with a strange sadness. *What would become of a girl like Suzie, a girl who had bought into Jimmy Nelson's brutal prank, played on Willard before a willful, jeering audience? What would become of any of them . . . of herself?*

"God, mind, stop working so hard," she said aloud.

The students at her table looked up, surprised.

"Sorry," she said, blushing, "Didn't mean to say that out loud. Got a lot on my mind this morning."

"Guess so," one of the students said, grinning.

She smiled back. The connection felt good.

⌘ ⌘ ⌘

Angie heard about the fight only minutes after the period was over.

She was drawn to a tight knot of students involved in an excited exchange. They were speaking with fierce animation and so loudly that their voices reverberated beneath the covered walkway that led from the library.

"Holy shit!" she heard a short, stocky redhead exclaim. "Willard Dunn, that kid from down South, just beat the crap out of Brad Browning. Broke his nose for sure."

"No shit! I saw the whole thing!" another chimed in, his voice quivering. "Blood squirted everywhere. Brad's nose looked like a goddamn fountain."

"What happened? What happened?" Angie scurried over to the group of students many of whom were familiar. Some of them probably had been at Jimmy's party; a few were in her classes. Her heart began beating hard.

"Willard? Brad? What the hell!" Angie stammered in disbelief.

"I saw the whole thing," the red-haired boy told her. "I was just walking out of the can over in the math wing when I saw Brad charge out of Ms. Cummins's room, all pissed off about something. You know how he puffs out his chest and clenches his fists when he's mad. Well, he came out just when that kid, Willard, the one Brad's always picking on, walked into the building. First thing Brad did was walk up to Willard and shove the dude backward through the door and flat onto the pavement. Then he kicked him . . . hard. He was aiming for . . . well, you can guess, but Willard moved faster than a goddamn rabbit. He was on his feet in a second. It was crazy. Willard just threw himself at Brad. Brad fell down, slipped on the wet pavement, maybe. Who knows? Anyway, Willard started beating the crap out of him. Must have hit him four or five times before Brad could get him off him. Brad got Willard too. Both of them were bleeding all over the place. Hey. Aren't you Brad's girlfriend?"

"Was," Angie said in a terse reply.

The boy clearly did not absorb her comment for he continued talking.

"Well, you won't be seeing Brad around school for a while, or Willard either. Campus supervisors dragged them both off to the office right after it happened. They'll be suspended for sure," the boy stated.

"Yeah, they will, no matter who started it," Angie agreed. "Anyone caught fighting at school gets suspended . . . probably for a week or two anyway," and then she added, "God, I hope he'll be all right."

"Brad? Yeah, he'll shake this off."

"I meant Willard," she admitted. "He's the one I was thinking about."

"Willard? Well, he got pounded pretty good too – black eye, cut lip. Brad's a strong fucker, but Willard, he didn't back down for one second. He was all over Brad like stink on shit. Surprised the hell out of me. Got my respect. Who knows, maybe Brad will back off the dude now. He'll either do that or take it to the next level."

"He'd better not," Angie replied, though she knew her words, or her wishes, would have no impact on Brad whatsoever. If Brad felt he had been embarrassed in front of his peers; he would plot to make Willard pay, again and again.

"Well, time will tell," the boy said. "One thing for sure, Willard won't go down easy. Think he's had enough of Brad Browning."

"Willard and I are on the same page there," Angie muttered as she turned around and walked slowly into the building away from the group She wandered into her government class and sat quietly, unable to erase the image that had been created by the red-haired boy of Brad and Willard thrashing each other in the pouring rain. She wanted to cry. *What's next? What, the hell, is next?*

⌘ ⌘ ⌘

Even at home, Angie could not relax. The entire school day had passed by in tedious increments. She didn't remember much other than the rain sheeting against the windows and being held over in Mr. Mitchell's class. In the last minutes, he had turned on his students like a rabid dog and had given them a ridiculous assignment just as the bell rang. *Just for spite! What a jerk! Just because everyone was all jacked up about Jimmy's party Saturday, and about the fight today, like it was any of his business.*

She had watched the teacher move about the room, listening in on conversations, hungry for information, eager in some perverted way to fit in with his students. The man disgusted her. Simply looking at him made her hands sweat and throat tighten. She trembled thinking of that late afternoon earlier in the year when he had cornered her in his classroom and then directed her to his truck after her fall. She could not erase the memory, and though she had escaped his clutches, the violation by a man as old as her father remained lasting and distinct. *The damage has been done, slime ball.*

Angie had retained every detail of the incident but had promised herself that no one would know, ever, especially her dad. It would kill him. What Angie did not realize, however, was that someone else did know. Florence Gray did. She had watched, alarmed and anxious, from a darkened doorway of a science classroom. She had been too afraid at that moment to move and too timid to utter a word, but like Angie, she had not forgotten.

⌘ ⌘ ⌘

Angie heard the kitchen door open. "Hey Angie, I'm home."

"Hey, Dad. How was your day?"

"It was okay. Routine. Asking questions right and left. And yours?"

"Crazy, kind of," she told him. "Found out Brad and Willard, remember I told you about him? Well, they got into a fight. Both got suspended. Don't really know what happened for sure but I'll find out soon enough. One of them will call, or both."

"Sounds as though the school has everything under control." George Murphy said, with only mild interest.

"Oh, yeah. They handle this kind of stuff all the time," Angie said. "Not that fights happen much. They're pretty rare at school, really. Guess Willard finally got tired of Brad pushing him around and fought back. Makes me kind of proud."

"Proud?"

"Yeah, that Willard had the guts to stand up."

George smiled. Angie did like this boy.

"From what you've told me, it was bound to happen. A person can be harassed only so much," George surmised. "By the way, honey, did you tell me Willard's last name?"

"I think I did. Dunn. It's Dunn," she told him.

"Met his dad a couple of weeks ago. Didn't connect, until I remembered you mentioning Willard's accent."

"You met Willard's dad? How? Where?"

"Sherry Mitchell's office. Remember, that Saturday morning when I got the call from the station and I told you to stay put? Think I told you Sherry had decided on the spur of the moment to close her office for the weekend; said she didn't need you to come in to work. Well, that wasn't true, I'm afraid to say, but I wanted to spare you until I knew more."

"I remember," Angie said. "And then you came home and told me." Her eyes filled with tears once again.

"I did what I thought best, and I believe I told you enough then . . . that she had been killed . . . that it was Sherry's handyman who had found her body and called 911. Police were on the scene in only minutes and the poor man was beside himself. Believe he was afraid he was going to be arrested. He was so shaken up when I got around to questioning him at the station he could hardly talk and when he did manage to say a word, that crazy accent was so heavy, I could hardly understand."

"I never met him," Angie mused. "I knew Sherry had hired someone to take care of her properties, but he was never in the office when I was. She called him Kirby, my Kirby boy, as if she owned him, like a dog. She really could be a witch with a capital *B*, Dad."

"I've had a few folks allude to that," he agreed.

"But what about Kirby Dunn, Willard's dad? Is he in trouble? He didn't do it, did he? Willard's dad wouldn't do such a thing."

"You don't know Willard's dad," George warned. "But, you must be a pretty good judge of character, because Kirby Dunn had nothing to do with the murder other than stumbling into the crime scene the morning he called 911."

⌘ ⌘ ⌘

George remembered vividly. As though fast-forwarding through a movie, he could replay the events of that Saturday morning, three weeks prior, with precision. He had compressed details of the incident into a compact file of sorts that he viewed over and over in his mind's eye. What had he missed?

The call came early, at 6:00 a. m. awakening George from a deep sleep. He had been dreaming of a flood. *Water rapidly was rising in his house, slowly receding, and then rising again; random people whose faces were obscure were climbing the stairway seeking safety. Linda, his bride, was there as well, smiling down from the top step, encouraging him, and then abruptly glowering at others who were blocking his way. Unquestionably she believed that George would make it to the top and keep her safe. His eyes were fixed on hers and he was clutching the bannister as the water swirled and eddied around his body. It was impeding his effort to move forward, up. Would he make it?*

"George, you awake?" The familiar, husky voice of his sergeant on the phone that morning was a shock to George's senses.

"Yeah, yeah. I am now. I was having a crazy dream."

"Well, you're about to get into a more bizarre one," the sergeant warned.

"What happened?"

"We have a murder on our hands. Got a call minutes ago. Fellow found his boss dead. Shot."

"Holy crap! Where? Who?"

"Real estate agent, the one whose mug is plastered up on the billboard out on the Interstate. Mitchell. Sherry Mitchell. Christ, the whole county must know who she is. Was. Dead now. Shot in the head, from what the guy who called said."

"Jesus," George muttered and thought immediately of his daughter. She was due to work at Sherry's office that day, just as she had every Saturday for several years. How in the hell was he going to tell her about this? Well, he wouldn't. Not now. He couldn't protect her from this horror forever though . . . but first things first.

"Get on down to the station. Now. Two squad cars are on the way over to the scene, as we speak. We'll head down when you get here."

"I'll meet you there. Sherry Mitchell's office is closer to my house than the station is. I know exactly where it is. My daughter works for her on Saturdays."

"Holy Mother of God. How are you going to explain this?"

"No clue. See you in a few," George replied. He could feel his heart racing as he moved into the bathroom to urinate and throw some water on his face. Shaving would have to wait. He grabbed fresh boxers, and threw on his clothes – slacks, a starched, white shirt, black tie, and sport coat. He charged into Angie's room then and fibbed.

"Angie, you awake?"

"Barely."

"Well, lucky you. You can go back to sleep. Just got a call from Ms. Mitchell. She said she'd been called away and is closing the office for the weekend. I'm heading down to the station, just for the morning; I'll give you a call later."

"Oh, that's kind of cool. More needed sleep. Bye Dad," Angie mumbled and snuggled deeper into her blankets.

"Sweet dreams."

When George arrived at Sherry Mitchell's modern, real estate office the place was a whirl of police activity. It was early, and Saturday, so the streets in the small town were virtually absent of traffic, affording George quick access to the place. He pulled in behind a squad car against which an officer and another man stood talking; then he ducked under the yellow, caution tape that cordoned off the building, and walked directly to the front door. It stood ajar.

Though he was a seasoned police office and detective, George could feel adrenaline amp his awareness. His breathing had elevated and he felt an uneasy energy surge through his body. He had felt this way before. What cop hadn't? Yet this was different. Intense. And he understood why. This crime scene was too close to home.

George pushed open the door and stepped into a large room that housed several plush, leather chairs, a row of oak bookcases filled to capacity with folders and books, and two desks, one located next to a wide, bay window, and the other tucked into a cubicle to one side. The larger of the desks held a computer, a telephone, and several, neat stacks of folders. Pencils and pens were stuffed into a bright, orange cup that was placed next to two photographs of a family, Sherry's secretary's George assumed. The smaller desk held a telephone, a towering stack of files, a note pad and pen, and two photos, one of Angie and Brad at the beach; the other was of George himself with his daughter. His large hand clutched her shoulder protectively and both were smiling widely at someone behind the camera. It likely had been Brad.

George continued to survey the front office for a moment more. The walls of the room had been painted green in two complementary shades that were inviting. They also were home to countless framed awards, Sherry's, of course, clearly promoting her as a real estate agent and broker extraordinaire. They also documented her involvement with the Chamber of Commerce, the National Association of Realtors, the American Business Women's Association, as well as honorary membership on the boards of several, philanthropic organizations. The array was impressive, if not a bit gauche.

Two doors were positioned at the back corners of the room. One obviously opened to a bathroom and the second to the personal office of Sherry Mitchell.

Two, sober officers stood just outside the inner office where Sherry's body lay. Another policeman was positioned inside the door. His face was serious, absent of color, and he had trouble for a moment finding his voice.

"Hell of a deal, Detective," he finally muttered.

George's attention was drawn immediately to the figure on the floor. Sherry lay in front of her desk, her head cocked backwards and wedged awkwardly between the leg of a leather chair and the desk. Her chin was thrust upward, her lips parted, and her eyes, as blue as the sky, were open wide. Her hands were clinched into fists. One single bullet hole exposed a dark, inch wide cavity in the center of her forehead. Only a trickle of blood had oozed from the bullet's entry point to the side of Sherry's nose, but the floor around her head and shoulders was inundated with the stuff. The dark, red plasma had plastered the woman's dark

hair to the carpeted floor. It looked as if her head was surrounded by a gory, crimson halo. And the smell . . . it was a
putrid, heady odor, sweet, musty, and metallic at the same
time, a stench George had experienced only once before in
his life on a foggy night years before when he had helped
drag, in pieces, the lifeless body of a women from the mangled mass that had been her pickup truck. A tinge of bitter
bile rose to George's throat, but he recovered quickly by
swallowing the acid taste with a proliferation of saliva that
had gathered in his mouth.

"Coroner's on the way," the officer said, as he took a
handkerchief and held it tightly over his nose. "God, I hate
the smell of death, of blood. Makes me sick to my stomach."
The man was telling the truth, for he began retching at that
moment and scurried out of the building where he vomited
voluminously onto the lawn.

George circled Sherry Mitchell's body, bent over it, and
simply looked. Even in death she was a beautiful woman.
He was deep in thought, remembering the times he had
said hello to Sherry in passing. She never had engaged him
in any long-lasting conversations but she had been polite,
and had seemed pleased with Angie's assistance and work
ethic. That had been enough.

"Detective?"

The coroner had arrived along with an ambulance and
two paramedics. George photographed various angles of
the murder scene, and then stepped away so that the others
could do their unenviable jobs.

The coroner knelt beside the woman's corpse. Wearing
protective gloves, he then touched the body – her chest,
her stomach, her arms, and her legs. He felt her neck, her
cheeks, and then her lips before shining a flashlight at her
eyes. They were doll's eyes, blue and fixed in place, lifeless

and seeing nothing. In a deft mechanical, yet gentle movement, the coroner pulled the lids shut.

"Rigor mortis indicates she died a good while ago," the coroner stated. The flat tenor of his voice and the lack of emotion on his face were grim evidence that he had been here before, assessing aspects of a death scene even before the autopsy.

"What does *a good while* mean?" George queried.

"I'd estimate she died immediately from the looks of the impact, and I suspect the time of death was between 9:00 p. m. and midnight, last night. Friday."

"Going to need a bullet," George told the coroner. "I'd be surprised if one is lodged into the floor; more likely it fragmented. A lot depends on what weapon was used too, and right now, we have no clue."

"Just looking here, from the amount of blood, the bullet was probably some kind of frangible type. When I do the autopsy, I'll know more. I definitely will extract any bullet fragments I find from the brain tissue," the coroner said. "God, what a shame," he added.

George snapped several more photographs of the room and took another long look at the items on Sherry's desk, that included numerous files, one spread open on top, pens, note pads, a half-eaten granola bar, a cold cup of coffee, a beautiful, blooming, potted orchid, and two photographs: one was a professional portrait of herself alone and the other a snapshot of Sherry holding a Siamese cat, its eyes an identical blue to her own. He donned protective gloves and gently touched the edge of the file that lay open and then thumbed through the pages. It was a refinance package for a person named Margaret McGrath, whoever she was. He jotted the name in his notepad, looked once more at Sherry's body, now blue-grey and stiff, deep in the throes of rigor mortis, and stepped out of the room, away from the stench.

Once outside the office, he stood silently for a moment, thinking, categorizing, and storing every detail he could remember. Two support technicians would be along soon to dust for fingerprints. Theirs would need to be a thorough job. It would be time-consuming but critical. Aside from the corpse, the blood, and the reek of death, it did not seem as though anything was out of order, quite the opposite of what George had anticipated when he had received the message that he was needed at the site immediately to investigate a woman's death. In actuality he had expected the place to be ransacked or to find that items of value were missing. The motive for this crime clearly had not been robbery; nor did it appear to have been random. No. Someone Sherry had known likely had planned and carried out this homicide.

Don't get ahead of yourself. It was a warning. *One step at a time . . . call it gut feeling, but from what I've seen thus far, this murder is in the first degree. Whoever did this must have known Sherry Mitchell personally.*

George looked in the direction of the parked squad car. The police officer was still positioned there with the man George had seen earlier. A woman who clearly had been crying had joined them. Perhaps it was the secretary. He sighed then, expelling a long breath of air as he did so. *Going to be a long day.*

⌘ ⌘ ⌘

George was correct. He learned quickly that the man leaning against the squad car was the handyman Sherry

Mitchell had employed to maintain her properties and her office, and the woman, yes, was her secretary. Both looked deeply shaken. The man, tall, thin, sandy-haired and ever so slightly balding, was pale, his lips almost blue. The woman, dressed in a shiny, black sweat suit and wearing purple, tennis shoes, looked as though she had just crawled out of bed. Her uncombed hair lay in clumps at her shoulders, her eyes were red-rimmed, and her face absent of color. Her lips quivered uncontrollably.

"I'm Detective Murphy," he said, unsmiling. His job required that a distance be established immediately between him and any would-be suspect. He was nobody's friend this morning and would sustain that countenance until the investigation was completed, the murder solved.

"My name's Kirby Dunn," the man offered in an accent so heavy, George had to lean in and ask for him to repeat.

"Curly, you say?" George asked.

"No, Sir. Kirby. It's K-I-R-B-Y, like the vacuum cleaner. And Dunn . . . D-U-N-N."

"All right, then. Got it, Mr. Dunn," George stated, jotting the name in his pad "Well, Mr. Dunn I'm going to be asking you some questions for a time down at the station. And you too, Miss?"

"I'm Stella Small, Sherry's secretary. Been with her forever," she sniveled as she wrapped her arms around her waist.

The name fit, all except for the woman's bosom. Stella couldn't have stood over five feet and although not fat, was well endowed indeed. George was a man. He noticed. *Wonder how she keeps from toppling over forward.*

He admonished himself. *Jesus, George. There's a murder here.*

⌘ ⌘ ⌘

At the station, George motioned for Kirby to follow him into a small room adjacent to his office.

"Ms. Small, you'll be next," he told the woman. "Just wait here." She looked at him blankly for a moment and then began to cry, softly sniffling into a handful of crumpled tissues.

"Here," he said, shoving a box of Kleenex at her. "Shouldn't be long."

"Keep an eye on Ms. Small," he told an officer on duty. "Get her what she needs."

He turned then, and directed his attention to Kirby Dunn who was seated at a wooden table. Kirby's hands lay like huge mitts in front of him, but when George entered for the questioning, he pulled them from sight.

"Tell me about yourself, Mr. Dunn."

"I'm a handyman by trade, Detective. Married. Got five kids. Live down on Locust Way, near the high school. I was hired on by Ms. Mitchell just shy of thirteen months ago when me an' my fam'ly settled in here from down yonder in Alabama. Brought the whole bunch of 'em out here hopin' for a better life for 'em," Kirby told George. "Had a hard time findin' work back home an', like I said, I got a wife an' five kids t' feed."

"How did you find the job, Mr. Dunn?"

"Seen an ad in the newspaper. Jumped on it. Ad called for a maintenance assistant, which I figured was a handyman, an' well, that's me. I can fix just 'bout anything that's broke. An' I'm a hard worker. Not one t' sit still. Like t' keep busy . . . get the job done." Kirby sounded a bit as though he was an interviewee for a position of employment, rather than a person being questioned about a murder.

"Did Ms. Mitchell hire you immediately?"

"She did. Told me I had t' cut my hair 'cause it was dustin' my shoulder, but otherwise, I'd do."

"Did you offer her a resumé?"

"Didn't have one of them. Just filled out an application best I could. Got everything right up here in my noggin. Just told her where I'd worked, who I'd worked for, what I could do. Filled her in real good. Gave her some numbers too . . . of folks back in Alabama who'd do right by me."

"And how was Ms. Mitchell as a boss?" George pried.

"She was nice enough, I reckon. Well, she wasn't the friendliest t' all folks, lest she was doing business with 'em. She could be a little snippy from time t' time with me too, 'specially if she wanted things done in a hurry. But that didn't bother me. She was the boss. She was kinda caught up in her own business, I reckon, but I wasn't 'round much. Came in on Mondays an' she'd fit me with a list of things t' do, places t' go for the week. Give me a charge card for supplies an' I brought back receipts t' her on Fridays. She was real organized, Ms. Mitchell was."

"And you have been working for her for thirteen months, you say?" George asked.

"Just shy, like I told ya'," Kirby replied.

"Today's Saturday, Kirby. You said you brought receipts back on Friday. Why did you come here on Saturday, and why so early?" George probed.

"Couldn't make it back in time on Friday, 'fore the office closed up. Was plannin' on it, but my littlest one, Massie, she's four, come down with another asthma attack. Mama called me, flat out hysterical. Told me Massie wasn't breathin' good an' said, in no uncertain terms, for me t' get on home. I did, just in time. Little Massie was wheezin' an' whimperin' t' beat the band. Got her t' the clinic 'bout four

o'clock. Mama an' me spent the entire night there, the two
of us with the baby. Charlie's the baby. Left the other two
girls home with my boy. He's up high school age. Figured
he could handle 'em whilst Mama an' me dealt with Massie.
Ya' can go on ahead an' check with the docs over t' the clinic. They'll tell ya'. My butt was glued t' a chair over there
watchin' my baby girl, just four years old, turn blue 'fore
she got her color back. Sat there all night long. Scared the
dickens out of Mama, an' me too. Told Mama this morning
'bout daybreak I was goin' t' be gone for just a short spell t'
drop the receipts off t' Ms. Mitchell's office, cause she'd be
wonderin' where on God's Earth I'd gone off t'. I'd called
her about nine o'clock last evenin' but she didn't pick up.
Left her a message though. Like I say, it was 'round 9:00
o'clock, 'round 'bout the time Massie was restin' more easy.
I wanted t' make certain Ms. Mitchell would be cotton t' the
fact that my baby girl was real sick. I reckon what I told her,
the words of it, must still be on her machine lest she erased
it last evenin'. An' now, I still ain't got back t' the clinic, t'
Mama an' the kids. Mama will be worryin' up one side an'
down the other, sure as shootin'. This here commotion's
pretty much set me on my ear, I mean t' tell ya'. I'm real
shook up. I mean, holy shit! Oh, I'm sorry Mr. Detective,
for cussin' but I ain't never seen such a sight as I walked in
on this mornin'. Don't reckon I'll ever shake it loose."

Kirby's face was knotted with the memory. His hands
had found each other in his lap under the table and they
held on, fingers tightly clasped, like best friends.

⌘ ⌘ ⌘

As George had assumed it would, Kirby's alibi panned out. Though George always had warned himself to avoid quick judgments about folks, judgments that could be deceiving and could come back to bite him in the ass, he had been convinced early on, that Kirby Dunn didn't have a mean bone in his body. He was not the culprit in this crime. George was certain. Kirby had a viable explanation for his whereabouts on the night of Sherry's death and it had been verified with a quick phone call or two. His lack of culpability in this crime was all too obvious, for Kirby was an open book. He had supplied detail after detail in that heavy, southern drawl of his, the lilt of which drew George in like a bee to honey. The poor guy had blabbered on for so long, that George had found himself sitting on the edge of his chair, leaning toward the would-be suspect, listening intently, his list of questions set aside. Kirby had handed unabashed answers over to the detective like unexpected presents. And when he finally stopped talking, they were done. Finished. George needed nothing more from Kirby Dunn.

"You can go now, Kirby," George told him, "but stay available. I may need to talk to you again."

Kirby's face softened with George's dismissal. He managed a quick, "Yes, Sir," and rushed out of the police station to his wife and children.

Stella Small's excuse exonerated her as well. She and her husband had returned home, only that morning, after a week's vacation in Maui where they had celebrated twenty-five years of marriage. They had landed in San Francisco just before midnight on Friday night. Their big Boeing had soared into the Bay Area, dropping through clouds of dense fog and landing perfectly. The overcast had been so thick Stella had not even been able to see the airport lights from the tiny airplane window until the wheels of the plane plunked down onto the tarmac without so much as a screech. San Francisco International Airport, lit brightly and bustling with activity, beckoned her inside. She couldn't wait. Flying took her completely out of her comfort zone. It always had taken two valiums and a glass of wine once onboard to settle her nerves.

After gathering their baggage and locating their car in the long-term parking lot, Stella and her husband had driven home. Stella had surmised that it would be another two hours, perhaps more, before they reached their final destination, for the heavy, tule fog and mist undulated in thick swirls ominously around their vehicle. Fingers of the ghostly vapor eerily circled so close to the ground that Stella felt she had entered a strange, new realm of existence.

"Going to be slow going," her husband had complained. "Can hardly see the road."

"We'll be fine. Drive slowly, honey," she had replied, gripping the armrest until her fingers ached. "We'll be home before you know it and everything will be back to normal."

How wrong she had been.

The two-hour drive home had increased to three, and when the two pushed open the front door finally, exhausted and tense, they sought nothing more than sleep. Stella could remember nestling into her pillow and closing her eyes just as a tepid sun was beginning to lighten the sky.

The rest was history. A phone call from the sergeant jostling her awake, a summons to the real estate office, a hasty drive there, the revelation of Sherry's murder, all, all of it, occurred in only half an hour. In thirty minutes, Stella's life had been turned upside down.

She sat at the wooden table, in the same chair that had been vacated by Kirby Dunn, and wept. Detective Murphy was patient.

"I realize you have just returned this morning from San Francisco, and Maui was it?"

"Yes."

"I just have a couple of questions then," he said formally. "How long did you work for Sherry Mitchell?"

"Fifteen years. A long time," she managed.

"And how was your relationship with Ms. Mitchell?" George was not sure what kind of reply to expect.

"Sherry was a unique person. I got use to her. She wanted everything perfect, or at least done her way, no deviation. She was bossy and curt sometimes, could hurt my feelings really, but, on the other hand, she was generous and made a point to do good things for people, you know, donations, fund raisers and the like. And she took good care of me. Paid well. Was honest, and to me, basically she was nice. She demanded respect though. Folks who did not respect her could get an earful. Or, a time or two, I've seen her hop up and walk out on a client who didn't see things her way. She was no nonsense that way. Taught me never to get on her bad side."

"Can you imagine anyone wanting to harm your boss, Stella?" George fished.

"Don't know, really," Stella said. "Sherry was a private person in many ways. She kept her feelings to herself. She never even talked much about her divorce from Jack."

"Jack?"

"Yeah, Jack Mitchell. Teaches over at the high school. They divorced about a year ago. Guess they were together six or seven years."

George jotted Jack's name in his notes.

"Anyone else?"

"I really don't know, Detective. She was a beautiful lady and she was a tough and thorough agent. Flawless when it came to real estate and brokering. But who knows, maybe a client was jealous or angry." She paused. "I'm just heart-sick, Detective Murphy. Sherry and I weren't what you'd call good friends but we relied on each other to keep the business going smoothly. If nothing else there was respect and frankly, I'm not sure what I'm going to do without her."

Stella laid her head on her crossed arms and sobbed.

George let her be.

⌘   ⌘   ⌘

The hardest part had been telling Angie.

George had climbed the stairs slowly, not wanting to face his daughter but knowing he had no choice. It was noon. The house was quiet. He could almost hear his own heartbeat.

Knocking softly on her door, he spoke her name, "Angie?"

"Yeah, Dad. I'm awake."

"Hey," he said softly. He shuffled next to the bed and sat in the familiar, wing-backed chair, the one Linda had adored curling into to read her books. It had been down-stairs then, next to the front window where natural light fell on her pages. In later years the chair had been moved upstairs at Angie's request. She could not possibly have known, but George had seen her there, in Linda's chair, tucked in just as Linda would have been, a blanket cocoon-ing her feet, a notebook wide open in her lap. The repli-cation of the bearing of the two was so uncanny it was as though Linda somehow had willed it from afar. A perfect picture of Angie folded into the chair formed in George's mind and then he saw Linda. He remembered her still, her golden hair sparkling in a beam of sunshine, and his throat tightened.

"Angie?" George said again.

"What's wrong, Dad?"

"I have to tell you something, and I'm not sure how, but you have to know."

"What?" Angie sat up in bed pulling her blanket to her neck.

"Somebody . . . someone . . . we don't know who yet . . . someone went to Sherry's office last night and shot her."

"Oh my God, Dad," Angie's eyes widened and filled immediately with tears.

"Is she okay? Is she hurt bad?"

"She's dead," George stated matter-of-factly. "One shot. To the head."

Color drained from Angie's face. A strange gurgle seemed to choke her for a moment before she gasped and burst into frantic sobs. George moved to the bed immediately and hugged her tightly.

"I'm so sorry, honey. And I'm so sorry I had to tell you." Of the two comments, for George, the latter held greater veracity.

He allowed Angie to cry for minutes and when she seemed finished, she slid back under her blankets and lay still, looking first at the ceiling and then at her dad, back and forth, back and forth. She finally spoke. "What's going to happen? How are you going to find out who did it?"

"The investigation is underway," he said, "but we'll find out. The answer is out there. Somewhere. It may take a little time."

Tears slid down Angie's cheeks, but she made no sound. When she spoke at last, her voice was flat. "The world's screwed up, Dad, but I never thought something like this would happen to someone we know."

"I know, baby. I'm so sorry." George was overcome with a sudden sense of sadness, not for Sherry, but for himself. He had not been able to protect Linda, nor Angie so many years ago, but he had been on the right track since then, hadn't he? God knows he had tried.

George, the protector . . . The truth was acid to his brain. *I can't protect shit.*

"I'll be back," he recalled telling his daughter.

He had backed in a hurry then out of her room, trudged down the hallway, firmly shut the door of the master bedroom, flown to the bathroom, and fallen in front of the open toilet. There he expelled the sight and the stench of Sherry Mitchell in a spew of stringy bile and vomit into the watery hole.

CHAPTER THIRTY-THREE

MELODY

Melody's head still throbbed. *I deserve it. Stupid. No running away from this one.* Though her memory was somewhat muddled, she was certain about one thing. She essentially had asked a man, a stranger, for sex. She knew it. What was his name? Tom. It was Tom. Tom, Dick, Harry. It didn't matter. All of the men Melody met and slept with on a whim, as she had with Tom, were basically the same. Except . . . except . . . Sunday night had been different. Melody could remember very little about what had taken place with Tom after she walked with him into the seedy, motel room and sipped her first taste of vodka from a paper cup. She recalled the feeling of reticence that had tapped into her conscience for a moment or two when Tom had ordered her to sit and then, like a seasoned, male stripper, had ripped off his shirt revealing a smooth, muscular body.

What the hell, Melody! What are you doing? The exact inner voice had warned her before, but she had ignored it, silenced it once again as she knew she could. He was a beautiful man.

She had taken the drink, licked the waxy lip of the cup, and smiled. She had savored the first sips . . . cold, and yet a bit bitter on her tongue. Instantly, magically, the drink had emboldened her, if only for short moments. It was enough. Had she undressed herself, or had he? She had no idea. She vaguely remembered her nakedness and the smells embedded in the folds of the sheets . . . urine, semen, feces, and stale perfume. The fusion of odors had caused her to gag and Tom had laughed at her. She remembered the sound, his deep voice chortling above her as she weakened below him, sinking, sinking. Tom was done with her, initially, very quickly, and then she was gone . . . unconscious . . . beyond . . . an insentient body of human flesh that would never in a thousand years know what Tom had decided would satiate him.

Melody did not remember one thing until the morning when she awoke, groggy, sore, bruised, and alone. In a haze she had fled the motel and made her way to school. It was Monday. She did have to teach after all, didn't she? No time to go home and change. She brushed her skirt with numb hands. *This will do.* She had looked nice last night, hadn't she? Of course she had. She had looked hot, incredibly hot.

She had managed to maneuver her way into the front door of the humanities wing of the building, somehow had climbed the stairs to the second floor, and had made it to her classroom door before she stopped, not having a clue what to do. The next hours escaped her just as the previous night had, although faces floated in an out of her consciousness to taunt her . . . Midge? Midge had been there, and that secretary, what was her name? Davies. Cora Davies. The name didn't matter. And there had been men, more men, grabbing her body, touching her, covering her with blankets, tying her down. "What are you doing?" she had mouthed, though no one heard; no one listened.

She did remember the clinic now . . . and the doctor, vaguely . . . and her mother who had arrived to collect her. Loretta Miller's eyes, red-rimmed and moist, had bored in on her daughter. Sadness, disgust, loathing, and exasperation were locked together in a glare that was not a stranger to Melody. She had come to expect it. Yet, in the presence of the medical staff, Loretta's voice took on the tone she feigned for the little children she taught. "Oh, Melody, dear, what has happened to my girl? Have you done something to embarrass yourself again? I believe maybe so. Looks as if we have a little dilemma to clean up, don't we, dear? Come on. I'll drive you to your apartment."

And so it had been. Loretta had done her duty. She had said all the right words in front of the medical staff while boiling inside and wishing secretly she had never given birth to the likes of Melody who had been disappointing her and her husband, Harold, for years. How had two, fine, educated, intelligent individuals produced such a child? At times it was too much to fathom. So Loretta, her lips pursed in disapproval, had chosen to say little more. Instead, she had dropped Melody off like a discarded puppy on the porch of her apartment in the rain and set off after Harold exactly as she had done for a lifetime.

⌘　⌘　⌘

Hours later, after having showered and examined the bruises and her other injuries, Melody sat cross-legged in the middle of her bed. She had brewed hot tea and sipped it slowly, the warm liquid soothing her irritated stomach. She had tried to nibble a cracker or two as well, but the pasty concoction gathered on her tongue taunting her to swallow. She deposited the goop into a tissue to keep from choking. Food would have to wait.

Though the pounding had begun to subside, and the queasiness had dissipated, Melody's entire body felt as though it had been pummeled. She had bruises on her inner thighs, her buttocks, her arms, and her breasts. One wrist was cut, and the sclera of her left eye was crimson. How had this happened? Her reasoning was jumbled at best for many minutes and then, remarkably, the answer became glaringly clear. *It was a roofie. The jackass slipped a roofie into my drink. He drugged me.*

Melody knew about date rape drugs. What young woman didn't? Awareness of the danger did not preclude unsuspecting targets succumbing to their use however. Stories of abuse were slipped into the back pages of newspapers at best and then forgotten. In most cases, the victim, ensconced with shame, said nothing. Seldom was any individual held accountable, and certainly, Tom would not be. Melody did not even know his last name. *Stupid . . . just plain stupid.*

Melody, as other women before her, and surely like a few entrapped men as well, would remain silent. She had no other recourse, really, for evidence of any wrongdoing had vanished with the night. Who would believe her? She had no proof although she knew. She would always know.

⌘ ⌘ ⌘

A pounding on the door of her apartment startled Melody from her musing.

Tom? Her skin immediately crawled with chills. *No, of course not. He has no clue where I live. But who is it? Mother? Certainly not Father.*

She scrambled awkwardly from atop the bed, tightened her robe around her, and tiptoed to the door as the knocking intensified. Melody's apartment was on the second floor of the building, the door sheltered from sight in a shallow alcove. Whoever was outside easily could be concealed from view, and it had grown dark. Her door had no peephole for viewing outside; nor was there a window adjacent. Cringing with fear, Melody slouched down against the wall, drew her legs to her chest, and wrapped her arms around them. She could hear heavy rain again beating on the roof and the wind whistled eerily, a restless siren in the night. *Go away whoever you are.*

"Melody?"

It was a man's voice, muffled but insistent. "Melody let me come in."

"Who?" she began, but her voice failed her.

"Melody! It's me, Jack. Let me in," he shouted.

Jack? What the hell? She was panicked by his presence and was mute momentarily.

"Melody. Let me come in. I'm soaked out here."

"Jack?" she called out at last.

"Yeah, it's me, Jack. Jack Mitchell. Open the door, Melody."

"Go away, Jack," she hollered. "I'm sick."

"Let me in, Melody. Need to talk to you."

"Go away," she shouted though her voice proffered only a weak insistence.

"Please," he said. "I heard about what happened. Think you could use some help."

"Help?" she replied, gagging on the word. She stared at the door before her as though she could see right through it and envisioned Jack Mitchell standing there – cold, wet hair, wild eyes, his jaw set, and his shoulders squared. Though his persistent pleading this night appeared sincere, Melody knew Jack was as earnest as a fox. Letting him inside her apartment would be yet another risk. After all, hadn't callous calculation always been at the very essence of his being? Of course, it had. She knew him. She knew him well . . . and he knew her. She clinched her fists and began banging them in manic, mechanical fashion into her thighs one after the other, first left, then right, left, right, over and over until they burned. She was a cuckoo clock set to unhinge.

"Melody! Come on. Open up." Jack's voice broke her rhythm.

"No."

"I'm not leaving," he threatened. "I'm going to knock on this door until you open it."

And she did.

⌘   ⌘   ⌘

With shaking hands, Melody unlatched the security bolt, twisted the knob to the dead bolt, and yanked the swollen door toward her. An angry screech accompanied its opening. Jack stood before her, serious and soaked.

"Get in, then," she ordered, grabbing Jack's arm and pulling him into the room with astonishing force. He stumbled slightly and staggered to the left, stopping his momentum with a strong hand on the wall. Melody released her clutch on him and peered out into the swirling rain and darkness before firmly pushing the door shut. She locked the dead bolt and then turned to face Jack.

The damp air from outside had followed him in like an invisible specter chilling the entryway. Melody shuddered.

"What do you want, Jack?" she asked bluntly. Her heart pounded and her head began to throb once more. She glared at the man who had been her lover only months before. What was he doing here? Why had he sought her out this rainy night? It couldn't have been for love, or even sex. He detested her. He had made that very clear.

"Jesus, Melody. What the hell happened to you?"

"I don't want to talk about it, not with you, Jack, or with anyone else. It's no one's business."

"You're wrong there, Melody. Dead wrong. When a teacher shows up at school, intoxicated . . . " he began.

"I wasn't drunk," she insisted. "Just hung over."

"Not a lot of difference," Jack asserted sternly, and then uncharacteristically his voice softened. "Look, I'm freezing," he said. "Could I have some coffee, tea, something hot to warm me up?"

Melody did not reply but moved to the kitchen and filled a teakettle with water. "We'll have tea," she told him. "Can't handle coffee just yet."

Jack smirked at her but said nothing. Rather, he went to the cabinet, set out two large mugs, garnered some tea bags from a canister, and waited. He had not been in Melody's apartment for months, yet it was as familiar as if he had been there all day. He sat down in a wooden chair next to the table, rubbed his hands together, and shivered.

"Look, Melody, I'm not trying to pull anything here, but I'm really cold. Do you have a blanket I could use? Maybe I could throw my wet clothes into your dryer?"

Why not? Can my life get any more bizarre? "Sure, Jack," she told him. "Blankets are in the closet there. You know where the bathroom is."

Jack re-entered the room minutes later wrapped in two blankets, one clamped around his waist with his belt, and the other draped over his shoulders. Clutching the blanket closed with one hand, he awkwardly shoved his sodden clothes into the small dryer at the rear of the kitchen with the other. He sat down at last across from Melody who, like a cat, had been following his every movement

"Been awhile, " he said.

"Yes."

"Thought you were doing all right until Roger dragged me into his office after school to fill me in on the latest. God, Melody. You sure pissed off a few people."

"Let me guess," she replied. "Midge McGrath, for one."

"Nailed it," he grinned.

"She hates me," Melody said. "And I hate myself for ever thinking she was a friend. I told her a few things I shouldn't have."

"Like what?"

"Oh, just stuff, about my past," Melody admitted. She had no intention of telling Jack he had been the central figure in their discussions. She continued. "I made a mistake with that witch. I admit it, but I'm new at this. Teaching is hard. I confided in her because I thought she'd help me. She's the veteran. Instead, she thinks my questions are silly, that I don't know the *canon*, oh my God, and that I'm a dumb shit."

"She doesn't even know you," Jack replied in a rare moment of defense for a woman who had been his own victim in the not-too-distant past.

"She thinks she does. Guess I didn't make a good impression. Said too much. She's always watching me . . . when I arrive at school, when I leave. She's been holding me hostage to her grandiose standards and I guess I just don't make the grade. And now, with what happened this morning . . . well, I'm sure she thinks I have shit for brains." Melody paused. "Maybe I do."

She smiled briefly and then looked at Jack, a forlorn expression shrouding her face.

"You look pretty bad," Jack admitted. "You have that bruise on your cheek and, well, what the hell happened to your eye? It's blood red."

"I know. I told you, Jack. I really don't want to talk about it."

Melody sipped her tea before continuing. "You know, Jack, I'm pretty tired. I don't feel so great and it would be best if you'd just take off once your clothes are dry. I'm not even sure why you're here anyway."

"Look, Melody, I know we've had our issues, and whether you believe me or not, I wanted to give you a heads up about what to expect when you go back to school. Roger's pretty upset. Cora Davies is all up in arms. She, sure as hell, is not on your side. She gave Roger an earful. Think Cora, rather than Roger, runs the damned school most of the time. And Midge? Well, she's out to get you in the worst way. She wants you gone. Is demanding it. She was on your case even before this mess, so you'd better come up with a good excuse."

Melody's eyes brimmed with tears as her words began spilling out despite her intentions to stay silent. "There is no excuse. I met this guy at Two Timers, left with him, and before I knew it, the night was over. The bastard slipped drugs into my drink, took my money, and God only know what else. I don't remember past the first half hour being with him. Woke up this morning confused and sick and he was gone. Somehow I knew it was Monday, so I went to school. By the time I reached my classroom I was so nauseous and dizzy . . . well, hell. I can't remember. I remember Midge, but barely . . . and that Cora woman . . . and some guys grabbing at me."

"Paramedics," Jack said.

"Well, whoever they were. Woke up at the clinic and stayed there until my mother picked me up and drove me here. My parents are disgusted too. My life pretty much sucks."

"Think maybe you should report this?" Jack asked.

"No way! And get the police involved? No way," she said again. "I went with the guy willingly. He didn't kidnap me. It's not his fault."

"He drugged you, Melody. That's not his fault? And look at you. Clearly he manhandled you," Jack stated.

"You know well enough, Jack," she hissed, "that I've been manhandled before. You ought to remember a little something about that! So, no, I'm not telling the police. Besides, they have enough on their hands with the murder and all."

Jack's face blanched at the mention of Sherry's murder. Melody noticed.

"Did you do it, Jack?" Melody blurted, the question rising out of nowhere. "Did you kill her?"

Jack's head jerked back as though she had slapped him.

"God, Melody, no. I can be a son of a bitch. You know that as well as anyone," he avowed, "but I'm not a killer."

"Me neither," Melody offered, "in case you were wondering. You know, that detective, Detective Murphy, was at my house on Sunday, all afternoon, asking question after question after question. By the time he left, I was drained. Empty. That's why I went to Two Timers . . . for a drink, for a little fun, to get my mind off of the day. What a mistake that was," she said, gently touching the bruise on her face.

She continued. "That cop scared me though, made me feel trapped although I didn't have a thing to do with Sherry's murder. I didn't even know her, just knew of her, from you. Detective Murphy asked about our relationship too, asked if I was jealous of Sherry. I don't know how he did it, but he made me question my own innocence because he was right. I was jealous, but not enough to hurt someone. I probably told him too much though like I always do. You know, Jack, I am pretty much a dumb shit."

"Murphy has cornered me three times so far," Jack said, ignoring Melody's self-deprecating assertion. "Think he's trying to trip me up, get me to admit to something I didn't do. The guy's desperate, so don't feel you're being singled out. Just because Sherry was married to me, and I'm a teacher at the high school, Murphy has been questioning everyone, every teacher, Roger, even the aides and custodians. Because he finally got around to you on Sunday doesn't mean a thing. The jerk is doing his job. I guess, but his lurking around is more than annoying."

"Do you think he'll figure out who did it?" she asked.

"Yeah, probably, in time. I don't think the murder was random though. I believe that whoever killed Sherry, knew her. I feel it in my gut," he replied.

Melody stared at Jack whose face suddenly bore a sadness that undoubtedly equated to the affection he had felt for his wife. Both emotions clearly were deep – the grief and the love. Melody was sure of it. She fought once more to quash the niggling feelings of envy and resentment that had been an undercurrent in her psyche from the moment she had learned that Jack Mitchell had had a wife, "*a beautiful wife*", named Sherry.

"Why are you here, Jack?" she asked again with rare, bold assertiveness.

"I told you. To give you a heads up."

Her gaze told him she did not believe.

"I'm not sure why I'm here," he admitted. "I wanted to warn you. That's true, but I also knew, from what Roger told me, that you must have been messed up over the weekend . . . you know, like you get sometimes."

Melody cast her eyes to the floor, staring seemingly at nothing until one, enormous tear rolled down her cheek, plopping like a raindrop into her lap. She understood completely. Her moods, her emotional outbursts, her lies, all, had ensnared her since she was a young teen, and certainly they had been at the root of her breakup with Jack. Yet he had manipulated her too, and he had been mean, abusive. *Perhaps he had no other way to deal with the likes of someone like me.*

Even at this moment, when it appeared that at least one person cared about her, if only superficially, she could not let herself off the hook. She remained trapped in the snare of self-loathing that had held her captive for a lifetime. Jack's voice startled her.

"The fact is, Melody, that I wanted companionship for a couple of hours. I wanted the company of someone who might just be as fucked up as I am. Ever since Sherry's death, I've been a wreck with nightmares, paranoia. I can't focus on shit."

Jack's forlorn features revealed his anguish, but he blurted a demand. "Don't you dare tell a soul what I just told you," he said. "I'll deny it."

"Who would I tell, Jack?" she answered. "I don't have a friend in the world."

CHAPTER THIRTY-FOUR

FLO

From her vantage point, Flo observed a tense and tacit interaction play out. It was a new Monday, just after lunch, and Flo had topped the stairs to the second floor of the building to begin the second week of her custodial duties there. A harried, young teacher had mounted the steps just ahead of Flo, and now stood fumbling with the lock of her classroom door. Only twenty feet away, an older woman had placed herself squarely in the hall clearly surveying the girl's every move. It was Midge McGrath who glared at the teacher sourly. Ms. McGrath's fists were rocks on her hips, her eyes had narrowed to slits, and her unflatteringly reddened lips were pursed tightly as if holding back years of pent up rage. Flo had come to anticipate Ms. McGrath's bearing, for it had altered very little in the week Flo had been her custodian. If the truth were known, Flo had begun to wonder if Midge's mouth weren't locked into that puckered position permanently. Flo observed the younger woman too. In the minute it took her to fight the lock, her shoulders visibly had tightened as if she was expecting to be struck; moreover, she had averted her eyes from the scowling face of her dubious colleague. When the door gave at last, she glanced quickly behind her, and escaped like a cornered rabbit into the classroom. *Those two are just a little uptight, not that I should judge. It's none of my business.*

The young woman, Flo discovered, was, indeed, Melody Miller, the teacher who, if gossip from Cora Davies held any veracity, had arrived at school exactly one week earlier intoxicated and sick. "Don't you tell a soul," Cora had nattered to Flo.

Flo, of course, had not been present to observe the incident, but had first-hand experience that some mishap undoubtedly had occurred because she had been ordered to clean up the sour, bile-infused vomit. Flo clearly remembered wondering if such an unpleasant duty might be a precursor of things to come as she embarked on her new assignment; she even longed, though only for a moment, to be back in the offensive, gas-infested environment of Mr. Lindsey's nasty, science lab. At least it was familiar territory. The week had panned out all right, however, with most teachers being politely pleasant or more-to-the-point, disinterested in the likes of Florence Gray. The only exception was Midge McGrath who adamantly had refused Flo admittance to her classroom until she left for the day. That suited Flo. She innately understood it best keep her distance.

Flo hurried to a small closet next to the bathrooms to retrieve the custodial cart that was housed there for second-floor use. She was purveying the supplies, when she was tapped sharply on the shoulder. She jumped, startled.

"I want to remind you, Ms. Gray, not to enter my class-room until I have left for the day. Is that clear?" Midge McGrath was scowling at her.

"I have done exactly as you requested," Flo stated, un-comfortable with the fact that she felt a need to defend herself.

"Simply making sure. I'm a stickler about my directions being followed to the nth degree," Midge insisted. Her fists remained on her hips and she leaned aggressively forward.

I'm not Ms. Miller. Flo had wanted to say the words, but simply answered, "Yes. You made your wishes perfectly clear."

"Well, one never can be too sure one is understood," Midge replied. "Not all employees such as those in your position fully understand such requests."

"There is protocol here," she added and then turned abruptly toward her classroom, not allowing Flo to respond.

Flo absorbed the abuse, certain that Midge McGrath was lashing out at her in the absence of access to the teach-er who now was holed up in her classroom. Midge's words stung nonetheless. *Had to take her anger out on someone. Can't fathom why she would harbor such obvious distaste for a new, young teacher though. I'd think she'd want to support her, but what do I know? I'm staying out of the middle of this conflict.*

⌘　⌘　⌘

Flo's first personal interaction with Melody Miller occurred just after the final bell rang that same day. Melody's room had emptied quickly during the prior week as substitute teachers generally had exited on the heels of the students every day. As a result, Flo had stepped into Melody's room to clean it first once the hall was clear of students. In one week it was routine.

"Hello," Flo said, poking her head into the room. "I'm Florence Gray, the new custodian."

Melody jumped visibly when she heard Flo's voice. Her eyes quickly scanned the room before she looked down again.

"Would you close the door?" she asked.

"Certainly. Do you want me to come back and clean later? I can do that," Flo offered.

"Oh no. It's okay," Melody muttered as she shuffled through a stack of papers on her desk. She had not looked up again.

"Well, some teachers don't want to be disturbed and would prefer I wait until they have left for the day."

"And that would be Midge McGrath no doubt," Melody said shifting her attention to Flo. "What did you say your name was?"

"Florence Gray. Folks call me Flo."

"What happened to Carlos?" Melody asked.

"Principal wanted to make some changes. I'm not sure why," Flo said. She had no intention of regurgitating Roger Cunningham's ridiculous reasoning to someone she did not know.

"Oh, too bad," Melody replied. "I liked Carlos. I could practice my Spanish with him. My Spanish needs all the help it can get."

She grinned then, "Sorry, Flo. I didn't mean to insult you. I'm going to miss Carlos, but what's life without a little change? My life is always in an uproar anyway. Wouldn't know what normalcy looked like if it slapped me in the face." She paused, and then added almost as an afterthought, "It's nice to meet you, by the way. I'm Melody

Miller, first year English teacher! Having the time of my life in this crazy place, as you can well imagine!" She snickered self-consciously.

Flo forced a timid smile as she dabbed at the black mole with a tissue.

"Seems teaching is hard work," Flo answered.

"It is for me," Melody admitted. "And I've been out for a week sick. It was the flu, I think."

The white lie was uttered simply but it slid out like a slippery snake. Flo would need to be wary of Melody Miller too. She too was likely a loose canon, as dangerous as Midge McGrath only in quite a different way: one the victim, the other bent on wielding her authority. Either was apt to go off like a shot without a moment's notice. It had taken Flo only one week and a day to figure out that possibility. Cora Davies' words came back to her in a rush: "The teachers in the humanities wing are quite the group . . . lots of sparring . . . power . . . control . . . don't step on toes."

"Well, glad you're better," Flo tendered. "That flu bug can be a booger."

"I'd say." Melody's round face darkened, a flush of crimson visible on her neck. Her brown eyes darted nervously.

Flo observed her. *Still worried about Midge McGrath. Can't blame her one bit.*

"Well, I'd better get to my duties," Flo said aloud. "Classrooms won't clean themselves."

CHAPTER THIRTY-FIVE

JACK

Jack left Melody Miller's apartment before midnight. He had not touched her, nor had he wanted to and that fact, in itself, was completely uncharacteristic of him. He was a man who seldom passed up an opportunity for sex, however remote the possibility, but he had been completely uninterested, and so had she, it was clear. Though the two had talked somewhat amicably intermittently while he was there, silence predominated the hour. They had looked across at each other like old friends sipping hot tea without a word between them for many minutes. Though each was lost in private thoughts, they ironically, for the first time in months, sat comfortably together at the small, kitchen table, drawn by a mysterious force neither could have articulated.

So why had he gone there, making a racket by pounding on her door, scaring her, demanding to be let in? Why in the hell, in the pouring rain, with no obvious reason had he been so anxious to reach her? The answer eluded him.

He had told Melody it was to warn her that she was making enemies at school, and that the likelihood of her retaining her position was waning. Her behavior both inside and outside of school had everyone up in arms, he had said. Yet, Jack knew such reasoning was a lie. He owed Melody no favors and the truth was that he had no feelings for the woman whatsoever. He wasn't even angry with her any more. He had gone because she was manic. Crazy. She was unstable enough, that in the throes of one of her episodes, she was as unpredictable as the sea. Jack always had imagined that Melody might become her own victim, harming herself as a result of the volatile bouts with anxiety and depression that plagued her; yet, the contrary could occur as well. If she could hurt herself, could she not hurt another? Jack realized he had sought out Melody, after being apprised of her drunken episode because he needed to know for sure. He had wondered, time and again, was it Melody Miller who had murdered his Sherry? He had believed her capable, oh so capable, until tonight.

Now he knew. Melody could not possibly murder anyone. She did not have an aggressive bone in her body. Rather, she was as frightened as a whipped puppy. He had watched her closely. Her wide, sad eyes dominated a face that bore an expression of such melancholy, he was afraid she might lapse into tears. Yet that did not happen. Instead, she maintained a stolid, almost aloof demeanor, her emotions bundled inside, and when his clothes had dried, she simply said, "Get dressed, Jack. Go home. I'm tired."

He had left her in the kitchen, letting himself out, this time trotting quietly down the stairs. It was pelting rain as it had all day so he rushed to his car and sat inside listening to raindrops nearly half the size of marbles splatter on the hood. He thought with sympathy of the girl upstairs, alone in the small apartment; or perhaps it was empathy he felt, for Jack understood. In recent weeks he had questioned his sanity as well. The dreams, the accidents, the deprecating self-dialogue, all pointed to a man who despite his projected arrogance and air of superiority was lost, simply lost.

Jack also knew he had gone to Melody because he needed to make sure of one other thing. Was he going crazy too? He knew Melody was a woman controlled by constant angst that she tended like a bad habit; she likely never had lived without it. And while his own tormented existence of late was new to him, his anguish surely mirrored hers. Her pain, he realized, was effectively too much for her to bear at times, and as a result, she ran from it, acting out in bizarre and inappropriate ways. For the first time in Jack's life he understood, for he had been flirting with a similar distress, not knowing which way to turn for relief. He absorbed the truth at last, that he was better than no one else, and though he comprehended that reality in the heart of his very being, he would never tell a soul. To do so would betray the character he had created and honed since he was an eight-year-old child. It was imperative that the lie he had conjured as to his implicit power remain buried inside; not one person could ever know that it was fear and absolute insecurity that had driven him. His life was a paradox of mammoth making.

CHAPTER THIRTY-SIX

MIDGE

Midge was fuming. That awful, new custodian was as bad, if not worse than Carlos Ortiz had been. Both had responded to her demands in the same conciliatory manner: *"Yes, Ms. McGrath." "Of course, Ms. McGrath." "I understand." "I'll do whatever you want."* It was infuriating. Of course she wanted them to do as she demanded, but responding to her so insipidly, without so much as a hateful look, made her blood boil. Her husband, Fred, had been the same way, a hapless oaf with no backbone. And what had he done? Left her, high and dry, without a target.

Midge had plopped herself in the chair behind her desk and clutched her own body, her clinched fists bearing down with vise-like intensity. She held that position until her heart stopped pounding and her breathing slowed; then she touched one of the keys on the lanyard around her neck and leaned forward to unlock her desk. She pulled open the wide drawer, releasing its hold on three, deep drawers to her right. Inside the top drawer were note pads, a stash of pens and pencils, staples, and other supplies. The second housed a first aid kit, lotion, a mirror, chewing gum, and her lunch bag, now empty. Midge took the same, cloth bag home each evening, refilling it routinely with a plain, cheese sandwich, a piece of fruit, and perhaps a cookie or two. She had carried her lunch to school daily for years; seldom had she entered the faculty room to lunch with her colleagues. She detested their meaningless banter and non-stop, unsubstantiated gossip, wondering all the while how some had been hired in the first place.

Melody Miller. Perfect example. What was that little fool doing back at work today? Had Roger Cunningham gone mad? Midge had been sure, after Monday's fiasco that she never would have to see the ridiculous girl again. Both Midge and Cora Davies had provided the principal with every possible, sordid detail in regard to Melody's condition the morning of the incident. How much evidence did a principal need to comprehend that she was incompetent, not to mention a threat to the school's reputation? What more information, indeed, did Roger require? Need the facts be spelled out in blood? *I can bet that Roger has allowed Melody to return to her classroom to teach without even a reprimand!* Her face flushed red and her lips found their position. *Well, I'm going to put a stop to this insanity right now. Roger is going to wonder what hit him.*

Midge pulled open the bottom drawer of her desk. Her purse was nestled there as it always was, safely tucked away from the eyes of teenagers, some of whom would have liked nothing more than to rummage through it in order to know her secrets. She tucked the bag under her arm, pushed papers into her briefcase with the other hand, slammed the desk drawer, and exited the room on a mission.

CHAPTER THIRTY-SEVEN

ANGIE

Brad called Angie first.

"Guess you heard about that jackass, Willard Dunn, attacking me from behind just for the hell of it," he blurted before even saying hello.

"Yeah. I heard there was a fight," she answered, her voice flat.

"Yeah, well, the dude is going to pay. Actually already has. I hammered him pretty bad. Send him home bloody and crying like a baby. You can ask anyone. Stupid jackass thought he could beat me up . . . me, of all people. Well, I showed him. He won't be able to show his face, or what's left of it, for a month."

Angie did not reply. Brad's version of the altercation clearly was very different from what more than a few students had told her. More importantly, however, it bore out what she knew already about him. The truth was a creation of his own making, and she understood, as never before, that his survival depended on actually believing it. She had heard it all many times: *"I crushed that fucking quarterback."* *"I had that loser teacher, Mr. Lindsey, shaking in his shoes."* *"Old Cunningham ain't gonna suspend me. He doesn't have the balls."* *"Watch out Angie. Suzie tried to get all over me at Zach's party."* *"That Ms. Miller's got a nice ass for a teacher and I've seen her looking too. Bet she'd give anything to have some of me."* *"I beat the shit out of that stupid geek when he was a freshman."* *"That bitch, Ms. Cummins can lick my balls."* Brad's only defense against his own hidden insecurity was the bravado he donned like a knight's armor. Inside, Angie believed, he was as weak, or perhaps weaker than anyone she had ever known.

"So, you're going to have to get my assignments, probably do a few of them too," he demanded. "I sure as hell don't plan to spend my five days off from school doing homework. Hell, I'll have more time to work out."

Angie remained silent.

"You there, Ang?" he asked. "What the fuck! Why aren't you talking? Are you listening to me?"

"I'm here."

"Well say something."

"Okay," she said with atypical, bold assertiveness . . . but she had been practicing. "I'm not getting anything for you, Brad. I told you on Sunday. I'm telling you again. I am breaking up with you."

"Look, Bitch. Don't start this shit again," he shouted.

"Do not yell at me, Brad, and do not call me names."

"I'll call you anything, the fuck, I want," he snarled.

"I can't stop you from referring to me as a bitch, or whatever else you think up," she said, "but I am stopping you from calling me your girlfriend. I'm done. It's over."

It was Brad's turn to be silent, although Angie could hear him breathing heavily.

"Don't call me again, Brad. If you do, you'll be speaking with the principal, or better yet, my dad," she threatened. "You don't want that to happen."

"Ang," he managed.

"Good-bye, Brad."

The call was over, and with it, finally, her relationship with Brad Browning. She sat very still, quivering, as an unexpected rush of adrenaline surged through her body.

⌘   ⌘   ⌘

Willard's call came later. Angie was ready.

"Hey Angie," he began. "Just called t' check up on ya' an' wanted t' let ya' know that I won't be able t' see ya' for a week. Grounded. My folks are real upset about the fight. Guess ya' heard."

"Hey, Willard. Yeah, I heard. How are you? Are you okay?"

"Yeah I am, I guess. Lip is a little swollen, black eye, but it was worth it."

"I heard Brad started it."

"He did. Came out of nowhere. Rushed right at me an' pushed me out the door. Landed on my back an' he started kickin'," Willard paused. "I reacted. I'm not takin' shit from Brad an' his buddies anymore. Don't care if I have t' fight 'em every day."

"Good for you, Willard, but I don't think you'll have to worry about Brad. He's going to keep his distance. He's going to walk around school like he's the coolest and pretend he got the best of you, but by the sound of it, everyone else knows better. I heard about the fight in detail from some kids who saw the whole thing."

"Doesn't matter t' my folks who started it," Willard replied. "My mama's all emotional an' my dad's upset, especially since he just got hired on by the school district."

"He did?"

"Yeah. He was hired as a custodian at school. He's goin' by his first name only though since I'm a student there. He knows about all the harassment an' shit. He's lettin' me work that out, but he figured if kids knew he was workin' at the high school as a janitor it would make things worse for me."

"Why didn't you tell me?"

"He just got hired on. Hadn't had a chance."

"I guess I don't understand why his being a custodian would make things worse," Angie said.

"Oh, it would, Angie. Think about it. Ya' know how some people are, kids like Brad or Jimmy, Suzie . . . they'd have a heyday if they knew. They look down on people they don't think are cool or aren't rich. Ya' know. It's stupid, but that's how they think."

"I guess you're right, but they're wrong. What a person does for a living doesn't mean shit about their character. Makes me sad for you, for your dad."

"Don't be sad, Angie. It's the way life is. People get all jacked up over the stupidest things . . . what people wear, how they talk, what they do for a livin', how smart they are. Folks judge all the time."

Angie took a moment to absorb what Willard was telling her.

"How did you figure all that out?" Angie asked.

"I know it. I've experienced it. I don't live in a bubble like some of the kids at school do."

"Do I live in a bubble?" she asked, afraid he might say yes.

"I don't think ya' do. Ya've had shit happen t' ya' too, like losin' your mama. At least ya' have a good father who takes care of ya'."

"I do, that," she agreed. "I worry about him though. He's working so hard these days, trying to solve this crime."

"Seems that way. My dad met him, ya' know."

"I know. He told me. Your dad found Sherry Mitchell dead, didn't he?"

"He did an' it shook him up real bad. Was talkin' about it again this mornin'. Said maybe we should have stayed put in Alabama. We no sooner get here than he finds his boss shot dead an' with all the shit that's been happenin' with me, he's wonderin' if we should move back. But he got the new job, so I reckon we won't be leavin' real soon."

"Don't you dare leave, Willard Dunn," Angie said softly. "I just found you."

⌘　⌘　⌘

George Murphy walked into the house to find Angie at the stove, stirring spaghetti sauce.

"Making dinner," she smiled.

"Smells great," he replied. "Thanks for doing that, honey. I'm about ready to drop."

"You look tired, Dad. Are you making any progress on the case?"

"Well. Some. I know who didn't kill Sherry. That list is getting longer, but a few people have pretty flimsy alibis. Can't make an arrest yet though. Not enough evidence, but the coroner was able to locate bullet fragments. Ballistics has them. They'll narrow down what kind of weapon was used. I suspect a .38 special or a 9 mm Beretta. Could have been any of a number of small or mid-sized pistols, a Glock maybe. It's a wait and see. Man, that smells good," he said again.

"I'll make a salad, put on some pasta. Dinner won't be long," Angie said, adding, "I'm sorry you're having to deal with this investigation, Dad. It's hard to realize a murder happened right here in town, isn't it?"

George sighed. "It is. Makes a person wonder if any of us really know our friends or neighbors that well. We might think we do, but I suppose everyone harbors a secret or two. And there's the old issue of the dark side. What was that book you read a year or so ago. *The Secret Sharer?*"

"Yeah, Written by Joseph Conrad. I was in Ms. McGrath's class. I remember we had a huge discussion about the fact that everyone must have a dark side. Some kids said, 'No way! People are either good or bad,' but others agreed with Ms. McGrath. She was sure of it. Remember? I came home still thinking about that class debate, and I really wanted to know what you thought."

"I do remember, and for some reason, that concept – that basically good people can have a mean streak or a dark side – came back to me during the past week or so. You know, I've talked to a number of individuals, some more than once, and most seem sincere and forthright, but I know people. Putting up a front is pretty common. And then there's the issue of perception. A person can be deceiving. What you see first is not always what is, if you know what I mean."

"Actually, I do," Angie answered, ready to tell her father about her conversation with Brad. "Brad's a perfect example. It took me a long time, Dad, but I realize what a jerk he really is. I broke up with him for good today. Think he finally got the message loud and clear."

"And how are you feeling about that?" George asked.

"I would say good, but that's not exactly true. It's more of a relief that I don't have to deal with him any more. He was becoming so demanding and on top of his arrogance, it was just too much. I'm glad I stood up to him. Made a decision. It was the right thing to do."

"And what about this other boy, Willard?"

She grinned. "Well, he's still in the picture."

George looked at his daughter lovingly. "I think you have a pretty good head on your shoulders, young lady," he smiled.

"I have a good teacher," she said. "You."

CHAPTER THIRTY-EIGHT

MELODY

Melody slipped out of her classroom on the heels of the new custodian, Flo. It was safer. The last thing she wanted was an encounter, much less a confrontation, with Midge McGrath. She scuttled down the hallway to the stairs, not turning to look behind; yet, whether it was the case or not, she imagined eyes tracking her movements. Her heart pounded. At the door of the building she finally glanced quickly over her shoulder. The hallway was empty.

"Thank God," she muttered to herself.

She had one more hurdle before she could go home though: the office and quite possibly, the principal, Roger Cunningham. Already that morning she had endured a hateful glare from Cora Davies, Roger's secretary, who sat daily like an engorged, recluse spider behind her desk, scoping out every movement. *Bitch*. Melody had remembered Jack's words, "Cora Davies is not on your side . . . gave Roger an earful."

Well, I'll take care of her. Melody had devised a plan.

That morning she had sidled up beside Cora's desk, had flashed a shy, sweet smile, and had said, "I so want to thank you, Ms. Davies for helping me out when I was so sick last Monday. I've been told you saved the day."

Cora's face had flushed and her eyes had narrowed. "I did as I was told," she had said, her voice icy.

"Well, I appreciate your kindness. I was sick all week with the flu," Melody had cooed. It wasn't quite a lie, was it? She had been sick. The absolute truth of what had precipitated the weeklong absence was left unspoken however, and that important detail implicitly lay like a bleeding wound in Melody's conscience.

"It's nice you're feeling better," Cora had managed before busying herself with paperwork, effectively dismissing Melody who quite simply made her blood boil.

⌘ ⌘ ⌘

Melody was unable to avoid the inevitable.

"Ms. Miller," Cora said snidely, "Mr. Cunningham would like to see you in his office immediately."

Melody's demeanor betrayed her. Her round face grew pale, her eyes darted, and she drew her purse to her chest like a shield. Her other hand clutched her briefcase so tightly her knuckles blanched.

"Now?" she asked inanely.

"Now."

Melody's stomach tensed, but she moved slowly towards the principal's office.

"Ms. Miller is here," she heard. Cora had notified Roger more quickly than it took Melody to shuffle twenty feet forward.

Someone pulled the office door open from inside. It was not Mr. Cunningham, for he was at his desk, gazing solemnly at her as she stepped into the room. Once inside, she felt the door brush past her back, closing with a soft thud. She turned.

"Jack," she muttered. "What are you doing here?"

"Sit down, Ms. Miller," Roger told her, ignoring her question to Jack. "We have some issues to discuss."

Melody set her briefcase on the floor and sat facing Roger Cunningham. Her throat had tightened uncomfortably. She continued to clutch her purse closely against her breasts, embracing a strange notion that if she let go of it, she simply might float to the ceiling and bobble there like a helium balloon, completely out of control.

"Yes, Sir," she murmured so quietly that Roger leaned forward, tilting his head to hear.

"You need to be straightforward with me, Ms. Miller," he began. "If you expect to be supported, if you want to be helped, you need to explain exactly why you came to school last Monday in, well, in quite a precarious and confounding condition."

He continued. "I will tell you up front that those who observed you were quite sure you arrived at school nauseous and confused as a result of intoxication. Furthermore, I have been told that your attire was completely inappropriate for a teacher to wear in a classroom. I have only hearsay to go on, but I am more than a bit concerned by what I have learned. Fortunately, Ms. Miller, you have a bit of luck on your side because for some reason, Jack Mitchell here, thinks you deserve a listen."

Melody gave a sideways glance toward Jack before she spoke. She stammered a bit at first, not knowing what to say.

"Start with Sunday afternoon," Jack prompted.

"Okay. Well . . ."

Melody explained first about being interviewed by Detective Murphy for what to her seemed to be needless hours. She had been frustrated, frightened, and made to feel guilty for something she had nothing to do with whatsoever.

"I could never hurt a flea," she said earnestly.

She resumed her story. In an attempt to forget the horrible afternoon of questioning, she had ventured off to Two Timers, she said.

"I just needed to relax," she reasoned. "But things went all haywire."

It took Melody almost half an hour to complete the tale, complete with the self-denigrating judgments that completed her. When it was done, when the story was finished and her words exhausted, she released the grip on her purse, looked at Jack, and began to sob.

Every pent up emotion – frustration, anger, fear, shame, despair, resentment, humiliation, and sadness – found an outlet that afternoon through her tears. Yet jumbled into the mix was gratitude and awe that two people, two men, had listened, not interrupting, and not openly judging. Neither of them wanted a thing from her other than the truth. She was undone by the raw reality of it.

⌘　⌘　⌘

Melody left Hollow Vista High School that day with her job intact, but with a warning and an assignment.

"Melody," Roger Cunningham had said. "I am giving you another chance, but if anything like this occurs again, you will not teach another day, not here, not anywhere. Do you understand?"

"Yes."

"And you need to take better care of yourself. Please seek some counseling; maybe have a thorough medical checkup, probably both. I am in no position to make you do either, but I would suggest you consider it very seriously. Can you see why? Do you understand?" he had added.

"Yes, and I will. I can."

"Also, I want you to check in with me every week, Mondays, during your prep period, just for a few minutes. We need to keep a dialogue."

"I will. Thank you Mr. Cunningham. I can't thank you enough. I've been so embarrassed and scared, and I'm relieved. Thank you." For the first time in months, Melody had felt as though she did not have to hide, that perhaps she had an ally. Maybe for once someone had believed in her.

Before she stood to leave, she had looked at Jack. "Thank you too, Jack. I'm not certain why you did this, why you helped me out."

"Out of character, isn't it?" he had chuckled, looking at Roger uncomfortably. He was about to bare his soul a bit too.

"The last few weeks have shaken me up," he had admitted. "Shit, I have to be honest. I know people think I had reason to kill Sherry. I didn't," he had stated, turning to look directly at his friend, Roger. "But I was afraid you might be the one, Melody . . . that you killed her. I know that couldn't possibly be true now, but I considered the possibility. I know how emotional you can be. Last night, when

I told you I was as messed up as you were, I meant it. As strange as it sounds though, talking to you helped. I wanted to return the favor, so I talked to Roger, here."

He had glanced again at his boss before he had added, "Maybe we all need help, or at least a second chance. So, here you go. This is yours. You can do this, Melody. Don't fuck it up."

"I won't," she had answered, offering a wan smile to the two men before her.

She left the office that day feeling a sense of unprecedented optimism. *You have to make a change, Melody Miller and you can.* Buoyed with new hope, she strolled through the main office without even a glance at Cora Davies.

CHAPTER THIRTY-NINE

FLO

Flo had dragged the heavy vacuum around every second floor classroom except Ms. McGrath's. The woman was still locked in her room, poring over papers and rifling through her desk drawers. Flo had peeked quickly through the window in the door several times, waiting, waiting. Finally she parked her cart that was filled with custodial supplies, adjacent to Ms. McGrath's room and moved to the ground floor to take on the art classrooms. As usual it was a challenge, but at least friendly Michael Campo made the task of cleaning his area easier.

"How are you doing, this afternoon, Flo?" he asked. One hand was filled with dripping paintbrushes; the other held a flimsy, watercolor-splashed paper.

Flo spotted a small puddle of greyish water spreading slightly with each drip from the brushes. She smiled sadly and shook her head. She knew artists. She had mopped up

Randall's messes for years and the memory made her feel, at this moment, oddly at home.

"What do you think?" Michael flipped the painting awkwardly so that Flo could see.

"Ah, nice. Pretty colors. It's a girl, isn't it? Pretty. Love the long blond hair. Seems to meld right into the sunshine," she said. "Who did it?"

"Willard Dunn."

"The kid who did the pen and ink I liked?"

"That's the one. I had a feeling you'd like this one too."

"He does have talent. Moving from pen and ink to watercolors takes an eye," she said. "My husband could do that too. Never sold a painting in his life though. Didn't have the gumption. Didn't want the attention. Just the way he was. Shame though."

As she spoke, Flo's head tilted ever so slightly as if, in that tick of time, she was measuring the intensity of a possibility, now as nonexistent as Randall was.

"Well, I plan to encourage this kid," Michael said. "He's shy too, but seems to be coming out of his shell. He told me this watercolor was of his friend. From the attention to composition and color, and to the care he took in completing it, I'd think she might be more."

Flo offered a tightlipped smile.

Michael grinned. "Guess I'm a romantic."

"Nothing wrong with that, Mr. Campo. The world could use a little more affection."

"Couldn't agree with you more, Flo."

⌘ ⌘ ⌘

The day had grown dusky when Flo joined Carlos and Kirby for a snack break. The three had agreed to meet at a sheltered patio just outside the science wing. It was a place many of the seniors commandeered during school breaks, but the students were long gone now. The place now belonged to the custodians and they sat quietly on a day that had begun to cool; the air had retained enough heat however to be comfortable.

"How's the first week been, Kirby?" she asked, ripping open a granola bar.

"Been okay. Busy though an' hectic. Guess ya' heard 'bout my boy."

"No."

"Got into a fight. From what I was told some kid jumped on him for no good reason, but Willard fought back. Reckon I would have too seein' as how he's been gettin' harassed some. Kid may be shy, but he's not goin' t' take gettin' picked on forever."

"That's too bad, Kirby."

"Yeah. I got called in t' Mr. Cunningham's office. There he was . . . Willard, a sight t' behold . . . bloody nose, cut lip, black eye. Looked like he'd swallowed a canary, when he saw me; he was so ashamed. Truth came out though. Trouble is, even though he didn't start the fracas, he fought back, so he got himself suspended for a week just like the other kid."

"Doesn't seem fair to me," Carlos said.

"I don't think so either, but that's the way the administration plays it 'round here. Lesson learned, I reckon," Kirby replied.

He was silent for a moment before he added, "Saw the other boy . . . big, muscular kid. His face looked like hamburger an' his nose was off kilter. I ought not say it, but I couldn't help but harbor a little bit of pride. Wouldn't tell Willard that though. Besides he has his mama t' contend with. She's fit t' be tied. Cried her eyes out when she heard what happened, but she's a tough woman. Gets real cranky if she's upset. She goin' t' have Willard doin' chores up, down, left, and right all week long."

"Sounds like a good plan," Carlos offered.

Flo did not respond directly to Kirby's comments about the fight, but she did not let the conversation about Willard die.

"Your son, Willard . . . it's Willard Dunn, right?" she began.

"Yeah," Kirby replied.

"Well, I don't know if you're aware of this, Kirby, but he's one hell of an artist."

"He's always liked t' draw," Kirby said looking at Flo quizzically. "Do ya' know somethin' I don't?"

"Well, no, but I've seen his work. Met one of the art teachers. Willard is in his class. First day there I spotted a nice piece of work, a pen and ink of a vineyard. It was well done. Then today, Mr. Campo, that's the teacher, showed me a watercolor Willard painted. It was beautiful. A girl."

"Willard painted a watercolor of a girl?" he asked.

"Yes, and a pretty one," Flo said with a slight smile. Her fingers reached up to cover the mole that resided high on her cheek before adding, "Guess there is something I know that you don't."

"Well, I'll be damned," Kirby declared. "Bet I have an inklin' who it might be."

⌘ ⌘ ⌘

Being in the vicinity of the science area of the building was strangely agitating to Flo. She couldn't put her finger on just why until Kirby began talking again.

"Bunch of interestin' folks teachin' science 'round here. That Mr. Lindsey's room stinks like the devil. Don't know how the kids stand walkin' into the place, much less sittin' for an hour listenin'."

"Hated cleaning his room," Flo admitted. "It's been foul smelling from day one. Mr. Lindsey says it's all the chemicals he has stored there, but I venture to say there's another reason."

Kirby sneered at his companions. "No doubt about it, I reckon. New guy has t' start at the bottom."

Carlos chucked at the innuendo. *Hiring Kirby Dunn was a good move.*

"How are you doing with Jack Mitchell?" Flo asked.

"He's decent enough. Seems real moody though. Never know if he'll be smilin' or frownin'. Reckon I can understand though, an' I feel kind of bad for the fella'. Heard he was married to Sherry Mitchell for a spell. Reckon he's pretty discombobulated about now with all that's happened. Ya' know I worked for her, Flo, before comin' here. Don't like recallin' it, but I'm the one found her that awful mornin'. Walked right in on her dead body. She was shot clean in the head. Blood ever'where. Haven't slept a full night since."

"I can imagine," Flo said, as she mindlessly slid her hand into the pocket of her frock. Her fingers folded over the photo of Jack and Sherry Mitchell, and at that moment Flo understood her discomfort. As inconsequential as a tiny photograph must be, she had stolen it. She had taken another person's property. Dropping the picture into her pocket had been an almost subconscious decision on her part and yet, at the same time, it ironically had been purposeful.

She slipped momentarily into her own world. She heard Carlos and Kirby's voices; she was sitting at the table with them, yet she was far away. *I stole . . . from Jack Mitchell. Why? Why Jack?*

The answer instantly materialized with vapor-less clarity, leaving her dumfounded by her ludicrous foolishness. Her random action had been an attempt at revenge on a man who had hurt her. For years Jack had been her tormentor, acutely when she had been a teenager, the flagrant taunts tearing at her self-image. And though never in adulthood had he offended her overtly, when they passed each other day after day in the halls of the very high school they both had attended, his passive dismissal of her made its cut. His very presence had become a constant reminder of his cruelty. She had hidden her pain inside, releasing it only when loving her husband, but then gathering it up again, a worthless booby prize she had never been able to relinquish.

That picture. That stupid photograph means nothing. How simplistic of me.

Landing in the right hands, maybe it would have incriminated Jack in the murder of Sherry, she must have reasoned. Perhaps the authorities would have looked more closely at him as a suspect if the picture were made public she must have thought. Her silly, little girl mind had made that ridiculous judgment on a whim, and for over a week, she had carried the photograph with her like a dead weight.

"Flo, are you okay?" Carlos asked. "You have that far away look again."

"Sorry, guys. My mind took a short trip to outer space," she chortled self-consciously.

"Hey, did you fix those cabinet doors for Jack Mitchell," Flo asked, taking the attention from herself.

"Yeah, I did. Came out real nice. Come take a look," Kirby invited.

The three friends wandered into the science wing to Jack's classroom.

"It's always so eerie when the students aren't around," Carlos said. "It's so quiet now. Come seven-thirty tomorrow, this place will be hopping."

They walked through Jack's classroom to the lab behind. The cabinet doors had been rehung perfectly. Kirby opened and closed each one, listening to the metal fasteners click with precision.

"Nice job," Carlos said.

"Looks good," Flo admitted. "Jack must be glad to have them fixed."

"Believe he is," Kirby replied, glancing up at the clock.

Flo's eyes followed.

"Guess I need to get back to work," Flo said, "I still have a couple of rooms to clean."

"Yeah, we'd all better get going," Carlos added.

Flo left the two men chatting behind her in the lab. Once in Jack's classroom, she made her way to his desk. She pulled the photograph of Jack and Sherry Mitchell out of her pocket, gave it a cursory glance, and then placed it carefully in the center of Jack Mitchell's desk. The simple doing of it filled her with instant relief.

"Done with that," she muttered. *Thank goodness. Lesson learned.*

CHAPTER FORTY

JACK

Jack cringed. The first person he saw when he drove into the high school parking lot was Detective Murphy, standing outside the front office as if on guard. It was early, the interior lights still off, the doors most certainly locked. *Not again. Does that jackass have nothing better to do than hang out around here questioning everyone in sight?*

Jack exited the car, slamming the door with force. He had awakened this day feeling relatively good. He had slept. No nightmares. No accidents. The conversation with Roger and Melody the afternoon prior had eased his tension, but seeing Detective Murphy filled him with instant fury. He was not even sure why.

George looked sharply in Jack's direction when he heard the car door slam.

"What are you looking at?" Jack muttered under his breath as he sauntered toward the office and to what he knew would be another, uncomfortable interaction with George Murphy.

"Morning, Jack," George said.

"Back at it?" Jack replied, a smirk twisting his mouth.

George smiled. Jack's animosity ironically was satisfying. *He's worried.* George was assured. *He's a tight-lipped son of a bitch, though.*

"I'll be at it as long as I need to be," George commented.

"Well, have at it," Jack snarled, brushing by the detective to enter the office. He jammed his master key into the lock, a noticeable click freeing the door. The office was empty. Neither Cora nor Roger had arrived yet. Jack scooted in, letting the door ease closed without inviting Detective Murphy inside. *Bastard can wait.*

The detective did not react. Rather he maintained his stance, his back to Jack, gazing at the near-empty lot, waiting, waiting.

⌘ ⌘ ⌘

Jack had no intention of hanging around the office anticipating Roger's appearance as he often did. It was clear the principal would be tied up with the detective all morning. *No wonder Roger's a bundle of nerves these days. Can't even run a school with all this shit going on.*

He grabbed a stack of papers from his mail slot, entered the bathroom to take a prolonged piss, and then slipped out the back door onto the campus. It would be another, long day. He hated teaching in the spring. The students were antsy and he was bored. It was too late in the year to begin a new unit, so he resorted to review of material half of his students could not remember after four, short months and that he knew inside and out having taught it for years.

"Maybe I'll throw on a video about the ecosystem," he muttered. *That should keep the kids quiet, at least.*

He flipped on the light and walked to his desk.

"What the hell! Where did this come from?" he said aloud. He was looking down at the smiling faces of himself and Sherry. He fingered the photograph gingerly as though touching it would sting. It did not, of course, but the memory, both of the moment the picture was taken, as well as the fact that the missing photo had reappeared in plain sight of anyone who might have looked, filled him with anxiety.

He stared at it for minutes until, right in his hand, Sherry's features seemed to come to life. Her deep, blue eyes, framed with long, dark lashes, sparkled and she was smiling, looking at him now longingly. His own face, though, alive with happiness then, taunted him now. How had life unfolded as it had? When he had spotted Sherry so many years before, he had fallen for her instantly, and he was quite sure the feeling had been reciprocated. She was the ultimate love, the perfect woman. Time became a torturer though. The first year of passion, love, and lust fell victim to reality. Jack had his classes to contend with and Sherry was consumed with her business, one that took precedence over everything else. Jack was placed on the proverbial back burner. Sherry's attention was focused on work, on money, on her clients, and on her reputation. She was driven. Any interest in Jack had waned more quickly than he ever could have imagined and with it came her crushing cruelty. It did not take long for every comment, every moment together to be tarnished by sneering insults, criticism, and ridicule. Sherry was arrogant, powerful, and caught in a trap of her own making. It appeared she could not help herself, and as a result, Jack suffered, for the first time since he was an eight-year-old child, at the hands of another human being. While his misery consumed him, she mocked his weakness, until, at last, the two parted, angry and disgusted with no one to blame but themselves.

Jack had not seen her for twelve months, although he had thought of her longingly often. Even in the arms of other women, he had imagined her there. His mind played those nasty tricks on him over and over, reinventing the hurt and eventually leaving him barren of feeling for anyone, perhaps even himself.

He flipped the photograph over. *Wedding Day, Sherry and Jack* still was visible in faded ink. More prominent, though, were his scrawling letters: *bitch.*

"And she was," he muttered mournfully. He tucked the photograph safely into his jacket pocket and zipped it shut. He would take it home where it belonged.

CHAPTER FORTY-ONE

MIDGE

Midge still was enraged when she climbed out of bed in the morning. She had not slept well. Her mind had been a tumble of troubled thoughts, and her heart heavy with myriad burdens she could not sort out or articulate even to herself. All of her plans had been going awry, the least of which had been her inability to confront Roger Cunningham the day before as she had so anticipated.

"He's in a meeting," Cora Davies had told her tersely when Midge had demanded to see him. "It will take quite awhile. You'll need to see him later this week. His schedule is jammed."

"Well, I hope it has something to do with Ms. Miller's dismissal," Midge had snapped.

"I wouldn't know," Cora had lied. "He's with Jack Mitchell."

It had been the veiled truth. Cora conveniently and purposefully had failed to mention that Melody also was involved in the discussion behind Roger's closed door. *Poor Roger doesn't need to deal with Midge McGrath on top of everything else. As much as I think Melody Miller needs a good reprimand if not worse, I can't bring myself to accommodate Midge for another second.*

It was true. Midge's demands on Cora on the morning of Melody's near disastrous blunder had been an affront to which Cora was still incensed. Midge had treated her as the hired help, lower than dog shit. *"You need to come over here . . . tell Roger . . . get over here . . . I have to teach . . . be with her until she's the hell out of here . . . now."* It basically had been a "Take-care-of-it-Cora-I-have-more-important-things-to-do," conversation, one that Cora had not appreciated then and the memory of which irked her to that very day.

⌘ ⌘ ⌘

Midge was in no mood to teach. No one wanted to face students this time of year. *Most of my kids are a mass of disinterested, self-indulgent brats who want nothing more than to be lying on a beach somewhere. God, what a bunch of dolts they are. I can count on my fingers the few who actually want an education. The rest? What a joke. I've spent my entire career wasting my time.*

She wandered into the kitchen, made coffee, and stood soberly staring out the kitchen window at a grey and weathered, redwood fence not six feet away. She looked at two dented and dirty garbage cans that had been placed on an expanse of ground that was completely barren save for tufts of brown grass stubbornly poking out next to the fence posts. "Ugly," Midge declared aloud. "Ugly as sin." Her loathing of the scene made her stomach burn with acid and she forced her mind elsewhere, to a recollection from the past.

She instantly managed to claim a memory file of a time, twenty years prior, when she and her husband, Fred, had lived farther from town. With meager savings and a bit of help from her parents, they had purchased a sprawling, ranch house that butted up to farmland. Not too much farther in the distance lay the foothills of the Sierra. The views from her windows then were oh so different: fields of willowy corn to the west, rows of dark, green tomato vines to the south, and queues of ropey grape vines perfectly placed on the hillsides to the east and north. She had loved the place in the beginning.

The initial moments of pseudo-happiness both with the house and Fred quickly morphed however into boredom, and eventually, Midge's ever-deepening aversion for her husband. His disinclination to have much of anything to do with his wife was the mirror. As a result, the couple had no children and Midge buried her outrage at what she considered an inane choice of her own making, into her job teaching high school students English. Both she and Fred endured twenty years of cohabitation until it was over, just like that. Fred had disappeared on a morning in May ten years prior to this very month and Midge was left to clean up the mess.

And here she was now in a tiny, rundown cottage she could barely afford to keep. She had sought financial help; she had seen a real estate agent; she had done what she needed to do, and for what? No one had been willing to help. She was bent up with sorrow, anger, and remorse at where life had taken her. Her angst was strangling her and she could tell no one of her torment.

CHAPTER FORTY-TWO

ANGIE

By the time Angie was ready for school, the sun was warming the day. Her dad had left much earlier when the fog barely was lifting from the valley floor.

"Do my best thinking early in the morning," he had told her.

"By the way, I'll be at the high school on and off this week, Angie," he had warned her, chuckling. "Will try and stay out of your way."

"The last thing I'm worried about is you," she had told him, thinking instead that in a very short time she would be seeing both Brad and Willard, perhaps at the same time. It made her nervous.

"See you later, Dad."

She was apprehensive with no idea what to expect as the day unfolded. Brad was not likely to go away easily. In fact, he had called twice several days before despite Angie's wishes; fortunately her dad had intercepted the calls. She had spoken to Willard though, although only briefly.

"My mama's on a mission t' teach me right from wrong, I guess," he had told her. "She allowin' me one phone call, just like jail, an' this is it. Wanted t' let ya' know. Can't do a thing but study an' do chores. 'Grounded' means 'grounded' 'round here. That's for certain. I'll be talkin' t' ya' soon, though. Don't forget me."

"Not a chance," she had said with a smile.

⌘　⌘　⌘

Angie's first class was English, and she was anxious. Both Brad and Willard were in the class as well. God only knew what would happen when they saw each other, or her. The class had had substitute teachers for a week because Ms. Miller had been sick, really sick apparently. Angie wasn't sure the poor woman would be up for a class full of rowdy students ready for the school year to end. That consideration took a back seat to her other concerns though.

Angie arrived to the classroom early. She sat in her desk, reading through her notes quietly after greeting her teacher who uncharacteristically was present on time.

"Hey, Ms. Miller. Hope you're feeling better," she said.

"I am. Thank you. That flu bug really got to me." Melody had come to believe her own story.

Ms. Miller was a bit pale, but she atypically appeared more focused than usual. Maybe a week away had given her time to prepare.

When Willard walked into the room just prior to the bell, Angie grinned. He took his seat several rows away and smiled at her. His face still bore a slight tinge of purple about one eye. Otherwise, he was simply Willard.

Brad did not appear until ten minutes after the bell had rung. He swaggered to Ms. Miller's desk, threw a yellow tardy pass at her and then turned toward the class full of students. His nose was slightly swollen and it sported a fat Band-Aid but otherwise he appeared unscathed. He glared quickly at Willard, and then took his assigned seat in the row next to Angie. He looked straight ahead though, ignoring her. Angie relaxed. *Good. I'll take being ignored. Rather like it.*

Ms. Miller managed to maintain the class's interest with a quick review of an author's background and a discussion about existentialism. The class had been assigned, *The Stranger.* "Albert Camus," she said, "often has been labeled an existentialist, though he insists he was not . . ."

"The ideas of existentialism, however, stem from a philosophy that brings up some pretty dicey questions about life," she added.

She began to write questions on the board: *Is life fair? Do bad things happen to good people? Should we label others? Can one be truly independent? Are we responsible for our own actions? Are we defined by how we act and by what we do willfully? Do we create our own values consciously? Should we be defined by our behavior? Must a person take responsibility for his or her own actions? Are we really free? How does one determine the meaning of life?*

"What do you think?" she asked, turning to the class. The students became engaged, as they had not been all year.

"People label others all the time."

"Yeah, but that's not fair."

"No one has the right to tell me how to act or how to be."

"People should just be responsible."

"Bad things happen to good people all the time."

"Look at what happened to that woman who was killed. Was she responsible for what happened to her?"

"Somebody who's evil is responsible."

"Now you're labeling."

"Isn't a murderer a criminal?"

"Couldn't a basically good person do a bad thing?"

"Doesn't matter. People need to have values."

"What about the concept of everyone having a dark side?"

Angie's mind drifted along with the debate until she could no longer focus. Bad things had happened in her life. Her mother had died delivering her; a warped kid had raped her; her boyfriend had been abusive; her boss recently had been killed. Where was the fairness in any of that? And how could she possibly be responsible? The mere consideration of any of it was confusing and suddenly filled her with sadness. Her eyes began to fill with tears. Thankfully the bell rang just in time. *Saved.*

"We'll continue this discussion tomorrow," Ms. Miller hollered over the commotion of the students charging or shuffling toward the door.

Angie remained seated, as did Willard until everyone was gone. Brad Browning fortunately was among them. She smiled up at Willard who had stood and walked to her side. *Maybe life isn't all that bad after all.*

⌘ ⌘ ⌘

Willard and Angie strolled into the hallway where Brad stood by the stairwell with three of his buddies. He glared at them.

"Get over here, Angie," he demanded.

"No," she said definitively.

"Ang. Don't make a scene," he pressed. "I want to talk to you."

"And I don't want to talk to you," she replied. "I have things to do."

"With ass wipe there?" he snarled, referring to Willard.

"Shut up, Brad," she said. "Don't make a bigger ass of yourself than you already have."

"Let's go," Willard urged quietly, touching her arm. "Don't play into this."

"You're right," she agreed.

The two walked quickly past the huddle of boys and trotted down the stairs. Angie's heart was beating hard. From behind her she heard crude laughter and Brad's voice, "It's not over yet, bitch."

"Oh yes it is," she muttered, otherwise not reacting.

When she and Willard reached the first floor and rounded the corner, they stopped and looked directly at each other for a moment. Angie reached up and gently touched his bruised cheek.

"I think you'll make it," she grinned.

"No doubt about it," he said, reaching over to touch her sparkling, blond hair.

An electric moment passed between them before Willard spoke.

"Hey, will you come with me to my art class for a second?" he asked. "I have something I want to show you."

⌘ ⌘ ⌘

Michael Campo looked on from a distance as Willard Dunn guided Angie Murphy to an array of artwork pinned to the wall.

Willard pointed first to the pen and ink drawing, now even more striking having been double matted in black and white.

"What do ya' think?" he asked.

"It's stunning," she said. "Oh my God, Willard. I didn't know you had this talent."

He grinned. "There's another one," he said, drawing her attention to the watercolor he had painted of her awash in sunlight in an imaginary garden.

"You," he said simply.

"Oh, Willard," she said. "It's amazing. You made me look beautiful."

"Ya' are," he said, pulling her closer to him. "Ya' are."

CHAPTER FORTY-THREE

FLO

Flo and Carlos met with George Murphy together. George did not suspect that either of the custodians had had anything to do with Sherry Mitchell's death. It was likely neither of them really knew her, and about that, he was correct. He was interested in their knowledge of Jack Mitchell, though. George's troubling feeling that Jack knew more than he had admitted, had him scrambling for answers.

"I've known Jack since our own high school days," Flo offered, while mindlessly directing her hand to her cheek in order to cover the black mole lodged there. "Both of us went to school right here, if you can believe that. He was an athlete. Cocky. Sure of himself. We didn't run in the same circles."

George nodded. He could well imagine that was the case though would never have said so out of respect for the woman. The two clearly were as different as day and night.

"And Carlos?" George pried. "How well do you know Jack Mitchell?"

"I've been acquainted with the man for years," Carlos said, "but that doesn't mean I know much about him. He's been teaching here forever, but like Flo says, he's not that friendly with the custodians. Tells us when he wants something done; otherwise spends time with the other teachers, or Mr. Cunningham. See him up there in the front office every morning and afternoon, unless Mr. Cunningham's not around for some reason. Mr. Mitchell fills in for him sometimes. That's all I know."

"So, nothing else?" George asked.

Flo looked away, afraid the detective would read her mind. She did know more, but could not bring herself to tell Detective Murphy that she was quite certain Jack had attempted to accost George's very own daughter. It had been only recently that Flo had learned George's relationship to Angie. She had overheard Midge McGrath spouting off, as though it were an awful truth, that Angie was, in fact, the detective's daughter.

"I knew it," Midge had hissed to a colleague. "Can you believe that little, blond cheerleader, Angie, is that dreadful detective's daughter? Had the girl in my class a year or so ago, but he never made an appearance in my classroom. Didn't bother to come to Back to School evening or Open House. Says something about his parenting if you ask me. Seems all he's interested in is that detective work of his. He's hell bent on badgering people; I do know that for a fact. Has he gotten to you yet?"

Flo did not recall the other teacher's response, but filed the information about Angie, and about Midge as well, for herself nonetheless. On this occasion, though, face to face with Angie's father, her knowledge played with her conscience a bit, but she would say nothing. In no way would she possibly be able to tell George Murphy about Jack's seemingly inappropriate confrontation of Angie. There was no proof anyway. And who was she to be spreading rumors? Besides, maybe the encounter between Jack and Angie Murphy had been less smarmy than she had imagined. Perhaps because she had always detested Jack, she had read more into the situation. Maybe she had been dead wrong. Flo's reasoning led her to one decision. She would remain silent.

CHAPTER FORTY-FOUR

MELODY

When the room had emptied, Melody sat quietly at her desk. *Class was great today. Can't believe the discussion. Those kids were really thinking, and I was the catalyst. Me. I am a teacher after all. I know it.*

Perhaps it was because her head finally had cleared; perhaps it was because Jack Mitchell, so uncharacteristically, had stood up for her; or perhaps it was because Roger Cunningham was willing to give her another chance – she was unsure of any of it – but Melody felt as though she could go on now, that she had some control, that she could teach, and that she could do it with her own sense of style.

Screw Midge McGrath, the old biddy. She wants me out of here. Well, screw her. I'm not going anywhere, and for the first time I'm going to teach my way. No more pages of vocabulary; no more pop quizzes; no more one essay a week requirement; no more, "You must have a lecture planned for every day." No more "Do as I say" from Midge McGrath.

Melody was bound up in emotion: exhilaration, optimism, resentment, and contempt. All her feelings were deeply embedded and not one of them could pull free of the others. *I'm going to talk to my students and listen to them, just like today. It was so cool, and I think I've finally turned the corner. So, Midge, you bitch, you can go to hell.*

As if on cue, a figure suddenly filled the doorway. Midge.

"So you wormed your way back, I see," she snarled.

"I am back," Melody stated flatly. "Bad flu."

"Who do you think you're kidding?" Midge snapped, pulling the door closed behind her. "Look, Melody Miller. Your behavior at this high school, this comprehensive high school, a school of distinction, I might add, has been a disgrace."

Melody stared at Midge, startled by the attack.

"I'm not perfect . . ." she began, but then fell silent, interrupted by an extended tirade.

"Teachers should be role models. Teachers should be prepared. Teachers should be learned, competent, disciplined. You are none of these, you little nitwit. You are an embarrassment to the English Department, to the school, to the district, to educators as a whole. Do you not understand how ridiculous your behavior has been? You disgust me. Why Roger has allowed you to show your face here again is beyond my comprehension."

Midge's face was crimson, and her eyes alive with fury. Her lips pursed for only a moment before she continued.

"Well, I'll tell you this. Roger may think he is in control, but he's wrong. I was an educator in this school long before that absurd, spineless principal ever set foot on this campus. I have power he doesn't realize and I plan to let him know, and soon. As for you Ms. Miller, watch your step. I'll be gunning for you too."

CHAPTER FORTY-FIVE

JACK

The day was dragging, just as Jack knew it would. Teaching in the spring was next to impossible. No one, not the students, nor the teachers, wanted to be stuck inside when the chilly, rainy winter finally gave way to spring. It had been a stubborn rendering this year however. The torrential rains the week prior proved the point. The heavy downpours, rather than the usual sporadic sprinkles, that had wracked the area were unprecedented, a mocking counterpart to Sherry's sudden death, the hallmark incident having stunned the community. Jack was not convinced normalcy ever would reign again. Certainly it would not for him, of that he was sure. It was grief that pestered him now, although the disintegration of his marriage, the final divorce, and his own outrageous reaction to his initial loss, had launched him into a tailspin. What had he been thinking? Countless trips to whores in San Francisco, months of risky sex with Melody Miller, fantasies of female students, and an actual attempt to lure Angie Murphy into his clutches were ludicrous. What was wrong with him? Was he insane?

Alone in his classroom, he sat at his desk staring outside at a cerulean sky, at a blue so deep and pure it was awesome. Not a cloud was visible anywhere. Clarity such as this had never been present in Jack's life and the reality of that fact was staggering, taunting him to take stock. It was no wonder Sherry had lost interest. The bravado he had presented early on in their relationship had been a sham and a façade she surely and quickly must have discovered was only the tip of the iceberg.

What a pretentious fool I've been, all my life.

He shuddered visibly as he faced the awful truth. From the childhood moment when he had been preyed upon by a monster in the night, he had made a decision. No one, not one person, would ever have control over him again. He had to make sure. The horrific incident in his mother's seedy trailer was the foundation for his revenge, and he understood, at this very moment, that he had spent a lifetime making others pay. Paramount to him had been his need to hide the fact that he had been vulnerable. For years, even as an adult, he had been unable to understand the veracity of one fact - that he had been a defenseless child. The grief for the loss of his innocence compounded his current pain. Tears stung his eyes. *Jesus, Jack. Don't fall apart again. Not here. Not now.*

He stood up, stumbled past the rows of empty desks to his lab and a small, private bathroom at the rear. From inside, he closed the door, leaned over the sink and retched. When he was done, he let water run from the faucet for a full minute until it warmed; then he splashed it on his face, finally righting himself to look in the mirror.

"I'm not normal," he mouthed to the reflection. *What was normal anyway? Was it Melody's uncanny unpredictability, Detective Murphy's dogged determination, Florence Gray's plodding presence, Midge McGrath's insistent demands, Roger's acquiescence to any confrontation, his colleagues' silent agendas, or his students' games?* Nothing, nothing quite made sense. His notion of normalcy had gone that awry.

Jack heard the bell signaling the end of the lunch break. Soon students, noisy and distracted, would enter his classroom, clamoring to their seats and he, equally unfocused, would be expected to teach them. He remembered his final words to Melody days before when Roger had given her another chance. "Don't fuck up," he had told her. He patently knew, as never before, the same for him was true.

CHAPTER FORTY-SIX

MIDGE

Midge had a prep period and it was a good thing. Her barrage of words toward Melody, only moments before, paradoxically had left her more shaken than it appeared the girl was. Melody, her mouth gaping, had simply stared dumfounded. She had not uttered one word of protest, to Midge's knowledge, and that fact in itself was infuriating. *What is it with people? I ran over that girl like a Mac truck and she didn't even respond.*

Midge had wanted a reaction in the worst way. A retort of any kind quite likely would have escalated into a full-blown confrontation giving Midge further fuel when she challenged Roger later.

"The girl has lost complete control," she could imagine herself saying. "You cannot imagine how she spoke to me,"

Melody had left her empty handed, though. Midge would have to try a different tactic. She was quite positive that she was capable of doing whatever it took to get rid of the young woman once and for all, however, with or without the principal's blessing. She had pull that Roger could not have imagined. Roger's unwillingness to immediately comply with Midge's wishes was a bitter pill, one that actually had been the impetus for her verbal assault on Melody in the first place.

Why certainly someone has to reprimand that silly, young teacher for her wanton and inappropriate behavior. Roger's lack of cooperation left Midge with a decision: to take matters into her own hands.

Clearly Roger also required a good talking-to, but finding access to him these days was proving to be difficult. That secretary of his protected him like a badger and of course that horrible detective seemed to have taken up residence in the office. He always appeared to be lurking around somewhere on campus, cornering teachers, spying, looking for evidence of any kind that would put him on the right track in solving the murder of Jack Mitchell's wife.

The very thought of Sherry Mitchell intensified Midge's edginess. Oh how she had detested the woman. Midge paced, back and forth, back and forth in front of the windows, hoping to slow her rapidly beating heart and to decide her next step.

CHAPTER FORTY-SEVEN

ANGIE

The last period of the day finally brought Angie and Willard together again. Since the uncomfortable, morning exchange with Brad after English, followed by the sweet, impromptu visit to the art class, both had gone their separate ways. Angie fortunately managed to avoid any further, direct contact with Brad. He and his friends were occupied anyway. At each break, they had begun their normal routine of prowling the campus like wild coyotes looking for fresh meat.

"Brad's not going away easily," Angie's friend, Cynthia, whispered at lunch. "He's over there staring at you right now."

"Yeah, and he has his hands all over Charlene's ass. She's as bad as Suzie," Angie countered.

"He's only trying to make you jealous," Cynthia said.

"Well, I'm not." Angie stated emphatically, "I don't care who Brad sees, feels up, or does. I'm done."

"What are you going to do about prom?" Cynthia questioned. "Weren't you supposed to go with Brad?"

"Was," Angie said. "I'm sure as hell not going with him now. Don't really care if I go at all, to tell you the truth. I just want to graduate and get on with life."

"I can't believe you'd want to miss out," Cynthia continued.

"After all that's happened lately, Cynthia, prom has lost its importance to me. My boss, Ms. Mitchell, is dead . . . killed by some creep out there, our so-called friends have taken harassment to a new low, and I'm sick of it all. I just want to be with people who don't have any trips," she said.

"Like Willard, maybe?" Cynthia asked.

"Yeah, maybe, and like my dad. He's been working his ass off trying to solve this murder. I watch what he does, know how exhausted he is, and it puts everything else in perspective. I don't know, Cynthia. I'm just tired of high school. That's all."

"Seems a shame. Hope you don't have regrets."

"If I do, I do, but I'm not expecting it. Need to get to class now. Willard wants to review my notes."

"Saw him this morning," Cynthia said. "Compared to Brad he looked pretty good after that fight. Think Brad got the worst of it."

"Yeah, looks that way to me too. Brad got what he asked for finally. Look, I have to go. Bye, Cynthia. See you later."

⌘　⌘　⌘

"Hey," Angie said when she walked up to Willard who already was seated at the lab table they shared.

"Hi," he grinned.

"How was your first day back?"

"Okay, I guess. Kids have been pretty cool actually."

"I think you gained some respect, Willard," Angie smiled. "Suspension or not, you did the right thing standing up to Brad."

"Has he bothered ya' any more today?" he asked.

"No. I've seen him a few times with his buddies and a girl or two. Had his hands all over Charlene. Don't worry, Willard, he's going to have no trouble at all moving on . . . and neither am I."

Willard smiled and beneath the tabletop, squeezed her hand, drawing it close to him.

⌘ ⌘ ⌘

"Okay, class, cut the chatter," Mr. Mitchell hollered above the noisy conversations in the room. "We're going to be watching a short video about the ecosystem. It'll be good review for your final," he added. "Listen up. We'll be discussing it during the second half of the period. Be ready to participate."

A student in the front row dimmed the lights and the video started. The drone of the narrator quieted the class some of whom watched as if in a stupor; others actually put their heads on their desks and slept. Mr. Mitchell ignored the behavior, slipped to a corner in the back of the room, and leaned against the wall. He was so tired he could have dozed in place. The video had been playing for only minutes when three, muffled, cracking sounds jarred Jack and his students . . . *pow, pow, pow!*

"Holy shit," Jack said, running to secure the door. "Everyone hit the deck," he ordered. "That was gunfire."

CHAPTER FORTY-EIGHT

FLO

"What in the hell was that?" The question was one shared by many.

Flo looked out from the custodial closet next to Michael Campo's art room at the exact moment he stepped into the hallway, a crowd of students right behind.

"Back," he yelled. "Get back. All of you! Flo, get in here."

She moved to his doorway as quickly as she could. He grabbed her arm firmly and yanked her inside before slamming the door and locking it.

"Everyone get down. Get behind a counter. Don't be moving around. Those were gun shots."

Flo's heart was in her throat. She inched on her knees to a counter next to the wall where two young girls were cowering. Both teens began crying, clearly overwhelmed with fear. One was shaking badly, almost convulsively. Flo reacted by reaching over gently and touching her hand. She wrapped her calloused fingers around the girl's soft hand and squeezed. Flo could not have verbalized why she made such a move; aside from her husband, Randall, human touch had been a rarity for her. The girl looked gratefully at Flo though, and in the dim light, Flo saw a slight smile appear on the teenager's tear-streaked face. She did not pull away and Flo did not let go.

"It'll be okay," Flo whispered, although her words were hollow. She knew they were. She could not possibly have had any way of knowing that *it*, whatever *it* was at this point, would be all right; on the contrary she doubted anything would be the same, ever. Her own experiences had taught her that the world could shift that quickly. Unpredictability was at the very heart of human existence. One could resist in some cases, of course; yet, more to the point, as in a predicament such as this, one more likely had little choice other than simply to go with it, let the situation play out.

Someone was in the school building with a gun, shooting. How many times had similar scenarios occurred in schools throughout the country? How many students, misfits, and crazies had sought revenge for myriad reasons, rational or otherwise, in this very way? Her own heart began to race as she listened to the whimpers of frightened students, strangers and friends, united in terror as never before.

CHAPTER FORTY-NINE

MELODY

Melody was alone for only a minute or two. She had sent her students to the library to work on their final research projects.

"I'll be right there to help you," she had told them, gathering materials to take with her. "Go on down. The librarian is waiting for you. Our class has the library to ourselves for the whole period."

The students, a rowdy group of freshmen, would need supervision. They had been a chatty, unruly bunch all year. At least in the library, hopefully, with a limited amount of time to work, they would be more focused.

When the last student was gone, Melody sorted through some papers, stashed a few, along with her class list, into a folder, grabbed her keys, and turned to leave. She was halfway to the door when it was pushed open.

Midge entered. She had a shabby-looking, cardigan sweater thrown haphazardly over her shoulders and she held a black, crocheted purse close to her breasts. *She looks old, so old and outdated.*

Midge took a few steps forward toward Melody before speaking, "I'm not finished with our conversation," she said.

"What conversation?" Melody asked. "You did all the talking this morning, and I don't have time to chat now, Midge. My class has gone to the library. I need to be there too."

"They can wait," Midge declared in a voice charged with venom.

Melody backed a few steps nearer to her desk, her eyes shifting from Midge to the door. "I have to go," she said.

"No."

Midge moved slightly closer, stood very still, and glowered at Melody with dark, angry eyes. She opened her mouth slightly as though she were going to speak once more but did not. Instead, she tilted her head to the left, her face baring a look of bewilderment, and dropped the purse. In her hand she held a gun.

Melody visibly started when she saw the weapon, but before she could flee, before she could utter a word, Midge fired . . . one, two, three times.

Melody's face went white and she cried out. The sound issuing forth from deep inside her was a combined moan and howl. Her body traveled backwards a few feet before she fell, hard onto the tile floor. Blood began to ooze from a wound in her shoulder, gore from her ear, a pulverized mass, soaked her hair. And then she was silent, save for an eerie, ongoing gurgle emanating from her throat.

Midge did not even look at Melody Miller's prone form on the ground. Instead she shoved the gun into her purse and ambled backwards out the door. She was not finished.

CHAPTER FIFTY

JACK

Jack had a responsibility . . . to his students first and foremost. He knew it, but the intensity of the current crisis, a shooter somewhere in one of the hallways of the school, caused him to falter from his primary duty. Instead, he was overcome with a deep-seated need to do whatever he could to make it stop. He simply could not control his compelling drive to take action. The individual, perhaps more than one, who was creating this chaos had to be stopped without delay and Jack was poised to intervene. From childhood, being victimized ended as an option for Jack Mitchell. It was as if he was on automatic pilot. He had no choice but to abandon his classroom and move forward.

"I don't want any of you to leave this room until you hear an *all clear*. Do you understand me?" he yelled over the sounds of students, some sobbing, a few comforting, all frightened. "I'm going to step into the hallway to check things out."

"No," a student demanded. "You can't do that Mr. Mitchell."

"You don't have to be a hero," another added.

"Stay with us," another pleaded, fumbling with her cell phone. "Help is coming. It has to be. Everyone's called home."

Jack was sure she was correct. The room had been abuzz with hushed cell conversations to parents, to friends, to the police. Jack was single-minded however; he was bound and determined to find out what was happening beyond the confines of his classroom. Now. Standing by, waiting, was not an option. It was as though this emergency had triggered in him an irrepressible resolve. He would not allow himself, or his students, to become prey to any other human being. As though forced by an unknown, he crept to the doorway and pushed the door open. He peered down the hallway, expecting to hear movement or to see a commotion. The place was deadly silent though. Not one person was in sight. Clearly everyone was holding in place as they had been instructed over and over.

He securely locked the classroom door and eased down the hallway, farther and farther, his back to the wall. He began to perspire, trickles of moisture surfacing on his neck before inching down his back and arms. He moved stealthily towards the main hallway and then, at last, to the heavy, double doors that led outside. Stationed in front of the monstrous, main building was the front office, an island to itself, oddly separate and isolated from the rest of the school, as though its function was poles apart from the task of educating children.

Jack searched for any movement, seeking out any person, but the campus was spookily quiet, disconcertingly still. He waited, unsure. Should he move forward? Certainly he would be held accountable for leaving his classroom, but that was a consequence he was willing to accept. He pushed on the door just as another gunshot rang out, shattering the silence. There was a pause before another, and another . . . three more in all. In the short course of twenty minutes a predator had shot six times. In his wildest dreams, Jack would not have been able to imagine who it was.

CHAPTER FIFTY-ONE

MIDGE

Midge felt strangely calm and very satisfied. For the second time in only a few weeks she had accomplished a feat she could never have fathomed performing only six months prior. Hers always had been a cerebral existence. She was brilliant, her mind a locked box into which she stored fact after fact, intellectual morsels filling her with gratification. She always had been a quick learner easily mastering skill upon skill from the time she was a small child. Her parents, in no way her intellectual equals, had somehow spawned a genius and they were in awe of her. Fortunately her mother had encouraged her in her academic pursuits, providing her with stacks of maps, games, and books not the least of which was the Good Book, a white, leather Bible that Midge was required to read nightly before bedtime. Failure to do so would provoke her mother to produce the switch, the branch of a willow that was propped behind the kitchen door for quick access. In fact, any lapse in obedience to her mother brought out the switch. Midge's legs still bore the scars from the lashings that occurred from time to time, often without warning. Physical domination was her mother's only power for she was a simple woman otherwise, a slave to her housekeeping, cooking, and gardening.

Midge's father, like so many other men in the community, worked long hours in one of the canneries that lined the rural highway. His job transformed him into an old man before he was fifty. He seldom spoke with any degree of substance to either Midge or her mother. Instead, when he was not working, he found solace in hunting for jackrabbits and squirrels that he said were a menace. He would gather the dead carcasses, toss them into a wire bin in the back yard and burn them to a crisp. The one skill he did teach his daughter was how to shoot a rifle. The fact was that he loved his guns, handling them like trophies and polishing them until they shone. When he died shortly after Midge married Fred, she inherited the gun collection, the only thing of value her father had given her, except for a small amount of money that assisted Fred and her in purchasing the country home she had adored.

Both parents were dead now, her mother passing only a year after her father. And of course Fred was gone too, away God only knew where. Midge had been alone for ten years. Though from time to time she contributed her services to a community fundraiser, it was primarily to be seen in the right place alongside an esteemed person or two; otherwise she was isolated from everyone. Contact with her students and collegial interactions with other teachers were the only outlets for her and she considered those trivial and boring. She found no alternative way to feed her overactive mind other than to study incessantly and to channel her energy by creating small dramas at school or by dominating any individual she could.

In recent months the solitude, combined with anger at where life had taken her, had her wound tight. She had lost everything: her parents, her husband, her home, and perhaps even her power, for clearly students were less inclined to listen and behave. On most days, Midge may as well have been lecturing to the wall. Even the few, bright scholars, the ones whose intelligence might almost have rivaled her own, were so egocentric that she found them repulsive. Simply dealing with any teenager had become a constant, frustrating battle of wills. On top of that some of the young teachers, including Melody Miller, had not heeded her instructions and counseling. Her deepening vexation carried even beyond the school environment though. Sherry Mitchell, for example, had stood up to Midge, ignoring her commands and, in essence, shoving her out the door of her office on more than one occasion when the woman had had enough of their arguing. When Sherry had informed Midge that her cottage was too slovenly and unkempt to qualify for refinancing, that the bank had refused, it was the last straw. Midge was undone, the invalidation complete.

⌘ ⌘ ⌘

Midge had had no choice really. She realized that. She had been pushed unceremoniously into a corner and left there to rot, just like garbage. On an evening only three weeks before, she finally realized she had reached her limit of tolerance. She indignantly wondered about Fred's disappearance and whereabouts; she thought angrily about her mother, an exemplar of contradiction, the abusive weakling; and she remembered her father, overworked, underappreciated, and hell bent on doing the one thing that gave him pleasure and power, exterminating the varmints that abounded around him. How ironic that he had become a model.

Sherry had been first, yet no one knew that. Not yet.

Melody was second.

And third?

⌘ ⌘ ⌘

Midge paced herself. She need not hurry too quickly. To do so would draw attention and that would be a mistake. Once in the hallway, outside of Melody's classroom, Midge looked blindly in both directions. No one was in sight. She had heard a chorus of screams and the frantic shuffling of footsteps before doors slammed, one after the other. A warning alarm had blared almost immediately after the gunshots. It was followed by a frantic, male voice, "Lockdown. Everyone shelter in place."

That was it. The school hallways were deserted and still.

Midge walked slowly down the staircase, her rubber-soled shoes not making a sound. She rounded the corner, stepped deliberately to the wide doors that opened to the outside, and pushed her way out. A gust of wind blew her cardigan from her shoulder, and she gathered it in her free hand, concealing the weapon still tight in her grip. She circled around the back of the library and then moved toward her target. Though the unforeseen and random timing of this day's events was somewhat astonishing even to her, everything now was unfolding exactly as she had envisioned.

The back, office door, fortuitously for Midge, had not been secured. She maneuvered quietly into the narrow hallway, passed the teachers' mailboxes and entered the office proper. She did not see anyone at first in the silent space; then she spied a shoe jutting out slightly from beneath a desk. Someone was hiding. She took aim, shot, and listened to a deafening scream. *Cora. Good.*

The principal's office door was ajar. Midge stepped gingerly to the opening and came face to face with Roger Cunningham. At that moment, for Midge McGrath, they were the only two people on Earth. She did not hesitate for a second. Instead, she raised the gun and fired twice in rapid succession. Roger fell to the ground at the exact moment she was rammed violently from behind by George Murphy. The impact propelled her forward slightly and her face jammed with force on the edge of the desk before she rolled to the floor. George's large hand wrestled the weapon from her before he deftly cinched handcuffs onto her wrists.

She stared up at the detective somewhat in shock and immediately began babbling incessantly, "Got them. Got them all . . . Sherry Mitchell, the bitch. Melody. Roger. Maybe even Cora Davies to boot. Good going, Midge McGrath," she gibbered. "They're vermin of the worst kind. Got them all." Her eyes rolled back suddenly then in dramatic fashion and she passed out cold.

Had her confession solved the crime? Had Midge, indeed, murdered Sherry Mitchell? Detective Murphy would have a short wait to be certain, but at that moment he felt assured. In time, to his satisfaction, a report from ballistics disclosed the awful fact. She had spoken the truth. Midge McGrath had murdered Jack Mitchell's wife, Sherry, in cold blood.

⌘ ⌘ ⌘

Detective Murphy efficiently had radioed to dispatch the status of the crisis as it was unfolding, quickly updating the circumstances as required. He had requested immediate, code three back up as well as emergency medical services. "Unclear of number or extent of injuries," he had reported.

"Roger, are you all right?" George asked scrambling to his feet to assess the principal's condition.

"Okay. I'm okay. Just grazed, I think," Roger managed, pulling himself up and then plopping into his leather chair. Blood began oozing from a surface wound at the crown of Roger's head but the flow intensified quickly soaking into the collar of his shirt.

"Grab a towel, handkerchief, something and apply pressure. Head traumas bleed like a son of a bitch," George ordered.

Within seconds the sirens that had been screaming in the distance filled the air. Roger and George could hear vehicles screeching into position, cruiser doors opening and then slamming shut, and rapid-fire instructions being given. At the same time a volley of loud knocks began vibrating the door of the building. George rushed from the inner office to find Jack Mitchell, his face red and intense banging, banging.

George threw open the door. "Get in, Jack. Go tend to Roger. Now," he ordered before adding, "Jesus, look at this."

Cora's face was chalk white, her eyes closed, and her breathing shallow. She was alive, though unconscious. The poor woman's foot had been severed almost completely from her leg. She was bleeding profusely. George gave way to a team of paramedics who barged through the door right

behind Jack and went to work. It took only minutes before
Cora had been stabilized somewhat, placed on a gurney,
and shoved securely into the back of an ambulance. The
vehicle squealed away, sirens blaring.

Roger was correct. His wound was superficial. Medical
staff treated him at the scene because he unconditionally
refused to leave the school site.

"I absolutely will not leave until I am certain every one
of my students and staff is safe," he told police.

Midge on the other hand was carted away in another
ambulance. Her destination was not to the hospital, however. She would take up temporary residence at the county
jail facility. Detective Murphy would deal with her in time.

⌘   ⌘   ⌘

A sweep of the entire campus by police officers led to the
discovery of Melody Miller. Though she had drifted into
and out of consciousness for more than an hour, her injuries, though significant, were not life threatening. The
force of the shoulder wound had shattered her left clavicle,
scapula, and snapped the humerus, her upper arm, in two
places. In severe pain, Melody simply whimpered when, at
last, paramedics knelt beside her in a puddle of blood and
urine to assess her injuries.

The shot to the head had missed its mark. Instead of
penetrating the skull, it had hit Melody's left ear, virtually
sheering it off. A pulpy mass was all that remained.

"I think I have a scratch on my head," she murmured to
the medic. "It hurts."

"Indeed you do," he said kindly, placing gauze to the
mangled ear and securing it gently. "We'll get you to the

hospital right away where a doctor can take care of it." The man knew that aside from probable hearing loss, the girl would need several operations and plastic surgery as well. It would be a long recovery.

Investigating officers located a third bullet lodged in the wall directly behind where Melody was found. An analysis of the trajectory indicated that it quite likely had missed her head by only an inch.

CHAPTER FIFTY-TWO

ANGIE

Angie was still huddled beneath the lab counter with Willard when the loudspeaker came alive.

Jack Mitchell gave the directive for his friend, Roger Cunningham, who though virtually unscathed physically, had been traumatized as never before.

"Teachers, students, all staff: the emergency is finally over. Thank you very much for your cooperation. Great job. You are free to leave the classrooms now, but please leave in an orderly fashion. Students, your parents have assembled at the front of the school."

"That was Mr. Mitchell," Angie noted.

"It was. He must have made it t' the office. Hope everyone's all right," Willard said, taking hold of Angie's hand and then touching her cheek with one finger.

"Thank you for keeping me calm," she smiled.

"I could say the same," he grinned.

They scooted from their hiding place and joined the other students who were hurrying into the hallway. Amazingly absent from the halls that day was the din of usual chatter and laughter. Instead, the students either were silent or they spoke in hushed, almost reverent tones. They were safe. None of them yet knew the details of what had occurred that day, but knowledge of the particulars unquestionably would alarm many of them as never before . . . the indelible memory haunting. Until authorities disseminated the official information however, they simply were comforted to be exiting the school unharmed.

⌘　⌘　⌘

Several police officers and numerous parents, all clamoring for information surrounded Angie's father. The detective was engaged, but he also was looking over their heads, searching. Angie spotted him first.

"Dad," she yelled. She dropped Willard's hand and threw herself into her father's arms. He squeezed her tight.

"Thank God, you're all right," he said.

"You too, Dad. What happened? Did anyone get hurt?"

"We can talk about everything soon, honey. It's a long story and, yes some people were hurt, but no students. This time around the shooting did not involve students." He looked fully at her face and then scanned the commotion surrounding them. "Look, I have a dilemma. Are you going to be able to get home safely? I have to stick around for awhile, as you can imagine, to wrap up the investigation," he said apologetically.

"I'll be okay," she said. "I'm with Willard."

She turned then to Willard who had been standing by quietly.

"Dad, this is my good friend, Willard Dunn."

"It's nice to finally meet you, Willard. I've been hearing your name quite a bit lately," George admitted.

"I like that," Willard grinned. "Nice t' meet ya' too, Sir."

"Well, can I count on you to see that Angie gets home?" George asked.

"No problem. My dad works here. He won't mind takin' us home."

"That's right," George said. "Kirby's your dad. Good man, your father."

"Thank ya', Sir." Willard looked in the direction of the custodial office. "Guess I'd best be findin' him. He'll be wonderin'."

"Good idea. I'm sure he's concerned like every other parent around here," George said before addressing Angie. "I'll be home as soon as I can, honey," he added. He hugged her once more before turning to face several more hours of work.

⌘ ⌘ ⌘

Angie and Willard made their way toward the small office that was an informal meeting place for the custodians and that housed myriad cleaning supplies. Kirby Dunn was at the door surveying the mob of still frightened students and stunned parents who were milling about as if they were not sure what to do: stay or go. When he saw Willard, he strode rapidly in his direction. Carlos and Flo followed on his heels.

"Willard. Never been happier t' see ya' in my life," he admitted. "Are ya' okay? Where were ya' hidin'?"

"I was in my biology class," he replied, "with Angie."

Before Willard could introduce her, Angie greeted Carlos and Flo. "Hey Carlos. Hey Ms. Flo."

It was not uncommon for some students, particularly those such as Angie who always had been involved in school functions, to call the custodians by name; after all the janitors often were on the fringe of their activities, setting up for assemblies, sweeping up debris after ball games, and always a presence in the cafeteria and hallways. In Angie's mind, they were as integral to the maintenance and functioning of the school as the teachers. The custodians didn't always know the students by name, but the kids knew theirs.

"An' where were ya'll, Dad?" Willard asked.

"Right here. Been holed up with Carlos in this place for an hour."

"And what about you, Ms. Flo?" Angie inquired.

"Scampered into an art class, Mr. Campo's room," she answered.

"My teacher," Willard said.

"I know," Flo replied. "Been admiring your artwork. Love the pen and ink of the vineyard. Reminds me of home. And the watercolor of the girl with the long, blond hair . . . beautiful," she prattled uncharacteristically.

"Ya' like art?" he asked Flo directly.

"My husband was an artist," she said, "a painter and an artist."

"Was?" Willard asked.

"He passed on some time ago," Flo said, her throat tightening.

"I'm real sorry," Willard replied simply and looked down, unsure. He reached for Angie's hand.

Kirby astutely ended the awkward moment. "Aren't ya' goin' t' introduce us t' your friend?"

Willard sighed and then grinned. "I am. Dad, this is my friend, Ang . . . my girlfriend, Angie."

"So happy t' meet ya', Angie. Willard's been tellin' us about ya'," Kirby said.

"I'm really happy to meet you as well, Mr. Dunn. I hope to meet all of Willard's family really soon." Her smile would have lit up a room.

She squeezed Willard's hand just slightly then, and for Willard and Angie the world stood still, if only for a second.

CHAPTER FIFTY-THREE

FLO

Flo's day of work, out of necessity, ended early. Most of the school was a crime scene. She wasn't allowed near the humanities wing, or the front office, and while Carlos surely could have given her an assignment, he did not and for good reason. After a horrendous experience like today's she needed a break. He had a great deal of respect for Flo's integrity, for her aversion to gossip, and to her professionalism in a thankless position that some folks dismissed as worthless. He often had mentioned Flo's work ethic to his wife, Carla.

"That woman works harder than anyone I've ever known," he said. "*Ella es una diamante en bruto.* Don't know what Hollow Vista High would do without her."

Carlos was correct. Indeed Flo was a diamond in the rough. Rather, than demonstrating unnecessary emotion, Flo worked doggedly, head down, minding her own business. The only indication that she truly had been deeply distraught this day was at her mention of her husband's passing. She had spoken quite quickly and very softly, almost indifferently, but Carlos had seen her eyes, a sparkle of light capturing the moisture there. Her voice too had betrayed her with an edgy tone of sadness, an emotion that evidently never had been expunged fully since her husband's death years before. And perhaps that is why Carlos had noticed Flo many times before seemingly in a tiny trance, a personal reverie, that caused her to gaze at nothing in particular as she was now. Was it a persistent, underlying grief that had its hold?

"Flo, you're doing it again."

"What, Carlos?"

"Staring into space."

"Oh, sorry. Just thinking."

"About?" he asked.

"About life. It's a conundrum," she said.

Carlos looked at her quizzically.

"A puzzle, confusing. You never quite know where it will take you." Flo's head was cocked to one side, her mouth open slightly, her eyes sad.

"Are you thinking about today, about everyone who was hurt? About Midge McGrath?" he questioned.

"Of course, I am, like you are too I would expect. Like anyone who knows about this craziness."

"You're right. I'll be thinking about this day for a long time. Just talked to Carla. She's been so worried. Gossip flew around this town like a wildfire."

Flo did not answer, but she nodded, understanding.

"Look, go home, Flo. There's nothing we can do around here now. Told Kirby to do the same. He left with the kids just now. Nice kid, that Willard . . . and the girl too."

"Yeah," Flo said, "A cute little couple. They seem so happy together."

"Go home."

"I am. Thanks Carlos. Hug your family."

"I will. I will do that."

⌘ ⌘ ⌘

At home Flo poured a hefty glass of wine and cried for the first time since the evening she had scattered Randall's ashes in the vineyard beside their modest, stucco home. For years she had bundled up her grief like a hidden gift that she tore into occasionally to pluck out a memory or two. Good or bad, it didn't matter. What was important to Flo was to remember the only man she had ever loved, Randall Gray with all his imperfections and all his perfections too. He had worked hard, had drunk like a fish, honed his talent, fought like the devil, and loved her until the day he died. She could not have asked for more.

⌘ ⌘ ⌘

When her tears finally dried, Flo sat numbly reflecting on the day's events. What would cause a person to become as mentally unstable as Midge McGrath obviously was and furthermore how was it that no one had noticed? *She was so arrogant and full of herself. I wanted to keep my distance, and she seemed to want that as well, distance, from everyone.*

What Flo could not possibly have known was that when anyone did make it beyond the fence Midge had created, as Melody Miller had, she attacked even more ruthlessly. It was a sinister truth. *What circumstances would cause a person to arrive at a point of behaving so insidiously? She must have been hurt dreadfully when she was a child.*

Flo was sickened to hear about Cora Davies' injury, and Melody's too. Cora had been Flo's friend for years, and Melody, though an unknown really to Flo, was young, with a full life ahead. Neither woman deserved this fate and neither would be the same again. The physical damage was only one side of the coin; the mental scars would last as well. And the poor principal, Roger Cunningham, had to be steeped in remorse, regret, and certainly a bit of rage. One of the most respected teachers on campus, and Roger's antagonist, as authorities learned later through their investigation, had done the unimaginable. She certainly would have to pay a heavy price though.

It was a fact. Midge was found guilty, and though clearly mentally unstable, not insane. She was ordered to live out the remainder of her days incarcerated, languishing in solitary confinement in the Central California Women's Facility. Her actions had assured that she would be much more alone there than she ever had been before.

"And so we're off, the three of us - me, myself, and I. So very curious, isn't it? The degrees of life's renderings are relative indeed, are they not?" were Midge's words following her sentencing. The judge, not understanding her eccentric babbling, had glared at her as if she were daft.

⌘   ⌘   ⌘

In time, of course, the community calmed but not one person forgot completely the nearly lethal rampage at Hollow Vista High School that was precipitated for reasons that would remain as ambiguous as the perpetrator. What the public did discover, however, was that Midge McGrath's act of vengeance on Sherry Mitchell had opened a floodgate of anger and resentment that she had not been able to restrain. The dark side had won its own sordid victory.

ABOUT THE AUTHOR

Judith DeChesere-Boyle was born in Elizabethtown, Kentucky and with the exception of living for three years both in England and Texas, was raised there. She first attended the University of Kentucky, and then moved to California, graduating from College of Marin with an AA degree in English with a Creative Writing emphasis and San Francisco State University with a BA degree in English. She attended Sonoma State University, earning two teaching credentials and an MA in Education with an English Curriculum emphasis. She taught English at the secondary level for many years, retiring early enough to pursue her love of writing more seriously. She raised two wonderful sons and now lives in Sonoma County, California with her husband, Rick. Besides writing, she reads avidly, gardens, adores her three grandchildren, and walks her German Shepherd and Chocolate Lab/Britney three miles a day. She dotes on her one-eyed cat and enjoys tending the family's pond full of koi. She is the author of two novels, *Big House Dreams* and *Nine Bucks and Change*, and a memoir, *Tumor Me: The Story Of My Firefighter.*